Streets of Nashville

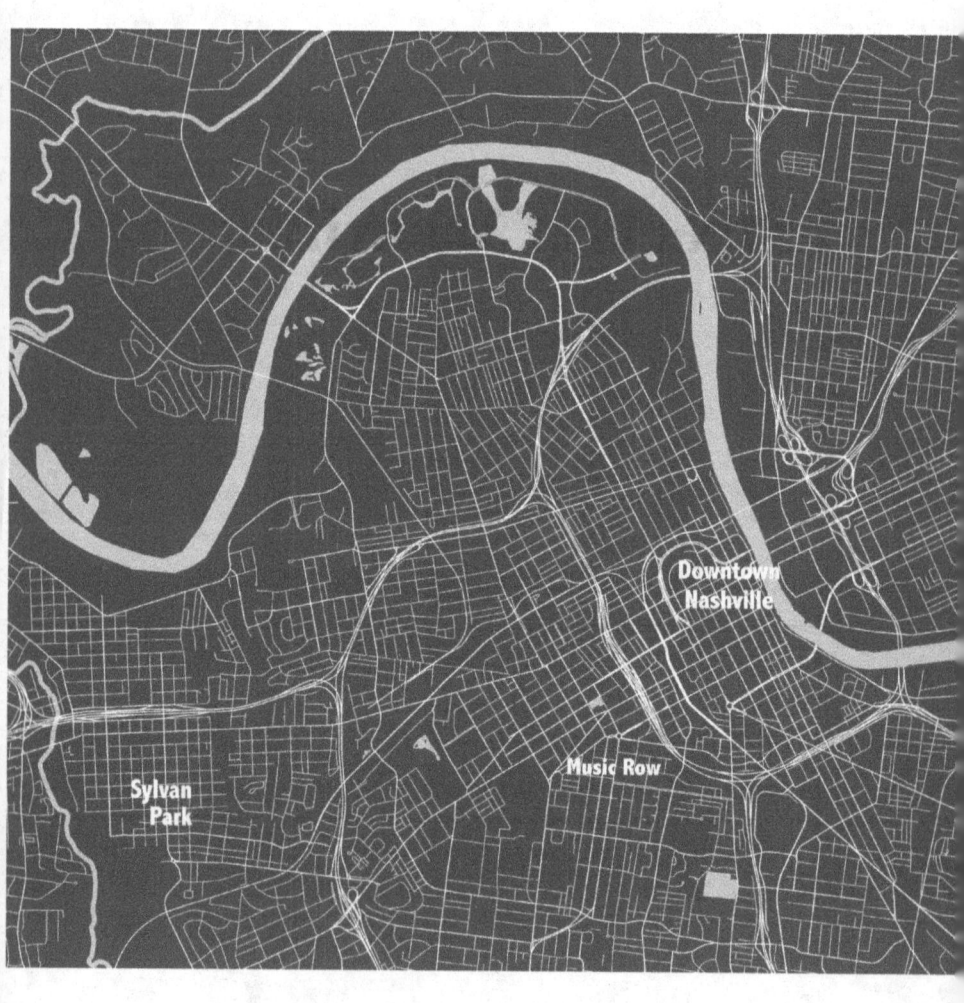

Streets of Nashville

Michael Amos Cody

Lake Dallas, Texas

FIRST EDITION

Streets of Nashville is a work of fiction. Names, characters, places, and incidents either are the products of the author's imagination or are used fictitiously.

Requests for permission to reprint material from this work should be sent to:

Permissions
Madville Publishing
P.O. Box 358
Lake Dallas, TX 75065

Author Photograph: Raleigh Cody

Cover Design: Sam Barnett and Kimberly Davis

Cover Photo: "The skyline of Nashville, Tennessee as seen from the Ellington Parkway." 1970 April 1, Tennessee State Library and Archives, Tennessee Virtual Archive, https://teva.contentdm.oclc.org/digital/collection/p15138coll28/id/5316, accessed 2024-07-29.

Cover Map: Map of the city of Nashville, Tennessee, by Tish11, licensed through Adobe Stock.

ISBN: 978-1-963695-17-5 paperback, 978-1-963695-18-2 ebook
Library of Congress Control Number: 2024945344

*For every Ezra and Benny Jack
on the streets of Nashville in the 1980s,
with the hope that they made it—or made it home*

I like making up a little song

—Maurice Manning, *Bucolics XVII*

Thursday, March 9, 1989

ONE

The streets of Nashville's Music Row lay night-lit and quiet, insensible to the rough mixes blasting on repeat in soundproofed recording studios tucked away inside office buildings and old houses. Occasional solitary vehicles rumbled north on 16th Avenue or south on 17th. A lone runner pounded through the intersection of 17th and Edgehill, crossing against the light as an approaching car blared its horn, the echoes jostling against nearby buildings and skittering past shadows lurking in the alleyways.

Two men in their early twenties emerged from Fireside Recording Studio on 18th and walked quickly to Grand Avenue, where they turned left. Staying close together, a magnetic tension infusing their bodies and hushed voices, they crossed 17th and turned right on 16th. After half a block, they disappeared into number 1021, the house that served as home to Evergreen Records.

The night quieted again, except for the tread and huff of the same lone runner who approached and passed along the sidewalk opposite Evergreen and faded north toward Division Street.

A few minutes after ten o'clock, lights went out in the Evergreen offices, the front door opened, and the two hurried down the steps and angled across the street. The taller one pulled jangling keys from his jacket pocket and led the way around the rear of a car to the passenger door, which he unlocked and opened for his friend. Then he turned to see a man—seemingly dressed in shadow—walking toward them.

1

The shadow man raised a revolver, and amber streetlight glinted along its barrel before disappearing as the muzzle flashed.

The first shot slammed into the shorter man's shoulder as he attempted to dive for the passenger seat, his dive becoming more of a wounded slump into the front floorboard.

His friend fled screaming toward Belmont College as bullet number two buried itself in his back. Bullet three joined it, and he stumbled to a stop and collapsed at the rear of a car parked in front of Blue Ridge Mountain Publishing and Bug Music. There, he lay bleeding, half on the sidewalk and half in the street.

The gunman strode to where his target gasped through sputtering sobs while scratching at the asphalt.

The whisper-call of a voice broke the stillness—"In here! Hurry!"

With the gun held against his thigh, the man in black turned his head and watched as the shoulder-shot man hobbled toward an apartment building and disappeared inside. He turned again to the man at his feet, leaned forward, and fired two point-blank shots into the back of his skull. Then he straightened and stood over the body for another moment, scanned the street in both directions, and disappeared into the shadows.

When the street returned to its normal Thursday quiet, the office manager for Blue Ridge Mountain Publishing rose from where she'd hidden in the floorboard of her car. She sat with her hands on the wheel at ten and two, shaking and staring straight ahead.

Across the street at Emerald Sound Studio, Willie Nelson, Kris Kristofferson, and producer Chips Moman worked undisturbed on vocal overdubs for *Highwayman 2*, Johnny Cash and Waylon Jennings having already finished their parts and gone home for the night.

TWO

Two hundred and twenty-five miles away as the crow flies from the murder on Music Row, Ezra MacRae and his best friend Melvin MacOde, known together as the "Big Macs" a dozen years earlier when they graduated from Runion High, sat across from each other in a booth at Runion Pizzeria, the remains of a large Appalachian Mountain Special—meatballs, mushrooms, spinach, and diced tomatoes—on the tabletop between them. Glutted with pizza and nostalgia, butts slid forward in their seats, they mirrored one another's sprawl and grin.

The pizzeria walls were hung with jerseys, posters, pennants, and other memorabilia in predominantly green for the Runion High Ridgerunners and red for the Runion State Redbirds. Interspersed among sports plaques were clichéd hillbilly caricatures, wall-eyed or cross-eyed, barefoot and gap-toothed. Crowded shelves held stuffed or plastic or ceramic figurines and trinkets from nearby Maggie Valley and Gatlinburg.

The jukebox standing between the cash register counter and the restrooms alcove played Debbie Gibson's "Lost in Your Eyes."

Outside the window by the Big Macs' booth, downtown Runion lay still in the glow of streetlights and sole blinking signal. The darkened display windows of Main Street businesses featured ghosted pictures of area real estate, new books and CDs, and mannequins decked out in flannel shirts of indeterminate colors. Directly across from the Big Macs' window, the south wall of Town Hall showed a mural in progress, with "Greetings from" curled in large loopy letters that wrapped around the small, barred windows of the second-floor jail cells.

"You suppose Mr. Harrell'll paint Li'l Abner and Snuffy Smith looking out those windows up yonder?" Ezra said.

Mel looked up as if considering. "Lord, I hope not," he said and turned back to Ezra. "Do you talk like that in front of your people in Nashville?"

"Like what?"

"You know, *yonder* and all. And *Harrell'll* or whatever the hell you said."

"Well, I don't reckon as how I do," Ezra said.

Both grinned again.

Hannah Henderson, the night's lone waitress, bussed the last table except for the one the Big Macs occupied. She put the dirty dishes in a plastic tub and carried it through the swinging door behind the cash register, then returned with a cart that she pushed around the dining room and loaded with shakers for salt, pepper, parmesan, and red pepper flakes. She misted the last tabletop, hung the spray bottle on the cart handle, picked up a rag, but then stopped. "Last call for root beer, Big Macs," she said over her shoulder. "Closing in seventeen minutes."

"Thanks, Hannah," Mel said. "I think we've probably hit our limit."

"Sure you'll be able to drive?" she said and bent to wipe the tabletop.

Ezra rubbed his belly. "I'll be okay to drive, long as I can squeeze behind the wheel."

The jukebox switched to "The Church on Cumberland Road," and the Big Macs sat for a moment and listened.

"This is a pretty big song," Mel said. "I'm guessing you can tell me who wrote it."

Ezra grinned. "Bob Dipiero, Dennis Robbins, and John Scott Sherrill."

4

"Knew you could," Mel said and saluted Ezra with his root beer.

"Big names on Music Row," Ezra said. "Put out an album a couple years ago under the name Billy Hill." He listened closely for a few bars, tracking the chord progression. Then, "You're the English major. What do you think about the lyrics?"

"I'm a farmer," Mel said.

"The most well-read farmer I know."

"And just how many farmers do you know these days?" Mel said. He reached out and touched the rim of the pizza pan and set it spinning slowly clockwise. "Well, you know the whole thing is mostly cliché, right? I mean, the girl, the truck, the drunk boys—it ain't much of a story."

"It 'ain't,' you say?" Ezra grinned and sat up. "That's worse than *yonder*, ain't it?"

"I reckon as how it might be," Mel said and also sat up with a grin. "But *ain't* and *yonder* and cliché aside, the song's probably true to life. A guy rarely gets that 'cutest little girl' the singer's after, particularly if he belittles her with such denigrating 'little girl' language."

Ezra raised his mug, and Mel met it with his.

"Now, that's what I'm talking about," Ezra said.

They tapped the mug bottoms on the table and drank.

Hannah came by with a large cup of root beer and poured half for each. "If y'all are gonna be toasting this, that, and the other thing," she said. Her eyes sparkled above a grin.

"Thanks, Hannah," Mel said again.

"Better get on with it. I gotta run y'all out of here in about eleven minutes."

They watched her sashay away between the clean tabletops, and then Ezra leaned in and half-whispered, "Why don't you take her out? She still married?"

Mel turned away from watching Hannah. "Caroline called me on Valentine's Day."

Ezra blinked twice and then stared open-mouthed.

"Exactly how I reacted," Mel said and took a sip of his root beer. "She almost hung up when I didn't say anything after hello."

"What the hell?" Ezra said.

"Also my reaction," Mel said. "I mean, I hadn't heard from her in almost ten years."

The guitar, synth, and percussion intro of .38 Special's "Second Chance" sounded from the jukebox, and both of them stopped to listen.

"Weird that coming on just now," Ezra said after the first chorus passed.

"Tell me about it," Mel said and sipped his root beer again.

"No, you tell me. What did she want?"

"Just to talk, I reckon," Mel said, "which we did—for almost three hours."

"What about? And what about her husband?"

"Well, there was the matter of a decade of catching up to do, Ez." He stopped and stared out the window as the second chorus began.

Ezra watched his friend and listened to the words singing from the jukebox, deciding—as he often did—that they were mostly sound without sense. "Melvin?" he said as the song slid into the first bridge. "Don't leave me hanging."

Mel stirred and shrugged. "She and her husband split up three or four years ago. Said it took her all that time to get up the nerve to call me."

"Well, pretty damned nervy to call you on Valentine's Day," Ezra said as the lead guitar took over the track.

"I thought so too."

"And what about the kid?"

Mel laced his fingers together and rested his hands on the edge of the table. "She lost the baby," he said. "Miscarried just like a month after the wedding."

"Geez Louise," Ezra said. "Sorry to hear that." He sipped

his root beer, looking over the top of the mug at Mel. Then he set it down and licked his lips. "You guys gonna get together?"

Mel didn't answer but looked up as Hannah appeared at their table, picked up the mostly empty pizza pan, and placed their bill between them.

"Time to get going, Big Macs," she said. "You want me to split this?"

Mel picked up the bill. "I've got it," he said as they scooted out of the booth. "You can leave the tip."

After Mel paid, they each hugged Hannah and stepped out into the cool late-winter night as the jukebox blasted the guitar intro to "Paradise City."

"So, you guys gonna get together?" Ezra asked again when the door closed behind them, muting Guns N' Roses.

"She wants to come up," Mel said. "I'm supposed to call her, but I haven't yet."

"Valentine's Day was three weeks ago, Chief."

"I know, I know." Mel shoved his hands down into the pockets of his jeans. "I know."

They crossed Lonesome Mountain Drive and walked down Main Street to their parked vehicles—Ezra's car in front of Ramsey's Funeral Home and Mel's truck across the street.

"Hey," Mel said when they stopped on the sidewalk. "We should've done a belated toast for Gabe's birthday. Didn't he join us in the thirties yesterday?"

"That's right, he did," Ezra said. "But it's bad luck to toast somebody without alcohol. Seems like I heard that somewhere."

"Only if you toast with water or an empty glass, I think," Mel said. "Do you see him much?"

"Not really. Maybe every three or four months." Ezra looked back up the street and saw the lights go out in the pizzeria. "He and his band are traveling a lot these days, and he's got some strange thing going on with his bass player."

"With his bass player?"

7

"It's a girl bass player, a woman," Ezra said. "Yvonne Moon. Cool name and hot as hell."

"Interesting." Mel yawned. "Guess I'm not the only one in a weird relationship space."

"Not by a long shot," Ezra said. "Gabe's got a new record coming out soon. I heard the single at his place a few weeks ago. Recorded it down in Muscle Shoals."

"That's cool. What's it called?"

"I don't know what the album is gonna be called, but the song is 'Catch That Train.' And despite his thing with the bass player, it's all about Eliza."

"Interesting," Mel said again through another yawn and a shiver.

Ezra grinned, knowing Mel was done for the evening. "Bring it in," he said.

As was their ritual when parting, they cupped the back of each other's neck with their left hands and touched foreheads together. Then Mel lifted Ezra in a bear hug.

"Love you, Chief," Ezra grunted.

"Love you, too, Ez." Mel set him down, and they stepped apart. "Drive safe tomorrow and watch your back in the big city."

Ezra yawned. "Don't worry. Nashville's generally as sleepy as Runion on a Thursday night."

Mel turned and crossed the street.

"Keep me posted on what happens with Caroline," Ezra called after him.

"Will do." Mel opened his truck door with a screech that echoed between the buildings. The truck rumbled to life as he slammed the door, and he waved and rolled away down Main Street.

With the moon still closer to new than to its first quarter, Ezra drove into the tunnel of light his headlights burrowed through the night. Alongside Highway 251, known locally as the

River Road, the French Broad flowed north in its channel, barely silvered by the waxing crescent moon and starlight. Beyond the shimmer of the river, the mountainous landscape stood ancient and august, a blackness blotting out much of the western sky. The shapes of river and hillside determined the curves he navigated and forced him to keep alert. He was glad to have had only root beer and grinned at that thought. Then he chuckled to himself at a remembered image of Granddaddy Brown, his mother's father from coastal Edenton, North Carolina, who on a rare visit sat wide-eyed and twisted in the front passenger seat, leaning away from the rockface in fear that the mountainside—"all that ground th'ow'd up in the air," he'd said—might collapse on top of him. Ezra felt the opposite. To him, instead of the potential for crushing destruction, the heights above and all around offered an embrace as strong and secure as Mel's hug.

For years he'd been certain that the songwriting life in Music City was his calling. But the streets of Nashville hadn't embraced him as he'd hoped they would, offering only occasional hinted promises to distract from the rejections. He could feel the pull of these mountains, that they and the people in them wanted him home. Mel had said as much while they waited for their pizza. He'd reminded Ezra of a summer evening a month or so before his move to Nashville, when they'd loaded themselves down with hotdog and s'mores fixings and too much beer and ridden horseback up Five Finger Mountain to the MacOde family cemetery. There they lay in sleeping bags among the gravestones, awake deep into the night talking. Mel mostly talked about working the farm and mourned Caroline, the woman who was to have been his helpmate but then walked away from that plan, and Ezra mostly talked about Nashville and songwriting. At some point, they'd sworn that if neither death nor marriage took them before they turned forty, Ezra would move to the farm where they could grow to be fat old bachelors together. They'd been laughing about that when Hannah delivered the Appalachian Mountain Special to their table.

"Why don't you come back and move to the farm now?" Mel had said, suddenly serious. "We can start our old bachelor life a decade early. You can write songs from here."

"Yeah, while I'm mucking out the stables and tending to the bees," Ezra said.

Then their mouths filled with pizza. By the time they could speak again, their minds had turned to other topics—Mel's little brother Curtis's recent move to New York City to find video production work, songs that played on the jukebox, and Caroline's call. Mel's mention of the fat-bachelors-gentleman-farmers dream, Ezra decided as he drove, might have been a means of distracting himself from the potential reappearance of Caroline in his life.

These thoughts then faded as if a curtain had been drawn in some part of his brain, and he turned left onto Sandy Bottoms. Four yawns later, he turned right onto Glory Ridge Trail. When he suddenly found himself in his parents' driveway, sitting in the car with the motor running, he felt sure he couldn't have navigated the last winding mile in his sleep. But he had no memory of it. He got out of the car and quietly pushed the door shut until it latched with a click.

The air was colder here than it had been in Runion, the night around him darker and quieter.

He started for the porch steps and smiled at the warm, familiar glow of the lamp's soft gleam in the window above him. But then he angled away from the house to relieve himself on the berm across the yard. He smelled mulch freshened on the worn heels of winter. He saw the outlines of small rhododendron, red twig dogwood, a number of dormant flowers awaiting warmer weather, Appalachian sedge grass, and river stones. Like a boy, he swiveled his hips and distributed his pee back and forth over the berm's inhabitants.

A distant cacophony of yips and howls rose from the direction of the river, and the word *coyotes* popped into his mind. When home for Thanksgiving, he'd listened to Mel talk about them as newcomers, having crossed the Mississippi and pushed east into Appalachia. He'd imagined himself on many a late-night drive along I-40 West, roaring toward Nashville while just beyond the guardrail a lone pair of coyotes trotted on tiptoe toward Runion. He shivered as image and sound joined to drive him back across the yard, up the porch steps, and into the house.

He stripped, brushed his teeth, and climbed into bed, leaving the bathroom fan on in the hope of lulling himself to sleep, the sound masking both further yips from the coyotes and the steady ticks from the living room's mantel clock. But a lurking embarrassment edged with anger constantly prodded him back to wakefulness. Something his mother had said earlier in the day, before he left to meet Mel downtown.

"Well, thirty's a milestone for most people, son," she'd said. "Your papa and I hoped you might come home and start looking for something more permanent."

Ezra gazed across the manicured bald of Glory Ridge. He clenched and then relaxed his jaw, caught a deep breath and cleared his throat. "I can't say that I've thought much about that, Mama."

"It's just the world's getting so evil and you seem so happy when you're here, son, here in the mountains and out with Mel. When you're in Nashville, you hardly ever sound that way."

She was right, he knew. As much as he loved Nashville and the promise it might hold, life there was lonely more often than not, even with the presence of Gabe and a few other friends he'd made. Living was happier here and close to Mel. He wrestled this shape-shifting dilemma back and forth and back and forth as he fell into an uneasy sleep.

Friday, March 10, 1989

THREE

He awoke later than he wanted to and shuffled barefoot into the kitchen just as his father was gathering his things to go to the church. "Don't you usually take Friday off, Papa?"

"Usually, but not this time of year." Ephraim MacRae pulled a jacket on over his sweater and settled a fedora on his head. "Well, drive safe, son, and come back soon."

"I'll be back in a couple of weeks for Easter, okay?"

"Fine." Reverend MacRae kissed Ezra's mother on the cheek. "Have a good day, my dear."

"Wash up and sit," she said when the door to the garage closed behind his father. "I've got breakfast for you." While he washed his hands and watched his father back out of the driveway, she opened the oven and removed a plate of biscuits and gravy, scrambled eggs, and bacon. She set the plate in front of him. "Oh, I forgot to get you a fork," she said and fetched him one from the silverware drawer. Then she poured his coffee and warmed her own and sat down across the table from him.

"Mama, Mama," he said and began cutting into a biscuit covered in gravy. "Thank you."

"Did you sleep well?"

"Not really," he said when he'd swallowed enough to speak. "I heard coyotes off toward the river when I came in, and they gave me the creeps."

"I know," she said. "They're awful seems like all of a sudden."

"And I couldn't stop thinking about what we were discussing yesterday."

"Satan and coyotes don't make good bedfellows?"

Ezra laughed. "I'm sure they don't, but I'm not really worried about either of them." He sipped his coffee and then forked a wad of eggs, touched it to the gravy, and stuffed it in his mouth. "I mean, the coyotes were creepy, but I didn't give another thought to old Satan after I left y'all on the porch."

She sipped her coffee and looked at him with an expression he read as partially concerned for his undefended soul and partially contented by his enjoyment of breakfast.

They didn't speak for a time.

"That was awesome, Mama," he said after he washed down the last bite with one last swallow of coffee. "Thanks."

She refilled his cup and carried his plate to the sink.

"Instead of coyotes and Satan, what I was thinking about was what y'all were saying about coming home and settling down."

"And what were you thinking about that?"

"Well, it feels a lot like giving up, and I'm not sure I want to do that yet." He waited a moment for a response that didn't come, so he cleared his throat. "What came to me before I finally went to sleep was that I'd keep at it just a little longer." He told her he could support himself with another season of cleaning pools. He already cleaned Barbara Mandrell's pool. He hadn't talked to her yet or even seen more than the blonde top of her head as she sat in a chair with its back turned to the outside world, but he'd chatted for a long time one day with her father, who walked around the pool with him as he cleaned. Other singing stars might come up on his weekly schedule.

"Give me seven months," he said. "If nothing's happened by the end of October, if I don't get any songs recorded or put on hold, then I'll fix Music City in my rearview and be a full-time Runionite by Christmas." He downed the last of his second cup. "How does that sound, Mama?"

"Good," Sarah MacRae said. "That sounds good, son."

Tuesday, March 14, 1989

FOUR

Detectives Darrin Hunt and Woody Davidson of the Metro Nashville Police Department slid into opposite sides of a booth in Brown's Diner. A Budweiser pheasant glowed above them in neon red, yellow, green, and white.

Davidson pushed the table a couple of inches away from his belly and toward Hunt. "You mind?"

"Make yourself comfortable." Hunt turned to the waitress as she approached.

"Well, Metro PD," Laurel Dauphin set down glasses of ice water. "We on duty or off?"

"A little of both," Davidson said.

"Beer?"

Davidson looked at Hunt with raised eyebrows.

"I might have one," Hunt said. "With my sandwich."

"How about a pitcher?" the waitress asked.

She returned with the drink order and then brought a cup of coffee for Hunt, who ordered a smoked turkey sandwich with potato chips and Coleslaw. Davidson ordered a cheeseburger and fries. She scribbled on an order pad, tucked the pen between her breasts and turned to the kitchen window, where she called out the order to Junior, the cook.

"Let me guess," Junior's voice came from somewhere unseen. "It's them boys in blue."

"You've got it, Junior," Laurel said.

Hunt and Davidson exchanged a look across the table. Hunt ran the knuckle of an index finger over both sides of his mustache. Davidson shrugged.

16

"Reckon maybe we come here too much?"

"Maybe." Hunt sipped his coffee.

While they waited, they made small talk about the people and politics within the offices and hallways of police headquarters, but they made no mention of their individual lives outside its walls. When their food arrived, they ate without talking.

Before Hunt finished the first half of his sandwich or more than half his glass of beer, Davidson pulled the paper napkin from his collar, pushed his greasy, ketchup-smeared plate to the side, and poured himself the last of the pitcher.

When the waitress came by to collect Davidson's empty plates and used silverware, Hunt asked for a to-go box.

"Hunt," Davidson said, "my Granny Woodrow would declare you don't eat enough to keep a bird alive."

"Thank you," Hunt said to the waitress as she handed him the Styrofoam box. He placed the remaining half of his sandwich in the largest compartment and scooped the leftover Coleslaw into one of the smaller ones, closed the top, and carved the date into the Styrofoam with his car key.

Davidson smiled, shook his head, and took out his notebook. "All right, back on duty."

Hunt likewise took out his notebook, leaned back from the table as Laurel cleared away, and leaned forward again. From between the notebook's pages, he unfolded a crime scene diagram clipped from Saturday's *Tennessean* and placed it on the tabletop between them.

It depicted the section of 16th Avenue between Evergreen Records and Kim's Market. Arrows showed the movements of both shooter and victims. Circled numbers were keyed to an inset describing the movements and positions of the wounded and the dead.

The detectives studied the image for a moment and then flipped open their notebooks to blank pages.

"Something feels different about this Music Row murder," Hunt said.

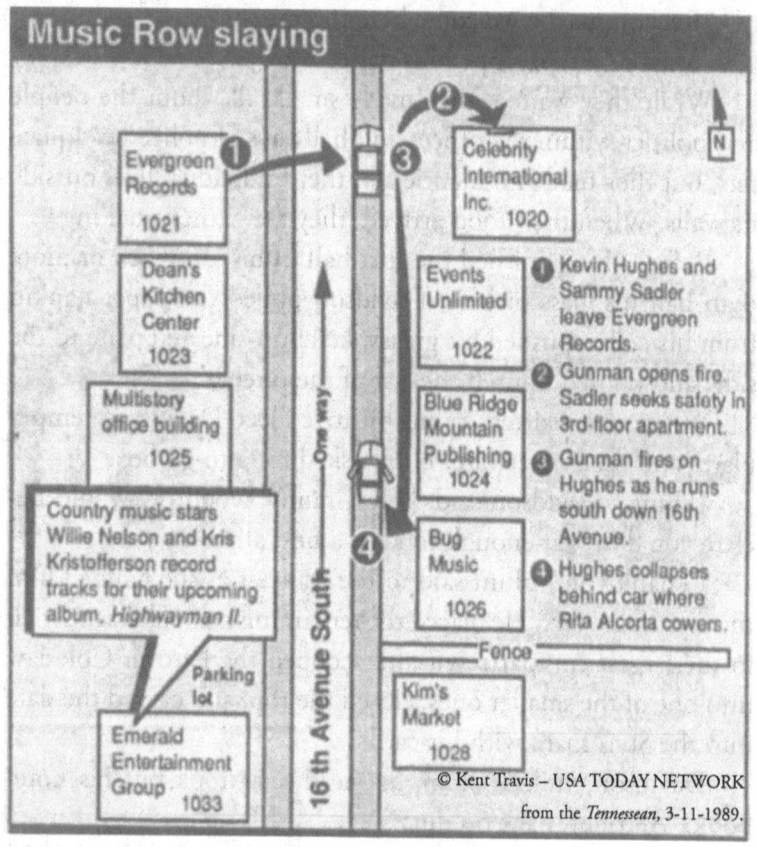

Music Row slaying

Evergreen Records 1021 ❶

Dean's Kitchen Center 1023

Multistory office building 1025

Country music stars Willie Nelson and Kris Kristofferson record tracks for their upcoming album, *Highwayman II.*

Parking lot

Emerald Entertainment Group 1033

One way — 16 th Avenue South

❸ ❷ Celebrity International Inc. 1020

Events Unlimited 1022

Blue Ridge Mountain Publishing 1024

❹ Bug Music 1026

Fence

Kim's Market 1028

N

❶ Kevin Hughes and Sammy Sadler leave Evergreen Records.

❷ Gunman opens fire. Sadler seeks safety in 3rd-floor apartment.

❸ Gunman fires on Hughes as he runs south down 16th Avenue.

❹ Hughes collapses behind car where Rita Alcorta cowers.

© Kent Travis – USA TODAY NETWORK
from the *Tennessean*, 3-11-1989.

"Different how?"

"I can't exactly say." Hunt brushed the heel of his hand to gather some crumbs in front of him and then wiped them toward the wall. He picked up his coffee cup. "Although I'm certain it's a target-driven act, the victim selection could be random—" He stopped and sipped his coffee. "Somehow it doesn't feel isolated."

"How do you mean?"

"Like it's not a stand-alone act," Hunt said. "But not like it's connected to anything, either. More like it's the beginning of something." He set the coffee cup down in its saucer. "A harbinger of things to come."

"That's some scary word choice, my friend." Davidson took a sip of water. "And yeah, I know what a harbinger is."

"I never doubted you for a moment." Hunt doodled a ski mask in the upper righthand corner of his notebook page. "So, what are we thinking? What are we hearing?"

Davidson drew the number one at the top of his page. "This lady who works at The Store down in Sylvan Park thinks it's part of the devil's work, like at those daycares all over the news."

"I've heard something similar," Hunt said. "But I don't believe things work like that, do you?"

"No, not exactly like that," Davidson said. "But I think there's scary shit to see and hear out there." He took another sip of water. "Maybe it's evil, I don't know."

"Maybe you're right. And I suppose that our thinking it's not real doesn't mean the perpetrator thinks the same." He picked up his own glass of water and sipped. "A man dressed in black might think any number of things about who he is and what he's doing."

The two detectives wrote in their notebooks for a moment, and then both leaned back from the table while Laurel topped off their waters and offered Hunt a coffee refill, which he declined. Davidson stared across the room at the Pistons vs. Pacers game playing on a small TV sitting atop a wooden buffet and hutch while Hunt people-watched.

"I hate that conspiracy shit," Davidson said at last.

"So do I," Hunt mused. "And I often wonder if the people creating stories about rings of child molesters and devil worshipers are laughing at the people they dupe or if they're ignorant enough to believe right alongside the rest."

"Well," Davidson said. "Those ignorant believers are out there either way, so I don't think we can completely dismiss the Satan idea." He picked up his water glass. "Like you say, we might not believe it, but the man in black or those around him might."

Hunt jotted something in his notebook and then looked up. "All right, what else?"

"Well, on the other end of the spectrum is the idea that the deceased worked at *Cash Box* and that this is connected to the magazine somehow. Music charts maybe." He finally sipped from the glass he'd picked up and then set it down. "Not as sexy as the Satan idea but probably more likely."

"Right—"

"Y'all want anything else?" the waitress said as she passed.

"No, thank you, Laurel," Hunt said. "Just the check."

"One check?"

"Yes."

When she brought the check and took away Hunt's coffee cup, Davidson sat hunched over his notebook, as if in prayer, then looked up at his partner. "You heard or thought of any other theories?"

Hunt stared at the check for a moment, then knuckled each side of his mustache. "I've got a couple of related things that land somewhere between the Satan and *Cash Box* ideas."

"Okay, tell me, and then I got to go get some shuteye."

"On the mundane *Cash Box* side of things, this might be the work of some disappointed and angry wannabe or maybe some has-been who thinks he'll get something out of removing one or both of Thursday's victims from the picture."

"Give me an example."

"I don't know enough about the music business, but I was thinking that maybe he got upset about Hughes's chart keeping, or maybe Sadler got the recording contract our killer believes he should have had."

Davidson nodded and wrote in his notebook. "And on the crazy Satan side?"

"I've heard that maybe the shooter was some current star—an upcoming one or even a legend—who attacked those guys to protect some ancient Music City secret."

"Like?"

"If we really run with the conspiracy thing, then maybe—I don't know—the regulars at the Grand Ole Opry prepare for the show with a black Mass."

"A black Mass?"

"Devil worship."

Davidson looked at Hunt for a moment and then wrote again in his notebook. He stopped. "Or how about this—somewhere between your mundane and conspiracy ideas." Davidson clicked the top of his pen three times. "What if one or more of the big country music stars was caught in some compromising sexual situation or something like that and Sadler or Hughes—"

"Or both."

"Or both found out about it and was planning to expose them."

They scribbled in their notebooks.

Davidson looked up. "Now that I see it on paper, that's probably a lot like the Satanic pedophile idea."

"Agreed," Hunt said. "So, that's enough for tonight." He pulled his wallet from the back pocket of his pants, took out a twenty, and placed it on top of the check. "We need to get out of here before we come up with anything else."

Saturday, March 25, 1989

FIVE

Ezra MacRae lumbered along the sidewalk, watching the cross-street signs for 16th Avenue South to become Music Square East. He figured he was probably lurching but hoped he wasn't, anxious to sleep in his own bed rather than take a backseat ride downtown to spend the night in the drunk tank. He wished Kate had come out to celebrate with him. Or at least to drive him to his place. Or to hers. But she hadn't. And that hurt.

Almost from the moment Gabe Tanner had introduced them three years earlier, Kate Hathaway had made no secret of the fact that she harbored reservations about Ezra's character. And yet in the last six months, they'd overflowed Jacuzzis and left lots of sweat-drenched bedding from Asheville to Little Rock and Louisville to Atlanta.

"We crossed state lines," he slurred to himself and then stopped on the sidewalk and shouted, "Oughta count for somethin', Kate!" Then, quieting himself with a long shush, he said in a whisper, "Shoutin' at trees's likely as lurchin' to—" He pressed his lips together and walked on.

A week and a half after some St. Patrick's Day indiscretion that he couldn't quite remember and she couldn't seem to forget, Kate still burned with an embarrassed indignation as vivid as her red hair. He'd validated her reservations about him, she said, but he knew only as much as she'd been willing—or able—to tell him through fits of characteristic seething rage and uncharacteristic heaving sobs. Despite her broken feelings, he knew she worried about him, about his body and mind and

23

soul, as did many others—his mother and father, Mel, his long-time sometime-friend-sometime-nemesis Gabe, and practically everybody else who was in his life for his own good. And he worried about himself as the wind pushed him north along 16th, blowing past him in its hurry to join the storm manifesting in flashes of lightning on the city's northwest horizon.

No way to make Utah before it hits. He began thinking of dry places he could duck into if needed. *Dry but not dry*, he thought, wondering how much celebration money he still had in his pocket.

After spending a few months shy of six years writing songs in Music City, he'd finally received some tangible encourage-ment—two savory morsels and one healthy serving of great news in a single week. All came from Ave Canora, the independent music publishing company to which he'd assigned a handful of songs the previous summer. The first morsel came Tuesday from his answering machine when he returned home after cleaning pools. The voice of Ave Canora's Mark Williamson reported that a Belgian country music star named Jurby Gibson had recorded "Somebody, Somewhere" for an album scheduled for release in May. Then on Wednesday, when Ezra stopped at a payphone between pools and returned Williamson's call, he learned that producer Rick West had just put "Blue Jeans Girl" on hold for an Epic Records project with country singer David Wills. Before Ezra hung up to hit his last couple of pools for the day, Williamson asked if he could stop by the office around two o'clock Thursday. When he did, Williamson and Ave Canora head honcho Burl Davies offered him a two-year exclusive songwriting contract guaranteeing him a salary of fifteen thousand dollars a year, with a possible increase to twenty thousand the second year if his pro-ductivity and further recordings warranted it. He'd signed and couldn't remember much since, except calling Kate at Billy Keith Productions and hearing her take him down a notch with her tone and her refusal to join his extended celebration.

As he approached the Edgehill intersection, the trees swayed, giving voice to the wind, their new leaves creating dizzying, shifting shadows beneath the streetlights.

Shit, Kate.

Then the wind and shadows stilled, as if somewhere the power failed and a fan stopped. The trees drooped, pinning humid shadows beneath them.

He looked up as he walked.

Directly above him between the streetlights and treetops, a few stars shimmered through the haze. But a straight line of fast-moving clouds was crossing the sky like a heavy eyelid closing, and flashes of lightning backlit the Nashville skyline.

He tripped on a curb and stumbled to a stop near the front of Kim's Market, where he sometimes met Gabe for eggrolls and Mountain Dew, which they would eat while strolling along Music Row and talking some about songs, but mostly about Runion—about home. Yet something else about this exact place—16th Avenue and Kim's Market—skulked in the shadows of his glowing inebriation. He stood with eyes squeezed shut and his right palm cupping his sweat-and-oil-slicked forehead, trying to track whatever it was. At the same time, he felt certain that he didn't really want to catch whatever the fleeting notion was. Just as he was about to give up and walk on, the memory emerged from a dark corner of his mind and rooted him to the sidewalk.

The memory of a map. A simple map of straight lines for a street, small rectangles for parked vehicles, and squares for buildings. This street—16th Avenue. And these buildings—Kim's Market beside him, Emerald Sound Studio just opposite, Evergreen Records farther down on the left. And among these places on the map, arrows represented movement. One arrow pointed from the Evergreen building to a car parked on the east side of 16th. Another ran from that car south along the sidewalk and then hooked to point behind a second parked car.

He'd seen the map in *The Tennessean* on the Saturday after

those two, Kevin Hughes and Sammy Sadler, were shot. On a regular Nashville Thursday night. The attack, he'd realized as he read the article accompanying the map, probably happened at the same time Mel and he were walking together from the pizzeria to their vehicles on Runion's Main Street. Sadler survived and might still lie in the Vandy hospital less than a mile away. Hughes died in the moment—*at the scene*—less than thirty feet along the sidewalk from where Ezra stood swaying in his tracks.

He imagined blood trailing along the sidewalk or pooling on the dirty asphalt. He wondered if he could walk on and not look down or if he should cross to the other side of the street. He wondered if anybody was recording over at Emerald and suddenly lurched to the opposite sidewalk, where he stood unsteadily and listened for a rumbling bass line from the studio. Then he turned to try and imagine the attack from this angle. "Jeez, jus' move 'long, Ez." *Nothin' to see here.*

He hurried up the sidewalk past where 16th at last changed to Music Square East. After another block, he turned left and stopped on the corner beneath the United Artists Tower. Across Music Square West stood the FISI building, where Bullet Recording was when he first moved to town—where Gabe and Billy Keith had recorded two unreleased albums. The studio space was still there, he knew, but it was now Norbert Putnam's Digital Recording. He continued along Music Square West and passed RCA's Studio B, where Elvis once recorded. *Tourist trap*, he thought with a drunken scowl. In another half block, Jamboree Music and Tree International Publishing rose on his right, their industry prestige and their physical buildings dwarfing Ave Canora's bungalow across the street.

Ezra stopped on the sidewalk, his back to Jamboree and Tree, and stood looking at little Ave Canora.

"No more cleaning pools for me," he said to the night that surrounded him and the darkness framed by the bungalow's windows. "This is where I work now." Even as he spoke, he felt the big publishing houses at his back loom over him. He was thrilled with his Ave Canora deal, but Tree and Jamboree embodied the dream, the big time for a Nashville songwriter.

"I'm happy with you," he said to the darkened bungalow. *For now.* He turned and continued along the sidewalk.

He passed the ASCAP building beyond Tree and felt another happy jolt at thinking he was finally a bona fide member, an ASCAP composer composing—on salary—for an ASCAP publisher. In contrast to these celebratory flashes brightening his beer-clouded brain, the sidewalk grew darker as he moved through bells of blueish light to Division Street, where he turned right, back toward Music Square East.

As he passed a small public park that adjoined the alleyway behind ASCAP and the near side of Spence Manor, with its guitar-shaped Webb Pierce swimming pool, he thought he heard a voice from somewhere beneath the park's trees. He glanced in that direction but didn't see anyone.

The voice came again. "I like your hat."

Ezra brought himself to a wavering stop and stared.

A little man sat still as a statue on a bench not too deep into the park. Then he stood and, mirroring Ezra's unsteadiness, motioned for him to come closer.

Money and cigarettes. Ezra almost continued walking but checked the sky instead and decided the rain was still a few minutes away, checked the area around the park—not very well lit but open—and decided he could give a couple minutes to a lonely soul. A little conversation might briefly mask the undertone of his own loneliness that hummed beneath the exultation over his recent good news. He left the sidewalk and lumbered across the grass toward the little man and his bench.

"Howdy, mister, howdy. Name's Benny Jack Boudreau from Appalachia, Virginia. You ever heard tell of Appalachia, Virginia?"

Ezra stepped closer to Benny Jack and stopped. "I think maybe I've seen signs for it somewhere."

"Hell, there ain't no signs for it. Ain't no signs for Appalachia, Virginia, nowheres."

"Well, I guess—"

"Without you're in it. If you ain't been in it, you ain't seen no signs." Benny Jack's walleyed stare shone glassy, and his body vibrated like a loose windowpane in a thunderstorm. He wore a huge T-shirt featuring Waylon Jennings's winged W logo, frayed and faded jeans and denim jacket, and shoes that matched only by both being brown and scuffed. A dirty and dented straw cowboy hat sat so low on his head that it nearly covered his ears.

"Big rain's coming, mister," he said. "Big rain."

Ezra looked up and to the west.

Twitching flashes lit up a wider part of the sky, and thunder followed more quickly, with a more percussive and extended rumble.

"I been in Nashville writin' songs and singin' 'em for twenty years," Benny Jack said in a tight fast voice. "I've all the time got words running through my head like crazy. Don't matter if it's day or night or I'm asleep or awake." He closed his eyes and scrunched up his face. His head quivered for a moment. When he opened his eyes, he said, "Yes, mister, yes, twenty years, me and my Lonely." His right hand made a jerky motion toward a Yamaha guitar in a battered and open Epiphone case propped up at one end of his bench, an open quart of Miller beer on the ground beneath. "That's what I call my guitar. My Lonely. I make it sing with this." The middle finger on his left hand was fully inserted in a small glass bottle. "Slide's my style," he said. "My hook." He swiveled his hand back and forth, as if admiring his dirty and chewed fingernails, and then bent all but the middle finger to his palm. "This here's the genuine Coricidin bottle Duane Allman used on 'Layla.'"

"Really?" Ezra grinned at the unintended rude gesture and

the lofty claim but didn't know what else to say. Even drunk himself, he wasn't in the mood to hear any drunken slide work, so he didn't want to offer encouragement that might lead to it.

"Yeah, me and my Lonely, we're the next big thing, I tell you. Song-making wonders is what we are. That's what Waylon says. I work for him. You could probably tell that from my shirt. He's gonna record one of my songs in that studio across the street there by the Country Music Hall of Fame, soon as I finish some work for him out at his house. He asked me where I wanted to record, and I told him in that studio just right beside the Country Music Hall of Fame. And he says, 'Okay, Benny Jack, that's where we'll do it.' And that's where I'll be before you know it, too, in the Country Music Hall of Fame with all the greats of country music of all times." He picked up his beer, his hand shaking as he lifted it to his lips, and drank with quick, violent pulls. "Want some of this here beer, mister?"

"No thanks," Ezra said. "You go ahead."

Benny Jack's eyes made him uneasy. While the right strayed around Ezra's face, the left looked steadily over his shoulder, and Ezra kept glancing back to be sure no one was there. Even though he'd checked the area, he began to feel like easy prey for a tag-team mugging.

Benny Jack wiped his mouth on the sleeve of his jacket and then reached into the back pocket of his jeans. He pulled out a flattened pack of Winstons. "Smoke, mister?" He pulled a mashed cigarette from the pack and held it out.

"Keep it. I've got some." Ezra reached for the Camel Lights in his shirt pocket.

"Can I bum one from you?" Benny Jack asked as he slid his pack back into his jeans and tucked the cigarette he'd pulled from it behind his ear.

"One what?"

"One of your smokes. I got a light for us."

"Sure." Ezra shook a single cigarette up from the pack.

"Jesus, you're good," Benny Jack said with a shuddering voice as he took the Camel Light. "You're good, I say." He reached into the breast pocket of his jacket and pulled out a silver lighter with a red, white, and blue eagle on it. "This here's a genuine bicentennial Zippo. Only two of 'em in the world, and Hank Jr.'s got the other one."

"How'd you come to have it?" Ezra asked as he leaned the tip of his cigarette into the shaky flame Benny Jack held up.

"Waylon give it to me. I work for him. He's gonna record one of my songs in that studio of his'n up down by Edgehill. He asked me where I wanted to record, and I told him wherever he records." He lit the cigarette Ezra had given him. "Yeah, this here lighter's been a good one. Only two of 'em made, too. Me and Hank Jr.'s all that owns one now that Waylon give his up." He took another draw from his beer. "My sweet mother died on April thirteen of nineteen and eighty-five."

"Pardon?"

"Just up and died of a sudden, and I don't know what of."

"I'm sorry to hear that, Benny Jack."

"I went back to South Carolina for the funeral. Her church sent me money to come on the Greyhound, praise God."

"South Carolina? That's a long ride."

"My goddamn cousins laughed at me, but I'll show 'em someday. Mama's watching me from Heaven right now, and she's so proud of me. And lordy, sure as I'm standing here, it'll rain her tears of joy from a clear blue sky the day they put me in the Country Music Hall of Fame." Benny Jack's voice rose and shook, and he turned into the wind and wiped his eyes. "Jesus, you got a cigarette?"

Ezra shook another Camel Light up from his pack, surprised that the small man hadn't yet asked for money.

But Benny Jack didn't say anything more. He took the offered cigarette and stood with his eyes closed and his body swaying in gritty wind that smelled of rain.

Ezra turned half away and looked up again.

The clouds had closed over the sky.

With one more glance at Benny Jack, he turned and angled toward the corner of Division and Music Square East, focused on beating the rain somewhere instead of getting home. The image of the googly-eyed little man gave him a sudden pang— hugging his guitar and trying to keep his cigarettes dry and the dregs of his beer from spilling while he scrambled to find shelter in some recessed doorway.

jesus came to see
my lonely and me
just before he made it rain
i asked him for a cigarette and he give me one
i offered him my beer and he said keep it son
i told him that i liked his hat
i told him my names benny jack
jesus just walked off while i was lookin tother way
wish he hadnt left
wish he had just kept
by me through the storm he made
i told him how my mama died some years ago
i told him how her church had paid to get me home
he said he needed to get back
twas nice to meet you benny jack
jesus just walked off while i was lookin tother way
yeah jesus just walked off while i was lookin tother way

Sunday, March 26, 1989
Easter

SIX

Ezra matched his pace with that of the big drops splattering on the sidewalk and street and thudding on the brim of his hat. The downpour began in earnest just as he crossed the Hall of Fame Motel's parking lot and passed through the doors into a lobby that rang with the strains of "Elvira."

In the motel's Sound Track Restaurant & Lounge, the band worked the crowd with a stir-'em-up breakdown of the Oak Ridge Boys hit. All five members stood along the front of the stage, clapping hands in rhythm, helping the singer lead the thirty or so wobbly patrons in an *a cappella* sing-along of the refrain.

Dallas Frazier, songwriter, Ezra thought, looking around.

At one table, a man and two women stood in their chairs, singing loud. All over the room, raised glasses reflected the yellowish stage lighting, and various alcoholic mixtures spilled down as if from a terraced fountain.

One by one the band members drifted back to their instruments and left the singer alone with the crowd. But he had trouble signaling the end of the song. He first tried to break out of the repeated lines with a kind of yodel. That didn't work. He stopped altogether. That didn't work either. He turned and took a swig from a beer that sat on the floor beside the kick drum and then rejoined the chorus and tried to lead an emphatic *ritard*. But the crowd plowed through his cue and reprised the "giddy up—oompoppaoompoppamowmow—giddy up!"

"A *ritard* means the end, y'all!" the singer yelled into his microphone.

Ezra found a clean table near the back of the room and sat down. As the slurred sing-along continued without the band, he kept glancing at the door, half expecting to see Benny Jack Boudreau standing there with his Lonely in his arms, his clothes and hair dripping rainwater and sweat onto the carpet. But he knew a guy like that couldn't get five feet into the lobby before security collared him and tossed him back out into the night and the rain.

He smelled the perfume first—a thick powdery smell, over-sweet and strong—then felt her hand on his shoulder.

"What're you drinking, honey?" she said.

He turned to find her leaning in close, long dark hair spilling down over her left ear and tickling his forearm. "Just a beer," he said to the shadowed face. "Whatever you have on tap."

"Be right back," she said, giving his shoulder a soft squeeze as she passed behind him.

"Heigh-ho, Silver, away, goddamn it!" the singer yelled into the microphone. "Hey, I know y'all don't give a shit right now, but we're signing with Epic Records here in a few days. This song'll be the one y'all drunks'll be crazy for next year." He turned his back to the crowd that still swayed and sang. "Hit it, boys!" he yelled, and the band kicked into a medium-tempo country shuffle, drowning out the drunken chorus of "Elvira." "A new songwriter named Jimmy Austin wrote this with us," the singer bellowed over the intro. "We're gonna do it in honor of all the women out there. It's called 'American Girl.'"

Ezra noted the name of the songwriter, smiled to himself, and shook his head. *With no apologies to Tom Petty.*

Some in the crowd sat down and started motioning for the waitress. Others gathered their things off tables and the backs of chairs and headed for the door.

Despite the comic brutishness of the band, Ezra figured it could happen for them. They had the look and the sound. The singer seemed a sinful version of George Strait. The guys on bass and keyboard were solid players and sang strong harmonies. The

34

drummer and lead guitarist approached the status of Nashville virtuoso. The people leaving might really be calling their local radio stations in a few months, asking to hear the song this as-yet-unknown band had launched into. They could be in the presence of superstars and not even realize it. He imagined the ghosts of the greats parading untouched by the rain down the sidewalk from the Country Music Hall of Fame, entering this bar, and lining the walls, smiling at each other for the simple pleasure of hearing again the music they helped create. *Wait'll y'all get a load of my songs*, he thought.

She brought his beer and stayed close beside him. She leaned down once and spoke close to his ear. He didn't understand her but smiled and nodded anyway.

Between the verse Ezra hadn't been listening to and the chorus coming up, the singer pulled the microphone from its holder and set the stand aside. He closed his eyes and placed his right hand on his chest.

You are sugar and spice
And everything nice in this world.
Like apple pie and mother,
I don't want no lover other than you, girl.
You're my American girl.

Ezra grimaced at the simile.

The guitarist ended the song with a smoldering lead that drew spontaneous applause from the ten or so remaining patrons, Ezra included.

"We're the Moonshine Rebels," the singer shouted into the microphone. "Happy Easter! And God bless America!"

Ezra downed his beer, stood up, handed the waitress five dollars, and excused himself. He headed for the door, trying to blow the smell of her perfume out of his nose and shake the words of the bar band's wanna-be hit song out of his head.

Before he stepped into the light drizzle that seemed like the storm's version of dust settling, he checked his watch and saw that it was a quarter to one on Easter Sunday morning.

when the rains come
i found a covered back door step
for my lonely and me
we made it a stage son
we played while the whole world slept
we give that show for free
then two devils dressed in black from head to toe
give fifty dollars for a second show
these two devils up from out the crowd
asked can you play your lonely really loud
i said sure
one was big and one was small
one was short and one was tall
the big and tall one talked like god
the short and small barked like a dog
then god whispered in his doggie's ear
give me fifty bucks and disappeared
i said cool

Easter? Ezra pulled his hat lower on his brow and walked across the parking lot, angling left and talking to himself. "Shit. I said I'd be home for Easter." In his mind, he laid out the hour-long walk to his apartment. He figured he ought to get to bed about the time his father rose for the sunrise service back home. He shoved his hands into the pockets of his denim jacket. *Hope this storm doesn't make it to Runion and rain him out.* He looked at the rainbow reflections of Nashville lights on the wet pavement, wiped his eyes, and kept walking.

On the corner of Music Square East and Division, he watched a car approach the intersection from his left. His pulse quickened for a moment when he recognized it as a sportscar like Kate's, and as it drew closer and the streetlight glare diminished, it became red like hers, too. He bent to look inside and saw that the driver was a beefy man sitting belly-to-the-wheel. "How's a big dude like you get in an RX-7?" he said as the car splashed through the green-light shine of the intersection and continued onto Demonbreun. *Like squeezing into a cupboard.* He checked left again and then crossed, continuing to look left and scanning the park for walleyed Benny Jack.

Big rain's coming.

Benny Jack's words flashed in Ezra's mind as clearly as he'd earlier heard "I like your hat" called from the park bench. Words with rhythm and a hint of melody followed, appearing unbidden in his mind—*He stepped out of the music and into the rain.* He stopped in the middle of the sidewalk. *Or maybe into the night,* he thought, *if rain's coming later in the song.* Then he pulled a pencil and pad from inside his jacket. He jotted down BIG RAIN'S COMING and HE STEPPED OUT OF THE MUSIC AND INTO THE RAIN/NIGHT.

"Could be he or she or I," he said aloud and added HE/SHE/I, followed by a question mark. He would need to decide about *rain* or *night* before the next line. *Need something about those tears from a clear blue sky.* He jotted down a couple more notes and put the pad and pencil back inside his jacket and continued walking, thinking it would be cool to make Benny Jack a co-writer on the song and surprise him someday with a royalty check. "If I can find him again."

At the corner of Music Square West and Division, he stopped and looked left once more, not for traffic this time—which would come from his right into this one-way street—but to gaze again with a thrill in his chest at 7 Music Square West, the 1930s bungalow that housed Ave Canora Music. Although the building had been dark when he passed it earlier, a light was on upstairs, and he wondered if maybe that was a writing room where some fellow night owl—a fellow Ave Canora songwriter—sat working, a room where in a month or two he might sit alone or with a co-writer and come up with a song for Clint Black or Kathy Mattea. *Maybe even the Moonshine Rebels.*

The light went out.

His planned route to Utah Avenue lay to the right and down to West End, but he turned left and moved along the sidewalk toward Ave Canora, passing again in front of the ASCAP building and hoping to see who came out of the bungalow. If Mark Williamson or Burl Davies or some songwriter he recognized, he might ask about a lift toward home.

The porchlight came on, and the front door opened. A woman and man Ezra didn't recognize stepped out, followed by Burl Davies, who reached in and turned off the porchlight and then pulled the door closed behind them.

My publisher, Ezra thought and smiled. He watched the three come down the steps and stop together on the bungalow's front walkway.

Then movement caught his attention.

Some twenty yards along the sidewalk from where he stood, Benny Jack stepped out of the darkness between Tree International and Jamboree Music. He had his Lonely strapped on and began a rattling vibrato with his pill bottle low on the neck, punching the sound out across Music Square West with strong strums.

Ezra turned to the gathering in front of Ave Canora and saw they'd stopped talking and were watching Benny Jack with expressions half-curious and half-annoyed.

Just as the little guitar man intensified his psychedelic vibrato to the point at which it seemed a string or two must break, another movement caught Ezra's attention, and from the side yard to the right of the Ave Canora bungalow, a figure stepped

38

out of the shadows and into the light from the street. A figure dressed all in black—black slacks, black turtleneck and leather jacket, a full-face black mask, and a big black cowboy hat.

Ezra thought he might laugh, but he sobered as the campy getup morphed toward sinister, seeming suddenly in communion with the shadows and the night. Then he thought he must shout a warning to the trio standing on the front walk of Ave Canora and watching Benny Jack, but a sudden tightness rose from his gut into his throat and trapped the breath in his chest.

Benny Jack abandoned the vibrato to execute a smooth glissando into the opening melodic phrase of "Free Bird," and the figure in black raised a pistol and fired.

Ezra swept the hat from his head and ducked behind a parked car as the man he didn't know went down first. He heard the woman scream and saw her reach toward the fallen man, but then at the sound of a second shot, she crumpled in a heap on top of him.

Burl Davies—a confused smile on his face—turned toward the sound of gunfire, and his expression widened into horror when his left shoulder flinched backward. He wheeled with the flinch and began to run toward Benny Jack, while the shooter followed at a walk with the pistol still raised.

Ezra watched, frozen in place and frozen inside, and wondered —strangely, he thought when he remembered it later—how a bear of a man like Burl Davies could put on such a burst of speed.

Two more shots sounded, and the guitar music stopped.

Davies stumbled to a stop and sank to his knees in the middle of the one-way street. He appeared to try to lean forward, as if to crawl away, but he winced sharply and remained upright.

The man in black walked up behind him.

Ezra heard Davies's ragged breathing and realized that his own breathing was coming hard and in sync.

The shooter turned gleaming eyes that appeared colorless

in the streetlight and looked directly at Ezra, who couldn't duck down further and couldn't look away. They stared at each other across a chasm of ten yards, and then the man in black winked and turned back to the kneeling Burl Davies. With little apparent concern about noise or the possibility of an approaching vehicle, he took off his cowboy hat and held it at his side, raised the pistol with his other hand, and shot Davies once in the back of the head.

Ezra's publisher pitched forward, falling hard on belly and face, and lay still.

The man looked toward where Benny Jack had stood.

Ezra glanced that way as well.

Benny Jack was gone.

When Ezra turned back, the man was staring at him again as he settled his black cowboy hat atop his mask, shifted the pistol to his left hand, and pointed it at Ezra. "Hey, good looking," he said. "Stand up."

Ezra remained crouched and staring.

"Stand up," the man said again, twice flicking his pistol muzzle upward. "Come on, now, let me get a good look at you."

Ezra braced himself with his right hand on the car's side mirror and stood slowly.

"Oh, boy," the man said with a breathy growl. He looked Ezra up and down once and then again. "I'll remember you, my handsome young man." Then he stepped over the body of Burl Davies and crossed the near lane, stepped up on the sidewalk, and disappeared into the shadows from which Benny Jack had emerged a minute or so before.

Ezra remained standing beside the car, afraid the killer might pop back out with "Just kidding!" or "I'm back!" and shoot him too. But when this didn't happen, he took a couple of steps forward on shaky legs and stopped. He looked at Burl Davies, face down in the middle of the street and unmoving. Then he looked across to where the unknown man and woman lay just as they'd fallen. He heard a groan, two coughs, and a sob. His eyes snapped back to Davies. *Dead.* He pulled his gaze away from Davies and looked where Benny Jack had stood with his Lonely.

Protruding from the pool of shadows was a brown-shoed foot and an ankle Ezra's earlier glance hadn't caught.

"Benny Jack?" he called, and his voice reverberated through the nighttime streets. He forced himself two more steps forward but stopped when he heard another groan and saw the foot twitch. Afraid of what bloody scene might lie in those shadows, he stood still—except for the tremors quaking through his body—and listened for approaching sirens.

Ezra sat on the curb, cross-legged and sobered, an empty Styrofoam cup in his hand, Ave Canora's dark-windowed bungalow behind him. He ran the tip of his tongue between his lips and wished he had more water. He wanted a cigarette, but somehow he couldn't bring himself to shake one up from the pack and light it.

The street in front of him—mostly dry now—stretched across two lanes to the Acura Integra he'd hidden behind when the shooting started. Police and EMT personnel, the Integra's body and glass, the restless leaves overhead, the walls and windows of Tree International and Jamboree Music—all pulsed in blue and red lights. Radios in open cars and walkie-talkies on belts squawked and fussed. Voices all around rose and fell with either urgency or deliberation.

The bodies of the dead lay still where they'd fallen.

"You want some more water?"

Ezra looked up at the uniformed officer who materialized in front of him. "Sure." He handed up the empty cup. "Thanks."

The officer returned with the refill and handed it back, then hiked up his trouser legs and sat on the curb to Ezra's right, somewhat shielding him from the two bodies heaped on Ave Canora's front walkway. "I keep some water bottles in the patrol car."

"Cool." Ezra took a shaky sip. "Much obliged."

The officer pulled a small pad and pencil from a pocket, held them in his left hand, and extended his right toward Ezra. "Name's Latt Edwards," he said.

Ezra shook the proffered hand. "Ezra MacRae."

"Spell that last name?"

"Big *m*, little *a-c*, big *r*, little *a-e*."

"Sounds like you have to spell that a lot."

"All the time," Ezra said as Officer Edwards scribbled on his pad. Then he tipped his cup toward the ambulance. "How's Benny Jack?"

"They're trying to stabilize him before they run around the corner to Vandy." Edwards stretched out his legs and crossed his ankles.

"At least he's alive," Ezra said.

"He got hit pretty hard, I think, but if he's got a chance, Vandy Trauma is the best place to be in Music City."

"What about his Lonely?"

"Come again?"

"His guitar. He calls it his Lonely."

"Oh," Latt Edwards said. "Shot right through the G string over the sound hole and exited out the back and into his lower abdomen."

Ezra felt a sudden, involuntary twist in his own belly. "You play?"

"Trying to learn."

Ezra nodded and attempted to keep his eyes away from the body of Burl Davies, but it haunted his peripheral vision.

"You all right?" Edwards said.

"Probably not." Ezra tried to sip the fresh water again, but his hand shook too much. "Definitely not."

"Understandable."

Before Ezra could nod again, Officer Edwards shot to his feet and stood facing a wiry man who'd appeared in front of them.

"Officer Edwards?" the man said.

Ezra was trying to rise from the curb, and Edwards caught him under the right arm and helped him stand.

"Detective Hunt, this is Ezra MacRae," Edwards said. "He was passing by when the shooting happened. Saw the whole thing."

"I see," Hunt said. "Are you all right, Mr. MacRae?"

Ezra almost said that he was fine but stopped himself. "A little shaky, I guess. Maybe a little woozy in the stomach."

Hunt looked down, and Ezra followed his gaze to shiny black wingtips that seemed to want to take a step back.

"I'm pretty sure I'm not gonna be sick," Ezra said.

Hunt nodded and stood his ground. "What were you doing here, Mr. MacRae?"

"Well, I'd been out celebrating," Ezra said, as both Detective Hunt and Officer Edwards began taking notes. "I had my first couple of songs get picked up this week, and I took myself out to the Songbird."

"You're a songwriter?" Edwards said but stopped. "Sorry, sir."

"Again, Mr. MacRae," the detective said, "what were you doing here?"

"Well, I'd sat out the storm in the lounge at the Hall of Fame Motel, and I was heading home to Utah Avenue. I wanted to walk by because that building"—he gestured with a tip of his head, back and to the right—"is the office of the publishing company I just signed with." With another tip of the head, forward and to the right, he said, "That's my publisher there in the street."

Hunt stared at him a moment. "Burl Davies?"

"Yeah," Ezra said. "I just signed a contract with him on Thursday."

"And you know those unfortunates?" The detective gestured in the direction of the bodies that lay in front of Ave Canora.

"I've never seen them," Ezra said without turning around. "I don't know who they are."

"And the young man in the ambulance?"

"Benny Jack," Ezra said. "Benny Jack Boudreau."

"And how do you know Mr. Boudreau?"

"Well, I don't," Ezra said. "Not really." He described their meeting a couple of hours before and then seeing him again with his guitar on the sidewalk just before the shooting started. "I don't know where he was in between, but he must've found some place around here to get out of the rain."

"You say you live over on Utah Avenue," Hunt said. "Do you consider that your permanent address?"

"For now—" Ezra said and stopped and tried to smile. "Which I guess means it's not permanent."

"So, what do you consider your permanent address, Mr. MacRae?"

"Well, I get tax mail and suchlike at my folks' address in Runion, North Carolina."

"Suchlike?" Detective Hunt said and then stopped. He turned to a husky policeman standing to his left.

"Officer Perras, do you need something?"

The big man stiffened to attention. "No, sir."

"Then as you are not part of this interview," Hunt said, "I suggest you make yourself busy elsewhere." He ran the knuckle of an index finger back and forth across his mustached upper lip. "In fact, take a light into those bushes where we found the live victim and see if you can track how he moved from the park over at Sixteenth and Division to here."

"Yessir." Officer Perras lumbered away.

Detective Hunt watched him go before turning back to Ezra. "Make sure Officer Edwards has both your Utah Avenue and your North Carolina contact information." He flipped a page in his notepad. "Now, you were explaining your presence here, which isn't on your way to Utah Avenue from the Hall of Fame Motel."

Music Row, 16th & 17th Ave South

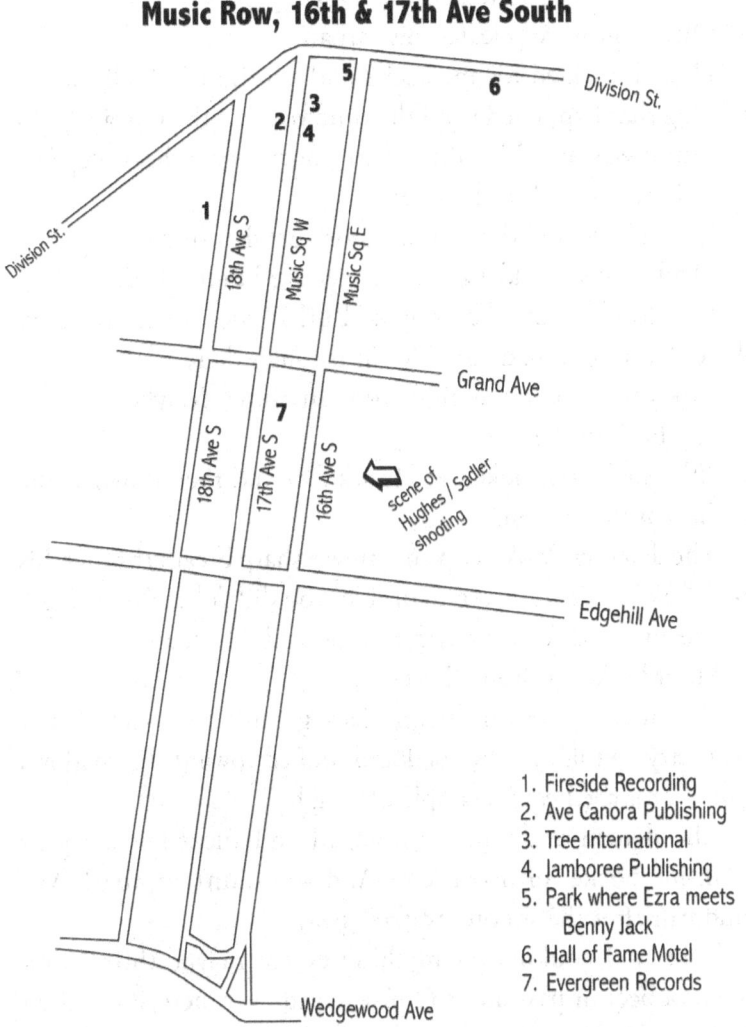

1. Fireside Recording
2. Ave Canora Publishing
3. Tree International
4. Jamboree Publishing
5. Park where Ezra meets
   Benny Jack
6. Hall of Fame Motel
7. Evergreen Records

Ezra pointed toward Division Street. "I got to the corner down yonder and saw a light on upstairs here." He again tipped his head back and to the right. "I thought if it was somebody I knew I might be able to get a ride."

"Down yonder?" Hunt said.

"Yessir." Ezra pointed again. "Down yonder."

Officer Edwards cleared his throat.

Hunt knuckled his mustache and continued. "Tell me everything that happened from the time you saw the upstairs light on until it was over." He flipped to a new page in his notepad.

Officer Edwards did the same.

Ezra stammered through the story of what he'd seen.

"And he just walked away?" Detective Hunt asked.

Ezra looked past the body of Burl Davies to the shadows where Benny Jack had lain. "Right through there."

"Are you certain you didn't hear anything? Maybe a vehicle start up back in the alley?"

"No, sir." Ezra looked at Hunt's face and then down at the pad he was writing on.

The detective looked up and drew a sharp breath through his nose. "'No' you're not certain or 'No' you didn't hear anything?"

"Yessir, I didn't hear anything," he said. "Except—"

Hunt looked at him. "Except?"

"I remember hearing Benny Jack groan," Ezra said. "That was pretty awful." He stopped and looked toward the shadows again. "I maybe heard a couple of coughs."

The detective closed his notepad and tucked it away in the inside pocket of his jacket. "And you didn't approach Mr. Boudreau after the shooter walked away?"

"I knew I couldn't do anything except maybe throw up a bunch of beer or pass out, so I just stayed over there and waited for the cavalry to arrive."

"The shooter's voice. Any accent or particular quality to it?"

Ezra paused, and Edwards opened his notepad again.

"I don't think so. Maybe a little bit of a growl, but deep like a good radio voice. Not a really heavy accent. Not Reba

McEntire heavy, I mean." *I'll remember you, my handsome young man,* he heard the voice say again. "Maybe that means the shooter's accent was more like mine. Since I didn't hear much of an accent in it?"

"That's a good point," Edwards said.

Hunt nodded. "I know it'll be difficult to forget what you've seen here," he said. "But I want you to give it as much thought as you can—think of anything you missed." He started to turn away but stopped. "Edwards, please give Mr. MacRae a ride home now, and if you're on shift Monday afternoon, you can get his formal statement and bring him to me at two o'clock."

"Yessir," Edwards said as Hunt turned and strode toward a group of men gathered near the body of Burl Davies. "Right this way, Mr. MacRae."

Ezra expected to be put into the back seat, but Edwards opened the front passenger door and waved him in. "Thanks," he said and collapsed into the warm and cushioned interior. He leaned back on the headrest and gripped the armrest on the door.

"So, you're a songwriter," Officer Edwards said as soon as they were clear of the crime scene and rolling up 17th toward Wedgewood.

"I guess I can say that officially now," Ezra said. "Or I guess I could before a few hours ago. I don't know what'll happen to my deal with Mr. Davies dead."

"I bet it'll be okay," Edwards said. "There was more than just him working there, right?"

"Yeah, a guy named Mark Williamson is my main contact."

"I'd say as long as he doesn't turn out to be the killer, then you should be good."

Ezra chuckled. "Yeah, there's that, I reckon."

Edwards turned right on Wedgewood, and then they were rolling down the hill toward 21st Avenue South and Hillsborough Village.

"I wish I'd've just stayed at the Songbird," Ezra said.

47

"Why didn't you?"

They rolled through the intersection with 21ˢᵗ, on the other side of which Wedgewood became Blakemore Avenue.

"Probably too drunk to think that straight. And then there's just something about walking on Music Row." He paused. "It's like it calls to me."

"I know what you mean," Edwards said. "But it's more dangerous nowadays, I think."

Ezra sat quietly for a few moments as they crossed Natchez Trace and Blakemore became 31ˢᵗ Avenue South. Then he cleared his throat. "While I was sitting on the curb back there, I heard folks around me saying things like 'same guy' and 'copy-cat.'" He paused again. "Do you think it was the same guy?"

Officer Edwards swung the patrol car left onto West End. "Man, I can't really comment on that right now, but it's gonna be on the whole city's mind soon as this hits the news."

"I thought about it—what happened a couple weeks ago, I mean—when I was walking up Sixteenth." He sat looking out his window and up at the nameless buildings of the Acklen Park area. "I wish I'd turned around and gone back to the Songbird right then."

"I bet you do," Edwards said as he veered right on Murphy Road.

Ezra straightened his back and drew a deep breath. "I keep hearing him say, 'I'll remember you.'" He shifted in the seat, so much larger than the one in his Ford Tempo. "Do you think he'll come after me?"

Officer Edwards let the car coast down into Sylvan Park. "Unless he's somebody you know and didn't recognize, I can't see how." He glanced up at his rearview mirror. "Or unless he's following us."

"What?" Ezra felt his breath catch and leaned forward to look in the side mirror.

"Sorry, man," Edwards chuckled. "I'm just messing with you."

"Well, stop it," Ezra said, feeling his face redden and his lips stretch in a half grin. "Take a right down here on Fortieth."

Sylvan Park Area

They turned off Murphy and glided over unmarked pavement, passing modest and darkened houses on either side.

"Left on Utah," Ezra said. "Then I'm at 4014, Youngstowne Square just down on the right." He yawned and sat up straight and rubbed his face hard.

They rolled to a stop, and Ezra fumbled for the handle, found it, and opened the door.

"Thanks for the ride, Officer Edwards."

"Latt," Edwards said as they shook hands again. "Double *t.*" He grinned. "Thanks for your help tonight, Mr. MacRae."

"Ezra. Means 'helper' in Hebrew."

"Well, that's appropriate," Latt Edwards said. "But MacRae doesn't sound Jewish."

"No, not Jewish, Scottish. Ezra's biblical. My dad's a Presbyterian minister."

"All right, then happy Easter to you."

"That's really where I should've been tonight," Ezra said. "Home in North Carolina." He yawned again. "I'd probably be getting up about now to go to sunrise service." He stood up, then bent down to say thanks again for the ride.

"See you Monday, Ezra. I'll be by at noon. Pick you up right here."

"All right, Latt. Be safe out there tonight." He closed the passenger door and turned to walk through the gravel entrance into his small apartment complex. Then he heard the car door open and turned back just as Edwards stood up and said his name. "Yeah?"

Edwards spoke softly. "That was some scary shit you saw go down tonight, and I'm sorry I messed with you just now." He patted the roof of the car three times with the palm of his hand. "I hope you can go to sleep all right, but if it gets to you, call somebody. Wake 'em up."

"Thanks," Ezra said. "I think I've got some beer in the fridge. Maybe I'll suck about three of them down real quick and pass out."

Latt nodded. "Normally I wouldn't condone that kind of thing. But tonight, yeah, that sounds like a plan." Then he dropped out of sight, closed the door, and rolled away.

Ezra stood and watched the taillights down Utah to 41st, where the patrol car turned left and disappeared. Feeling naked and exposed in the city-bright dark, he hurried into his apartment, where he turned on all the lights and looked in every closet and under every piece of furniture. Suddenly chilling like he had a fever, he turned up the heat before opening the refrigerator.

The three-beer tranquilizer soon laid him out fully dressed on the wreck of his unmade bed.

He sits on the curb—a Styrofoam cup of beer held between thumb and forefinger of his left hand, a cigarette gripped between thumb and forefinger of his right.

Behind him squats Ave Canora's dark bungalow, and in front, the buildings of Jamboree and Tree stand ablaze with light. The street is empty of vehicles—none parked, none passing. But it isn't absolutely empty. The body of Burl Davies lies there, and a faceless man of shadow stands over it.

Beyond him, Benny Jack sprawls on the sidewalk.

The unknown man and woman behind him begin to move— rustle of clothing, scrape of shoe soles, throat noises.

He cannot turn.

He cannot rise as he knows they are rising.

As Burl is rising in the middle of the street. The big man pushes up to his knees, climbs the shadow man like a downed fighter desperately climbs the ring ropes.

Beyond Davies and the shadow man, Benny Jack pops up like a jack-in-the-box, his bloodied body tilting this way and that until it stills. His googly eyes open and twirl until the right eye locks on him.

And then all five move toward where he sits too weak to rise. They point pistols at him, fingers twitching at triggers.

He cannot stand to run or raise arms to protect himself. In his peripheral, he senses a distant lighted stage where the Moonshine Rebels play a silent song.

High up in the darkness and far beyond the band he hears other voices singing—"Up from the grave He arose!"

"Papa!"

51

His shout awakened him to a gray Easter Sunday soaked in gentle rain, beer sweat, and piss.

"Sorry, Papa," he said to the quiet room. He rolled out of bed and shed his clothes, stripped off the sheets and stuffed them in the pillowcase. He pulled a box fan from his closet and set it up to blow on the mattress, which, he was relieved to feel, was far less wet than the clothes he'd slept in. He put damp and dirty clothes together in a garbage bag, topped them with his paperback of *The Neon Rain*, and set the bag near the front door. He shaved, showered, brushed his teeth for a long time, and dressed as if he might go to church. But he collapsed in a dining room chair and sat with the kitchen door open and stared out across the brick patio, through the disheveled hedge, and into the tidy, deserted backyard of the yellow house next door. He considered calling home but knew that his folks would be busy with Easter activities for another couple of hours. He considered fetching his guitar and working but seemed unable to muster the energy.

Why am I alive and sitting here at this kitchen table?

Less than three days before, Burl Davies hunched over his desk to sign Ezra's exclusive songwriter's agreement with Ave Canora. He'd been a hefty man, reminding Ezra of "Never Been to Spain" songwriter Hoyt Axton or heavyweight wrestling champion Homer Alexander. When Davies offered his hand after the signing, Ezra felt great strength in the meaty grip and wondered if Burl's parents had given him the name with foreknowledge that he was destined to grow into a man burly enough to own it.

Why am I alive and sitting here?

Less than twelve hours before, Davies crumpled into a heap of flesh and bone and bloody hair and clothes in the middle of Music Square West. All power and personality fled from him in one horrific instant, leaving him still and cooling like the asphalt he lay on as the Medical Examiner's people photographed his helplessness and police investigators spoke of his body in the present tense and his life and identity in the past.

Why am I alive?

And now Burl Davies probably lay in the city morgue, alone at last this Easter Sunday morning—unresurrected and silent in cold storage, his nakedness mountainous beneath a white sheet, a manila nametag dangling from the big toe of one exposed foot.

Why am I—

A quiet rustling sounded somewhere nearby, a brief susurrus that stopped with a muted thud.

Ezra froze—his breath caught, his ears deadened and rang, his vision tunneled to a nightmarish still life of five pistols pointing.

He willed himself to unfreeze and breathe, stood and steadied his mind by the same will. The thud seemed dull and distant enough that it might have come from a neighboring apartment, but the whispering sound had come from inside his place. He drew a breath and held it and listened again. Then in one impulsive movement, he stepped from the kitchen to the living room.

His laugh burst out with the breath he'd held.

The bag of dirty clothes lay flopped on its side with some of its jumbled contents spilled and settled to an angle of repose. The Burke novel—probably the source of the thud—lay on the carpet next to a balled-up pair of white socks.

In the bedroom, he picked up a plastic Metamucil canister half filled with change and screwed on the lid. He checked that the window was locked and then loaded his pockets with wallet, keys, writing pad, and a pencil. Back in the living room, he re-stuffed clothes and novel in the garbage bag and dropped in the change container. He opened the front door and made sure to reset the lock. Then he stepped out onto the apartment's front stoop, pulled the door closed, turned, and froze again.

Even in the sunshine of a late Sunday morning he sensed it—the same palpable nakedness and exposure he'd felt in those early morning moments after Officer Edwards rolled away into the dark of Sylvan Park. He almost stumbled backward into the apartment door, but stood firm on the stoop, gripped his laundry tighter, and drew a deep breath.

One foot in front of the other.

He drove to the corner of Nebraska and Murphy and parked across from a market known only as The Store. He scanned his surroundings—forward, to the sides, and all he could see behind in the three mirrors. Then he got out and hurried across the street.

"Good morning, Young MacRae," the clerk clucked her usual greeting.

"Morning, Penny." He veered left toward the grocery aisles then stopped. "Hey, you're not usually here on Sundays."

"Ain't going to church today."

"On Easter?"

"On Easter."

"Why the hell not?"

Penny stared at him a moment. "That crooked grin you've got, Young MacRae," she said. "You get by with a lot on account of it, don't you?"

"Right much, I reckon," he said, exaggerating both his accent and his grin.

"Like our young preacher," she said as she turned her gaze to the front windows and the street.

"What's up with him?"

Penny drew a breath and released it in a sigh. "Reason we're not having church on Easter of all days," she said without looking at Ezra, "is that he give in to the devil and showed his wiener to Deacon Bussard's twins." At this she turned back to him. "And Deacon Bussard nigh killed him with a hatchet."

"Jesus."

"Satan's more like it." She turned again to the window and the world framed in it. "He's everywhere."

Satan in the preacher's wiener or the deacon's hatchet? Without

54

voicing that thought, Ezra left Penny staring out the front window of the store, the trembling fingers of her right hand raised to a quivering chin.

When he returned with the smallest, cheapest detergent he could find, a honeybun, a Moon Pie, and a pint of chocolate milk, he found her still standing as he'd left her.

She shook off her apparent reverie and rang up his items without speaking, totaled the purchase, and stiffened. "He's everywhere," she whispered, echoing herself.

"What?"

"He's everywhere," she said a third time, turning a wide-eyed stare to him.

"Who's everywhere?"

She swiveled her cash register's digital display to face him. Its red numbers indicated a total charge of $6.66.

Ezra looked at her.

"I can't let that number stay on my register," she said.

"What?"

"You need to put something back or buy something else."

"Seriously?"

"Yes, Young MacRae. I can't—I cannot—let the number of the Beast into the world like this." She turned the digital display around again. "He's everywhere, but he ain't gonna be in my cash register."

Ezra searched her face and drew a deep breath. "Okay, Penny," he sighed. "Give me a pack of Camel Lights, and I'll take this piece of bubblegum too." As she added the items to his total, he watched her relax.

"Thank you," she said as he handed her a ten.

"Maybe next time we'll go for all sevens or all threes," he said.

"Go on now," Penny said. "I've got work to do, and you've got clothes to wash."

He looked at her with a raised eyebrow, and she tapped a side of her nose with a finger.

"I see." He picked up the purchases she'd bagged for him and turned toward the entrance. "See you, Penny."

"Happy Easter to you, Young MacRae."

He turned again when he got to the door and pushed it open with a bump of his butt. "In spite of the devil and all his minions and your preacher's penis," he said, "Happy Easter to you too, Penny."

She grimaced and motioned him outside with a terse wave.

SEVEN

Hugo Rodgers awoke with no movement other than the upward fluttering of his eyelids. He lay naked and fully stretched out in his recliner, head resting on palms and interlocked fingers. With his gaze searching the stippled ceiling for face-like patterns, he listened to the quiet house and took note of the rumble of the central heat just a moment before the thermostat clicked and the whispering hum faded away. He listened then for Lucio and was grateful to hear only the sounds of sleep instead of the continuous coughing that had driven him to his recliner in the hour or so before dawn.

He lowered the footrest as quietly as he could, stood and stretched to brush his fingertips on the ceiling, and stepped into the bathroom, where he peed without flushing and turned to the mirror. At first glance, he regretted his thinning hair, where some of his natural reddish blond still lingered among the gray and silver, but then he picked up a comb and swiped straight back from forehead to crown, consoled as he did so by having kept the promise to himself that he would never resort to the combover style his father had worn. He put down the comb and leaned close to the mirror. *Bleary-eyed.* He pulled down on his right cheek and looked closer at the eye. *Red and watery like the old man's.*

Then he noticed the smell. He thought at first it might be his breath and cupped a palm and fingers over his nose and inhaled, but before he could exhale, he knew that the stink came from his hand. *Cigarettes, gunpowder, sweat, dried spit.* The smell included other bodily contributions as well, and while he'd been turned on by these in the middle of the night, they stank to him in daylight. He picked up a slimy bar of Irish Spring and washed his hands three times before his nose was satisfied.

After tiptoeing into the bedroom to gather some clothes, he dressed in the kitchen and slipped out the back door. He got in Lucio's ratty red Taurus and drove to the grocery store at the corner of 21st and Blair, where he backed into a space and cut the engine. He sat for a moment and scanned the lot and the vehicles parked in it, taking particular notice of a Metro PD cruiser before getting out of the Taurus. Just inside the store, he picked up a basket and made his way to the dairy section, where he selected a pint of whole milk. He picked up two plain glazed doughnuts from the bakery, opened the milk, hung the basket in the crook of his elbow, and wandered the aisles, eating a doughnut as he went.

In the freezer section, he found Officer Murdoch Perras loading frozen pizzas into a shopping cart mostly full of soft drinks, milk, bread, chips, cookies, and TV dinners. Perras still wore his uniform and moved slowly, as if his husky body were already half asleep.

"Officer Perras," Hugo said around the last bite of his first doughnut. "You just now getting off work?"

Perras visibly flinched. "Hugo," he said after a moment. "Yeah, hell of a night."

"Lucie and me heard a lot of sirens and saw a lot of blue lights run across our bedroom walls."

Perras turned to grab one more pizza. "And where is Lucky?"

"Still in bed," Hugo said and winked. "Had a rough night with that cough." He stuffed half the second doughnut in his mouth and turned to walk with Perras toward the front of the store. When Perras stopped to take a half gallon of Rocky Road from the freezer, Hugo took a long swig of milk and wiped his mouth with the back of his hand. "Tell me about last night."

"Outside," Perras said. "But I've got ice cream, so it'll have to be quick."

"All right." As Perras joined the shortest of the checkout lines, Hugo finished the second doughnut and chased it with the last of the milk. He put the cap back on the empty plastic bottle and dropped it in the basket, which he then set on a barren shelf in a jumbled section of leftover Easter candy and walked out. He saw open spaces on either side of Perras's cruiser, so he moved the Taurus to the space on the passenger-side and then got out just as Perras exited the store with his buggy.

"Did you pay for that doughnut and milk?" Perras asked as he stopped the buggy and opened the trunk of his vehicle.

Hugo looked down and nodded toward Perras's groceries. "You know, Murdoch, you really ought to eat better than that."

"Yeah, well, I don't have a live-in Italian cook like you do."

"Hey, we can't all have a Lucky Lucie." Hugo reached out his left hand and steadied the buggy as Perras began to unload it. "So, tell me about last night on the Row."

Perras settled grocery bags in his trunk. "I can't believe—"

"There was a witness, I think," Hugo said. "Handsome young man."

"Yeah, a guy named MacRae. Here from someplace in North Carolina. Lives over on Utah Avenue. But that's about all I got on him before Hunt kicked me out of the interview."

"Hunt?"

"Lead detective." Perras closed the trunk. "Asshole from New York. Head of the Murder Squad."

Hugo spun the empty buggy around and held it with both hands on the handle. "So, four shot," he said. "All dead."

"Yeah, well, no, actually. The little guy with the guitar is still alive. In surgery at Vandy last I heard."

Hugo looked across the parking lot toward the buggy corral. "Well, we'll pray for him to pull through."

"Yeah, right," Perras said. "You do a lot of praying, do you?"

Hugo pointed the buggy toward the corral but stopped and half turned. "We good, Murdoch? You seem agitated."

Perras balled his meaty hands into fists and then planted them on his hips. "I don't know, Hugo. I really don't." He paused. "I don't know how long I can—"

"Remember you're doing it for Lucie, too."

"That's the only reason," Perras said. "To keep Lucky safe."

"Is it, Murdoch? That's the only reason?" Hugo whipped the buggy around as if he would ram it into Perras's belly, but he stopped and held it between them. "Son, I don't care what you don't know as long as you remember what I know." His large hands tightened on the handle of the buggy. "And I know who's most likely interested to learn about your thorn in the flesh."

"I don't care anymore."

"Yeah, I bet you don't."

Perras pulled mirrored sunglasses from his uniform shirt pocket and put them on. "I don't know what Lucky sees in you or why he's going along with what you've done." He pulled keys from his pants pocket. "Hell, I don't know why I'm going along with it either."

"Shame," Hugo said. "We're all of us ashamed here in the sunny South, and your fear of shame trumps your desire to do what you think's right." He jerked the buggy back around and started across the parking lot. When he banged it into the others in the corral, he turned and noticed the noise had drawn the attention of customers in the parking lot. He ignored their stares and watched Murdoch Perras's patrol car slowly turn left on Blair.

EIGHT

While machines pumped full of quarters washed and dried almost his entire wardrobe, Ezra sat slumped in one of the blue plastic chairs mounted in a line along a wall of Sylvan Park's 24-hour laundromat. He'd chosen a seat from which he could keep an eye on the wooden, windowless door at the back, and, through the dazzled and reversed "A Squeaky-Clean Laundry" painted on the front window, he could see the laundromat's parking spaces and the Murphy Road traffic beyond. Between glances at the unmoving back door and at every movement from the front and the street, he tried to focus on his Burke novel, but he'd held it open to the same two pages since putting the second load in the dryer, the words on those pages continually blurring and swirling into images of a gunman dressed in black and bodies draped in white. He finally closed the book and dropped it in the plastic bag atop his roughly folded first load, crossed his arms, and sat watching through the dryer's window as jeans, underwear, and socks tumbled over and over and over.

The words again appeared in his mind—*He stepped out of the music and into the night.* He recognized that somewhere in his songwriting brain his muse had made the choice between *rain* and *night.* He picked up his writing pad and pencil from the seat beside him and flipped it open to the jottings from the earliest hours of his long Easter Sunday. *Before all this,* he thought. Where he'd written RAIN/NIGHT, he drew a line through RAIN/ and another through /SHE/I. Then he sat still, watching his clothes tumble inside the dryer drum.

He stepped out of the music and into the night,
from the rumble of the bass and drums into the city quiet.

He stared at the misted dryer window but closed his eyes when a full-body chill shook him so hard that he dropped his pencil. He pushed himself back into the chair to sit upright, then leaned down to fish the pencil from the floor. He looked again at his pad and drew a block against its right edge. Inside this he wrote, TEARS, SHADOWS, DANGER, ANGER, and RINGING EARS. He drew an arrow downward from the last on the list and wrote, FROM LOUD MUSIC OR GUNFIRE, then returned his gaze to the dryer just as the machine buzzed and the clothes collapsed to the bottom of the drum.

He caught himself staring again at the dark and misted window. His hands still held pad and pencil, so he looked down, flipped to a fresh page, and wrote, MAYBE THERE'S A CLEANNESS BEYOND THE MIST and underneath that added, I DON'T KNOW WHAT THAT MEANS. Then he stood up, tucked the pencil behind his ear, shoved the pad into his back pocket, and began pulling hot clothes into a rolling laundry basket.

NINE

As the movie played in the living room of 1619 16th Avenue South, Lucio Centopani, dressed only in khaki trousers, lay stretched out in his recliner. A two-day beard shadowed his finely chiseled face. The pouf of his thick black hair was lopsided. He snored, and twitches teased the length of his compact and muscular body—an eyelid, a corner of his mouth, an index finger, a foot.

The movie played on a small Panasonic TV/VCR combo that sat atop a short stack of two empty wooden crates from Cat's Records. Scene changes that flickered across the screen flashed in the room's dusky corners. Tinny voices and a soundtrack of strings bounced around a living room spartanly furnished with the recliner in which Centopani slept and a matching but empty one beside it. A third Cat's crate stood upended between these and held a dented Miller Lite can and a rusted '36 Plymouth hubcap overflowing with cigarette butts.

Lucio Centopani—stage name Lucky Baker—had arrived in Nashville some five years before as part of Dreamer, a five-piece country-pop band out of New Jersey. They soon landed gigs around Music City and began getting attention from independent record companies with a demo tape they'd made at a studio in Asbury Park. Ultimately, Billy Keith Productions offered a deal on spec and recorded a few songs to shop around to the major record labels. But after two years of rising and falling hopes, Dreamer found its contract terminated without warning. The band broke up. While three of its members returned north, Lucky and co-lead singer Nancy Castellano stayed and eventually ended up in this house together with Hugo Rodgers, a record promoter working with secondary radio markets but looking to get into the creative side of the business.

Two heavy steps thudded on the porch, and Centopani snored and choked and raised his head just as the front door shuddered open.

"What the hell, Lucie?" Hugo said as he leaned back against the door to close it. "You already started the movie?" He kicked off his shoes and bent to strip off one sock and then the other.

Lucio rubbed his face hard with both hands. Then he snuffled and coughed once. "Well," he said through a yawn. "Obviously, I wasn't fucking watching." He muscled the recliner back into its upright position and landed his bare feet on the floor. "We can rewind it and start over."

Hugo picked up the TV remote from the seat of his recliner and sat down with his shoulders hunched forward, elbows on thighs, and held the remote in cupped hands between his knees. With Lucio, he watched as an elevator car quickly descended its shaft while the adjacent car—with the movie star riding on top, barefoot in a dirty white tank undershirt—ascended at the same speed. Just when the man on the roof of the rising car realized that the lift couldn't be endless and looked up to see the ceiling fast approaching, Hugo pointed the remote and pressed the mute button.

Lucio looked from the screen to Hugo's hand and then to his face.

"I caught Officer Perras just as he was coming off his shift a while ago," Hugo said. "The runt ain't dead."

"What runt?"

"The crazy-eyed runt with the guitar."

"Fuck," Lucio said.

"You got that right," Hugo said. "He's in intensive care over at Vandy."

"He gonna make it?"

"Perras just said he's alive." Hugo pulled a pack of Marlboros from the inside pocket of his leather jacket, shook one up, lipped it, and lit it. "Still in surgery the last he heard," he said, the smoke of his first drag billowing out with his words.

"So, he's probably not talking yet," Lucio said, "even if he's out of surgery."

"And when he can talk, who knows how long before Hunt'll be able to make any sense of his gibberish?"

"Who the fuck's Hunt?"

"Lead detective, Perras says."

Without taking his eyes from the small screen, Lucio reached with his right hand and snapped his fingers twice. Hugo shook up another Marlboro for him to grab, tucked the pack away, and struck a light. Lucio leaned in and touched his cigarette to the flame, puffed a couple of times, and drew a sharp drag as Hugo lay the lighter by the hubcap ashtray and began unbuttoning his shirt. Smoke exploded from Lucio's mouth as he hunched over in a fit of coughing. Hugo watched him for a moment, shook his head, turned back to the screen, and unmuted the sound just as Sergeant Al Powell dumped an armload of Twinkies on a convenience store counter.

"I thought you guys just ate doughnuts," the clerk said as he began to ring up the purchase.

"I love that line," Hugo said and worked his way out of his black leather jacket and Hawaiian shirt at the same time. He stood, hung the jacket on the coatrack by the door, and lay the shirt across the back of his recliner.

With one more cough that shook his whole body, Lucio stopped and sat quietly for a moment, drawing in short, tentative breaths. Then, "Yeah, that's fucking hilar—" he said before exploding in another fit of coughing and a half inch of cigarette ash fell to the floor between his feet.

Hugo pressed the mute button again and laid the remote on

the arm of his recliner. "Maybe you shouldn't cuss so much like a Jersey sailor." He didn't smile or look away from the TV. "Not on Sundays, at least. And especially not on Easter."

"Fuck you," Lucio said when he caught his breath. Then he took his second drag from the cigarette.

Onscreen, three terrorists chased John McClane around the roof and down the upper floors of Nakatomi Tower, the flashes of muted machinegun fire strobe-lighting Hugo and Lucio and the room around them. The two watched until Officer Powell's cruiser rolled into the traffic circle far below the action.

"What about the other guy?" Lucio blew out his last drag and stubbed out the cigarette.

"What other guy?" Hugo asked, eyes still locked on the screen.

"Goddammit, the other guy from last night? The fucking witness?"

"Oh, him." Hugo cut his eyes at Lucio without turning his face from the screen. *Handsome young man.* He scooted back in the recliner, popped up the footrest, and squeezed his hands together between his thighs. "Perras says his name's MacRae. Lives somewhere over on Utah Avenue."

"Where's that?"

"Don't you mean, where the fuck's that?" Hugo chuckled. Then he folded his arms across his chest with his fingers buried in his pits. "Utah's over on the other side of West End. Sylvan Park area. Half the streets over there are named for states."

Lucio also stretched out in his recliner and laced his fingers behind his head. "You cold or something?" he asked.

Hugo didn't answer. *Handsome young man,* he thought again.

"You should've popped his ass while you had the chance," Lucio said. "Now you've got two loose ends if that crazy-eyed runt lives."

"Put your arms down," Hugo said. "Your pits are stinking up the room." He pulled his fingers from his own pits, sniffed them, and then again clasped his hands together between his thighs. "Maybe go take a shower or something before we head to Green Hills."

"Fuck you."

"I wasn't there to kill MacRae. And besides, I was empty."

All hell was breaking loose at Nakatomi Plaza. A dead body fell through Sgt. Powell's windshield, and bullets rained down on him as he backed madly away from the building and shouted at his radio for backup.

Hugo picked up the remote and pointed it at the TV. "We'll get those guys when the time comes." He stopped the tape just as a fleet of police cruisers was screeching to a halt at a short distance from the high-rise action. "Now, I mean it, take a shower. We'll go tan, and then I'm gonna order pizza. After that, we'll kick back and pay this movie proper attention."

Lucio collapsed the footrest and stood up from his recliner, turned without a word, and disappeared through the dark bedroom doorway.

Hugo shook his head and pressed the rewind button on the remote.

TEN

Ezra's apartment was cold when he returned from the laundromat, and he froze with the realization that, careful as he'd been to check the bedroom windows and make sure to lock the front door, he'd grabbed his dirty clothes bag and left without remembering to close the kitchen door. He stood in the dark living room and listened for a few moments, wondering what kinds of critters or monsters might have been in and out during the afternoon. When he'd set down the bag of clean laundry, stepped into the kitchen, and closed the door, he steeled himself through another search of the apartment and was relieved to find his guitars and electronic keyboard still on their stands in the second bedroom.

Satisfied that he was alone, he put away his clean clothes and the box fan and made his bed, then sat again in the kitchen with the cordless telephone handset lying on the tabletop in front of him. He took a deep breath, picked it up, and punched in his parents' number.

"We're leaving early in the morning for Charleston," his mother said, her voice slowed, Ezra recognized, by the distraction of choosing outfits to put in the single suitcase his parents packed for such trips. "Your father can hardly wait to get his shrimp and grits."

Ezra apologized for not coming home to spend Easter in Runion as he'd said he would, and he confessed that he had no good reason for his absence. He could tell they were disappointed but, at the same time, not surprised. They knew the good news about "Somebody, Somewhere" and "Blue Jeans Girl" and about his contract with Ave Canora. And while they seemed genuinely happy about these validations of his talent and aspirations, they also seemed to understand that each success made the possibility of his returning home for good less and less likely.

He didn't tell them that less than twenty-four hours earlier three people—four if Benny Jack died—had been murdered in front of him or that the killer had spoken to him or that he had no idea why he hadn't become the fifth victim. They might come across a report in the news, and while he was certain his name wouldn't be included, that of Burl Davies might. He thought it possible they would make the connection, especially if such a report mentioned both Davies and Ave Canora, but he would talk them through that if necessary. Their conversation soon ran out of steam, so he told his mother he loved her, asked her to pass his love on to Papa, wished them a fun and restful vacation, and said goodbye.

Mel's line was busy. But when Ezra's telephone began ringing immediately after he disconnected the call, he smiled and waited through three rings, and then answered. "Happy Easter, Chief," he said.

"I'm not your Chief," Kate Hathaway said.

"Oh, hey, Kate, I was expecting a call from a friend back home."

"Sorry not to be him, assuming this friend is a he," she said.

"It's Mel. I just called, and he didn't answer. He's a farmer, so he might be gone to bed already." He paused for her to respond to that, but she didn't. "I'll talk to him later."

"Did you hear what happened on Music Row last night?" Kate asked. "In front of Ave Canora?" She also paused. "That's the publishing company you signed with, right?"

His mind had seized up, and no words came.

"MacRae?" she said. "Burl Davies is dead."

"I know," he said. "I saw it happen."

"What?"

"I was there—" His breath and voice choked to a stop, and he felt his cheeks and eyes redden and crumple into each other as the tears came. He couldn't stop them, as much as he wanted to. All he could do was try and keep it to a silent crying without breaking into outright blubbering.

Kate waited without speaking.

After a few moments that felt like many minutes, he drew a shaky breath that didn't release in another wave of half-stifled sobs. "I'm sorry," he said, his voice tremulous. Then he drew a steadier breath. "I don't know where that came from."

"Hey, don't worry about it," Kate said. "You saw something terrible."

"It's embarrassing."

"Don't worry, I said."

He heard the lingering edge of anger or hurt reasserting itself in her voice and wondered again what had happened between them—what he'd done—on Saint Patrick's Day. "Hang on a second." He lay the handset on the tabletop. He stood and tore off a paper towel, stepped into the living room and blew his nose. Then he banked the wadded towel into the wastebasket by the kitchen door and picked up the handset. "You still there?"

"Still here," she said.

He heard her light a cigarette and blow out the long first drag.

"So," she said at last. "When did this happen?"

"About one o'clock this morning."

"What were you doing at Ave Canora at that time of night?"

"I was walking home," he said, feeling the edge in his voice. "From the Songbird."

"Seriously?" She took another drag of her cigarette. "Ever heard of calling a cab?"

"Seriously? Ever heard of coming out to celebrate with a

70

friend?" *Shit*, he thought as he pictured an abrupt draw on her cigarette, the O her lips formed as they released the butt for the inhale, the squint in her left eye. He heard her blow smoke.

"I'm not sure we're friends anymore," she said.

Shit shit shit, he thought, but he bit his lip and waited.

"Let's not get into that again now," she said. "Can you tell me what happened?"

"You mean, like, can I tell you without crying like a fucking baby?" He slammed his eyes shut and slapped himself in the forehead.

"No, that's not what I mean," she said. "I want to know."

He took a deep breath, exhaled, and opened his eyes. Then he shook a Camel up from his pack and lit it. "Okay, but I've gotta back up to when I met this odd character in that park across 16th from the Hall of Fame."

"I know the place," she said. "However you want to tell it."

He began with Benny Jack's compliment on his hat. She stopped him only once, to ask who the man and woman with Davies were, and he said he didn't know. When he finished with the ride home in Officer Edwards's patrol car, he waited for her to speak again, but she didn't.

"Still awake?" he said.

"Wide awake."

"Can I come over?" The words spilled out of his mind and into the receiver. *Shit*, he thought again. *Shit, shit, shit.*

"No, I'm coming over there." She ended the call.

Ezra held the phone to his ear for a moment as if waiting for her to come back on the line and say she was just messing with him and ask why she would come over when they weren't even friends anymore. Then he pulled the receiver from his ear, looked at it, and startled so when it rang that he dropped it on the table. He glanced at the digital clock on the electric range. 8:05.

On the fourth ring the answering machine kicked on, and

he heard himself speaking to the caller. He wondered if he would hear Kate after the beep—*Hey, MacRae, you didn't really think I was coming over, did you?*—or another voice—*Hey, I'll remember you, my handsome young man.* When the beep sounded from the machine in the living room, he heard his favorite voice—"Hey, Ez, it's Mel"—and picked up the receiver and pressed the button to talk.

They were on the line together for almost an hour.

Mel had been awake since before dawn and saw the sun rise from the graveyard of Ephraim MacRae's Presbyterian church. "Your papa gave a good little sermon," he said and reckoned around twenty people attended and sang hymns *a cappella.* He'd gone with the hope that Ezra would be there, but he said he probably benefited from hearing a bit of the Word and from being out in the world so early for something besides chores. Afterward, he went home to do those chores and then drove to Asheville for lunch and a mid-afternoon matinee of *Rain Man.* Evening chores followed his return home, and then he read *Lonesome Dove* until a call came from Caroline.

"How's that going?" Ezra asked. "You must've been talking to her when I called a little while ago."

"Well, phone calls have become a regular thing, but we haven't gotten together yet." He enjoyed getting to know her again, he said, but he still didn't understand where their over-the-phone reunion was leading. "So, I really did think you were coming home for Easter. Your folks thought so, too."

"Yeah, well." Ezra launched again into the story of the past twenty-four hours.

"Ez, you really need to get out of there and come home," Mel said when he'd heard all of it.

Ezra agreed as a loud knock sounded at his front door. "Somebody's here." He turned to the range just as 8:59 changed to 9:00.

"Ten o'clock on a Sunday's late for visiting," Mel said.

"Well, it's just gone nine here, but still—"

Another knocking came even louder as Mel said, "Why do I always forget that?"

"MacRae," Kate's voice sounded from the front stoop. "I've got perishables."

"It's Kate," Ezra said.

"Kate? I thought she didn't like you?"

"Yeah, I was meaning to tell you that'd changed, but she's—" Ezra stopped. "I don't have a good handle on this situation."

"Better go then," Mel said. "Tell me later."

"Love you, Chief."

"Love you, too, Ez," Mel said. "And you really ought to come home." Then he was gone.

"What are you doing, MacRae?" Kate said when he opened the door. "Take these." She handed him two plastic bags from the grocery store in Lion's Head Village.

"Sorry, I was on a call with Mel." Ezra took the bags and closed and locked the door behind her. "What's in these?"

"Makings for a Lowcountry breakfast. Some stuff I brought from my apartment, some I picked up on the way here."

"I'm a fan of breakfast for supper."

She opened the refrigerator and set her bag on the floor in front of it. "This is for in the morning." She bent down to pull shrimp, andouille sausage, and eggs from the bag and set them on the nearly empty refrigerator shelves. "If you're hungry, eat a Moon Pie." She straightened up, wiped her hands down the front of a black sweatshirt from Michael Jackson's *Bad* tour, and closed the refrigerator door. Then she turned away from Ezra and crossed the living room toward the alcove where doorways led to the music room, bathroom, and bedroom. "Check the locks and come to bed, MacRae."

He did as he was told, and after brushing his teeth, he found her waiting under the covers, her back against the wall. He first stripped down to his briefs and then took them off when she said, "Go Adamite." Leaving on the bedside lamp, he lifted the covers to lie down and found her naked as well.

"Don't say anything." She took him in hand for the moment it took. Then she threw her left leg across him, rose to straddle his middle, her calves and thighs cool against his skin, and settled down, guiding him into her. She planted her palms on his chest and dug her fingers into the black hair there. "More than this," she said. "There's nothing."

Bryan Ferry— His mind overheated. *Damn*—

She leaned heavily into her press on his chest, and he felt pinned and thrilled. As the corners of her mouth turned downward and her eyelids closed, he felt a deep swirl of heated energy that rose in him like lava. As she voiced one shuddering whimper and something in him gripped and growled and gushed upward, they came together.

Sometime later, still on his back, Ezra half awoke to the distant chirping of the telephone. He heard and felt the clicking and clunking of the answering machine's mechanics, heard his outgoing message mumble into the darkness of the empty living room followed by the beep and then nothing—no message he could hear. When the machine clicked and clunked to a stop, he reached up and turned off the bedside lamp, rolled onto his side, spooned Kate's warm body, and fell back to sleep.

Monday, March 27, 1989

ELEVEN

He awoke to the mingled smells of sausage cooking on the stovetop and coffee making. He lay still a moment, remembering with both mind and body the unexpected pleasures of the previous evening—*"More than this, there's nothing."* He raised his hands and rubbed his face hard, breathing the voluptuous fragrances on fingers and palms. *"More than This,"* he remembered with a smile of satisfaction. *Bryan Ferry, songwriter.*

"Breakfast!" she called from the kitchen.

He pulled on clean jeans and a blue Nashville Songwriters Association International T-shirt with the organization's motto emblazoned on the back—"It All Begins with a Song"—and left the bedroom. She stood at the range and worked over a skillet, and seeing her dressed in only her Michael Jackson sweatshirt, he thought—not for the first time—that she had the beautiful, powerful legs of a volleyballer. But despite the energetic intimacy of their late-night lovemaking, he still heard her words—"I'm not sure we're friends anymore"—and wasn't certain what was okay to say to her now. "You're not working today?" he asked.

"I took Easter Monday off." She picked up her cigarette from the Nashville, Tennessee cowboy hat ashtray he kept by the stovetop, took a drag, and put it down again.

"That's cool." He looked over her shoulder without touching her. "And that smells and looks awesome."

"Lowcountry shrimp and andouille sausage, like my mother used to make."

"Can I help?"

"This part's finished." She removed the skillet from the heat and partially covered it with its silver lid askew. "The eggs won't take long, so you can pour the coffee and set the table." She cracked an egg into a second skillet already prepped with butter, waited a few seconds, and cracked another. She did this twice more and had four eggs frying together. "How do you like yours?"

"My eggs?" He stood close beside her to take silverware from the drawer. "Over-medium." He turned away to the table and completed two place settings beside—rather than across from—each other, hoping she wouldn't mind.

"Bring the plates," she said.

He set them on the counter at the edge of the stovetop and stood close again as she flipped the fourth egg and then let them continue frying while she uncovered the first skillet and halved and plated its contents. "Lowcountry," he said, still unsure what he should or could say to her. "That's a lot of South Carolina, right?"

"Right," she said. "Charleston especially, but I grew up in a little town called Yemassee." She reached for her cigarette and, after taking a last drag, stubbed it out in the crown of the cream-colored cowboy hat. "We really haven't gotten to know each other."

"No, that hasn't been—" he said and stopped. "No."

She lifted the egg skillet and slid two over-medium eggs on top of his plate of shrimp and sausage and two over-well eggs on top of hers. "Let's eat," she said.

Ezra looked at his breakfast plate and then at her. "Beautiful."

"Most people in Yemassee use corn instead of mushrooms, but Mama always used mushrooms for some reason." She sprinkled a few additional drops of Texas Pete across her plate. "I guess corn would add some nice color."

Ezra closed his eyes and inhaled deeply, then whispered "Thank you" as he exhaled.

Kate looked at him. "Was that a prayer?"

"Just thanks to you for being here and doing this."

"It sounded like you were saying grace," she said. "You're the son of a preacher, right?"

Dusty Springfield's voice flitted through Ezra's mind—"*The only one who could ever reach me . . .*"—*John Hurley and Ronnie Wilkins, songwriters.* "Yes, I am," he said, dousing portions of his plate with Texas Pete and then setting down the bottle. "Presbyterian." He forked pieces of potato and sausage together. "In fact, he and Mama are on their way to your Lowcountry right about now. Going down to Charleston for vacation." He stuffed the first forkful in his mouth to stop himself talking, but he couldn't help himself. "Good Lord, Kate, this is delicious."

"I thought you'd like it." She took another bite and drank a sip of coffee. "Charleston's really become quite the destination these days." She forked up another bite and stared out the kitchen door for a moment. "Yemassee's a little over an hour west of there."

"I think Runion's around twelve hundred people not counting the Runion State students," Ezra said. "Is Yemassee about the same?"

"A little smaller, I think. Maybe a thousand. No college. I went to USC-Beaufort."

"Well, I didn't go to RSU," Ezra said. "In fact, I never even finished high school."

Kate stared at him a moment, and Ezra wished he hadn't shared that. They sat quietly together and ate until their plates lay empty in front of them. Kate scooted her chair back, crossed her bare legs, and lit a cigarette. Ezra lit one, too, then stood up, retrieved the ceramic cowboy hat from beside the stovetop, dumped old butts in the trash, and set it within her reach. Then he picked up their plates and put them in the sink.

"I'll wash these later." He picked up the coffee pot. "More?"

"Yes." She slid her cup closer to him.

As he began to refill it, something caught his eye. He looked up to see the message light on his answering machine flashing. Then he remembered the call that had come in late, sometime after they'd gone to sleep.

"Shit, MacRae, watch it!"

Startled back to the moment, he leveled the coffee pot and swung it to the counter, tore off two paper towels at once and corralled and covered the spillage before it dripped on her naked legs or splattered on the floor. "Shit. Sorry." He picked up her cup and, holding it over the wadded towels, turned and tipped the excess into the sink. He tore off another sheet to dry the cup's side and set it back down in front of her. "Sorry," he said again. "I just saw the light blinking on the answering machine and remembered a call came in after we were asleep last night."

Kate turned toward the living room. "Looks like they left a message."

Ezra stubbed out his mostly unsmoked cigarette and walked into the living room. "I remember hearing my outgoing message, but I don't remember hearing anybody say anything." He bent down and pressed the button to retrieve messages. "Maybe I fell asleep again before—"

The machine began to play what it had recorded, which was only few seconds of breathy, tuneless humming. The recording ended, and the mechanism clunked to a stop.

Ezra turned around to Kate. "Normally, I wouldn't think much about that."

She stubbed out the remainder of her cigarette, took one more sip of coffee, and came to stand beside him. "Do you have something like Caller ID or that Star 69 thing?"

"Just Call Waiting."

"Probably a wrong number." She pulled twice on the hem of his T-shirt. "Let's go take a nap."

She stepped around him and moved toward the bedroom, and he watched her Michael Jackson sweatshirt rise and come off over her head with a spill of red hair on her naked shoulders and back as she disappeared through the door.

He looked toward the kitchen and checked the time.

9:02.

"I have to get ready to go to the police station to make my statement," he said, again looking down at the answering machine.

"When?"

"Officer Edwards is picking me up out front at noon."

"Plenty of time," she said, her voice slightly muffled. "Get your ass bare and get in this bed."

After riding with Latt Edwards to Metro Nashville Police headquarters, making his statement, learning that Detective Hunt wasn't available, and riding back to Utah Avenue, Ezra called the offices of Ave Canora. When nobody answered, he wondered if that was due to Easter Monday or to the events of the weekend. Feeling sure it was the latter, he left a message for Mark Williamson and then changed clothes to begin what he hoped would be his last week of cleaning pools, figuring that before dark he could clean at least four of the ones he'd recently opened for the season.

Between his front door and his car, without Kate waiting in his apartment or Officer Edwards waiting on the verge of Utah, he experienced again the agoraphobic breathlessness that made him conscious of his feet and legs as they stuttered him forward. He collapsed into the driver's seat of the Tempo and quickly locked the doors. He swallowed hard and backed out of his space—small gravel popping beneath his tires. Twenty minutes later, he turned right onto Glen Leven in Oak Hill's Brookhaven Estates and then took the first long driveway to the right, followed it past the left side of a large, blue-shuttered colonial mansion, and nosed up to the fence behind.

He cut the engine and sat for a moment, studying the pool, thinking that it looked good and shouldn't take him too long. He opened the door and stood up and glanced across the roof of his car to the house's sunroom, where he saw just the blonde top of Mrs. Cora Pigott's head above the back of a plush loveseat. After popping the trunk and removing his kit, he let himself in by the gate to the pool area and immediately set about brushing the steps, underwater benches, pool walls, and waterline tiles. When he finished brushing, he began vacuuming the bottom.

He worked to keep his back to the expansive patio and the house so that he could watch the trees lining a small creek that bordered the back of the property. In places, he could see through the trees enough to glimpse the backyards of two estates that fronted Crestridge Drive, and, to his right, monitor the sparse traffic on McConnell Street. He didn't know what to be looking for. If a man appeared at the tree line but wore khakis and a gold Vandy sweatshirt instead of all black with mask and cowboy hat to match, Ezra wouldn't recognize him as the killer until the man called to him across the lawn—"Hey, good looking"—or raised a pistol and began firing.

After a few minutes he willed himself to turn away from the trees and the street, to watch only his work—the illusion of a waterline bend in the vacuum wand, the movement of the vacuum nozzle into gatherings of small black leaves and other debris, the leaving of a clean pool floor behind it. He felt the usual twinge of satisfaction at the stark contrast between the before and after of each vacuum stroke toward the pool's center. He stopped and pulled the notebook from his back pocket and took the pencil from behind his ear. He flipped to the last page he'd written on and saw his laundromat notes—MAYBE THERE'S A CLEANNESS BEYOND THE MIST? and I DON'T KNOW WHAT THAT MEANS. Below that he wrote, GETTING CLEAN ON THE BRAIN—TELL PAPA ABOUT VACUUMING POOL FOR SERMON IDEA. Then he added, MAYBE ABOUT THE DRYER DOOR/MIST

TOO. He almost closed the notebook but stopped and scribbled, OR DON'T—KEEP IDEAS FOR SONGS. With the notebook tucked again into his pocket and the pencil stuck behind his ear, he emptied the vacuum cleaner bag and removed debris from the skimmer baskets. He'd backwashed the pump filter when he opened the pool the week before, so he cleaned the pump basket and eyeballed the pressure gauge. He skimmed a few bits of debris from the pool's surface and then tested the balance of the water's chemicals.

Just as he was putting away his kit, he heard the sliding glass door whisper-rumble open and turned to see Mrs. Pigott step out onto the patio, barefoot and wearing a purple-and-gold silk kimono. *And maybe nothing else*, he thought.

"Hey, pool boy," she said as she padded toward him.

"Hey, Cora," he said. "You're gonna catch your death out here barefoot."

She and he were the same age, something they'd discovered in a poolside conversation the previous summer. She was almost as tall as he, with a solid build that filled out the one-piece swimsuits he'd seen her wear over the two years he'd been cleaning her pool. This physique combined with a cascading abundance of golden blonde hair put him in mind of Dolly Parton or Debbie Combs, a lady wrestler his papa relished watching in her rare Saturday appearances on Channel 4's *Mid-Atlantic Championship Wrestling*.

"Oh, my God, it's almost eighty degrees." She laughed and stopped beside him at the pool's edge. "Looking good."

"Yeah, but it'd be a polar bear event to jump in now." He bent to his kit and grabbed his clipboard and a pen. "We're hitting the seventies like this pretty regular these days, so it shouldn't be long."

"Has the company told you we're getting a heater in a couple of weeks?"

"No, they haven't said." He looked down at the form on the

clipboard. "I've got other heaters on my client list, so I'm sure yours won't be a problem." He scribbled a couple of notes and began checking off items.

Cora suddenly grabbed his forearm—causing one of his checkmarks to shoot across the page—and stretched a toe down into the water. "Oh, that's really cold," she said, her grip tightening. Then she kicked an arc of droplets across the pool, released his arm, and flashed a brilliant, dimpled smile.

"Told you." He handed the clipboard and pen to her. "Need your signature, ma'am."

She laughed and whipped her name across the bottom of the page and gave the items back to him. Then her face turned serious.

"Did you see the paper this morning?" she asked, touching his arm again. "About the new murders on Music Row?"

Ezra hung fire and looked into green eyes that sparkled in the late afternoon light. After a moment, he said, "I didn't see the paper, but I knew about it." He knelt away from her touch and returned the clipboard and pen to his kit, then stood again. "A friend of mine called last night to tell me."

"Did your friend say who was shot? The article just mentioned one name, and now I can't remember who it was."

"Probably Burl Davies."

"That was it," she said. "I remembered just as you were saying it." She moved her touch from forearm to bicep. "Did you know him?"

"I did, actually," he said. "In fact, I just signed a publishing contract with him last week."

She twisted his shirt sleeve in the sudden fist she made. "Ezra, that's awful." She released his shirt and smoothed it, lightly rubbing his arm between shoulder and elbow. "Was he a good friend?"

"Not yet," he said, trying to rescue his focus from the sensation of her touch. "But I was hoping, I guess."

"Sure you were." She patted his arm. "Sure you were." She withdrew her hand. "Did you know the rest of the people who were killed? The paper didn't give any other names, but I think it said there were two more shot."

Tears weren't part of his relationship with her, which inched forward—toward Ezra knew not what—through weekly pool-side flirtations and seemingly casual touches, so, remembering his embarrassing breakdown on the phone with Kate, he decided not to tell Cora he was there. "I doubt I knew them." He bent down, picked up his kit, and straightened up smiling at her. "I better get going or I'll be doing my last one in the dark."

"Save mine for last next week," she said, smiling in return with just the hint of a wink. "I hope things go well with your songwriting business after all this." She hooked a finger inside the cuff of his shirt sleeve and gave it three short tugs. "Get my number off your paperwork and call me if you want to talk." She turned and began walking back toward the sliding glass doors. Then, over her shoulder and through bouncing golden blonde waves, she said, "Call during the day, okay?"

Ezra reached the end of the driveway to find Rick Pigott, Doctor of Chiropractic, sitting in his BMW on Glen Leven, turn signal blinking. Dr. Pigott flashed a grin and two thumbs up. Ezra mirrored the gestures, turned right, and glanced in his rearview to see the chiropractor swing into his driveway. He drove less than a quarter mile to service an oval pool on the opposite side of Glen Leven, after which he hit one on Curtiswood Circle and another on Pasadena Drive before pointing the Tempo toward Sylvan Park and home. By the time he reached The Store, the sky was dark above the wash of city lights.

"Got any copies of today's paper?" he said as he pushed through the door.

Penny looked up at him with a glint of the overhead lights in her eyeglasses. "And a good evening to you, too, Young MacRae."

"Hey, Penny, sorry," he said. "Do you?"

"I ain't got any new left, but I've got a used copy." She bent down to look beneath her cash register and retrieved disheveled sections of *The Tennessean* and slapped them down on the checkout conveyer belt.

Ezra dug in his pocket. "How much?"

"Free with purchase."

"Fair enough." He went to the cooler, pulled out a Diet Mountain Dew, and grabbed a Moon Pie from a snack rack on his way back to the cash register.

"I hope that ain't your supper," Penny said.

"So do I."

She rang up his purchases and put them on top of the newspaper. "Can you stay away from Music Row, Young MacRae?" she said, looking out the front window at a passing car.

"What? Why?"

"Them murders." She looked directly at him and slid her hands into the pockets of her smock. "Satan's gobbling that place up." She turned toward the window again as a truck rumbled past. Then, in a whisper tinged with what he heard as a mixture of wonder and fear, "Even on a Easter Sunday."

"You said something like that yesterday," he said as he gathered up his stuff. "You're sounding like my mama."

"I reckon your mama and me'd agree on a lot," Penny said. "Like Satan"—she nodded toward his Diet Mountain Dew and Moon Pie—"and that supper."

He chuckled. "You know you shouldn't say shit like that to a songwriter, or you might end up in a song." Then he tried to soften his look. "I'll be all right, Penny." He likewise nodded toward the paper and his purchases. "Got a poke for that?"

Penny stared at him a moment before her face crinkled with a grin. "Lord, I haven't heard a soul use that word in I don't know when." She pulled a paper bag from under the cash register, stood the newspaper in it, and then added the other two items. "Here's your poke-full," she said and held the bag out to him.

He took it and turned away.

"The devil's everywhere, Young MacRae," she said after him. "I promise you that."

He turned again, walking backward toward the door. "Well then, you need to be careful, too." He rumped the door open. "What's the latest on your preacher's penis?"

She motioned him out the door with a dismissive wave.

Flirting with Cora Pigott, servicing her pool and the others, listening to Bruce Hornsby's *Scenes from the Southside* on the ride back to Sylvan Park, bantering with Penny—these had kept his fear at bay through the afternoon and past sunset. But when he parked at Youngstowne Square and cut the motor, fear returned full force. He sat in his locked car for a long time and scanned the shadow-haunted surroundings until he was as certain as possible that nothing was moving that shouldn't be. Then he took a deep breath and shouldered open the door, reset the locks and hurried into his apartment.

The message light flashed on his answering machine.

He stood with his back against the door but couldn't listen to the apartment, couldn't hear anything for the sudden rush of his own blood and the blaring klaxon horn that kept time in his brain with the machine's flashing light. He forced himself to breathe as he fumbled with the lock button on the doorknob, then stumbled across the room and collapsed onto the couch. He set his grocery poke on the cushion next to him and glanced into the kitchen.

7:23.

He turned on the lamp and stared at the flashing light as the klaxon and the rush of his blood faded to the sound of his breathing in the quiet apartment. He heard a bump and a muffled voice from the other side of his kitchen wall, and then the click at the thermostat followed by the breathy hum of the heat pump. With the warming air whispering up from the floor vents, he pressed the button to play the message.

"Hey, Ezra, I had a chance to check on Mr. Boudreau. He's critical but stable, and they've got him in surgical stepdown, room nine-zero-two-three. I couldn't get his guitar for you yet. This is Latt Edwards, by the way. Later."

The machine ran through its end-of-message noise and then rattled into a second message.

"Hey, it's Latt again. Listen, I gotta have a Whataburger. I could grab us a couple and come hang out if you're up for that. Let me know at the number on the card I gave you the other night. The other morning. Whenever it was. Later."

Ezra smiled to himself and picked up the telephone. He reached Latt in the parking lot of One Hundred Oaks Mall, gave him his Whataburger order, and said he'd leave the light on for him. Then he opened his Diet Mountain Dew and his Moon Pie and spread the newspaper on his lap.

He studied the smiling image of Burl Davies, who in the newspaper picture again reminded him of Hoyt Axton, this time crossed with Mel MacOde. The picture captured the warmth in Davies's eyes and smile, and Ezra remembered the feel of that same warmth in the man's mighty handshake after the signing of the songwriting contract. He scanned the crime scene map in the corner of the page opposite the picture of Davies, a map much like the one he remembered from the March 11 issue—one-way street, square boxes for buildings, arrows for the movement of victims and perpetrators. He saw his own position represented with X and labeled "WITNESS #1."

TWELVE

MUSIC ROW BECOMES MURDER ROW ... AGAIN
SHEILA WISSNER and ROBERT OERMANN
Staff Writers

NASHVILLE - Shots rang out on Music Row for the second time this month when, at approximately 1 a.m. on Easter Sunday morning, a masked man murdered three people and wounded a fourth.

Police said the gunman stepped out of the shadows and opened fire on publisher Burl Davies and two others, a man and a woman, as they exited Davies' publishing company offices—Ave Canora Music, 7 Music Square West. Davies, along with the man and woman whose identifications are being withheld pending notification of next of kin, were pronounced dead at the scene. The wounded man was rushed to Emergency at Vanderbilt University Medical Center, where he is reported to be in critical condition.

While the assailant seems to have taken no valuables from those attacked, a police source claims that robbery has not yet been ruled out as a motive.

"No motive has been established or even surmised," said Metro murder squad detective Darrin Hunt. "Maybe robbery was intended, but the perpetrator was interrupted. We simply do not know at this point."

According to witnesses, the two individuals with Davies fell first. Davies attempted to flee across Music

Square West, toward publishing house Jamboree Music, where lights were on, but was shot twice, fell to his knees in the middle of the street and then was shot once in the head at close range.

According to Hunt, the unidentified bystander seems to have been wounded by a stray bullet from the volley of shots that brought down Davies.

The gunman fled the scene on foot.

Unlike the March 9 shooting on 16th Avenue South when 11 people were available for questioning by police, only two witnesses could provide details about Sunday morning's shooting. Curly Crocker was in an office in the Jamboree Music building.

"I heard the first shots and went to the window. When Burl (Davies) started toward me before he went down, I realized the fellow with the gun could see me, so I turned out the light real fast," said Crocker, a staff songwriter at Jamboree.

"I seen the guy on my side of the street, the little guy with the guitar, go down about the same time Burl did. He just dropped," said Crocker.

According to police, a second witness was passing by on foot and saw the shooter as soon as he emerged from the shadows between Ave Canora and its neighbor Half Moon Magic, a beauty salon at 5 Music Square West. This witness watched events from behind a parked car on the east side of the street.

The gunman is described as approximately 6'2" and 250 pounds. He was last seen dressed completely in black, including a black ski mask and black cowboy hat. Witnesses say he spoke with a local or regional accent, according to police.

Davies, who lived in the Berry Hill area with his wife Daisy, was a longtime fixture of the Music City song publishing community. He began his Nashville career in 1963 as a songplugger for iconic Acuff-Rose Music.

"He had a great ear for songwriting talent and for matching the right song to the right recording artist," said Wesley Rose, president of Acuff-Rose from 1954 until he and Roy Acuff sold the song catalogue to Gaylord Entertainment in 1985. After 31 years, Davies left the company just before its sale to start his own publishing enterprise, Ave Canora, which is Spanish for "songbird".

Dr. Charles Harlan, Metro Medical Examiner, said Davies' cause of death appears to have been the final gunshot wound to the head. Dr. Harlan added the other two apparently also died of single gunshot wounds, the male to the head and the female to the heart. More test results should be available in approximately three weeks, said Dr. Harlan.

Contributing to this story:

Cindy Rowland

THIRTEEN

Hugo sat shirtless and barefoot in the kitchen at 1619 16th Avenue South, Nashville's *Tennessean* spread on the tabletop in front of him. His booth-tanned belly, carried well when standing and hidden in black, ballooned over his thighs as he leaned above the article about the Easter Sunday morning shootings.

Lucio, also barefoot and shirtless, wearing a vertically striped butcher's apron and gray Sansabelt slacks, moved back and forth between the sink, countertop, and stovetop.

"According to Bob Oermann, there was another witness the other night," Hugo said.

"What?" Lucio asked without turning. "Besides fucking MacRae, you mean?"

"Yeah, it appears Curly Crocker saw everything from the Jamboree offices." Hugo shook a Marlboro up from his pack and took it between his lips. "Hell, I didn't even notice a light on at Jamboree, did you?"

Lucio stood still and stared out the window above the sink. Then he shook his head, turned to the stovetop, and pushed at the breasts with a slotted spatula.

The sizzle of chicken frying filled the kitchen until Hugo cleared his throat. "*Ave Canora* means *songbird* in Spanish," he said out the side of his mouth. He caught the unlit cigarette between two fingers, pulled it from his lips, and took a sip from his bottle of Schlitz. "Did you know that?"

"Know what?" Lucio turned away from four browning breasts to face Hugo.

91

"The name of Burl's publishing company, Ave Canora. In Spanish it means *songbird*."

Lucio stared, his cheeks shiny from shaving, his jaws working as he clenched and unclenched his teeth. "Well, fuck me." He turned back to his pan of chicken. "Ain't that the shit."

Hugo drew in a deep breath through his mouth and blew it out through his nostrils. He folded the newspaper and lay it atop the stack growing from the seat of a table chair they hadn't used in more than a year.

Without looking away from the chicken, Lucio stretched his right hand back toward Hugo and snapped his fingers three times. After lighting his own cigarette with a couple of quick draws and puffs, Hugo stacked the pack and lighter on the tabletop nearer to Lucio, who turned enough to see he couldn't reach them.

"What the hell, Hugo? I'm slaving for you over here."

"What do you call a songbird in Italian?"

"What?"

"What's a songbird called in Italian?" Hugo retrieved the Marlboros and the lighter, leaned left in his chair and pushed them down into the pocket of his pajama pants.

"Oh, my fucking god." Lucio slammed the spatula down beside the skillet and turned down the heat of the stove eye. After he opened the oven and checked his bread, he picked up a bowl into which he dumped Alfredo sauce, minced garlic, sun-dried tomatoes, some Parmesan cheese, and seasoning. These he stirred together noisily, his jaws working again.

"Tell me the Italian for songbird," Hugo said. "Come on, now. I wanna know, and you wanna *sigaretta*." He drew another drag from his own cigarette and pulled another swig from the Schlitz.

"You are such an annoying fucking mook, Hugo. Have I ever told you that?" Lucio poured his sauce on top of the chicken and stirred everything together. He leaned over his work and took a deep breath before covering the skillet and looking at his watch. Then he turned and leaned back against the counter. "All right, lemme think." He put one hand in a pocket of his slacks and thrust the other inside the apron to rub his chest. Then the rubbing stopped. "It's *uccello canoro*," he said. "That's what we call a songbird in Italian."

"Say it again."

"*Uccello canoro*," Lucio said with exaggerated lilt.

Hugo growled a little and stood up. "One more time," he grunted as he pulled the Marlboros and lighter from his pocket. He took another swig from his beer, picked up his half-burned cigarette, and stepped around the corner of the table. "Come on, now, say it one more time for me."

"*Uccello canoro, uccello canoro*," Lucio sang when Hugo stood in front of him.

Hugo lipped another cigarette from the pack and lit it with the burning tip of his own, then took it from his lips and placed it between Lucio's. "*Uccello canoro*," he echoed.

"You need to go wash up while I set the table," Lucio said, one eye squinting against the smoke.

Hugo snaked his left hand inside his pajama bottoms to adjust himself, vented another growl, and turned away. He dropped the remainder of his cigarette in the Schlitz bottle as Lucio suddenly laughed out loud. "What's funny?" Hugo said as he left the kitchen.

"Know what else that can mean?" Lucio called after him. "*Uccello canoro?*"

"What?"

"Singing dick."

"Say what?" Hugo called from the other room.

"Singing dick," Lucio said louder as he opened a cabinet and reached for the plates. "*Uccello canoro!*" he sang to the tune of "Per Tutta la Vita."

When Hugo had washed his face and hands and Lucio had

filled their plates and glasses and removed his apron, they sat across from each other and ate.

"Damn good, Lucie," Hugo said after he'd chased his third bite with a third sip of wine.

Lucio tipped his head from side to side. "It ain't my nonna's, but it's all right."

They ate without speaking until their plates and the wine bottle were empty, then pushed back their chairs, lit cigarettes, and looked at each other through the haze between them.

"You're doing the fucking dishes, right?" Lucio said.

"Fair enough."

Lucio's breath caught in the middle of his next drag, and he turned sideways in his chair, away from the range and refrigerator, and coughed until his face was red and his eyes were wet.

"Why don't you go take a walk while I'm cleaning up your mess?" Hugo said. "Get yourself some fresh air."

Lucio gathered his breath in stuttering inhalations, drew one last time on his cigarette, and stubbed it out in a leftover dollop of Alfredo sauce. "Don't need no fucking fresh air." He cleared his throat again. "I'm gonna do my teeth and get in bed."

"It's only quarter past nine," Hugo said. "I ain't ready for bed yet." He looked at the black mess Lucio had made with the cigarette. "I think I'll clean the kitchen and then go for a walk myself." He reached across the table, lifted Lucio's plate, and set it on top of his own. "I'll get to bed after that."

"Suit yourself." Lucio stood. "Just keep the fucking noise down."

"Sure," Hugo said as Lucio disappeared through the door and into the darkness of the living room. He sat for another moment, rubbing his naked chest and full belly. Then he stood and walked to the sink, started the water to let it warm, and turned back to the table and gathered up the dishes.

FOURTEEN

Ezra stuffed wadded-up napkins and the ketchup-and-grease-smeared debris of his burger and fries into the Whataburger bag, crumpled the whole into a ball, and banked it into the trash can by the kitchen door.

"Nice shot," Latt Edwards said and did the same.

"You too." Ezra pulled a sip of unsweet tea through his straw. "And that's the dishes done." He braced his hands on the tabletop, ready to push up to his feet. "Smoke?"

"No, never got 'round to that habit."

Ezra remained ready to stand.

"But don't let me stop you," Latt said.

"I'll have one later." Ezra stood. "Let's adjourn to the living room."

They sat on opposite ends of the couch, Ezra slumped into his cushion by the telephone table, Latt seeming barely seated on the front edge of his.

"You don't have a TV?" Latt said. "Or a stereo?"

"My stereo's in the music room. Supposed to be a second bedroom." Ezra looked at the black cable that still curled out of the wall and into a coil on the floor in the otherwise empty space between the front door and the entranceway to the kitchen. "I got rid of the TV when I got poor back in the winter. I get more reading and writing done now." He drew another sip of tea and looked again at the empty space. "Maybe I should put a plant or something there."

"Do you miss it? Even just for the noise if not the news?"

"Now, that's a pair of words that sound right together—*noise* and *news*." Ezra drew on the straw again, slurping the last of the tea and ice melt. He shook the cup, heard nothing but the end of the straw tapping the insides, and set it on the telephone table. "I used to be obsessed with MTV and pro wrestling. But wrestling's turned into a bad cartoon circus and most music's become mostly image. Music videos are stealing our imagination."

"Not sure I follow you."

"Well, you know, Hulk Hogan and—"

"I get the cartoon wrestling part," Latt said. "What about music videos?"

"Hang on a sec." Ezra stood and disappeared into his music room, then came back with his six-string Guild and sat down again. "Okay, remember before MTV when you could hear a great song and picture yourself in the story?" He pulled the guitar across his lap. "I'm thinking good story songs like 'Brandy' or 'Year of the Cat.' Maybe 'Midnight Train to Georgia' or 'The Gambler.'"

Latt nodded. "'Jolene' or 'Papa Was a Rolling Stone'?"

"Exactly," Ezra said. "So, see why I got rid of the TV."

"Not really."

"Well, what could you imagine about 'Billie Jean' if MTV hadn't clogged your brain with Michael Jackson dancing across squares of light in pink socks and white shoes with black tips?"

"Okay," Latt said, "I'm starting to get it, but I'm not giving up my cable TV."

"I ain't looking for converts." Ezra strummed a G chord and then took the Guild by the neck and handed it toward Latt. "You said you're trying to learn?"

Latt took the guitar and pulled it onto his lap.

"Show me what you've got, Officer Edwards."

With the tip of his tongue barely visible between his lips,

Latt positioned the fingers of his left hand and strummed a C just as the telephone chirped in tune with it.

"That was cool," Ezra said. "Probably my pal Mel from back home."

"Go ahead and take it," Latt said as he strummed the chord again. "I need to go in a minute anyway."

Ezra picked up on the third ring. "Hello?" Instead of Mel's friendly *Hey, Ez, it's Mel*, he heard an inhalation, followed by breathy humming. But this time the humming wasn't tuneless like the message he'd found that morning. He caught Latt's eyes with a glance.

Latt lay the Guild carefully on the carpeted floor and scooted over next to Ezra, who tipped the receiver away from his ear so that both could listen.

At first, only the humming was heard. Then it broke into breathy singing touched with tremolo. "*You are always on my mind,*" the caller sang. "*You are always on my mind.*"

Ezra and Latt pulled back and cut their eyes at each other across the mouthpiece.

Wayne Carson, Johnny Christopher, and Mark James, songwriters, Ezra thought despite the growing panic in his mind.

The voice stopped, and a whooshing sound interrupted the quiet.

Latt mouthed the word *payphone*, and Ezra nodded.

"Hey, Mr. X, Mr. Witness," the baritone voice said in an exaggerated Southern drawl. "I know it ain't even been forty-eight hours, but I just wanted you to know I remember you like I said I would."

Ezra sat still, stunned, barely able to breathe, but then Latt rolled a finger in the air, motioning for him to keep the conversation going.

"I was just reading the story of that recent unpleasantness on Music Row and saw your X on the little map. Thought I'd give you a call."

Another whoosh sounded through the receiver.

"You there, MacRae?"

"How—" Ezra started and stopped, then cleared his throat. "How do you know my name?"

"Got it from a friend who said you live over on Utah Avenue. Your details are in the phone book."

Another vehicle whooshed by.

"Here's a random question," the man said. "Do you speak Italian?"

"What?"

"Can you speak Italian?"

"No."

"Maybe a little Spanish or French?"

When Ezra didn't respond, Latt motioned again.

"No, not those either," he said and stopped. He heard the scrape of a lighter, followed by an exhalation that sounded smoky even through the telephone line.

"Well, that's disappointing," the caller growled. "Hey, don't you want to ask who I am or where I'm calling from?"

"Why would I ask that?" Ezra said. "You wouldn't tell me, would you?"

"No, I don't imagine I would."

"So, why did you kill Burl Davies?"

Ezra and Latt heard another vehicle pass by the payphone, this time accompanied by the sound of a horn.

"Gotta get off here, MacRae," the man said. "I'll call again soon or maybe just come by. I'd like to press flesh with a handsome young man like you."

The line went dead.

Ezra slowly hung up the receiver, while Latt rose and stood in the middle of the living room.

"Wow," Latt said. "That was exciting."

"Exciting?"

"Yeah, man, we were just on the phone with a murderer."

"Okay, exciting for you, maybe, but he knows about me, Latt." Ezra pushed up from the couch and felt his entire body shaking. "I think I'm gonna puke."

"Come on, man, just breathe. Don't lose that good Whataburger." Latt smiled and put a supporting hand on Ezra's shoulder. "You're all right," he said. "You're all right." He bent down and picked up the guitar and put it on the couch. "Just breathe, Ezra—"

Both men startled when the telephone rang again. They looked at each other on the second ring, and Latt gave a terse nod. Ezra again answered on the third.

"Hello?"

"Hey, MacRae, just calling to check on you." Kate's voice sounded warm and slightly slurred with wine or sleep or both.

"Kate," Ezra said and nodded at Latt. "Hey, can I call you back in a minute?"

"Why?"

"I've got one of the police officers working the case over here, but he's getting ready to leave."

"Okay, but I can't guarantee I'll answer."

Ezra hung up, and when he turned back around, he found Latt Edwards putting on his jacket.

"You be all right?" Latt asked.

"I don't really know."

"He's messing with you," Latt said. "My guess is he just left wherever he lives and walked to a payphone. Entertaining himself as much as anything." He zipped up the front of his jacket and turned toward the door. "I'll bet the car horn spooked him, and that's why he hung up so quick." He stepped out on the stoop, stopped, and looked up. "The moon's in the middle of its Waning Gibbous phase," he said. "So, still plenty of light out."

"What does that mean?" Ezra stood in the open door.

"I've been trying to keep track of whether more bad shit happens the darker it is or the fuller the moon is, but I can't

99

tell much difference." Latt stepped down to the walkway. "I'd say that if our guy gets nervous at a honking car then he's not likely to come into a neighborhood he probably don't know and under this moon and the streetlights." He jingled his change and keys.

"Thanks for the burger and the company," Ezra said. "I'll buy next time."

"Deal."

"And if you've got a guitar, bring it when you come."

Ezra closed the door and locked it. Then he turned off all the lights except for the small lamp on the telephone table. He sat on the couch just listening to the apartment, then called Kate back. He wished her answering machine a good night, disconnected the call, and dialed Mel, who answered full of inconclusive news about Caroline and questions about Ezra's day as a murder witness.

"If the police haven't told you not to leave town, you should come home and stay with me," Mel said. "That guy'll never find you here on the farm."

They talked until it was nearly midnight in Runion, and when he hung up, Ezra turned off the telephone table lamp. Feeling unsettled, he stepped into the kitchen, where he lit a cigarette and drew the smoke deep into his lungs. Then, he set his jaw and walked around the table, unlocked the kitchen door and opened it, and stepped down onto the loose bricks of the patio. He stood smoking, looking at the silver-dark stillness of the adjacent house and its backyard, listening to night in the neighborhood and the indistinct rumble of the city beyond. Standing there in the open, he felt he was being brave in the face of certain danger, but on a deeper level, he couldn't help feeling a disquieting confusion at his yearning for the hideaway Mel offered in the mountains.

i sleep they beep
machines surround me with their flashing light
she creeps i peeps
to see her fussing over me so quiet
how did i get here
i dont remember anything at all
did i walk did i crawl
i maybe seen these lights and climbed the wall
last thing i remember
i was moving through the dark
my lonely and me
following gods doggie
by its nasty black lung bark
we hardly could see
then black doggie said get ready benny jack
and pushed me on the stage said dont look back
the crowd was waiting just across the street
gods doggie walked away on jingling feet
i dont remember nothing after that
till i woke up not knowing where im at
i cant help wondering if this heres a tomb
with angels going in and out the room

FIFTEEN

Hugo returned to his dark house and stood for a moment just inside the front door, watching the street and breathing in the lingering aromas of supper. Then he kicked off his shoes and peeled off his socks. In the bathroom, he dropped the socks in the hamper and peed. After he flushed, he went into the bedroom and sat on the edge of the mattress.

"You awake?"

"Leave me the fuck alone so I can sleep."

Hugo sat grinding his teeth and growling deep in his chest. "You can sleep in a little while," he said at last. "But right now I want to make you sing like a"—he paused and bit his bottom lip—"a *uccello canoro*."

Lucio didn't respond other than to roll over onto his side with his back to Hugo.

Make you sing like a uccello canoro. Hugo found he could say in the darkness what he couldn't say when they sat shirtless in their recliners and watched *Die Hard* or when—in the bright, warm kitchen—Lucio stirred him up with Italian food and Italian words. On the dark bed, with Lucio within reach, he could say such things without the death grip of his raising closing on his throat and choking him, without the uproar of voices—his father, his mother, preacher after preacher, coach after coach—drowning his desire in angry words that as good as proclaimed they would sooner condone his cold-blooded killing of three or four people than condone a single moment of passion and pleasure with little Lucio Centopani. Or with big

Ezra MacRae, for that matter, who'd loomed large in his imagination for almost forty-eight hours.

The house settled into nighttime quiet, its wood periodically popping as it cooled. A LifeFlight helicopter passed overhead on approach to the rooftop helipad at Vandy Medical Center. A vehicle rumbled past on 16th, followed by another. Now and then, a siren wailed in the distance. And in that dark bedroom, the staggered breathing of the two men ebbed and flowed through the intervals between those sounds from the world outside.

At last, Hugo stood and stripped off his shirt and stepped into the living room. He tossed the shirt onto the back of his recliner as he passed through to the kitchen to draw a glass of water at the sink.

Thursday, March 30, 1989

SIXTEEN

Ezra startled awake to an almost simultaneous blast of light and clap of thunder. Shudders rippled through his body like the shockwaves that reached him from higher and higher along the lightning's trail. As the rumble rolled and reverberated for long seconds through the pre-dawn sky above Nashville, he realized that the approach of the storm had entered his dreams as slow-motion gunfire that pursued him as he fled, exposed and afoot, up and down Music Row's empty sidewalks and in and out of abandoned offices. He thought the city beautiful in rain, with its greens and reds and yellows shining on wet streets, but after almost six years, he still hadn't gotten used to the intensity of thunderstorms that frequently roared across middle Tennessee's gently rolling landscape.

He moved the covers aside, swung his feet to the floor and sat up on the edge of the mattress.

The red numerals on his bedside clock read 5:10.

He waited for a break in the rumbling and then listened to his apartment for any unusual sounds. But after two shallow breaths, the room around him lit again with blinding light and another explosive thunderclap shook the walls. *No pools this morning*, he thought as he lay back down and nestled into his warm bedding. The murmurings of the retreating storm lulled him to sleep again, and he slept without remembered dreams until the telephone awakened him. On the second ring, he opened his eyes and wondered if this might be another payphone call from the killer. On the third ring, he raised up on an elbow and looked at the clock.

9:23.

On the fourth ring, the answering machine clunked and clicked into action, and following Ezra's outgoing message, Ave Canora's Mark Williamson began speaking.

Ezra threw off the covers, launched out of bed, and grabbed the receiver. "Hello, Mark?"

"Hey, Ezra, sorry to be so long returning your call. It's been crazy around here."

"I can imagine."

"I guess you were calling to see what's going on with your publishing contract."

"Well, that sounds callous given what you folks are going through, but yeah."

Williamson cleared his throat. "Well, the honest truth is that I don't know what's going on for the long term. Not yet anyway."

Ezra began to pace back and forth in front of his couch.

"I'm gonna get together a business meeting with Burl's wife Daisy as soon as possible," Williamson said. "Maybe sometime next week if she's up to it."

"Do you reckon I'll still have a contract?"

"Oh, you've got a contract. That's a done deal."

Williamson paused, and Ezra pictured him taking a sip of coffee.

"In fact, you can come by tomorrow afternoon and pick up your first paycheck."

Ezra felt a thrill course through his body. "Mark, that's awesome," he said, his throat tight with relief and excitement. "So, Mrs. Davies will keep the publishing company going?"

"Well, that's what I've got to meet with her about." Williamson paused again. "Daisy used to be in the industry as a singer but never quite hit it big. She's got a bit of a chip on her shoulder about it."

"Okay."

"But she's a businesswoman and she loved Burl. That's hopeful." A beep sounded in the background. "Both our positions with Ave Canora depend on her decision to keep things going, so for now, I suggest you keep your day job, just in case." A second beep sounded. "Listen, Ezra, I've got to go. Holler at me if I'm here when you stop by tomorrow."

Ezra got in the shower, thinking that a clean body and a cup of strong coffee would wake him up enough to dress and step into his music room and try to write a new song for his new publisher. As he leaned the top of his head into the spray and felt the hot water streaming through his hair and around his ears and down his face and body, he heard the telephone ring again. He stood straight and let the spray dance on his chest while he listened. He relaxed after hearing a voice pitched like that of a young woman. He finished washing and rinsing, turned off the water, and stood in the tub to dry himself. Finished but still naked, he stepped into the living room to hear his message.

"Hello, Mr. MacRae? This is Hope Hayes at Ave Canora. Mark Williamson asked me to call and say he forgot to let you know that the funeral for Mr. Davies will be two o'clock this afternoon at West End United Methodist Church, with the Reverend Russell T. Montfort officiating." She paused, and the message tape hissed for a moment. "I don't suppose you need to know that last part. But I go to church there, and Dr. Montfort is amazing." She stopped again. "That's all, I guess. Bye."

Ezra smiled when he thought he heard her whisper to herself, "Jesus, Hope," before she disconnected the call. He felt certain that Ave Canora's receptionist was named Tina Joseph, and he didn't remember meeting a Hope Hayes there. He decided she was either a temp or somebody who worked—as he'd done during his earliest days in Nashville—in some back room with the mail or with demo tapes and lyric sheets.

He stepped to the kitchen door. Gray as the day was, he imagined that the air might still feel clean and fresh on his skin, like a cool version of the shower steam he'd left drifting in the bathroom. He opened the door and drew in a deep breath, which caught in his chest when his gaze fell on the single concrete step leading down to the small brick patio.

The center of the step held one wet footprint.

He slammed the door and turned the lock, then leaned left and right to see as much of the outside as possible. At last, he took another deep breath and released it, then unlocked the door and pulled it open.

The wet footprint gleamed on the otherwise dry concrete step.

He crouched to look closer. *Less tread than a sneaker*, he thought. *Definitely not a cowboy boot.* He braced himself with a hand on the door frame and, still crouched, leaned and put his head out and looked left and right. He scanned the backyard of the yellow house beyond the hedge. *Empty as usual.* He stood stiffly, stepped back, and closed and locked the door. He thought about rigging a towel to cover the window but decided if anybody came snooping around again he wanted to meet him eye to eye.

SEVENTEEN

Hugo stood beside the bed where Benny Jack lay with eyes closed, a defenseless body—*small like Lucie's*—beneath a white sheet, completely still except for the left foot that flexed and unflexed at the ankle like the curling and uncurling tip of a cat's tail. Hugo looked up from the pallid face with its scraggly gray-brown beard and watched the lights and digital numbers flash as the surrounding machines beeped and clicked.

"You shouldn't be in here," a voice said from the doorway. She wore blue scrubs and gray soft-soled shoes, her curly blonde hair pulled back. "I'm sorry, but it's not visiting hours yet."

Hugo turned his face toward her and bared his teeth in a grin. "Hey, good looking." He ogled her from eyes to thighs. "Lucky guy to have a such a beautiful nurse." He turned back to the bed. "He ought to wake up and get a load of you."

Benny Jack's nurse crinkled her nose slightly but didn't smile. "Visiting hours on this floor don't start until ten o'clock."

Hugo looked at his watch. "Ten's just twenty minutes from now." He looked her over again. "Come on, sweetheart."

"I have to check his vitals and give him a quick sponge bath before—"

"Luckier and luckier," Hugo said. "I'm sorry, Nurse—?"

"Sally Evans."

"Nurse Sally, I apologize." He clasped his hands behind his back. "I'll just go downstairs for a cup of coffee and come back up at ten o'clock." He grinned again. "Can I bring you anything?"

"You might want to wait until a quarter after or so," she said as she stepped to the opposite side of Benny Jack's bed. "The police usually show up around ten to check on him."

"I see," Hugo said. "Thank you." He turned away but paused and turned back. "Has he been awake at all?"

Sally looked at him with a raised eyebrow.

"It's just that him and his guitar are always so lively. I hate to see him like this."

"You know him?"

"I live over on Sixteenth, and he's around that area a lot." He again turned away and again turned back. "When he's ready, could he come stay with me?" He cleared his throat. "It'll be hard trying to get well living on the streets."

"It's not time for him to leave yet, but when he goes, I think he'll go to rehab for a while." She began checking the various connections between her patient and his machines. "I don't know what happens after that." She looked up at a clock on the wall. "Now, if you'll excuse us."

"Sure." Hugo left the room and made his way to the elevator. He pressed the button to go down and, while he waited for the arrival of the car, stood and scanned the layout of the hospital floor. When Sally Evans came out of Benny Jack's room, he grinned and waved as the elevator's arrival tone sounded and the doors opened. "Hey, good looking," he said under his breath as the nurse glanced at him and turned away.

"Hey, yourself," Detective Woody Davidson said with a chuckle as he stepped out of the elevator and lumbered toward Benny Jack's room.

Hugo stood and watched the man pass the nurse's station. *How'd it be to bed that hoss?* he wondered and felt his cheeks flush at the thought. Lucio was much smaller, powerfully built from weightlifting but still almost like a plaything at times. Hugo imagined that he and the big man disappearing into Benny Jack's room—*certainly a police detective*—would be much more evenly matched, and he again wondered what that would be like.

The elevator doors began to close, and he shot out a hand to stop them, shouldered his way into the car, and pressed the button to descend to the parking garage.

As a tinny string section overhead whitewashed the strolling rhythm of "Ain't That a Shame," he tried to recall ever having had such a thought—*to bed that hoss*—about another man before that drunken night he and Lucio had crash-landed like fallen angels into a broken, burning heap on his bed.

Then the elevator bottomed, the doors hissed apart, and the apparition of Gilbert Dooley stood before him spectral and smiling and blocking his way, semitranslucent in the garage's murky light.

Big Gil Dooley, looking just as he had that October night in 1955 when the two of them were second-string offensive linemen for Mississippi State. The Maroons had just defeated the Crimson Tide 26-7, and he and Big Gil had gotten to play the final three possessions in front of twenty-eight thousand people in Tuscaloosa. Giddy over crushing their rival and drunk on Clyde May's bootleg moonshine, they sat in the back of the bus, jostling hotly against each other on the two-hour ride back to Starkville. At some point in their drunkenness, in the darkness between Coal Fire and Columbus, when all the voices of teammates had stilled and silhouetted heads lolled this way or that with the curves on the highway, he and Gil found themselves with their hands down each other's pants. After they came together and sat stupefied a moment, Gil laughed and wiped his palm on Hugo's thigh, turned to the window, and went to sleep while Hugo stared straight ahead, his father's slurred curses and hammering fists rattling his brain and a Soso Baptist preacher's thunderous voice echoing inside his skull as inside a cinderblock church. The cursing and beating and sermonizing urged and belittled him until at a point in the walk across campus to their

111

dorm, he turned on Dooley with stunning ferocity and dragged the big boy into the darkness beneath a Southern magnolia, where he continued the beating until his mind calmed and the only rage remaining was that of his heart thumping against his ribcage. He'd left Gilbert Dooley there for dead, returned to his room to shower and pack his belongings, and then drove out of Starkville heading north.

The elevator doors began to close, and again he shot out a hand to stop them. He charged through Dooley's apparition—like an offensive lineman off the snap—and stumbled into the parking garage. As he regained his balance and hurried to the Taurus, he sensed something settle like congestion in his barrel chest and felt again in his loins and fists those moments in the back of the bus and beneath the magnolia. *Almost thirty-four years ago,* he thought as he settled behind the wheel. He couldn't remember how long the fear had pursued him—not the fear of being a murderer on the lam if Dooley died but the fear of rousing the murderous monstrosity he believed he'd become that night as he yanked at the drawstring of his teammate's sweatpants and wrestled his meaty right hand down inside the waistband.

EIGHTEEN

hey jesus
our father wert in my room
not more n a minute ago
watching over
where i lay me playing possum
with my crazy eyes closed
my ears open
hey jesus
our father wast here for me
to take me home with him
but i cant die before i wake
because i aint asleep
i cant give him my soul to take
heres where i need to keep
angel come in sayin it aint time for me
but it was time she said for god to hit the street
hey jesus hey jesus hey

Ezra parked in the back corner of the lot behind West End United Methodist Church. He took the sidewalk around to the church's main entrance. From a table just inside the porte cochere, he picked up a program for the service—featuring a photograph of Burl Davies, smiling—and then stepped through the open double doorway and felt the dim coolness of the nave on his face.

Two rows of nearly thirty pews each stretched away to the chancel railing. At the opposite end of the center aisle, between lectern and pulpit, a closed mauve casket stood hedged with floral arrangements, a fleeting exuberance of color in contrast to the church's muted tones of wood and stone. Beyond that centerpiece, on the backside of the chancel and beneath a subtly pointed arch, a balding organist sat with his back to the nave—only his head and shoulders visible—and played a confident but not bombastic version of "A Mighty Fortress Is Our God." Still farther on, in the apse at the end of this long, vaulted space, quiet light filtered through stained glass and colored the empty choir loft, the back wall a garden of singing silver organ pipes.

Ezra felt the pressure of others entering behind him. He stepped back from the center aisle doorway, excusing himself, moved to his right, and passed through a door to the side aisle. He spotted an isolated seat at the end of an unoccupied pew—eleven or twelve from the front—and made his way there, where he first stepped around a stout concrete pillar and then took a seat beneath the soft opal gleam of a pillar-mounted gothic sconce trimmed in copper.

Murmuring people filled the front seven or eight pews on both sides of the center aisle. Some heads leaned together in whispered conversation, while others—even though shoulder-to-shoulder with their neighbors—remained still and somehow solitary. Behind this crowd, mourners and curious congregants and on-lookers scattered themselves through the pews around him.

He supposed the woman sitting alone in the center of the front pew to be Daisy Davies, and he wondered if she and Burl had no children. The man sitting a discreet distance from her on that same pew he recognized to be Mark Williamson and beside him two hairdos Ezra thought likely to be Ave Canora's Tina Joseph and Hope Hayes.

Another woman a couple of pews nearer to him caught his eye when she turned to look back toward the entrance, and he saw that it was Pam Tillis, a singer-songwriter—and daughter of entertainer Mel Tillis—he'd met recently at Dalt's in Lion's Head Village. Those around her faced forward or leaned together without turning and so remained only balding heads and cascades of hair. Off to his left, he could see profiles, and he recognized a few. He saw Rodney Crowell and Rosanne Cash, who sat just shoulders away from singer-songwriters John Hiatt and Ashley Cleveland. He glimpsed the profiles of Kathy Mattea and Harvey McDibb—*writer of "Common Girl" for Don Williams.* Fred Carter Jr. and Jim Isbell sat together, musicians he'd met once when hanging out with Gabe Tanner during one of his first recording sessions with Billy Keith. Redheaded Dottie West sat near them, arguably the biggest country music star in attendance, with the possible exception of Rosanne Cash. He recalled meeting Dottie briefly the same night he'd met Carter and Isbell, when she and her people were booked into Bullet Recording's studio B while Gabe recorded in studio A.

Movement tugged at the corner of his eye, and he turned to see songwriter Dallas Frazier—*writer of 'Elvira,' by the Oak Ridge Boys and those Moonshine Rebels*—and Alabama producer Harold Shedd, who, after a quick, whispered conversation, took seats together beside a scooting and smiling Vince Gill. Directly to Ezra's left, David Wills sat beneath the opposite copper-trimmed sconce. Ezra wondered for a moment if he should try to bump into the performer after the service and mention "Blue Jeans Girl," the song Mark Williamson had said was on hold for Wills's new recording project.

The organ fell silent. The murmurs and whispers among the mourners faded. Somebody somewhere behind Ezra coughed twice.

A fireplug of a man in a black robe and purple stole stood up from a chancel chair and climbed into the pulpit.

"Jesus said, I am the resurrection, and I am life." The preacher spoke into the quiet with a rich and measured baritone that rose from a barrel chest. He paused for a moment, and the reverberations of his voice scattered to the distant corners of the nave and dissipated. "Friends, we have gathered here to praise God and to witness to our faith as we celebrate the life of Burleson Christian 'Burl' Davies." He looked down at the front row—at Daisy Davies—with a small smile. "We come together in grief," he said, still seeming to speak to the widow, "acknowledging our human loss." Then he returned his gaze to the gathered. "May God grant us grace, that in pain we may find comfort, in sorrow hope, in death resurrection."

Three coughs sounded like barks from what seemed the same troubled chest as the two coughs a couple of minutes before.

When the organist began again, Ezra checked the order of service, pulled a hymnal from the rack on the back of the pew in front of him, and rose with the congregation. He turned to number 526 and joined in the singing.

> *What a friend we have in Jesus,*
> *all our sins and griefs to bear!*

He stopped after these first two phrases and stood listening while Nashville voices swelled in the nave, creating a tension between their front-porch, cinderblock-church rhythms and the strict 4/4-meter trumpeting from the silver organ pipes. He wondered if the singers heard in their minds shuffling guitars and drums, a bass touching the tonic and the five. He wondered what the white-robed organist and black-robed minister thought as the hymn entered its bridge lines—

> *O what peace we often forfeit,*
> *O what needless pain we bear. . . .*

—and powerful Grand Ole Opry harmonies ascended through glissandos of moans and wails. The spirited grappling between the natural, untrained voices of many a country music stage and studio and the organ's solemn nineteenth-century hymnody seemed a musical enactment of the tensions between Music Row's Nashville as "Music City, U.S.A." and Belle Meade's Nashville as "Athens of the South."

When the hymn ended, Dr. Montfort stood again in the pulpit, bid the Lord be with them all, and led a congregational prayer.

Ezra listened to the voices—the communal hum of them rich and harmonious, their individual enunciation of consonance and sibilance knocking and hissing in the struggle to keep pace with each other. After a few phrases, he looked down at his program and joined in. "Give to us now your grace, that as we shrink before the mystery of death, we may see the light of eternity. Speak to us—" He froze. From some distance directly behind him but not far, he heard the same voice that'd spoken to him in the wee hours of Sunday morning—*I'll remember you, my handsome young man.* He swiveled at his hips and thighs with the impulse to turn and look, but he kept his feet planted and remained facing forward. As the prayer ended, he found himself unable, for a panicky moment, to bend his knees and sit, but he forced himself to focus on the man in the pulpit, who seemed to be returning his gaze.

"Out of the depths I cry unto thee, O Lord!" Dr. Montfort said as Ezra's knees relented and he collapsed to the pew with a thump and a wooden creak that turned a few heads in his direction. "Lord, hear my cry," the preacher continued.

NINETEEN

Lucio sat muscleman-straight in a black Armani suit, its padded left shoulder pushed against the right shoulder of Hugo's Rai Nani Hawaiian shirt.

"If this had been a Catholic funeral, no way you'd wear that shit shirt," Lucio whispered without turning his head. He bent slightly forward and looked down at Hugo's sandaled feet. He leaned back again, drew a breath, and blew it out his nose. "You need a fucking pedicure." Then he coughed twice but was able to stifle a fit.

"At least I didn't wear shorts," Hugo said. "But I am going commando."

"Jesus Christ."

Hugo scanned the crowd and then inclined his head toward Lucio and pointed. "Look, yonder's Rosanne Cash."

Lucio turned slightly and coughed once. "*'Yonder's Rosanne Cash?'* Can you not just nod her way? I know who the fuck she is."

"Shush now, Lucie. This is my favorite part."

"What is sown is perishable, what is raised is imperishable," the minister read. "It is sown in dishonor, it is raised in glory. It is sown in weakness, it is raised in power. It is sown a physical body, it is raised a spiritual body."

"Now, that right there's what we did for Nancy and Burl," Hugo whispered. "We sown them so God can raise them up."

"Whatever," Lucio whispered. He crossed his arms over his chest, coughed three times, and settled into the pew.

TWENTY

When Dr. Montfort pronounced his final "Amen" and the organist began what Ezra thought a surprisingly bluesy rendition of "Soon and Very Soon," men in black suits swarmed the coffin of Burl Davies, turned it from the chancel and began guiding it along the center aisle toward the exit. Ezra watched Daisy Davies rise and follow. The mourners, already standing after the dismissal, began to turn and gather their things and solemnly wait for Burl's coffin and his wife to pass. Then they made their way out of the pews and back along the center and side aisles.

Ezra hesitated—afraid to turn around and join the flow of exiting mourners. He nodded at Mark Williamson as he and the young women with him passed along the crowded center aisle. Then he stepped to his right and forward to put the stout pillar between himself and the back half of the nave, his breath quick with the realization that the gunman knew his face, could pick him out of the thinning crowd outside on the West End sidewalk and follow him home. The wet footprint he'd found on his back step that morning could mean that he'd been there already. With his back against the cool concrete, Ezra stared at the empty, softly lit chancel and forced himself to breathe and be still. After a few moments braced by the solid pillar and surrounded by the nave's immense quiet, he felt steady. He peeked around the column to his left and right and saw that nobody remained among the pews or in the aisles. Then he moved quietly forward toward the south transept.

The aisle in front of him—dappled with rainbow light from

the bordering stained-glass windows—ended just past the pulpit at a tall door of dark wood. It stood slightly ajar, and he stopped and listened, thinking that either through it or through the matching door on the opposite side of the chancel he would find a safe way into the interior of the church and out to the parking lot in the rear. When he didn't hear anything, he gently pushed the door open and entered a narrow room dimly lit and partially filled with hanging robes and other garments. Too late he noticed Dr. Montfort standing in shadow at the other end of the narrow room, his back to the door and to Ezra as he draped the purple stole on a padded hanger.

Having apparently noticed some shift in the air or the light of the vestry, the preacher turned and gave Ezra a practiced but genuine smile. "Hello," he said, his voice as rich as it'd been in the nave's sound system. "Are you lost, young man?"

"Not exactly," Ezra said after a moment. "I'm looking for a back way out of here?"

Dr. Montfort chuckled as he tucked his chin and peered over the top of his glasses. "That sounds ominous." His smile widened. "Should I be concerned?"

Ezra wiped his palms on the back pockets of his jeans and tried to smile in return. "I don't think so. Just being cautious."

"That also sounds ominous," Dr. Montfort said with raised eyebrows, the smile not fading from his voice. "There is indeed a back way out of here." He reached to his left, opened a door, and held it. "My car's in the back, so I can just walk you out if that's all right."

TWENTY-ONE

Hugo stood with Lucio in the breezeway between the church's main wings.

"Our boy was in there," Hugo said. "Just a few seats in front of us."

"What boy?" Lucio said between wheezing coughs.

"MacRae, Lucie. Jesus. Ezra MacRae." Hugo eyed the exit from the porte cochere.

"Fucking allergies," Lucio wheezed.

"Yeah, I know, they're bad this year." Hugo turned and looked into the cloister garden and then at Lucio. "Why don't you get back to the house and get your shoes and shirt off. Maybe take a hot shower and a nap." He crossed his arms over his chest. "I'll wait and then walk back."

"You sure?" Lucio said and took a short breath. "It don't look like he's coming out."

"He might've gone looking for a bathroom."

"And he might have made us and found another way out."

"Made us how?"

"I don't fucking know, Hugo. Maybe he recognized your voice."

"Well, if he did, then we've already spooked him, and that's what I wanted anyway."

Lucio broke into a brief fit of coughing. Then he turned away toward 23rd Avenue North, his coughs giving him a momentary stagger.

"You gonna be all right?" Hugo called after him.

Lucio turned without stopping, walking backward and looking at Hugo. "I'm gonna stop by Cat's and pick up two more crates. You can put them together later, right?"

"Sure, Lucie," Hugo said, feeling the usual effects of the younger man's name on his tongue, of his deep brown eyes and the sight of his body in motion.

Keys in hand, Lucio thumbed the direction over his left shoulder. "You sure you don't want to ride?"

"I'm fine. You go on. I'll see you later."

"Whatever." Lucio coughed once as he turned away.

Hugo watched him past the church's front entrance. "Allergies, my ass," he said aloud to himself. He drew a sharp breath. "You'll be dead come another spring." He clapped his right hand over his mouth and squeezed his nostrils as if to stifle a sneeze. *To lose you—lose this—so soon*, he thought.

The greatest loss he'd known in his fifty-three years emerged from the trainwreck of embarrassments in that moment when Nancy had walked out of the house on 16th and slammed the front door behind her, never to return. It had been a loss more complicated than just a break-up. He'd not only failed as her husband but, unable to land a Music Row recording contract for her, as a businessman and her hero as well. And from that first unexpected taste of Lucio, even before she caught them, he believed he'd failed to be a man for her too. Putting a bullet in her heart hadn't been revenge or recovery but erasure of failure. He wasn't sure how—or if—he could stand to lose Lucio, much less care for him through the stress and ugliness of his dying. He decided in that moment as he turned toward downtown, that he wouldn't do it. Couldn't do it.

TWENTY-TWO

what have you been up to lately sally
you bending over me with beeps and hisses
pushing up my sleeping eyelids sally
you see my brains filled up with dreams of kisses
o sally youre so cute
in your blue hospital suit
o sally youre so fine
i just need you to be mine
im used to waking up at your touch sally
how will i ever sleep again without it
youre an angel and im a devil sally
if you don't mind then i don't care about it
o sally youre so cute
in your blue hospital suit
o sally youre so fine
i just need you to be mine
im in the hospital so i aint got health
i sleep out on the streets so i aint got wealth
but listen heres a thing or two
i got a healthy wealthy love for you
this place has got a chapel aint it sally
we need a little minister and fiddler
you and me can go get married sally
my best man stands all full of piss and vinegar
o sally youre so cute
in your blue hospital suit
o sally youre so fine
i just need you to be mine

Ezra followed Dr. Montfort around a corner and down the first flight of a stairwell.

"How did you know Burl Davies?" the minister asked over his shoulder.

"I'm a songwriter," Ezra said. "I write for his publishing company."

"Have you written anything I might have heard?" Dr. Montfort stepped down onto the landing and made the turn and started down the second flight.

"Not yet." Ezra stopped on the landing and looked into the cloister garden, identified by a small sign mounted next to double doors. "I'm working on it." He could see the breezeway beyond the garden, on the other side of which, he knew, was busy West End Avenue. He thought a figure stood framed in one of the breezeway arches, but the small panes in the door were too hazy with condensation and pollen to be certain.

"I really am in a bit of a hurry," Dr. Montfort said.

Ezra turned to see the minister smiling up at him. "Sorry," he said and started down.

At the foot of the stairs, they bore left across the vestibule to glass double doors through which the parking lot appeared, and in a moment, they stood outside beneath greening trees and a gray sky. Ezra quickly glanced right toward his car, Louise Avenue, and Elliston Place, then left toward 23rd.

"God, I hope it doesn't rain at the graveside," the minister said as he stretched, his arms reaching toward the sky.

Ezra looked at him with a raised eyebrow.

"Prayer," Dr. Montfort said, the soft light of day glinting off his eyeglasses. "That was a prayer."

"Well, brother, I hope you get the weather you seek." Ezra smiled.

A sudden burst of coughing sounded from the direction of 23rd, and they turned to see a well-dressed and well-groomed man veer from the sidewalk into the parking lot without looking their way, staggering slightly from the coughing fit toward a dull red Ford Taurus with a blue license plate with yellow lettering.

"Allergies are bad this year," Dr. Montfort said. "Probably a lot in the air here that isn't a problem in New Jersey."

Ezra nodded in response but kept watching the coughing man. "New Jersey?" he said and turned back to the preacher.

"That's a New Jersey tag, if I'm not mistaken."

Ezra squinted to try and read the state name and number but couldn't make them out. "You've got better eyesight than I do," he said.

"I was stuck in Philadelphia traffic recently and saw a number of those blue and yellow tags up close and personal."

Ezra turned back to see the smile and the extended right hand, which he took and shook.

"I'm glad to have seen you safely out of the building," Dr. Montfort said. "You'll be all right from here?"

"Oh, yeah," Ezra said. "Thanks."

"I have to go," Dr. Montfort said. "But I have a feeling you're an interesting young man." He turned away but added over his shoulder. "Come visit me anytime or come worship with us some Sunday morning."

"I'll do that." Ezra watched the minister get into his car and hurry out of the parking lot. Then he turned back to the coughing man in the red Taurus.

The man sat behind the wheel staring at Ezra but then turned away as his face folded into another painful-looking bout of coughing, leaving him hunched over the steering wheel.

Ezra hurried to his car and left the lot, keeping an eye on his rearview for anybody following.

The sky continued to threaten rain for the late afternoon, so, after checking with the pool company and arranging to do two days' work the following day, a Friday, with a late lunch break during which he would collect his check from Ave Canora, Ezra settled on his couch with his Guild and a pad of paper. He wrote the lines he had from Sunday's distracted work at the laundromat.

> *He stepped out of the music*
> *And into the night*
> *From the rumble of the bass and drums*
> *Into the city quiet*

He laid down his pen and finger-picked a tentative chord progression in a minor key, whisper-humming a wordless melody as he scanned the drafted lyrics. While he continued the progression, he considered images from that Saturday night and Sunday morning prior to the horrors of gunfire and the man in black—the approaching storm beyond downtown, Benny Jack Boudreau, the lounge band's music and lights. He kept his left hand on the neck of the guitar and picked up the pen.

> *Lightning strobed the skyline*
> *And thunder shook his heart*
> *Big rain's coming*

He laid down his pen again, set the butt of the guitar on the floor, and leaned the neck against the couch. Then he stood and went to the kitchen door and opened it. With a downward glance, he confirmed that the morning's shoeprint had evaporated and then stepped onto the patio. He moved between the apartments and the hedge until he could see the parking lot and most of the street.

No red Taurus, he thought and then listened. *No coughing.*

Back on the couch with the Guild again in his lap and the pen again in his hand, he jotted down a line every few minutes over the next couple of hours.

She sat up in darkness
Turned on the bedside light
A warm palm smoothed the cool and empty
Pillow by her side
Distant thunder mumbled low
Lightning lit the window
Big rain's coming

Staring at the night now fallen outside and trying to think what might come next in the song, he startled when the telephone on the table beside him rang.

After the machine had gone through its processes, a familiar and friendly voice spoke into the room. "Hey, Ezra, it's Latt Edwards. You there?"

Ezra picked up the receiver. "Yeah, I'm here. How's it going, Latt?"

"I'll call it so-so. Some good, some not so good."

"What's up?"

"I've got Benny Jack's permission to get the guitar for you," Latt said. "I'll try to get Detective Hunt to help me take it out of property and evidence tomorrow morning if you can stop by. Or we can arrange to meet somewhere."

"You spoke to Benny Jack?"

"Yeah, they think he's more or less out of danger now, but he'll still be in the hospital for a few days." Latt took a bite of something and continued, talking around whatever was in his mouth. "Did you know he calls you Jesus?"

Ezra chuckled. "Well, that's good news he's out of danger, but, no, I didn't know he calls me that." He laid the Guild on the couch beside him, its neck on the opposite armrest. "Can we do another Whataburger meal when I get the guitar? I'll buy this time."

Latt's end of the line remained quiet a moment. "Well, that's the not-so-good news, man. When I reported our meeting the other night and the phone call you got, my bosses chewed my ass out. Apparently, we can't be hanging out while it's an active case and you're a witness."

"Well, shit," Ezra said. "That's a bummer."

"Yeah, so for now, I'd better just hand over the guitar and leave it at that."

Before the call ended, they agreed to meet sometime during Ezra's late lunch break and possibly in the vicinity of Ave Canora.

Ezra replaced the receiver in its cradle and took a cigarette to the front stoop, where he lit up and allowed his mind to drift like the smoke he blew toward a lowering sky aglow with the Music City lights—drifting thoughts of the new song and the initial publishing successes he hoped were ushering him into a profession; of Mel and the promise of safe haven at MacOde Farm; the intrusion of Caroline into that haven; of Burl's killer at the funeral; of the threatening, haunting mystery of the Taurus man; of good Dr. Montfort; of Latt Edwards and the possibility of friendship; of Benny Jack and his Lonely, both wounded and in need of healing.

Tires suddenly ground their way across Youngstowne Square's gravel lot, and headlights swept the walkway and grass between the duplexes.

Ezra finger-flicked the ember from the remains of his cigarette and inched back into the shadow beneath the stoop's awning.

A single car door thudded shut. Then a second.

He waited, listening, his hand slowly feeling behind him for the doorknob. When a single set of footsteps sounded on the concrete walkway, he immediately imagined a second set tiptoeing through grass toward his back patio. The lighting between the Youngstowne buildings was dim, good for sleeping but not so much, Ezra realized, for identifying people on the property.

He recognized her volleyballer legs first. Then his gaze climbed Kate's body, and he registered that her arms were wrapped around two grocery bags.

She stopped in the middle of the walkway. "MacRae? What are you doing?" She shifted to adjust the balance of the bags. "A little help?"

Once inside with the door locked behind them and the groceries unbagged, she wrapped him in a warm embrace.

"Breakfast?" he said.

"Nope. I have to be gone before your ass'll be awake." She began sorting groceries on the countertop and table—chicken thighs, a can of chicken stock, olive oil, a box of Uncle Ben's rice, and several flavorings from onions to bay leaves. "This will be just a basic Lowcountry chicken bog."

"Chicken bog doesn't sound very appetizing."

"It's just a name, MacRae. You'll love it."

"All right, what can I do to help?"

"Nothing," she said. "I'm wound too tight at the moment to supervise you." She began opening packages. "So, why don't you go call Mel and talk to him while I cook?" She opened a cabinet and pulled out a bowl and a metal measuring cup. "But be ready to hang up when I say, because once this goes in the oven, we're going in the bed for thirty-five minutes." She took him in her arms again and, for a moment, held him tight and then pulled back to look him in the face. "You haven't eaten yet, have you?"

"I wouldn't tell you if I had."

"Smart man." She released him and turned to preheat the oven.

TWENTY-THREE

Hugo sat in a rocking chair and watched the nighttime traffic pass. Two newly assembled Cat's Records crates stood stacked beside him on the concrete slab of the front porch. He flicked the butt of his cigarette out into grass past ready for its first spring mowing, then stood and stretched and turned to the picture window.

The living room was lit but empty.

After the funeral for Burl Davies, Lucio had picked up two videos at Cat's along with the crates, and before Hugo knew anything about it, he'd planned a movie night at Perras's place. Hugo had refused to go despite Lucio's frustrated pleading and Murdoch's grudging invitation, and he did his best to hide his disappointment and jealousy that the two of them were going ahead without him.

"What movies did you get?" he'd asked.

"*The Breakfast Club*," Lucio said.

"A little young for me." Hugo opened the door to take the unassembled crates out onto the front porch. "Like you," he'd added with a wink that felt awkward and stupid. Then he came back in to retrieve his small hammer from the closet in the bedroom. "What's the other movie?"

"*Torch Song Trilogy*."

"What's that about?"

Lucio read the description from the label on the black plastic rental box.

Hugo almost said that was a little too queer for him but

130

didn't. "I don't think I'm ready for that," he said instead. "You boys enjoy." When he saw Lucio's cheeks take on a soft blush, he added, "I trust you."

"What the fuck's that supposed to mean, Hugo?" Lucio said, his voice suddenly angry and tight.

Hugo felt his gaze harden, but he drew a slow breath. "It don't mean anything, Lucie. Forget I said it."

"Fuck you." Lucio brushed past Hugo and grabbed his jacket from the coatrack by the front door.

"Hey," Hugo had said. "Come on, now." He looked at the intense red risen to Lucio's cheeks and a brimming of tears in his dark eyes. His mind flashed on a couple of slaps that he could see escalating out of control, and he heard his father's tight voice growl, *"Boy, I'll give you something to cry about."* But while Hugo had stood with gritted teeth, Lucio brushed past him again, grabbed the videos, and in moments was on the other side of the slammed back door. He'd heard the Taurus start up, followed by its back tires slinging gravel.

The drama framed in the picture window—*like a scene from a movie*—faded, and he picked up the small hammer and pushed the handle down into his back pocket, feeling the steel head cold against his skin. He carried the assembled crates through the front door and stacked them beside Lucio's recliner. In the bedroom, he returned the hammer to the toolbox in the closet, and when he raised up again, he stood and stared a moment at a black case on the shelf above the hanging clothes. He took it down, popped the latches as he backed up, and sat on the bed with the case open in his lap. He lifted his revolver from the textured gray foam and laid it aside. Then he tipped one bullet from the ammo box into his palm and laid it with the gun. When he'd closed the case and reset the latches, he stood and returned the case to the shelf. Already shirtless, he stripped off his pants and put on black jeans, black socks and shoes, and a black sweatshirt. He dug around in his underwear drawer for the black mask bought years before in a San Antonio *luchador* shop and stuffed it in a back pocket. Figuring he had at least a couple of hours before Lucio came home, he loaded the revolver with the single bullet, spun the cylinder, tucked the piece into the back waistband of his jeans, and left the house.

Friday, March 31, 1989

TWENTY-FOUR

In the minutes after midnight, they lay sated with chicken bog, white wine, and both pre- and post-prandial orgasms, sleepily sharing conciliating banter in a slowing circling of slurred words, fingers and palms lightly lighting here and there on naked bodies. With telephone and answering machine unplugged, their night settled to a fearless stillness.

Kate had been quiet for a long time, and Ezra, believing she'd gone to sleep, felt himself following her.

"Cassie Nance."

Ezra startled awake. "What?"

"Why did you jerk like that?"

"I thought you were asleep," he said. "You scared the shit out of me."

"Sorry." She nestled more tightly into the curves of him.

"Who's Cassie Nance?" he asked.

"According to the scuttlebutt on the Row, she's the woman who was killed with Burl Davies. She's apparently been making the rounds looking for a record deal." Kate yawned. "If it was her, then the other guy that got shot was probably Earl Hill, acting as her manager or producer or something like that."

"She any good?"

"I've heard she's okay." Kate yawned again, and her hand floated beneath the covers to settle on the flat of his hip. "God, your skin is so soft."

Ezra didn't know how to respond to that, so he lay still a moment and focused on her touch.

"Anyway, my friends are sure they know her from sometime in the past," Kate said as her hand left him. "But they said she'd had some kind of serious makeover—not plastic surgery but not just a beauty treatment either."

"What, some kind of *Educating Rita* scenario?"

"Crude, MacRae, but, yeah, something like that." She paused. "Bonnie's sure that, if it's the same person she's trying to remember, she wasn't named Cassie Nance."

"Interesting." He breathed in the cherry almond scent of her hair. "Maybe they were at Ave Canora listening to songs for her."

"Maybe."

Maybe my songs. Ezra browsed through the handful of his titles in the Ave Canora catalog, but none of them struck him as easily adaptable for a female singer. *Have to work on that.* He pulled her closer and kissed the crown of her head. "I'm glad you're here, Kate. It feels good."

"Don't get maudlin." She yawned a third time. "We didn't have dessert. Let's go make some naked pancakes."

"What are naked pancakes?"

"Pancakes you make while naked, dumbass."

He rolled partially onto his back, laughing, twisting at the hips so that he maintained their spooning from the waist down. He imagined them moving around the kitchen together, pulling items from the fridge and the cabinets, pouring and mixing, flesh jiggling as they stirred batter—and all the while the never-present family of four from the little yellow house next door peering through the hedge.

"All right, I'm game," he said as he unspooned and sat up on the side of the bed. "But I've gotta pee first." He stood and left the bedroom, glancing at the dark answering machine and smiling to himself as he entered the bathroom. The moment felt good, almost as happy, safe, and at peace as he'd imagined he would feel with Mel at the farm. After he finished and flushed, he stepped to the bedroom door. "Okay, let's do it."

No movement or sound.

"Kate?"

She snored lightly.

He smiled to himself again, put the thought of naked pancakes out of his mind, and gingerly lay down beside her, wondering how she could possibly wake up in time without an alarm.

TWENTY-FIVE

Hugo glided along the sidewalk bordering Portland Avenue on the west side of 21st. Although only half a mile as the crow flies from his house on 16th, he'd traveled almost twenty-five minutes and covered over a mile of ground on the way, staying in the shadows as much as possible and avoiding the wider and brighter streets. After a few more steps, he turned right on Calhoun Avenue and saw Lucio's Taurus parked on the street fifty yards ahead. Hugo angled across Calhoun to the car and glanced inside. Then he turned, recrossed the street, and stopped in front of Murdoch's IROC-Z and Metro PD patrol car, parked together in the lot of the condo complex. Hugo tilted his wrist toward the nearest streetlight and checked his watch and saw that it was 12:33. Number 2122 appeared dark at first, and he felt his neck and face flush red with suspicion and jealousy. But then he noticed the flicker of television light through partially closed first-floor blinds and moved closer for a better look.

He wasn't halfway across the lot when the light came on in the front room, and before he could stop in his tracks, the outside light stung his eyes. He turned sharply left and trotted a few steps until he heard Murdoch's front door opening behind him. At that point he turned left again, passed between a pickup and a minivan, and hid behind one of the trees in the line that separated the condo lot from Calhoun.

Lucio stepped out onto Murdoch's front stoop. He turned at something Murdoch said and then opened his arms and was lifted in the big policeman's bearhug.

Hugo's breath caught. *Don't y'all fucking kiss.* He exhaled a relieved sigh when Lucio—freed from the hug—turned away and trotted toward the Taurus. Hugo ducked down and duck-walked from behind the tree to a position between the pickup and the minivan. He waited until he heard the Taurus start and saw it roll past on Calhoun. Then he pulled the mask out of his pocket and down over his face, adjusted it, and raised slowly up to peer through the windows of the pickup's cab.

Although Murdoch stood looking in the direction of the pickup and minivan, Hugo knew he was watching Lucio up the street to the stop sign and out of sight. He reached back and wrapped his fingers around the revolver's grip, then positioned himself so that a portion of the cab frame shaded his eyes from the stoop light. He had a clear shot, diagonally across the hood and just to the right of the windshield's lower edge. He drew a deep breath, let half of it out slowly, stopped and held the rest, and squeezed the trigger.

Click.

When Murdoch stiffened and seemed peering into the area where he crouched masked in shadow, Hugo imagined that they stared each other down across the intervening distance, perhaps holding Lucio between them.

But then without turning away, Murdoch stepped backward into the condo and closed the doors.

Hugo stood up in the dark when the stoop light went out and waited for an upstairs light to come on. When it did, he watched for Murdoch to cast a shadow against the blinds. The window frame remained lighted but empty of the big man's shape, so Hugo turned and strode away in the direction Lucio had gone. At the intersection, he turned right on Fairfax as Lucio had done, walked half a block, and then stepped into the middle of the street. He stopped and spun the revolver's cylinder and waited for the first vehicle to come from either direction. He checked his watch again. 12:44. A sportscar crossed 21ˢᵗ and rolled slowly toward him along Fairfax. When he felt the headlights fully on him so that even dressed in black he must be visible to the driver, he raised the pistol, pointed it at the right side of the front windshield, and squeezed the trigger again.

Click.

The car lurched to a stop and then began accelerating backward.

Hugo spun the cylinder and pushed the revolver back into the waistband of his jeans—this time just to the right of his belly—and ducked into #815 Alley. He trotted toward Acklen, stopping halfway to pull off his wrestling mask and look back. When he neared the street, he stopped again and stuffed the mask into the front-left pocket of his jeans, then turned right on Acklen and recrossed 21ˢᵗ against the light. He wound his way to 19ᵗʰ, then jaywalked across Wedgewood. All the while, he thought about Lucio—picturing him coming in the back door and being quiet until he discovered Hugo gone, picturing the curiosity on that expressive face, imagining him naked and erect and brushing his teeth in front of the bathroom mirror, then lying in the dark bedroom, listening, waiting. Hugo quickened his pace as he continued along the portion of 19ᵗʰ that dead-ended at Capers less than a hundred yards in front of him.

But before he closed the distance, he saw the intersection begin to glow with headlights. He stepped up into the yard of a large, whitewashed brick house and hid behind three tree trunks that grew close together, all tightly wound with ivy. He again pulled out his mask and put it on, then pulled out his revolver. When the vehicle turned from Capers onto 19ᵗʰ, he saw that it was a police car. He glanced behind to be sure that the house remained dark. Then he turned again and raised his gun between two of the ivy-covered trunks. By streetlight, he saw that the driver's window was down and that a beefy arm lay along the bottom of the window frame. He heard Alabama singing "Song of the South" and saw the cop's open hand patting time on top of the sideview mirror. Although he couldn't see the driver, he wished him to be Murdoch Perras. But this thought unleashed an explosion of tangled images—Murdoch and Lucio and, strangely, Ezra MacRae and himself. Just as he felt the swelling in his crotch, he pulled the trigger.

Click.

The beefy hand didn't stop patting time on the mirror, and the patrol car rolled past to the stop sign at Wedgewood, where it sped left and disappeared.

Hugo again glanced over his shoulder at the dark house, then peeled off his mask and spun the cylinder and tucked the gun into the back waistband of his jeans. He returned to the sidewalk and hurried on toward Capers.

Less than ten minutes later, he turned left off of Dorothy Place and entered the alley that ran behind his house. Within a few paces of his back lot, he heard a noise and stopped in his tracks and listened. When he heard the sound again, he located the source near the trashcans in their rotting wooden frames at the edge of the back entrance to his place. *Coons*, he thought. Without putting on his mask, he pulled out the gun and pointed it toward the sounds. He watched the lid of one can rise and drop and then rise again, and the streetlight revealed the masked face and gleaming blue eyes that looked directly at him. Hugo aimed and began to squeeze the trigger but stopped and released it.

The racoon launched out of the can and scrambled into the hedge that lined the alley.

"Reckon we ain't that different tonight," Hugo said.

Inside the house, he sat on the closed toilet lid, alternately brushing his teeth and removing his shoes and socks. Then he stood on his side of the bed and stripped off his sweatshirt. He slid the gun beneath his pillow and dropped his jeans and underwear. He wanted to say something or hear something said to him, but the bedroom remained quiet as he slid beneath the covers and turned on his right side. He lay there, glad for the quiet in the absence of the coughing fits that lately seemed to punctuate their life together.

Lucio stirred. Then, with a couple of scoots, he curled his nakedness into Hugo's, and without a word, he reached back with his left hand and wrapped palm and fingers around Hugo's erection.

Hugo's breath caught at the touch, and his eyes fluttered shut. He couldn't breathe again until Lucio's massaging settled into a slow and rhythmic stroke. Then he reached around to touch Lucio and found him flaccid. His breath caught again in surprise.

Without releasing his grip, Lucio elbowed Hugo's arm away. "No," he whispered. "Let me."

Then, as if these three whispered words were a trigger, Lucio shuddered into a coughing fit, the first bark tightening his grip so that Hugo jerked his hips away in pain. As Lucio curled into himself and shook with coughing, Hugo felt a sudden flash of rage. He snaked his right hand underneath his pillow and touched the cold steel of the revolver, sensing the single bullet's desire for release. But he controlled himself, and while the fingers of his right hand remained weakly stroking the revolver's smooth barrel, he placed a steadying left palm against Lucio's quaking back and began a gentle rubbing up and down, feeling the muscles tense and release with each barking cough.

"Fucking allergies," he whispered.

TWENTY-SIX

She'd been gone when he sat up on the side of the bed at seven past seven. He remembered her climbing over him at some point while it was still dark outside. She'd paused without word or whisper or kiss and just lay atop him for a few deep breaths. And then her weight lifted. He thought he remembered hearing the toilet flush and wondered if she'd dressed and left instead of coming back to bed. But even if that was what happened, it didn't bother him, as their long evening together had seemed a healing time.

By ten o'clock in the morning, he knew he was unlikely to make Mel's farm before midnight. Because of the previous day's stormy weather, he had fourteen pools on his schedule. He was lucky with neighborhood groupings and relatively easy traffic to cut his travel time between stops, but the pools themselves were messier and took longer to clean than he'd anticipated. Those he could typically make pristine in fifteen to twenty minutes were taking thirty-five to forty as he cleared the water and the machinery and the surrounds of debris from a variety of plants and bugs. A couple of stops had taken more than an hour. At one, the visitation of a gaggle of geese left the pool littered with feathers and feces. At another, that of a family who insisted on keeping a birdfeeder at the edge of the surround, the usual mess of seeds and droppings lay covered with blood and feathers where a hawk had caught some portly diner—probably a dove—unawares.

By two o'clock in the afternoon, Ezra knew he wouldn't make it to Mel's farm at all that night. He needed a break to eat something, to meet Latt Edwards and get Benny Jack's Lonely, and to pick up and deposit his first check from Ave Canora. Another five pools remained to clean after all that.

Latt couldn't meet him with the guitar for another half hour, so he sped from the neighborhood around Woodmont Park toward Ave Canora. He realized as he drove up 16th that if he parked on Music Square West in front of the bungalow he would be revisiting the scene of the horror he'd witnessed less than a week before. Without signaling, he swerved across the lefthand lane to make a sharp turn onto Edgehill, cutting off a red Cadillac with steer horns mounted on its grill. The Caddy swerved into the righthand lane to avoid him, the driver gesturing and shouting something unintelligible out her open window. Ezra caught a green light at Edgehill and 17th and a couple of streets later turned left into the alley and parked behind Ave Canora.

The silhouette of Tina Joseph appeared in the hallway in response to the button he pressed.

"Hi, Ezra," she said and held open the door for him.

"Hey, Tina. Sorry, I couldn't bring myself to come in the front."

"I understand completely." She closed the door behind him, checked the lock, and led him through the long hallway to reception, saying over her shoulder, "The back entrance has been a mercy this week."

Watching her move ahead of him in a black shirtwaist dress with white polka dots, sheer black nylons, and black patent leather pumps, Ezra was suddenly aware that his sweatshirt and jeans were filthy from cleaning pools all morning.

"I guess you've come for your check?" Tina eased herself down onto her desk chair.

"Yeah." He stopped in the middle of the front room.

"Mark had to leave for a meeting down in Berry Hill, but he said your check is on his desk." She stood again—"I'll get it"—and disappeared down the hallway.

Ezra listened to the sound of her climbing the stairs to

Mark's second-floor office as he gazed through the front windows to the yard and the street.

On each side of the front walkway stood a large three-by-five-foot banner, both set up there since the shooting took place. The words and images facing the street shone through in reverse on the banners' white backs. The image of Zack Thigpen—a songwriter Ezra had met once when dropping off a demo—filled one-third of the banner on the left. Beside his image, the larger lines read,

AVE CANORA MUSIC PUBLISHING
CONGRATULATES
ZACK THIGPEN
ON HIS NUMBER ONE HIT
I'M ON THE LOOSE

He could make out the smaller print beneath Thigpen's name—"Greg Watson, Sylvia Mack, & Marty South"—and figured them to be the song's co-writers. At the bottom, another line read, "Thanks to Stallion Records & Marty South."

The banner on the opposite side of the walkway read,

FOREVER
in our hearts
BURL DAVIES
February 23, 1926—March 26, 1989

Beside these lines, the banner featured the photograph of Burl from the funeral program. Visible at each end of the banner and creating shadows along the bottom, bunches of flowers had been laid in memory.

He heard her descend the stairs and come closer along the hallway, but still he startled when she spoke.

"Here," she said, handing him a plain white envelope with his name scrawled on it.

"That's gotta be hard to look at," Ezra said, jutting his chin toward the scene outside as he took the envelope from her.

"It is," Tina said with a sigh. "I do my best to keep turned away from it."

Ezra nodded but didn't speak. He couldn't keep from scanning the scene, seeing it again from the perspective of the bungalow—two dead crumpled where the banners now stood, Burl lying in the street, Benny Jack gone down on the opposite sidewalk. He imagined the windows of Ave Canora as eyes, wide open in horror as the shooting began, seeing him hiding in place and doing nothing.

"Are you the only one here?" he said at last.

"Yes, and I keep imagining I hear Burl." She spread her hands on the desktop. "It's creepy."

"Where's Hope? I mean, I don't know her, but she works here, right?"

"Speaking of creepy," Tina said, and her eyes crinkled in a smile.

"I know, I know. It's just that she called to let me know about Burl's funeral, and I figure if I'm gonna be working here then I should know everybody. That was her with you and Mark at the funeral, right?"

Tina swiveled her chair toward the front windows but quickly back again. "Yes, that was Hope. She works mostly upstairs, with demos and lyric sheets, sending things out and making sure Mark and Burl—" She paused and drew a breath that caught midway. "—making sure Mark has what he needs for pitching songs around the Row." Her telephone began to ring, and she lay her left hand on the receiver. "She's actually out singing a demo for somebody else this afternoon, I think."

He pointed toward the hallway, and as she waved and nodded, he turned to leave.

"Ave Canora, this is Tina," she said behind him.

He stepped into the midafternoon sunshine and stopped,

145

lifted his face to the blue sky, closed his eyes, and inhaled deeply. He wondered how many times Burl Davies might have done the same, standing in the same spot. Then he tore open the envelope and removed the check for $1,250 just as Officer Edwards rolled into the lot and parked beside the Tempo.

Latt popped up from the driver's side, pushed his mirrored sunglasses up to his forehead, and smiled at Ezra across the patrol car's roof. "It seems Lattimore Edwards's perfect timing strikes again," he said.

Ezra tucked his check into the back pocket of his jeans. "Good to see you, Latt." He stepped around the rear of the patrol car.

"You get your check?" Latt extended his right hand for Ezra to shake and with his left opened the back door.

Ezra shook his friend's hand and looked down at Benny Jack's Lonely lying across the back seat. "It doesn't look as bad as I thought it would."

Latt leaned and picked up the guitar, straightened, and handed it to Ezra.

The bullet appeared to have passed cleanly through the G string and sound hole, exiting out the back of the guitar's body. It left a smaller hole in the wood than Ezra expected, and none of the interior braces seemed damaged. The biggest problem apparent to Ezra's eye was that the rear of the bridge had come loose from the spruce top.

"Yeah, this is not nearly as bad as I imagined," Ezra said. "I bet Stone R can fix this for just one dime bag and a twenty."

"What?" Latt said.

"I can—" Ezra stopped. "I shouldn't have said that out loud."

"No, you absolutely should not have."

Ezra pulled the envelope holding his check from his pocket. "If we were still friends, I could cash this and make you forget what I said with Whataburgers and beers back at my place."

"And that would add bribery to possession," Latt said.

"Forget about it." He pushed the patrol car's back door closed.

"No, we're still friends, Ezra. We just shouldn't hang out until this case is closed."

Ezra refolded the envelope and stuffed it in his front pocket. "Speaking of the case, where's the guitar case?"

"What?"

"The night I met Benny Jack, he had an old Epiphone guitar case with him."

"We didn't find a case at the scene." Latt pushed both thumbs into the waistband of his uniform trousers, one at each hip, pinched the belt, and shimmied up the waistline. "Officer Perras reported that he'd found where Mr. Boudreau had sheltered from the rain, but he didn't mention a guitar case." He turned and dropped behind the wheel. "Maybe he didn't find the case 'cause he never found the place."

"Watch out," Ezra said. "Your songwriter's showing."

Latt grinned up at him. "I'm just saying that maybe Perras just pretended he found the place but—check this out—never even tried and so he lied." He winked, pulled his mirrored sunglasses down from his forehead, and closed the door. He backed out of the parking space and gave Ezra a wave as he exited the lot.

Ezra drove to his bank in Hillsboro Village and deposited the check. He made a quick run into the neighborhood behind Belmont College and ate a late lunch at the International Market, a small Asian grocery and cafeteria that he liked. Then, with just under three hours remaining before sunset, he headed south toward Brentwood and his five remaining pools.

TWENTY-SEVEN

Just over a third of a mile as the crow flies from the table Ezra had just left after wolfing eggrolls, fried rice, and chicken sticks, Hugo sat shirtless and shoeless at the kitchen table, cleaning his revolver and listening to Ricky Van Shelton's *Loving Proof* on the boombox. He'd retrieved the gun from under his pillow and the cleaning materials from the closet in the bedroom, keeping an eye on the lump of bedding beneath which Lucio had been sleeping most of the day. Hugo pressed PLAY on the boombox as he passed from the living room to the kitchen and sat down at the table with everything spread in front of him. While the first song—the up-tempo "Swimming Upstream"—rollicked along, he picked up the .45 bore brush and attached it to a cleaning rod. He dipped the brush in solvent and then gently pushed it through the barrel and pulled it out again. He'd done this twice and begun the same process with the chambers of the cylinder by the time the piano and steel guitar intro to *I'll Leave This World Loving You* began. When Shelton's vocal entered, Hugo sang with him.

"Walk away, leave with my bless—"

"What the fuck, Hugo?" Lucio shouted over the music.

Hugo turned in his seat with raised eyebrows and an amused grin but didn't say anything.

Lucio stood in the kitchen doorway, wearing nothing but red bikini briefs and a pair of tube socks with three black stripes around the top. "Hold on a sec." He turned away with a "fucking douchebag." The music stopped, and in a moment, he was back with a dirty towel, which he doubled and spread at the end of the table. "Put your shit on this." When Hugo didn't move or speak, Lucio slid the towel over next to the spread of gun and cleaning materials. He leaned over Hugo's shoulder and moved everything a piece at a time from the tabletop to the towel. "Now you won't get shit all over my fucking table." He turned and stomped out of the kitchen.

He made it only halfway to the bedroom before Hugo caught him from behind in a chokehold. Hugo's right arm noosed around Lucio's throat, and his left hand clamped the back of the smaller man's neck. Lucio clawed at the elbow crook and forearm that squeezed his throat. Hugo ignored the clawing and with his right hand locked on his own left bicep arched his back to apply more pressure.

"Don't you ever call me a fucking douchebag," he spat into Lucio's ear, his naked chest and belly firm against the smaller man's back. "And if I want to get shit on the table, I'll get shit on it, 'cause it's my table, Lucie boy. It ain't yours." He cinched the choke tighter so that Lucio's hands seemed trying to caress and pacify rather than claw free. "And one more thing," Hugo panted, his erection pushing hard at his zipper and Lucio's buttocks. "Don't you ever mess with my music, especially when I'm in a mood." He huffed a sigh in Lucio's ear. "You could see that I'm in a mood, right?" He grunted the last word and tightened the hold with a sudden jerk.

Lucio's hands fell away, his legs spasmed and then collapsed.

Hugo released the chokehold and caught Lucio around the waist as he slumped. He hoisted the unconscious body over his shoulders in a fireman's carry and lugged it into the bedroom. Just as a reviving Lucio began sputtering and squirming, Hugo flipped him over onto the bed, where a coughing fit began in earnest. Hugo stood and rolled his shoulders and neck, then left the room.

He turned on the boombox as he passed it, and Ricky Van Shelton sang, *Oh, but life would be lonesome without you. . . .*

He again sat down to the cleaning of his gun, finishing several minutes later with a careful polishing of its low-reflecting stainless-steel frame as Shelton sang the tag line to "Don't Send Me No Angels." He threw the dirty towel in the trash, loaded the revolver, and turned off the boombox.

Lucio coughed twice and fell quiet.

Hugo set the revolver atop the boombox, sat in his recliner, and put on socks and shoes. Then he stood and went to the door of the bedroom. "Hey, Lucie, I'm going to San Antonio Taco," he said. "You want your usual?"

"Fuck you," Lucio wheezed.

"We'll talk about that when I get back." Hugo hovered in the doorway. Then, "See you in a bit." He turned and took the shirt from the back of his recliner and put it on unbuttoned, picked up the revolver and left the house.

Bobby Boone was twenty-three years old and couldn't remember a time when he hadn't sung at least two Sundays a month at the Ninety Six Church of God back home in Ninety Six, South Carolina. His fellow congregants claimed he had the voice of an angel when he sang. These days, he left the bouncy gospel songs to his mother and her sisters, who patted their free hands—on the one and the three—against the hands that clutched their microphones, keeping approximate time with the rollicking drums, bass, and piano. Bobby preferred to accompany himself on acoustic guitar as he let his voice soar on songs by Michael W. Smith, Buddy Greene, and Dallas Holm, whose "Rise Again"—on which his mother and her sisters harmonized—was a favorite and often requested. But Bobby's other selections from David Meece or Stephen Curtis Chapman or Rich Mullins raised eyebrows and prompted some church members to whisper to the preacher at the door as he saw them out after the service.

As an avid reader of CD liner notes and lyrics, Bobby had

learned that all his favorite Contemporary Christian singers worked out of Nashville, recording in Nashville studios for Nashville-based record labels. So, he'd saved up for a five-day, four-night trip to get a feel for the place—Tuesday to Saturday in a motel near the airport, then home for church on Sunday. He'd spent Wednesday at Opryland U.S.A., riding the rides and attending all the shows. He spent Thursday morning visiting Church of God locations, but he found many of them to be smaller Black congregations, which he hadn't expected. Thursday afternoon he sought out those churches he'd discovered his favorite singers used as their home bases and then browsed various stores for a Music City guitar strap and CDs he couldn't find around Ninety Six.

While Wednesday and Thursday temperatures had felt like home, reaching nearly eighty degrees by the afternoons, Friday morning was in the forties. The day never warmed above forty-seven, so he kept his University of South Carolina sweatshirt on as he slowly walked the Music Row streets between Division and Wedgewood, amazed at all the music businesses—record labels, song publishers, management companies, law offices—and imagining all the music industry processes taking place behind their closed doors.

On the advice of a college-aged couple he'd chatted with as suppertime approached, he ate at San Antonio Taco Company, sitting at a table on the tree-covered deck, watching the traffic on 21st Avenue and the people coming and eating and leaving. He decided in the middle of his second taco that he liked this city, and he began doodling on a napkin and making notes about how and when he might manage a move.

He folded the napkin and slid it into the back pocket of his jeans. Then he emptied the red tray into the trash and walked—hands in pockets and shivering slightly—along 21st until it bent right and became Broadway. A few steps beyond the bend, he found Division again, which—and it pleased him that he already knew this—would take him up to the Country Music Hall of Fame and 16th Avenue, near where he'd parked his car several hours before.

On the opposite side of Division, between 19th and 18th, he saw a plain blue-gray, one-level building identified only with a small sign that read "Omnisound Studio."

"Oh, man," he said aloud, recognizing that he'd seen this recording studio credited often in liner notes of albums he listened to all the time, particularly his favorite country band Restless Heart and his favorite Christian songwriter Rich Mullins.

Bobby crossed the street and stepped up on Omnisound's front stoop. All afternoon, he'd been too shy to approach any of the music business doorways he passed, but here he thought he might encounter one of his heroes rather than anonymous receptionists. He pressed the lighted doorbell button and waited. He pressed it again and listened, thinking that he could hear music somewhere inside. Although the front windows were opaque, he saw clear seams edging the frames, and he leaned in close to these and cupped his hands around his eyes.

Focused as he was on catching a glimpse of movement inside and straining to catch more of the music he thought he heard, he didn't see or hear the faded red Taurus that rolled to a quiet stop just feet across the sidewalk behind him, didn't see either the glint of mixed twilight and streetlight on steel or the two quick muzzle flashes.

TWENTY-EIGHT

i was petting my lonely
while it purred out the blues
when those devils i saw
a-coming for me
though i thought about running
where on earth could i go
i just sat and waited
and booked me a show
i remember the night
i got paid fifty dollars
to split between lonely and me
i was gonna use my half
on my pretty girl sally
but im in the grave cold as can be
you cant rassle with a bullet
and you cant change its mind
when its made up to be
a-coming for you
dont you cry now pretty sally
well then maybe one tear
o jesus is waiting
we wont long be blue
i remember the night
i got paid fifty dollars
to split between lonely and me
i was gonna use my half
on my pretty girl sally
but im in the grave cold as can be

153

With the aid of exterior and underwater lights, Ezra finished his last job—a kidney-shaped pool at the corner of Brentwood's Long Valley Road and Paddock Place. The owners at his previous stop had been bothered that he was there so near sunset. But they hadn't been belligerent or threatened to complain to the pool company. He was grateful that these last homeowners were away, their mansion brightly lit by spotlights on the front lawn but quiet and dark inside. He stored the "stays-here" equipment in the pool house and carried his kit and "with-me" gear back to the Tempo, where he settled everything into the trunk. He checked the address's info sheet on his clipboard to be certain that he wasn't supposed to turn out the lights in the pool or along the surround, then placed the clipboard next to his kit and closed the trunk lid.

The sky above him displayed a band of deep lavender at the horizon, from which rose layers of magenta and peach to a bursting bubble of gold that gently dissipated into a starfield of lighter lavender and a faded indigo blue. He stood beneath that beauty and breathed in the relative quiet and security of the place, imagining that he might have something like this after he'd strung together a few hit songs.

As he cooled down from his work, he began to feel the sharp chill in the air, so he grabbed his jacket from the backseat before he dropped in behind the wheel and left the property. He navigated from Brentwood to a Vandy Med Center parking garage, then walked to a hospital entrance, the evening around him almost more like winter than spring and alive with sirens.

"Friday night in the big city," he said aloud as the automatic doors hissed open. *Glad it's not a full moon.*

At an info desk, he learned that visiting hours for Benny Jack's unit had ended just minutes before at seven-thirty. He stood a little while and chatted with the white-haired woman in the volunteer vest. Yes, she told him, he could visit tomorrow between the hours of ten in the morning and two in the afternoon. No, he didn't need to be an immediate family member, but only one person was allowed in the room at a time.

"So, I heard lots of sirens when I came in," he said.

"As per usual," the woman said. "But something bad must've happened. They're going crazy in Emergency."

"Do you know what?"

"No, the gossip hasn't trickled out to me yet."

"Guess I'll see it the paper."

"If you come back tomorrow, be prepared to wait a few minutes," she said. "The police have been here a lot to talk with Mr. Boudreau when he's awake." She sighed. "Which isn't often, I hear. That's another thing you might expect—he could sleep through your visit."

Ezra looked at her name tag. "Thank you, Miss Donna," he said. "Hope the rest of your night is calm." He rapped the desktop twice with his knuckles and turned away.

Then he was outside again beneath a black sky awash with city light and quieter than before. He got in his car and drove to The Store—Vienna sausages, saltines, and a six-pack of Sam Adams on his mind. On the way, he met three separate Metro Police cars speeding toward downtown with a rush of swirling blue light. He wondered again what was happening, wondered if Latt was driving one of the cars he met. When he rolled to a stop in front of The Store, he sat looking through the plate-glass window at Penny, who stood facing his direction but focusing on a small, rabbit-eared TV set on the end of her checkout counter.

He picked up pad and pen and jotted down two lines that came to him—

It's the night of the stranger
You better not ignore the danger

—then hooked the pen on the pad and tossed them into the passenger seat, got out of his car, and went in The Store.

"It's happened again, Young MacRae," Penny said as soon as he pushed through the door. "Satan is let loose on Music Row."

"What?"

"It's breaking news." Penny nodded toward her TV and then turned down the volume. "Satan has stepped out of the daycares and shot another child of God on the streets of Nashville."

Ezra stood across the checkout counter from her and looked at the small screen on which a reporter spoke into her microphone, turning once to glance over her shoulder to indicate a scene flooded with flashing emergency lights.

"That's outside Omnisound," he said. "Who got shot?"

"Some unidentified male."

"Dead? Somebody from the studio?"

"Don't know."

Ezra turned away, a roiling in his belly and a catch in his breath.

He remembered he had chicken bog in his fridge, but he still picked up two cans of Vienna sausages and a four-sleeve box of saltines. He took a six-pack of Samuel Adams Boston Lager from the cooler and added a liter of Diet Mountain Dew and two Moon Pies on his way back to Penny's register.

Her TV had disappeared.

He spread his purchases on the checkout counter.

"Dear God, Young MacRae," Penny said. "What're you doing to yourself?"

TWENTY-NINE

Hugo sat alone at the kitchen table with his tacos and a bottle of Schlitz from the fridge. He stared at the darkness framed in the window above the sink. When a cough from Lucio seemed to stir him out of a reverie, he picked up a taco and took a bite, picked up the beer and took a swig. Then he winced, reached back and pulled the revolver from his waistband and laid it next to the bottle and continued eating.

When he finished, he fished the dirty towel from the waste basket, dumped in his trash, and left Lucio's tacos bagged in the center of the tabletop. He retrieved his gun-cleaning kit, dropped the revolver in his pants pocket, grabbed another beer from the fridge, and went out onto the covered back porch. He turned on the overhead light and turned it off again, then tested a squat lamp that stood among dead houseplants on a dusty card table and moved it to the edge of the equally dusty glass-top breakfast table that had gone unused since Nancy left. A temperature already into the mid-forties goosed the flesh on his bare arms and chest as he folded and lay the dirty towel as Lucio had done earlier and removed from his kit those pieces he would need to clean his gun again. Then he pulled the revolver from his pocket and sat down to work.

The sound of crinkling paper came from the kitchen.

Hugo swigged his Schlitz and then dipped a green tooth-brush in the solvent and brushed around the muzzle, the sides and ends of the cylinder, and the extractor rod. He redipped the brush and cocked the hammer to clean it. By the time the

157

crinkling of paper stopped and the back door creaked open a few inches, he was applying gun lubricant to all the low-reflecting stainless-steel surfaces.

"Didn't you just clean that gun?" Lucio said.

Hugo turned to look at him.

Lucio had put on khakis and a tank undershirt.

"I was distracted earlier," Hugo said. "Besides, I let it go too long the last time. It wanted more." He took another long pull from his beer, picked up the silicone cloth, and began polishing the revolver's frame. "You're welcome for the tacos, by the way."

"What the fuck was going on with all those sirens while you were out? You see anything?"

"Something down on the other end of the Row. Or maybe on Broadway." He turned the gun in the yellowish light of the lamp. "I went down to Division and around to San Antonio before all that commotion started. Must've just missed it." With the cloth, he touched up a spot on the cylinder and turned the gun in the light again. "I heard it after I got the food and came home through the backstreets."

"Aren't you fucking cold, Hugo? Jesus Christ." Lucio squinted at the thermometer attached to the door frame. "This says it's forty-three degrees, and it's probably even colder 'cause I been standing here with the fucking door open."

"Keeps my beer chilled and my nipples hard," Hugo said with a chuckle, followed by a last pull from his beer. "We'll be wishing for this come July and August, and Nashville's ninety-nine degrees at midnight." He leaned back and to his right and pulled six .45 rounds from the front pocket of his blue jeans and pushed them into the chambers. Then he eased the cylinder back in place. "You feeling better?"

Lucio hesitated. "You mean the allergies?"

"Yeah, you're sounding better at least."

"The cough has eased off for now."

"Why don't you go take yourself a hot shower? We can watch *Die Hard* again."

"I took it back when I got the other movies."

"What'd you do that for?"

"It was fucking due back, Hugo."

"Well, shit." Hugo began returning the cleaning materials to his kit. "What about one of the other movies?"

"I left them with Murdoch."

"Well, shit again," Hugo said. "Want to go back to Cat's and get another one?"

"Why don't you do that while I take a shower? You can pick up that *Young Guns* you've been wanting to see," Lucio said. "I wanted to get the latest *Nightmare on Elm Street*, but I know you don't like the scary stuff."

"Well, I'll think about old—Freddy, is it?" Hugo said. "Now, go take your shower. Make it steamy as you can stand it and breathe deep through your mouth."

THIRTY

Ezra sat at the kitchen table, Guild across his lap. On the righthand side of the tabletop lay a legal pad of scrawled lyrics and on the lefthand side a few cooling bites of leftover chicken bog in a bowl, one empty Vienna Sausages can, one mostly empty sleeve of saltines, a crumpled Moon Pie wrapper, and three empty Sam Adams bottles. He swigged from his fourth bottle, blinked, and gathered his jottings into a verse.

> *You say you hear a knock,*
> *But nobody's there—*
> *Must be your emotions.*
> *Somewhere in the night*
> *Underneath a light,*
> *Somebody's waiting.*
> *Keep your door locked,*
> *'Cause out in the dark*
> *A voice is calling.*
> *He knows what he wants—*
> *He knows what you need—*
> *He knows that your heart is weak.*

Below this he added the two lines he'd first thought of, which now turned out to be the beginning of a chorus.

> *It's the night of the stranger.*
> *You better not ignore the danger.*

He lay down his pen and drew off the remainder of the beer and belched. "Excuse me," he said. For a few minutes he sat tinkering with chord progressions and melodies that might begin to make the words a song.

Then he set the butt of the guitar on the kitchen linoleum and leaned the neck against the other dining chair. He glanced at the range's digital clock—10:55—and stood up slowly, keeping a hand on the tabletop to steady himself before lumbering across the living room to collapse on the couch. He called Mel and Kate, but neither answered. He tried Gabe Tanner, and when that call went unanswered too, he figured Gabe and Lonesome Star were probably onstage somewhere. He called the number that Latt had given him, but he hung up before the Metro Police dispatcher answered. He considered calling his parents but remembered they were still in Charleston, so he sat in the quiet another moment and then pushed up from the couch with enough momentum to carry him to the refrigerator. He grabbed and opened a fifth beer and looked again at what he'd written. Then he turned out the light, opened the kitchen door, stepped outside, and crumbled downward to sit cross-legged on the patio in the cold night.

He stumbles through the darkness of Music Row—drawn forward along a faint ribbon of sidewalk that glows as if touched by fox fire, pushed from behind by the trailing, tapping footfalls of some dreaded pursuer.

Bursts of light haunt the edges of his sight—blue and red of police and rescue, strobe of heat lightning, muzzle flash of silent gunfire.

And then he is sprawled on his belly, pinned on a cold, hard surface beneath some naked and immeasurable weight, a blackness intent on pressing him to death.

He feels the panic of suffocation, the fear of breathlessness.

The black weight that pins him down becomes a man with raven hands that seek holds on his throbbing throat, his pulsing erection.

The darkness roars with fear and thrill and panic and desire— strange but not unwelcome, unexpected but not unlonged-for.

And then what was cold and hard and heavy softens and warms into flesh—skin and muscle of chest, belly, thighs.

Again the darkness roars—its voice become that of a river rolling along, on the mossy bank of which he wrestles in the night, not with a murderous, raven-handed angel of death but with one whose strength and warmth and sweat-slicked flesh pulse with love and life.

Saturday, April 1, 1989

April Fools' Day

THIRTY-ONE

When Ezra woke up atop his jumbled bedding at a quarter to three in the morning, sick to his stomach and naked to the waist, he couldn't remember taking off his shirt or moving from patio to bedroom. He sat up on the edge of the mattress, elbows on knees and face in hands, relieved that he hadn't pissed himself this time. And then he was hunched over the open toilet, where he vomited and gagged and heaved for longer than he could tell. When the sickness finally passed, he stripped off his jeans and sticky briefs and peed a steady stream for another long time. Then he flushed everything and showered.

He stepped out of the bathroom and felt a chill on his skin and stopped when he saw the kitchen door standing open. *Damn, that's twice!* He stood and listened to the night but heard nothing out of place, so he moved to the door and closed and locked it. Again he turned on every light and looked everywhere a killer might hide. Finally assured that he was as alone as he'd been before he blacked out, he turned off all the lights and opened the refrigerator. With its interior glow filling the kitchen, he dropped ice in a glass and covered the cubes with Diet Mountain Dew, then leaned against the countertop and ate the second Moon Pie.

The red light on the answering machine blinked in the darkness, so he tossed the pie's cellophane wrapper in the trash and refilled his glass, closed the refrigerator, and stepped into the living room to retrieve his messages.

"Hey, Ez, it's Mel."

The final images of his dream bloomed in his mind and warmed his cheeks.

"Hoped you might be here tonight, but it doesn't look like you're coming," Mel's message continued. "It's, uh, it's about half past midnight in Runion. I've been on the phone with Caroline for the last couple of hours. Um, believe it or not, she's coming to the farm tomorrow afternoon. Not to stay but just for a visit, maybe a supper in town. I haven't seen her in—what, almost ten years? It's weird."

When Mel paused, Ezra felt a tightening in his throat and a slight shivering along his inner thighs.

"Anyway, I hope you're being smart and staying safe," Mel's voice said. "Remember, Ez, nobody loves you better than me. Not your mama, not your papa, not your three-eyed cousin Whoppa. Call me."

Ezra ached for home, but the sudden confusion of desire to be with Mel and an old jealousy of Caroline was short-lived as the machine clicked and clunked into a second message.

The recording lasted five seconds—a shaky breath and a half and some small noise at the end just before the machine clicked off.

He'd heard no street noises like those in the background of the killer's previous calls, but maybe no cars had passed at that time of night and during so short a connection. The man himself hadn't been so shy before as not to hum or sing or speak. *And that noise at the end?* Ezra wondered and was surprised to find himself so accustomed to his fear—in the space of less than a week—as to be almost dozing on his feet in the face of it. He listened to both messages again and then listened to Mel's a third time while he rechecked the doors. He turned off the machine at "Call me" and stumbled back to bed.

He awoke to sunshine streaming through his bedroom window but lay still and ran through his hangover self-check. *Light doesn't hurt.* He swallowed. *Dry and thirsty.* He cupped a hand over his mouth and nose. *Breath stinks.* He closed his eyes—*No*

165

headache—and opened them again and sat up slowly. *Not dizzy. Sore belly muscles.* He got to his feet and stood a moment to confirm he was steady. In the bathroom, he fixed his toothbrush and stepped, brushing, into the living room and listened again to the late-night messages, hearing Mel's with less jumbled feelings and still wondering about the other—the differences between it and the previous messages from the killer of Burl Davies. When the machine clunked to a stop, he showered and dressed, grabbed Benny Jack's Lonely, and stepped out of the apartment into a bright and chilly morning.

He drove first to The Store and picked up a pint of chocolate milk, another Moon Pie, and a newspaper. Penny wasn't working, so he didn't linger but returned to his car to eat his breakfast and scan the brief frontpage notice of the previous evening's shooting on Division Street.

At press time, little information had been available—that it was the third area incident in March, that it happened at dusk on Division, that the one unnamed male victim had been rushed to Vandy Med Center and was in surgery. The only witness was a young mother who'd just come out of Virginia's Market, fifty or more yards up the hill from the scene. She'd been loading her baby into his car seat when she heard two pops. With the baby secured, she stood and turned and looked down the street in the direction of the sound and saw a car moving slowly away. She didn't know the make or model. She thought it was a dark reddish but said it was difficult to tell in the low light. She hadn't seen the body fallen in front of Omnisound and had driven home. Then she'd called Metro Police when she saw the breaking news broadcast from the location. The brief article concluded with speculation about possible connections between this shooting and those that took place in the Music Row area on March 9 and March 26 and some irrelevant information on Omnisound. An inset stock photo of the studio accompanied the piece.

Downtown, Ezra found a place to park on 4th Avenue North

and put Benny Jack's Lonely in the trunk and walked the streets in search of pawn shops. He found fewer than expected, and although the windows and walls of those he did find displayed an embarrassment of guitars, none had a replacement case that suited Ezra. At last, he went in Gruhn Guitars on Broadway and bought a case that worked and a set of strings. As he moved toward the exit, he heard an electric guitar lick performed with a dexterity he could barely imagine and veered toward the sound as if pulled by a cord attached to his earlobe.

Wearing nothing but gray-striped bib overalls and pink flipflops, a wiry, bearded man Ezra knew as River Ben stood in front of a Marshall JCM 800 combo amp, a 1979 anniversary Stratocaster strapped on, its strings singing for his fingers.

River Ben saw Ezra and winked. "What's up, man?"

"Just listening to the genius of Tennessee State," Ezra said.

"The penitentiary." River Ben launched into an unaccompanied version of the outro guitar solo from Stevie Ray Vaughan's "Pride and Joy."

As the guitarist whammied the last low note, Ezra finished the popular phrase, "Not the university." Then, "Hey, do you know Stone R the guitar tech?"

River Ben switched off the Marshall, set the Stratocaster in a stand, folded the strap, stuffed it in a big back pocket. "Do you know who you're talking to, MacRae?" he asked. "Of course, I know Stone R."

"I need some work done on a guitar," Ezra said.

"It's in the case?" River Ben headed for the exit. "Thanks, Gruhners," he called over his shoulder.

"Always a pleasure to hear you play, RB," one of the staff said.

"Come by anytime they let you out," another said, and they all laughed.

River Ben laughed too and led Ezra out of the store. He stopped on the Broadway sidewalk and looked down at the case. "Okay, let's see it," he said.

"Oh, no, this is empty." Ezra shook the case by its handle. "The guitar's in the trunk of my car."

"Where you parked?"

"Up on Fourth near Printer's."

"Do you have Stone R.'s number?" River Ben asked as they turned left on 4th Avenue and started up the hill.

"Yeah, I got it from this guy named Hayes who plays in Gabriel Tanner's band."

"I think I've heard of that guy," River Ben said. "This Hayes tell you Stone R.'s payment plan?"

"He did." Ezra lowered his voice. "I've got the cash but not the other."

"I can fix you up with the dimes," River Ben said. "Both of them, no problem."

Back at the Tempo, Ezra unlocked and opened the trunk. "Man, I don't want you to end up back at Tennessee State."

"Don't worry about it, MacRae." River Ben leaned down toward the trunk as if to examine the guitar. "Clear?"

"What?"

"Anybody looking at us?"

"Oh, no."

River Ben pulled two plastic baggies from the front pocket of his overalls and pushed them through the sound hole where the G string had been. "I think Stone R. can fix you up."

"You need a ride anywhere?" Ezra said.

"How about down to 7th and Demonbreun?"

"Get in." Ezra sat down behind the wheel and moved the newspaper and his breakfast trash to the back floorboard before unlocking the passenger door.

When they stopped for the light at River Ben's destination, Ezra handed him thirty dollars. "Twenty for the dimes," he said. "And another ten for playing that Stevie Ray lead so sweet."

River Ben opened the door while the light was still red.

"You're an awesome guitar player," Ezra said. "You should start a band and take it to the top."

River Ben winked and smiled and stuffed the cash in his bib pocket. "Later, MacRae."

THIRTY-TWO

"Anything in the paper about the sirens last night?" Lucio sat across from Hugo at the kitchen table, where they'd just breakfasted on steak, sauteed onions and mushrooms, and eggs—scrambled for Hugo, fried over easy for Lucio.

"Something on the front page about a random shooting," Hugo said and yawned. He rested an elbow on the table and held his coffee cup suspended above the personal ads section.

"Give," Lucio said and snapped his fingers twice.

Hugo huffed a sigh and separated the first section of the paper and pushed it across the table. "Below the fold."

Lucio righted the paper in front of him and read. After a couple of minutes, he looked up to find Hugo staring at him across the top of his coffee cup. "What the hell?" he said. "I thought you were just going to get fucking tacos."

"I did get fucking tacos, Lucie. I got you some, too, remember?" Hugo set the coffee cup down, leaned forward with elbows on the table, and laced his fingers together. "But I also had my gun with me, and there was this boy and nobody around."

"What boy?"

"I don't know," Hugo said. "Just some boy with a mullet. Never even saw me."

Lucio pushed the newspaper aside and lay his hands flat on the table. He stretched his fingers wide, and goose flesh spread from both biceps to the center of his bare chest.

"Nobody saw me," Hugo said.

"The woman with the kid?"

"Says right there that she didn't see anything but a car she don't even know the color of."

"I don't give a fuck what it says, Hugo. What if she knows more than the cops let her tell?"

"She don't, Lucie," Hugo said. "She don't know any more than Curly Crocker knows."

"Why the fuck didn't you go hunting him instead of shooting this boy?"

"I'll get Crocker whenever I decide to," Hugo said. "Maybe tomorrow."

"And MacRae?"

"I can have him, too, whenever I want him."

Lucio stared across the table, seemed about to say something but didn't. He stood abruptly and began clattering their dishes together. "Everything was supposed to look connected to the music business."

"Outside a recording studio and practically on the Row," Hugo said. "Close enough."

"I don't fucking believe you." Lucio slammed the dishes on the countertop beside the sink, turned on the hot water, and added dishwashing liquid.

"I don't see why you're so pissed, Lucie." Hugo pushed his chair back from the table, then pushed it up onto its two back legs, and relaced his fingers over his belly. "Banging around here like you got a cobb up your ass."

Lucio turned off the hot water, braced his hands on the edge of the sink, stared out the window, and drew a shaky breath. "I thought you were going to kill me yesterday, and then you go out and shoot some boy." He turned and stood with his arms crossed.

Hugo lipped the cigarette shaken up from the pack and touched a flame to the end, squinting one eye against the smoke and glaring at Lucio with the other. "Yesterday was yesterday." He stood and slid the lighter and the pack of Marlboros into his pants pocket, disappeared into the living room, and then was back in the kitchen doorway putting on a shirt. "I'm going for a walk down the Row." He winked. "Everything's cool, Lucie boy."

"What about the kid you shot?"

"What about him?"

"He dead?"

"How should I know?" He turned from the doorway. "Why don't you go over to Vandy and see if you can find out," he said from the living room. "And don't get one of your hacking jags, or they might just commit you." When Lucio didn't respond, Hugo began to hum a Dolly Parton melody, and the front door shuddered open and then closed.

THIRTY-THREE

Ezra sat watching Benny Jack Boudreau sleep through visitation hours. In daylight, the man looked older and smaller than in Ezra's week-old memory of the night they met, and while that seemed reasonable given what Benny Jack had been through since, he thought it might also be an illusion created by the oversized pillows and the machines looming around the head of the bed. He leaned forward and pulled his notebook from a back pocket. When it fell open to the last lyric he'd worked on, "Night of the Stranger," he read through what he'd written so far. Then he flipped back to the previous notes for "Big Rain's Coming" and read through those. He'd somehow failed to attach a pen to his notebook, so he stood up and looked around the room for something to write with and was just before going to the nurse's station when a nurse entered Benny Jack's room.

She saw him and stopped. For a moment she seemed confused, looking him up and down with a curious tilt to her head. "Who might you be?"

"I'm Ezra," he said. "Ezra MacRae."

"And I'm Sally, Sally Evans," she said with a hint of a smile. "And I'm so glad he has a visitor who isn't a policeman." She stepped to the side of the bed and began checking the tubes and wires attached to Benny Jack's body, the readouts on the machinery. "Or a creep."

"What?"

"Are you a friend or a member of his family?"

"Well, neither really. We met the night this happened to him."

He paused. "My friend Latt—one of the policemen on the case —said Benny Jack calls me Jesus."

"Oh, so, you're Jesus. I've been wondering if you were real." Sally adjusted a piece of tape on the back of Benny Jack's hand. "He talks about you a lot whether he's awake or dreaming. It's hard to tell when he means, you know, the famous Jesus and when he means you." She looked closely at a setting on the machinery and then at the IV drip. "You're not famous, are you?"

"Not yet."

She moved quietly to the door. "If the police come, you'll have to step out. Otherwise, stay until two o'clock if you like."

"Thanks, Sally," Ezra said. "Hey, do you have an extra pen or pencil I could borrow?"

She fished in the pockets of her smock and came up with a pen and handed it to him. "It's a freebie from one of the drug companies, so keep it. We've got more than enough around here." Then she left the room.

Ezra took his seat again and looked at the pen, which was imprinted with Marion Laboratories. He clicked the button a couple of times and sat staring at the tinted window that made the sunny day outside appear like a big rain really was coming. Then he clicked the button again and began to write.

> *Storm clouds roll down from the mountains*
> *Big rain's welling up inside like tears*
> *Two hearts caught out in the open*
> *Two hearts on the run and broken*
> *Beneath a sky that's looked like rain for years*

He clicked the pen's button against the tip of his nose and read through what he'd written. *Not bad*, he thought just as Sally came back in the room.

"Ten more minutes, Son of man," she said.

"Already?"

"I looked in a couple of times, but Mr. Boudreau was sleeping and you seemed to be in some kind of trance." She stepped to the bedside and stood with a hand on Benny Jack's forearm and looked down at the sleeping face.

Ezra suddenly wondered if she'd seen Benny Jack's eyes open.

"I don't see many people writing these days," she said. "Some read—magazines usually—but most just sit and watch TV, whether the patient is conscious or not."

"I don't much care for TV," Ezra said.

"I'm not surprised," she said and left the room.

Ezra read again what he'd just written. Then he read it in context with the verses he'd written before. When he heard movement coming from the bed, he looked up and saw the slow penduluming of Benny Jack's left calf and foot beneath the bedding.

"Ain't she awesome, Jesus?" the little man said and then opened his eyes.

"Hey, there you are." Ezra rose and stepped to the side of the bed. "You remember me?"

Benny Jack squirmed both legs for a moment and rolled his eyes, then closed them and turned his face away. "You got a nice hat, but you ain't got it on right now, and you smoke Camel Lights."

"That's right, Benny Jack."

"Ain't she awesome?" Benny Jack said again. "I've been making little songs about her."

"Who, Nurse Evans?"

"I call her Sally." He grinned and turned and opened his eyes again. "Sweet Sally of my dreams."

"She sure is," Ezra said.

"You ain't gonna try to take her from me, are you?"

"She only has eyes for you, I think," Ezra said and thought, *I Only Have Eyes for You,* Al Dubin and Harry Warren, *songwriters.* "Anyway, I just met her."

"My sweet mother used to sing me that song." Benny Jack made a wheezing sound. "Jesus, I'm thirsty."

Ezra stepped around the foot of the bed to a nightstand on the other side and picked up a plastic cup of water. He held the bendy straw to Benny Jack's lips.

"Thank you, Jesus," Benny Jack said as he relaxed onto his pillow again. Then he closed his eyes and in a voice somehow childish and operatic at once, he sang, "I only have eyes for you!"

"Wow!" Sally said from the doorway.

Ezra turned toward her and smiled.

"I didn't know we were having a concert this afternoon," she said as she came into the room and stood across the bed from Ezra. "Very nice."

Ezra looked down at Benny Jack, who still held his eyes closed as he grinned and blushed. "A real crooner." He winked at the nurse.

Benny Jack's body suddenly tensed.

"Hey, are you hurting?" Sally asked, leaning over him, her hand on his forearm again. "Benny Jack?"

"My Lonely, Jesus," Benny Jack said. "Where's my Lonely?"

"His guitar," Ezra told Sally. He looked down at a face gone pale and eyes now half opened. "I've got your Lonely, amigo. It was hurt like you were, so I'm taking it to a guitar doctor."

Benny Jack's face relaxed. "I ain't stupid, Jesus. You can say *repairman.*"

"All right then," Ezra said. "I'm taking your Lonely to a guitar repairman."

"And my slide?" Benny Jack slurred.

"I'll find it," Ezra said.

The three were quiet together for a minute, and then Benny Jack began lightly snoring.

"Visitation hours are over, Jesus," Sally whispered. "Slide?"

"It's a guitar thing," Ezra said. "Do you have his stuff here?"

"Most of it was ruined, but—" She stopped and nodded toward a chest of drawers by the bathroom door.

Ezra opened the top drawer and found a large white plastic bag with only a few items inside—a crumpled pack of Winstons, a falling-apart wallet with a fifty-dollar bill inside, the bicentennial Zippo, and the Coricidin bottle. "This is his slide." He held up the bottle for Sally to see. He looked again at Benny Jack's possessions. "I wonder where he got fifty dollars."

Sally shrugged. "I thought that was odd, too, considering."

"Do you know what size any of his clothes were?"

"Come on, Jesus, you need to go now," she said with a smile. "I'll walk you to the elevator, unless you intend to just disappear or float out the window."

Ezra grinned. "I'll do the elevator, just for the company and the hell of it."

"Jesus!" she said.

At the nurse's station, she stopped and pulled a sheet from a heart-shaped pad bearing the same Marion Laboratories logo.

"What's your number?" Sally asked. "I'll call you with sizes for clothes and shoes when I figure them out." She wrote down the number as he recited it and slipped the pale red note into a pocket of her smock. "Maybe we can go thrifting for him."

"Sounds fun."

"The elevator's down this way." She began walking. "But you know that already, right?"

"Verily," Ezra said with a chuckle and a wink she didn't see. At the elevator, he pressed the call button, and they stood together waiting for the car to rise. Then, "Hey, do you know anything about last night's incident on Division Street?"

"Nothing specific—nothing I can talk about, I mean."

"Is the guy dead or alive?"

"Alive, last time I heard."

"That's good."

"Do you think it was the same person who shot Benny Jack?"

"Seems likely."

An electronic ping sounded, and the elevator doors opened.

"This is me, I guess," he said.

"Thanks for the visitation, Jesus," she said as he stepped into the car and found the button to keep the doors open. "Really, that's the best he's been so far."

"Glad to help," he said. "And call me Ezra, which means helper in Hebrew."

"I'll call you, Ezra." She winked and turned away.

He watched her out of sight before he released the DOOR OPEN button.

On the main floor, he stepped past a family of three waiting to enter the elevator. As soon as the doors shut behind him, he heard somebody coughing and recognized the man from the funeral of Burl Davies—the man who'd come coughing into the back parking lot where Ezra and Dr. Montfort were taking leave of each other, the man who'd gotten behind the wheel of a faded red Taurus with a New Jersey tag. While the coughing man stood at the information desk speaking with the volunteer who sat there, Ezra moved—head down—to a position where he could be close to the exit and watch the man without seeming to.

He appeared to be about the same age as Ezra, perhaps a year or two older. His black hair was trimmed short on the sides but grew poufed on top, making him look taller than he actually was. The black tank top he wore revealed both sculpted muscle and olive skin. In contrast to the tight top, he wore multicolored parachute pants—an abstract design that included turquoise lizards sporting pink sunglasses—and starkly white athletic shoes.

When his conversation with the volunteer broke down in a fit of coughing, the man excused himself and moved in the direction of the restroom.

Once he was out of sight, Ezra stepped quickly to the desk. "Is that guy okay?"

"Lord, I don't know," the woman said. "He wanted me to think it was allergies, but I don't believe that." She stopped and looked around, then looked specifically toward the restrooms. "My guess is it's something more serious."

"Was he asking about my friend Benny Jack Boudreau up on the ninth floor? I just came down from seeing him."

She looked toward the restroom again and then leaned toward Ezra. "No, he was asking about that young feller brought in last night. Another shooting."

"Really?"

"I told him I didn't know nothing about that and couldn't tell him even if I did."

Ezra saw the man step out of the restroom and bend to the water fountain. "Thanks," he said, and in a moment, he was outside the front doors and into the shadows of a parking garage, where he moved among concrete pillars and parked vehicles and found a vantage point from which he could watch the entrance.

"You lurkin' or jerkin'?" a voice said behind him.

Ezra whirled, still in a crouch, and looked up into the inquisitive face of Latt Edwards.

"Latt," he said. "Awesome." He turned back around to face the hospital entrance and then turned again to Latt. "Wait, what are you doing here?"

"We now have two shooting victims in this hospital," Latt said. "Just checking on them."

"Is your car close? Mine's over on Eighteenth." When Latt didn't respond, Ezra continued. "Are you interested in following a guy who might lead us to Burl's killer?"

"What guy?"

"He's in there." Ezra nodded back over his left shoulder. "Might be coming out in a minute."

"Who's in there?"

"I don't know for sure," Ezra said. "I've got stuff to tell you, but there's no time."

"Okay, tell me what he looks like," Latt said. "I'll go have a looksee."

Ezra described the man and the clothes he'd seen. "Pretty easy to spot."

"Sounds like it," Latt said, and with a "Stay here" he disappeared through the hospital entrance.

Ezra stayed. But after a few minutes, he felt weird about loitering among the vehicles in the garage, so, feeling bolder with Latt on the scene, he moved to a shaded bench to the left of the entrance. After several more minutes, he saw Latt coming out of the shadows in the parking garage.

"He wasn't in there," Latt said as he took a seat on the bench beside Ezra. "I talked to the info desk and then rode the elevator upstairs to check on Mr. Boudreau and our other victim." He fussed with the button on his shirt pocket. "I figure your guy took the elevator down to the lower level and exited out the back to Twenty-First. Went down to check." He finally got the pocket flap unbuttoned and took out a notepad. "So, tell me what you know about this guy and how he's involved."

While Latt scribbled notes, Ezra told him how he thought he'd heard the voice of the killer among the congregation at Burl's funeral, how he'd waited in the church for everybody to leave, how he'd encountered Dr. Montfort and found a back way out.

"Sounds like something you might've seen on that TV you don't have."

"I guess." Ezra stood and turned and looked up the windowed stories of the hospital. "When Dr. Montfort and I were talking at the back entrance of the church, this guy dressed to the nines—"

"Like he's been at the funeral," Latt said.

"Right. This guy comes down the sidewalk coughing his damned head off."

"Hang on." Latt continued scribbling for a moment. "Okay, go ahead."

"He got in a red Ford Taurus."

"Red?"

"Yeah, but the paint job was really faded." Ezra waited for Latt's scribbling to stop again. "Anyway, I don't think I would've thought much about it except that after Montfort left to go to Burl's graveside, I looked back at the Taurus and the guy was just staring a hole through me."

"He didn't say anything?"

"No, he was like twenty yards away with the window rolled up. Then he broke into another coughing fit, and while he was busy with that, I ran to my car and got out of there."

"Okay, wait," Latt said. "If you didn't see your man in black, how did you make a connection between him and this guy with the cough?"

"It was mostly just the way he stared at me from his car." Ezra sat down on the bench again. "I felt like the killer was staring at me during the funeral, and then, you know, there was this guy's stare on top of that."

Latt scribbled for a moment. "Okay, I think that makes sense, but I wish you'd've told me this on Thursday night."

"Well, it was slow coming together in my head, and then when you said we weren't supposed to hang out anymore, I guess that threw me."

"Yeah, but that's about pal stuff. This is witness stuff." Latt made another note. "Detective Hunt's gonna be pissed when he hears about this." He circled something and drew an arrow. "All right, what else?"

"How about the red Taurus? Didn't your witness last night say she saw a red car drive away?"

"She thought it might be red but said she couldn't be sure. She wasn't real close to it, and she was distracted with her kid."

Ezra sat still for a moment. "Anyway, when I came out of the elevator after seeing Benny Jack, I heard this coughing, and there's the guy from the red Taurus talking to the lady at the information desk." He stood again and wiped his palms on the thighs of his jeans. "When he went to the restroom, she told me he was asking about the guy that got shot last night." He looked down at Latt and watched him flip a page of his notepad. "Does all that make sense?"

"It does," Latt said. "It does." He returned his notepad to his shirt pocket and stood up from the bench. "Did you talk to Mr. Boudreau?"

"Yeah, we talked in the last few minutes I was there."

"And did he call you Jesus?"

"He did," Ezra said. "And so did his nurse, which was weird."

"What did you and Mr. Boudreau talk about?"

"His nurse at first. I think he's in love with her."

"Nurse Sally?" Latt said. "She's a beauty."

"Don't you have a girlfriend already, Officer Edwards?"

"Don't you?" Latt said and stopped. "What else did y'all talk about?"

"His guitar mostly." Ezra looked up the side of the building again and tried to pick out Sally Evans's floor. "Then he went back to sleep."

"And you left?"

"Not immediately. I hung around and talked with Sally for a few minutes. We're gonna go thrifting—that's what she called it—to find Benny Jack some new clothes."

"Mm-hmm," Latt said with a raised eyebrow.

Ezra shrugged. "Hey, since I'm not involved with last night's shooting, can we talk about it?"

"Maybe," Latt said. "Maybe later. I'll get with you." He straightened his duty belt. "But now I'm going back up to see if I can talk to Mr. Boudreau."

"Visiting hours are over."

Latt put on mirrored sunglasses and a smirk.

"Oh, I see," Ezra said. "Well, tell Sally Jesus says hey."

"Mm-hmm," Latt said again and walked inside.

Ezra's stomach growled, and he found his way to 21st Avenue and then down the hill to San Antonio Taco Company, where

182

he ordered three chicken tacos, chips and salsa, and, eventually, three Coronas. On San Antonio's deck, he sat alone at a table beneath the trees. While he ate, he watched the traffic on both street and sidewalk, nodding to the few diners he recognized— or thought he recognized. He finished his food and the second beer, cleared his tabletop and bought a third beer, then sat with his notebook opened to "Night of the Stranger."

He'd written a verse warning the hearer—a woman, he reckoned—about what's dangerous out in the night. But then he thought that if the singer is out there, then he could also be the dangerous stranger. Images of the Big Bad Wolf circled just beyond the tree line in his mind, and with the first verse and the chorus already shaping themselves into a cautionary tale, he began jotting notes. By the time he'd drained the third beer, he had a draft of a second verse.

> *I've been standing here,*
> *Aching for your touch,*
> *Lonely in the shadows,*
> *Wondering if you see*
> *All that love could be*
> *If you'd just reach out.*
> *But the rhythm of the clock*
> *And the silence of the phone*
> *Are my only answers.*
> *Now I'm knocking at your door,*
> *Calling in the night—*
> *Hey, you know me, there's no need to hide.*

He held his small notebook open on the table in front of him and with his pen lightly tapped a rhythm on the empty Corona bottle until other diners began staring at him.

Musing upon the bedtime-story imagery embedded between the lines, he imagined that behind one door waited the forbidding Kate Hathaway. A stranger could knock all night and not gain entrance. And if the door did suddenly fly open, he would likely find his plans to terrorize and overwhelm her turned on himself. Behind another door waited the forbidden Cora Pigott, stretched out by her pool. A stranger might easily be admitted to find the aura of her desires as alluring as her body but the house of cards in which he thought to keep her blown apart the moment her husband's key scraped in the lock. Behind a third door lay a sleeping beauty, an angel, in blue scrubs.

He smiled to himself and jotted down some lines to flesh out the piece of a chorus he'd already written.

> *It's the night of the stranger.*
> *You better not ignore the danger.*
> *You know he could steal your heart tonight.*
> *It's the night of the stranger,*
> *And it's no place for an angel.*
> *So, just come into my arms, it'll be all right to hide*
> *On the night of the stranger.*

He snapped the notebook shut, put his last beer bottle in the trash, and headed for the Tempo, intending to find Stone R.'s place and drop off Benny Jack's Lonely before returning home.

THIRTY-FOUR

Lucio took the alley between 16th and 17th and parked the Taurus behind the house. He climbed the steps, crossed the back porch, and entered the kitchen. Through a doorway to his right, he saw Hugo napping in his recliner while Portland's Trail Blazers played Charlotte's Hornets. Lucio coughed twice and hurried back outside and down the steps before the full fit hit and had him bent over with hands on knees and body in convulsions, spit and phlegm and blood dripping from his lips. When he could get a breath, he wiped his mouth and stood upright to see Hugo standing in the back door, his left shoulder leaned against the jamb.

"Fucking allergies," Lucio said.

Hugo turned without a word and went back inside.

Lucio followed.

"What did you find out?" Hugo sat down in his recliner and leaned back.

"Not much," Lucio said from the kitchen doorway. "The volunteer lady seemed like a stupid fucking hillbilly, but she was tough and not giving out any info." He disappeared into the kitchen and returned with a glass of red wine. He passed behind Hugo's recliner, trailing his fingertips lightly across the older man's scalp, and then sat in his own recliner. "Ezra MacRae was there—"

"MacRae was there?"

"Yeah, and that Black cop Murdoch told us about."

"Edwards," Hugo said. "You draw attention to yourself?"

185

"It ain't like I can fucking control it, Hugo." Lucio took a sip of wine. "I excused myself to the john, and when I came out, I saw MacRae talking to the info lady but made like I didn't." He cleared his throat without starting another coughing fit. "I watched MacRae trying to hide from me in the parking garage—waiting for me to come out or whatever. And then fucking Edwards came out of nowhere and was there talking to him, so I split—took the elevator down to the lower level and just drove out of the garage."

Hugo sat and watched the last minute of the basketball game. "Looks like it's going into overtime," he said. While the teams and announcers prepared for the extra period, he drew a deep breath and sighed through his nose. "Lucie, honey, you know that cough ain't from allergies, right?" He paused and drew another deep breath. "I'm scared it's something serious. And I'm scared you're gonna get us caught."

"That ain't gonna fucking happen."

Hugo watched the Hornets run the floor. "I know," he said. "I know. But if there's one thing I can't take at this point in my life, it's getting caught." When Lucio didn't respond, Hugo stood and stretched, touched his fingertips to the ceiling, and then dropped his hands by his sides. "How's about I go in the kitchen and whip us up some pancakes for supper? Then we get in bed early tonight?" He turned and leaned down over Lucio and kissed him on the forehead. "I love you, Lucie boy," he said. "Sorry I don't say that more." He straightened, took off his already-unbuttoned shirt, and tossed it over the back of his recliner.

"You ain't gonna watch the overtime?" Lucio asked.

"I don't care nothing about that," Hugo said and disappeared into the kitchen.

THIRTY-FIVE

Somewhere along the drive to find Stone R.'s shop, "Another Saturday Night"—*Sam Cooke, songwriter*—emerged from the jukebox in Ezra's brain and began playing in randomly repeating snippets the rest of the way to the guitar repairman's place and then back to his own. He sang the opening lines to himself as he locked the Tempo and walked to his apartment. Once inside, he continued to hum as he performed the checks that had become routine over the past week. He glanced at the answering machine—*a message*—and then at the kitchen door—*closed, locked, no broken glass.*

He had two messages, and something sparked low in his belly when the first voice belonged to Mel, who had called a few minutes before noon—*Runion time*—to say Caroline was coming at two o'clock.

"Give me a call sometime tomorrow afternoon," Mel said. "That's Sunday afternoon. Love you, Ez."

Ezra glanced into the kitchen to check the clock on the range's control panel.

4:12.

If Caroline had followed through and arrived when she said she would, then she and Mel had been together about three hours. Given his love for his friend and the memory of the hurt Caroline had caused ten years before, Ezra couldn't decide if he wanted this reunion in Runion to go well or not. A warm and perplexing resonance from the previous night's drunken dream and visceral memories of wrestling Mel in field and barn loft and bedroom throughout their growing-up years mixed to make something in him tighten jealously around the spark burning in his belly.

His mother's voice broke the breathless tension. She had called a couple of hours after Mel to say that she and his father were back home, that they had a good time in Charleston, that they'd rested well and eaten some amazing food, that Papa was already in his study working on the next morning's sermon, that they hoped he would be home the following weekend or the one after that.

He felt his belly tightening again as soon as she finished and wanted the machine to keep going and play a distracting message from Kate, maybe even one from Benny Jack's nurse Sally Evans, but it clunked to a stop. With a hand that felt shaky but wasn't, he jotted two notes on the pad beside the telephone— CALL M and CALL FOLKS. He wrote SUNDAY PM and circled it. He took a deep breath and let it out slowly, then pulled his notebook from his pocket and went to the music room, where he sat with his Guild six-string and read the words he'd drafted for "Night of the Stranger." Some melodic notions began to fill his mind and form around his manuscript lyrics. He grabbed an A minor and lost track of the world and time.

Over two hours later, he began to emerge from writing mode and noticed three things—he was hungry again, the sun had set, and somebody was knocking on his door. A sudden nervous tension joined the growling in his belly as he recognized that the song he'd been writing was likewise filled with night and knocking. He set the guitar in its stand and stepped into the darkened living room, where another set of knocks startled him to a stop. He couldn't make himself go further. He looked into the kitchen and saw the time.

6:15.

"Who is it?" He heard a noise but couldn't tell what it was. "Who is it?"

"Open up, Mr. MacRae, it's the police."

He opened the door to find Officer Latt Edwards standing on the stoop holding Whataburger bags.

"Well, ain't this some synchronicity," Ezra said. "I'm starving, and you're delivering."

"Grab those drinks, will you?" Latt nodded toward two lidded Styrofoam cups on the stoop by his feet and stepped through the door. "How about we get some lights on in here?"

Ezra picked up the cups, closed and locked the door, and went into the kitchen, where he set the cups on the table and turned on the light. "What's this about, officer?" he said.

"It's about suppertime, citizen," Latt said. "Since I'm just a uniform and not officially on the investigative team, I've decided that what my superiors don't know won't hurt them." He set the bags on the table. "Or us."

"Awesome," Ezra said, "but I was supposed to buy the next round."

Latt took out the burgers, and Ezra dumped all the fries in a pile together on top of a flattened bag. They pushed straws into their drinks and began to eat.

"Did you get to talk to Benny Jack?" Ezra asked after a couple of minutes.

Latt swallowed his bite of burger and fries and washed it down with a sip of soda. "Depends on how you define 'talk to,' I guess."

When they'd finished their meals and cleaned away the trash, except for Latt's drink cup, Ezra lifted the garbage bag from the can and pulled an empty from a box in a cabinet under the countertop. He tossed the empty to Latt. "Make yourself useful." He took the full bag out to the Youngstowne Square dumpster. When he returned, he opened the fridge and looked at Latt across the top of the door. "Beer?"

"Better not. I'm back on the clock in a few." Latt laced his fingers together behind his head and stretched out in his chair.

"But we go into Daylight Savings Time tonight, so my shift is short by an hour."

"Good for you." Ezra grabbed a Sam Adams and popped the top. "So, did Benny Jack say anything useful?" He took a swig from his beer.

"It's hard to know." Latt slurped the last sip of his drink.

"Water?" Ezra asked.

Latt removed the lid and handed him the cup. "Nurse Sally told me he was more lucid when you were there."

As Ezra filled the cup, he wondered if Sally Evans had said anything more about him but decided not to ask. He turned off the tap and returned the cup. "Maybe it's the Jesus thing."

Latt chuckled as he refitted the lid. "That's probably it." He pulled a sip through the straw. "Kept going on about Jesus, some of which was about you, I'm sure. But he was also going on about devils—two of them, one big as Jesus or bigger and one smaller like him—coming out of the storm that Jesus made." Latt looked at his watch. "It was hard to follow."

"I can imagine."

"But apparently these devils offered him fifty bucks if he'd play his guitar when they told him to."

"Did you see that he had a fifty in his stuff?" Ezra asked.

"Mm-hmm," Latt said. "Anyway, maybe the most interesting thing he said was that they were black from working in Satan's coal mines and that the smaller one had black lung from it."

Ezra took another swig of beer. "Seriously?"

"He drifted off after that," Latt said. "But I think what he might've meant was that the little devil had a cough like your Taurus man."

THIRTY-SIX

Music Row lay largely deserted, emptied of its weekend workers and its daytime tourists as the cool blue afternoon had faded into a cooler pastel twilight and then into a cold city-bright night. Here and there, a large or small dog tugged at a leash only to stop and sniff in the grass of the verge or pee at the base of a light pole. Now and then a jogger huffed along the sidewalk, rubber soles slapping concrete, tinny strains of music leaking from Walkman headphones. The occasional vehicle traveled north on 16th or south on 17th, while Bobby's Idle Hour Tavern, with its light and laughter and music, offered the Row's only steady signs of life.

In the dark bedroom of 1619 16th Avenue South, Lucio lay naked on his right side, his back curled against Hugo's naked belly and chest, his head pillowed on the soft skin inside Hugo's right bicep. Only half covered with a sheet, they lay still as sweat cooled and dried on their skin and their breaths and heartrates slowed.

"Goddammit," Hugo sighed.

Lucio jerked as if waking from a nightmare but lay quiet a few breaths. "Don't fucking worry about, Hugo. You probably just got overheated again."

Hugo huffed another sigh—this time half growl—into the black pouf of Lucio's hair, over top of which he watched images his mind projected across the blank wall on the opposite side of their bed—a forearm and calloused hand dangling a leather belt; a steeple and cross against a troubled April sky; Gil Dooley's face covered in blood; Nancy in the bedroom

191

doorway, eyes and mouth wide open with disbelief and disgust; Ezra MacRae crouched behind a car, his face and lush body bunched with fear.

A helicopter flew over the Row, headed east.

Lucio stirred and lay still again, then cleared his throat. "For once, why don't you let me—"

"No." Hugo's *No* echoed off the wall of flashing, fading images to reverberate inside his head.

Lucio coughed once. Coughed a second time. Then he shuddered into yet another fit.

The coughing and Hugo's *No* combined and multiplied into a pulsing cacophony of rejection and denial and rage. The hammering in Hugo's brain became thundered curses that rose into the night sky above Music Row to break apart and rain down as contemptuous laughter at his impotence—Victor Rodgers's laugh and Pastor Riley Mangrum's laugh, Coach Royal's laugh and Gil Dooley's laugh, Earl Hill's laugh and Nancy's laugh, Murdoch Perras's laugh and Lucio's laugh. This downpour became an angry, sobbing flood that filled and overwhelmed the darkest and lowest places in Hugo's soul.

At a moment when Lucio had coughed his lungs empty of air and was about to draw breath for another fit, Hugo kissed his ear and whispered, "That's enough," then brought his right forearm down past Lucio's face and noosed his neck. With his left hand, he cupped the back of Lucio's head and locked his right hand inside the crook of his left elbow. "There, there," Hugo murmured and tightened the chokehold and held it. "It's all right, Lucie boy, just go to sleep." Then he buried his face between the pillow and the back of Lucio's head to protect himself from clawing attempts to break the choke. He leaned the greater weight of his chest and belly into the smaller man's back and threw a heavy thigh across his hip to help hold him down.

Lucio's legs thrashed uselessly, becoming more and more snarled in the sheet.

Even when all resistance ceased, Hugo held tight to the chokehold, as if unable to let go, and kept his face buried between the poufed black hair and the silk pillowcase. But after a few still minutes, he raised his face from its hiding place, took a deep, shuddering breath, and with his right arm still crooked around Lucio Centopani's dead throat, rolled onto his back, covered his mouth with his left hand, and stifled bitter lamentations.

Sunday, April 2, 1989

THIRTY-SEVEN

Just after five o'clock in the morning, Officer Latt Edwards cruised Love Circle, admiring the waning crescent moon that had risen from the horizon into the Nashville skyline a few minutes earlier and noticing the different feel to astronomical twilight following the arrival of Daylight Savings Time. He was thinking about pulling over and checking that all was well in Love Park when he received a call about a possible dead body at the rear of 21 Music Circle East. He acknowledged the call, confirmed himself *en route*, and hurried to the scene with flashing blue emergency lights but without shattering Sunday morning with a siren.

"Curiouser and curiouser," he said aloud to himself when he saw that the scene was in the rear lot of the building housing *Cash Box*, the music industry magazine linked to the March 9th shootings on the Row.

Officers Lashonda Stinnett and Archie Moody were already on the scene and had established the perimeter with yellow caution tape. Officer John Reavis Calloway rolled in on Officer Edwards's bumper.

"Johnny Reav," Latt said as the two rose up from their patrol cars at the same time.

"Lattimore," Calloway said in a western Kentucky drawl.

Latt held up a section of tape, allowed Calloway to go under, and then ducked under himself. He nodded a greeting to Stinnett and Moody as they approached, and the four gathered to confer on how to proceed. A breakfast cook coming to work at the Hall of Fame Motel had discovered the body, and a series of flipped coins decided that Moody would keep her company in the motel lobby until the investigative team arrived to speak with her.

"She's sort of pretty at least," Moody said. He gave them a casual salute and walked away toward the motel as Stinnett shook her head.

Latt turned for a first look at the victim.

The naked male lay curled on his side. Chest, arm, and leg muscles appeared well defined like a weightlifter's, even in death. The skin appeared tanned or olive, though fading with a grayish tinge. Hair on both head and genitals appeared to be black. The head lay cradled in the crook of the right arm, as if sleeping, but the face was a bloody pulp with no recognizable human features other than one bare eyeball and a few broken teeth.

Latt swallowed hard and turned away as a siren approaching from the southern part of downtown grew steadily louder in the quiet morning.

"Fucking Perras," Calloway said.

"Ass," Stinnett said.

Perras screeched to a stop on the near side of Division Street between the *Cash Box* parking lot and the Hall of Fame Motel. He let the siren blare a few more seconds before he cut it and got out, leaving the blue lights whirling.

"We should've said last on the scene sits with the cook," Latt said. He looked beyond Perras and saw that in at least eight windows of the motel's street-facing rooms the curtains were thrown wide open and guests in varied states of dress or undress watched the proceedings. "We'll have to knock on half the damned rooms over there before anybody can check out."

"All of 'em," Calloway said.

"We need to tell Moody to stop anybody who tries to check out before we get to the door-to-door."

"I'll do it." Stinnett hustled away with a jingling of keys and a creaking of leather.

"Thanks," Latt called after her and then watched Perras

196

duck under the tape at the back side of the parking lot and approach with his husky swagger, not even looking at Stinnett as she passed and obviously paying no attention to what evidence might be underfoot.

Perras ignored Edwards and Calloway, too, and walked straight toward the body, but when he got within a dozen feet, he stopped and bent and threw up.

"What the fuck!"

The angry voice rose from behind them, and Latt knew before he turned that the outrage was that of Detective Sergeant Darrin Hunt.

"Goddammit, Perras!" Hunt yelled. "Get your pansy-ass stomach the fuck off my crime scene!" He ducked under the caution tape Calloway held up for him. As Perras, Calloway, and Edwards scurried to security positions along the perimeter, Hunt strode toward the center of the scene and looked down at Perras's vomit and shook his head.

The forensics team arrived and began at the Division Street end of the scene, examining the parking lot surface according to an imagined grid. Medical Examiner Dr. Charles Harlan was on hand moments later and, after a brief consultation with Detective Hunt, began his initial examination of the body.

Hunt hovered over Dr. Harlan's work for a moment and then stepped away. He watched Stinnett return from the motel and take up her position on the perimeter and then motioned for Latt Edwards to join him.

"Yessir?" Latt said.

"Give me a rundown of everything before I got here."

"Yessir." Latt took the notepad from his uniform shirt pocket. "At some point around four-thirty, a young woman who cooks breakfast at the Hall of Fame Motel—sorry, I don't have her name yet—was arriving for work when she saw the body and called it in. Officers Stinnett and Moody were first on the scene, and Officer Calloway and I arrived soon after. Officer Moody is with the cook in the motel lobby. Officer Perras showed up just before you did, sir."

"Anything else?"

Latt turned toward the motel and pointed. "Sir, as you can see, we have several spectators in the windows yonder, so it's—"

"*Yonder*? Again with the *yonder*? You sound like Mr. MacRae."

"Sorry, sir." Latt continued with hint of a smile. "I figured you'd want to interview the occupants of all the rooms with windows facing this way, so Officer Moody is making sure nobody checks out before talking to y'all."

Hunt's lips twitched behind the mustache. He looked like he might make another comment on Edwards's word choices, but instead he turned away to check on Dr. Harlan and then turned back. "What's your take on Officer Perras's actions?"

"You mean him throwing up, sir?"

"Yes, that in particular."

"Well, it's only speculation, sir."

"Understood."

"I was watching him approach the body, 'cause he wasn't doing so as carefully as I thought he should." Latt paused, but when Hunt didn't comment, he continued. "His reaction seemed to be about more than the body's state of mutilation." He paused again. "Anyway, in that split second before his breakfast came up, I thought it looked like he recognized the victim."

Hunt turned again to watch Dr. Harlan for a moment, then turned to look at Perras, who leaned against the front of his patrol car, his head turned toward the motel and its spectator-filled windows, now numbering several more than eight. "Duly noted." He turned back to Latt. "Thank you, Officer Edwards." Hunt knuckled both sides of his mustache. "I heard that you've been to visit the surviving victim of last Sunday morning's shooting."

"Yessir, I wanted to get his permission for Mr. MacRae to take his guitar and get it fixed."

"But you've seen him more than once."

Latt drew breath to speak, but Hunt held up a hand.

"I don't have time for an explanation right now. Write up anything you've learned and get it in my hands soonest."

"Yessir."

"And if you're still meeting MacRae—"

"Detective Hunt?" Dr. Harlan called out.

Hunt turned toward the Medical Examiner and the body.

"Ready for you now," Dr. Harlan said.

Hunt turned back to Latt. "Carry on."

"Yessir," Latt said and then joined Perras to watch a small crowd of early walkers and joggers gathering across Division Street.

Hunt stood with the M.E. as both looked down at the body. "No I.D. on a naked man, obviously," Dr. Harlan said. "But I'm fairly certain of three basic things you've probably already guessed, the most certain of which is that this is a dump site and not the murder scene."

Hunt wrote in his pad and then looked away for a moment to watch the workings of the forensics personnel as they scanned the surface of the parking lot. He wrote another note. "Go ahead," he said to the M.E.

"The second thing is that the significant mutilation of the facial area occurred postmortem." He paused and swallowed audibly. "If such brutal disfiguration had been inflicted upon this man while he was living, we'd have much more blood on the body."

Hunt wrote a note. "Third?"

"The bruising on the neck suggests manual strangulation but not by the hands or a ligature. Most likely a chokehold from behind and most likely with the assailant's arms." As he spoke, he leaned down and pointed to the bruising on the neck. "See?" Then he straightened up again. "Though I suppose such a choke could be applied with the legs. Autopsy measurements of the bruises will tell us more."

"So, no gunshot involved?" Hunt said, looking up from his notepad.

"Nothing I've seen yet," Dr. Harlan said, his voice growing ragged. "I rolled him over as best I could. He doesn't appear to be lying on an entry wound." He cleared his throat. "Again, the autopsy will tell."

"Thank you," Hunt said. "I look forward to reading your report. Soonest, of course."

"Of course," Dr. Harlan said. "But as this is Sunday, like last week, it'll be tomorrow. By midday, I expect." Then he turned away and told his assistants to load up the body and deliver it to the morgue. "I'll be at the Pancake Pantry for a couple hours."

Hunt started toward Detective Davidson but then turned to the retreating M.E. again. "Dr. Harlan," he said. "Do you have an estimate on the time of death and how long the body might have been here?"

The M.E. stopped short of the crime scene tape and looked at his watch. "I'll give your latter question some thought during the autopsy," Dr. Harlan said without facing Hunt. "As for time of death, my best guess at this point is six to ten hours ago, so, sometime last night between eight o'clock and midnight."

"Thank you." Hunt turned back to the waiting detective. "Detective Davidson, I count forty rooms facing the crime scene. Maybe somebody was up to pee or had insomnia or morning desire and either saw or heard something." He stopped and scanned the lot. "Take Officer Stinnett to the motel and start knocking on doors."

"You got it," Davidson said and started across the lot.

"Oh, Woody, one more thing," Hunt said.

Davidson stopped and turned. "Yeah?"

"Talk to the cook who found the body. Officer Moody is with her in the lobby. If she seems on the up-and-up, get her contact info and release her to go to work or home, whichever she chooses."

"Sure thing." Davidson turned again and lumbered toward Division Street. "Officer Stinnett," he sang out. "With me."

Latt watched Davidson and Stinnett approach and nodded to them after they ducked under the tape. He and Perras watched them cross Division and pass through the small crowd milling about on the opposite sidewalk.

"I'd hit that ass," Perras said.

"Which one?"

Perras turned a mirrored glare on Latt. "Go to hell, Edwards."

Latt crossed his arms over his chest. "Damn, Murdoch, don't be so touchy. We've all had Hunt pissed off at us."

Perras huffed and turned back toward the thinning crowd and the motel, where the windows still had their curtains pulled aside but were now—since removal of the body—mostly empty of spectators.

"So, what got into you over there?" Latt asked. "And don't say you drank some bad chocolate milk."

Perras dropped his gaze to the pavement. "What's up, Edwards? Did Hunt tell you to interrogate me?"

"No, man, I'm just curious," Latt said. "You've never struck me as the kind to lose your breakfast over a little mutilation." He patted his own muscled belly and nodded toward the swell of Perras's. "I mean, you've got a hefty tank there. Cast iron, ain't it?"

"Again, bub, go to hell." Perras stood up from where he'd leaned on the front of his vehicle, his mirrored gaze seeming to take in the crime scene. "Looks like they're done here, so this conversation is over." He got in his vehicle, turned off the blue lights, and screeched away from the curb, flipping Latt the finger as a parting gesture.

THIRTY-EIGHT

White morning light cut through the bedroom window and crossed jumbled bedding. A sharply etched swath glowed on the opposite wall beneath songwriting awards—plaques and framed certificates—that surrounded a George Jones gold record for *Still the Same Ole Me*. The room smelled strongly of Davidoff Cool Water cologne. On the nightstand, a SleepMate 900 whispered white noise.

Despite the tangled condition of sheet and blanket, Curly Crocker lay unmoving on his back with his head deep in a pillow so thick and soft that its sides wrapped up around his ears. His mouth hung slightly open, and a light snore mixed with the shush from the sound machine.

Hugo stood beside the bed, alternately watching Crocker sleep—the swath of early sunlight cutting through the still air between them—and taking in the wall of awards. Still shirtless, his torso spattered with dried blood, he undid the drawstring at his waist and let his sweatpants collapse around his feet. He stepped free of the pool of cotton and closer to the low bed, feeling the light from the window warm the backs of his thighs, his buttocks, and lower back. He gently lifted Crocker's covers to find the man wearing a gray tank undershirt with his thin arms along his sides and his hands palms-down on his lower abdomen, thumb tips nearly touching below his navel and fingers buried inside his white briefs. With his eyes on Crocker's face, Hugo raised his left knee and leaned forward to drop his left shin across the sleeper's belly, pinning the thin and delicate hands in place. Almost at the same moment that Crocker's eyes and mouth startled open,

202

Hugo thrust the right shin across the man's throat, found his center of gravity, and settled heavily atop the ribby chest.

"Wakey wakey, eggs and bakey," he chuckled and then shuddered with a gaped-mouth yawn. "Hellfire, son, what do you weigh, like, one twenty?" He roughly rubbed a large palm over Crocker's reddening face, rapped his knuckles twice on the songwriter's balding head, and gave a light tug to the sparse hair. "I guess 'Curly' is a bit of a bad joke."

Crocker squirmed and attempted to buck, but Hugo was a stable and unmovable weight pressing him down. In moments, Crocker's eyes began struggling to focus.

Hugo leaned slightly to his left and somewhat eased the pressure on the man's throat. He watched the horror return to the eyes. "If you had yourself a wife, you wouldn't be in this situation," he said. "Or if you had some good meat and muscle like my MacRae, you might could buck me off."

He then leaned right and planted his palm on Crocker's forehead, redistributing the bulk of his weight atop the shin barred across the thin throat. He watched the eyes glaze within a few seconds and then snaked his left hand into his black bikini briefs. After a few awkward jerks, he straightened up again, switched hands, and rose to knees and shins, his face turned up toward the ceiling and his own eyes closed.

When finished, he settled down on the breathless chest beneath him and for a few minutes scanned the wall of awards, reading each one slowly. When his breathing and heartrate grew calm and even, he leaned forward to all fours, yawned deeply and shuddered again, and backed off body and bed, smearing semen on Curly Crocker's dead face as he closed the eyelids.

"No more a witness," Hugo said as he stood. He steadied himself a moment and looked at the body. "If you'd kept your mouth shut or told the paper not to use your name, I might've never known you saw what I did on Easter." Then he bent and picked up his sweatpants and turned away from the white light and white noise.

THIRTY-NINE

Ezra was surprised to find himself awake and seated in West End United Methodist Church for the 8:45 a.m. service. He sat where he'd sat for the funeral of Burl Davies. When all was said and sung, he blew a sigh of relief that the man in black and his coughing accomplice hadn't been in attendance again, and he wondered what such men would be doing on a Sunday morning.

He remained seated with his pocket notebook open on his knee and jotted down ideas from Dr. Montfort's sermon on Acts 5:27-32. The preacher had taken as his title Peter's words in the thirty-second verse, "We Are Witnesses," and Ezra wrote down points he remembered. He sketched beneath each point any connection between Dr. Montfort's exegesis of Peter's claim to being a witness and his own experience as a witness to brutal crime and evil afoot in the world.

"We have seen this momentous, life-changing thing, and we cannot but talk about it," Dr. Montfort had paraphrased Peter. "We are witnesses."

Ezra finished a final thought and drew a large question mark under his musings. When he stood up, he caught Dr. Montfort's eye and waved but decided not to join the line of congregants waiting to speak to the minister. He exited through the south transept and descended the stairs to the lower lobby and stepped out into a parking lot dappled with moving mid-morning shade and sunshine. He took West End to White Bridge Road and went to Dalt's in Lion's Head Village, where he sat at the bar and ordered the club sandwich with fries and an unsweet tea, then doodled around the morning's sermon notes while he waited for his order to arrive.

FORTY

Perras had gone off patrol a little over an hour after speeding away from Latt Edwards and the *Cash Box* crime scene. At his apartment, he'd spent the next three hours wrestling with his bedding, sweating, and failing to find sleep in his bedroom darkened with blackout curtains. Just before noon he stood in plain clothes—green sweatpants and a white long-sleeved Bush/Quayle t-shirt—and pounded on the back door of 1619 16th Avenue South. Between poundings he stood quiet, looking left and right, looking back toward the alley, cupping his hands against the back door's glass to see inside. After a couple of minutes, he turned and started down the back steps.

The door behind him creaked open.

Hugo stepped out onto the porch wearing only unbuttoned jeans and stood looking at his visitor through darkly bloodshot eyes. "Perras?" he growled. "What the hell?"

"Hugo," Perras said and stepped back up onto the porch, so close to Hugo that their bellies almost pressed against each other as they breathed. "Where's Lucky?"

Hugo turned away and stepped back into the kitchen. "I don't know," he said. "He went out to get groceries for brunch and ain't come back." He positioned himself at the opposite end of the kitchen table from where Perras stood. "Thought he might be with you."

"Why would he be with me, Hugo?" Perras closed the back porch door behind himself. "If he went to the store, why's the car here?"

"You want coffee? I'm gonna make some."

"Why is the car here, Hugo?"

Hugo began filling the carafe, then abruptly shut off the tap. "Listen, pup, you don't come into my house and take that tone with me." He turned on the water again.

Perras stood with arms crossed over his barrel chest and watched as Hugo tucked a filter into the coffee maker's basket and then measured out the grounds, poured in the water, closed the dust cover, and turned on the machine. "Well?" he said.

Hugo took a seat at the opposite end of the table, leaned forward, and pulled his cigarette pack, lighter, and an ashtray from the center of the tabletop and arranged them in front of himself. "We had a fight over the car. He'd told me that MacRae had seen him in it at the funeral for Burl Davies, and I told him that MacRae'd probably told that Black officer." He lipped a cigarette from the pack and lit it. "How's about you sit—"

"Cut the bullshit, Hugo." Perras loomed over his end of the table, bracing himself with both hands on the back of the chair in front of him. "Goddamn it!" he said as he lifted the chair off the floor and slammed it back down. "Lucky wasn't with me last night, but I sure as shit saw him this morning."

"You're gonna rip my linoleum," Hugo said. "So, I'll ask you kindly not to do that with the chair again."

"Fuck your linoleum, Hugo."

"And keep your voice down, Murdoch." Hugo began mashing out the half-smoked cigarette. "The neighbors don't all go to church and eat out after."

"I threw up at the goddamned crime scene."

Hugo stood and pulled two clean coffee mugs from the drainer beside the sink. "I mean it about your voice." He tipped the carafe to fill one cup. "Coffee?"

Perras drew a deep breath, pulled the chair from under the table, and sat with elbows on the tabletop and his forehead bowed into upturned palms. "I was meant to keep him safe," he said with a shaky voice. Then he raised his head and looked at Hugo.

"You weren't meant for shit," Hugo growled and set the full cup in front of Perras without getting too close, poured another for himself, and sat down again. "Safe how?"

"What?"

"How were you supposed to keep him safe?" Hugo said.

"Safe from what?"

"From you, old man. He thought you were losing it, and he was scared."

"You're lying."

"I don't think either of us really expected you to kill Nancy, and then we were in it when you did. I don't think he wanted to come back here Thursday night." Perras blinked hard. "I shouldn't have let him."

Hugo settled his elbows and forearms on the table and wrapped the coffee cup in both hands. He'd imagined cheating going on between Lucie and this big man across the table. But instead of baring his body, Lucie had been baring his soul and revealing his fears. *Afraid of me.* He drew a shaking breath and turned away from that thought. "How'd you recognized him?" he said after a moment. "You couldn't know his face." He took a cautious sip of coffee and again said, "How'd you recognize him?"

Perras squinted and stared, his head cocked to one side. "I've seen his body plenty," he said at last. He picked up his cup, but his hand shook so much that he set it down without sipping. "I don't know of a time I've been here when you guys had your shirts on." He rubbed a big hand back and forth across close-cropped blond hair.

Hugo stared and then looked down at his coffee cup. "Fair enough."

"I just want to know why," Perras said, his voice shaking like his hand. "Why in hell would you do all that? Kill him and do that to his face?"

Hugo drew a deep breath and then lipped another cigarette from his pack. "Ever hear the story of when John Wesley Hardin shot a man for snoring too loud—" He stopped and lit his cigarette. "Maybe that's making light of it." He expelled smoke in little puffs as he spoke. "Lucie's coughing fits were gonna get us caught. All of us. I couldn't abide that." He tipped the chair onto its back legs, pinched the bridge of his nose, and squeezed shut his eyes. "But he was sick, Murdoch. Dear God, he was sick. Did you know he'd started coughing up blood?" He sat quiet a moment. "He went on a coughing jag in bed last night, and I just couldn't take it anymore." He opened his eyes and snuffled loudly. "Can't say why about—"

"Goddamn it, he was my friend!" Perras moaned and buried his face in his hands again. "You're a fucking monster."

Hugo didn't say anything but leaned forward to let the front legs of his chair settle back on the floor. He took a sip of coffee and a drag, secured the cigarette in a slot on the ashtray's rim, and sat staring at Perras, breathing evenly, belly waxing and waning in steady rhythm.

Perras bolted up and knocked the chair over backward. His hip jolted the corner of the table as he lumbered toward Hugo, who stood to meet him, growling as he rose, "He was my boy, goddammit!" Hugo drove a left uppercut into the husky policeman's chin and followed it with a quick right hook to the jaw. When Perras's face snapped back into place and he stood stunned and teetering, Hugo landed a headbutt between his eyes.

FORTY-ONE

Ezra left Dalt's and drove to Fountain Square, thinking he might take in a movie. But first showings of the day were still an hour away, and none of the movies particularly appealed to his restlessness. He drove to Vandy Med Center, hoping the Sunday visiting hours were the same as Saturday's. They were, but Benny Jack was sleeping deeply after what his current nurse—*decidedly not Sally Evans*—said was a rough night. He asked about Nurse Evans and was told with a wink that she was generally off on Sundays and Mondays. Then he drove over to 1602 16th where his hometown friend Gabe Tanner lived in an upstairs apartment. He climbed the steps and knocked on the door a couple of times, but nobody answered. "*On the road again,*" Ezra thought. *Willie Nelson, songwriter.*

The day was warming into the upper sixties, so he left the Tempo parked in front of Gabe's place and walked 16th in the direction of Division Street, planning to swing left at Division and return via 17th. Beneath a vivid blue sky, he moved along with a growing sense of bewilderment that these beloved streets of Nashville—streets that had always seemed a kind of wonderland to his creative mind—had become blood-haunted and threatening. He passed place after place—bungalow, house, small office building—identified as housing publishers, independent record labels, artist management and booking agencies, recording studios, record promoters, salons-to-the-stars, and more. He finally had his own publishing deal, but these places still inspired him to wonder what work he could do with the

209

people in this office or that. Yet even as that old wondering stirred, he felt a new dread at what might hide behind those front doors, behind interior office doors, behind closet doors closed on some darkness within.

When he'd come this way little more than a week before, he was drunk, and a storm brewed to the northwest of the Nashville skyline. He passed again the scene where the life of Kevin Hughes had seeped into the cracked pavement and that of Sammy Sadler had been temporarily wrecked both physically and psychologically, he guessed, but in contrast to that stormy walk, the spot now seemed somehow more deviant and heart-breaking in the contexts of a beautiful day and of life's having picked itself up, brushed itself off, and moved on.

When he reached Division, he turned left for a block and then stopped on the corner. Instead of turning left again on 17th as he'd planned, he continued through the intersection and walked down the hill toward Broadway, curious to see that yesterday's barricades at 18th and 19th had disappeared. He hesitated beside the parking lot of Virginia's Market, looking at Omnisound from the vantage point of Friday evening's witness, then crossed the street and soon stood in front of the studio. As he took in the scene, scrubbed clean of catastrophe, he felt a constriction of his throat almost as if an unseen hand had taken hold of it. He imagined the young man—still nameless to him—as being much like himself before those shots rang out that might forever taint the wonderland of Music Row, might even taint the music and his love of it.

He retreated up the hill and turned right on 17th. At first, he was on the side of the street that would bring him directly in front of the Ave Canora bungalow. He slowed for a few steps, drew a deep breath, and then crossed to the opposite sidewalk, seeking the exact vantage point from which he'd watched a killer in black end the lives of Burl Davies and his acquaintances and blast Benny Jack Boudreau into a struggle for survival. He found the spot, and as if on cue the scene darkened. The promotional and memorial banners winging Ave Canora's front walk disappeared. The grass in the yard and along the verge between sidewalk and street faded from a lush green to the washed-out lavender gray it took on beneath streetlights. As the afternoon's blue sky likewise faded to a blackness glowing without stars, he watched ghosts in motion before him, falling and running and falling. He heard the maddening slide of glass across guitar strings, punctuated with six beats from a pistol. Suddenly he was aware that no car now separated him from the horror taking place in his mind's eye. He stood frozen in a fear greater than he remembered feeling at that senseless, violent moment. Again, as in his dream on the morning after, everybody in the scene leveled a gun at him, and his vision blurred with a wash of tears.

He blinked them away to run down his cheeks, and the sunlight and blue sky and green grass of Sunday afternoon surrounded him once more. He stood and drew a few breaths, sadly returning Burl's banner smile, reading again Ave Canora's congratulations to Zack Thigpin, feeling once more his own aspirations to success as the excitement of being a Nashville songwriter crept back into his chest. Then he wiped away his tears and turned and continued down 17th in the direction of the Belmont Mansion and the college.

Walk it off, Ez, he thought in Mel's voice, just as he'd heard him say many times over the years.

Near the Belmont end of 17th, he angled left onto Dorothy Place toward 16th. In the middle of Dorothy Place, as he crossed the entrance to the alley that ran the length of Music Row between the two one-way streets, he caught a glimpse of red through the landscaping and undergrowth. He stopped. Thinking *No way!* was this the coughing man's faded red car, he stretched to his tiptoes and then dipped to a crouch, attempting to get a better look. He crept deeper into the alley, and before he realized, he was standing in the open opposite the alley access of a small gray house with dark gray shingles and a light gray stone foundation. Its low-roofed back porch sported white posts, railings, and pickets. Four steps descended into the dirt and gravel area where two cars were parked—a dusty black Chevy IROC-Z backed up to the right of the porch steps and the faded red Ford Taurus nosed in to the left of them, its blue license plate with yellow lettering clearly visible—"New Jersey" and "Garden State." Ezra pulled out his notepad and jotted down the number—ZZT-622.

FORTY-TWO

Hugo stood in the shower for the second time that day, lathering himself with Irish Spring and watching Ezra MacRae, who stood out back with pen and notepad. Hugo braced his left hand against the wall beside the small window and with his right hand swirled the fragrant lather over his chest and belly and genitals. He began to harden and growl as he studied MacRae, imagining, as he worked on himself, how the young man might look without his shirt. After another minute, he scooped lather up from his body and washed his face and thinning hair. Eyes closed, he bent into the spray from the showerhead and rinsed from the top down. When he stood upright again and thumbed water from his eyes, MacRae was gone. He turned off the shower, toweled himself dry, and stepped naked into the bedroom.

"Murdoch?"

Perras startled as if Hugo had poked him in the ribs.

"Murdoch," Hugo said again. "We got stuff to do, so get up and take a shower. I'm gonna make some pancakes."

Perras rolled over on his back and moved to rub the sleep from his eyes, but his hands sprung away from his face as he winced. "Goddammit," he grunted.

"You'll feel better after a shower and something to eat." Hugo opened the top drawer in a chest of drawers. "But don't expect to look better."

Perras rolled over and sat up. "What stuff?"

"We're gonna ride up to Springfield and get rid of the Taurus."

He pulled a pair of blue bikini briefs from the drawer. "MacRae was outside while I was in the shower."

"Ezra MacRae?"

"You know another?" Hugo sat down on the foot of the bed and rocked backward, shot both feet through the leg holes, and rocked forward and stood, pulling the briefs up tightly as he rose. He dipped a hand in and adjusted himself. "He saw the Taurus and wrote down the tag number, so we need to get it gone before he comes back with his Black friend or Hunt."

Perras stood slowly. "Oh, man." He nearly fell back in the bed but caught himself with a hand on the nightstand.

"Like I said, a shower and something to eat. You can grab one of my T-shirts from the second drawer here if you want, any except the Waylon shirts, but I don't think yours has any blood on it." He pulled open his T-shirt drawer. "Now get in the shower, and I'll have a stack ready on the table." He turned and walked out of the bedroom.

FORTY-THREE

When he pushed through the door of The Store, Ezra found Penny standing at her checkout counter and staring out the plate-glass front window. "What's up, Penny?" he said and headed for the aisles, but when she didn't respond, he stopped. "You okay?"

"Lord, Young MacRae," she said as she seemed to catch up to the moment. "Satan has our city by the throat, and he's shaking it like a dog."

"Your pastor's penis again?"

"What?" she said. "No, don't be vulgar, boy." She put both hands over her mouth and drew a deep breath, then pressed her fingers against her cheeks. "You ain't heard?"

"Heard what?"

"There's another killed," she said. "Found early this morning."

"What? On Music Row?"

"Near enough. Down across from that Hall of Fame Motel."

"Haven't heard anything about it." He picked up two Moon Pies and laid them on the counter. "Another shooting?"

"I don't know, but there was this fellow in here who said the dead man didn't have a stitch on."

"Naked?"

"It gets worser," Penny said. "Didn't have a face either. Radio Rick said it was like somebody just mashed the man's face off."

"Good Lord." Ezra stood a moment staring out the plate-glass window as he'd found Penny doing. Then he shuddered and shook himself. "Hang on a sec." He made a pass through the center aisle and returned to Penny's checkout with another

215

two-liter of Diet Mountain Dew and a Chef Boyardee pepperoni pizza kit. "Radio Rick?"

"Works for WLAC. He was in here earlier." She began tallying up Ezra's purchases. "Folks do go on when they're buying their milk and cigarettes. Like I was their hairdresser or something." She finished the charges and bagged the items. "Where you been that you didn't hear?"

Ezra handed her a twenty-dollar bill. "Let's see," he said. "I went to West End Methodist for their early service, had brunch at Dalt's, and eventually ended up walking around Music Row."

Penny stood, holding his change in her hands. "Don't know nothing about Dalt's," she said. "But going to a cult church don't seem like a great way to start your Sunday." She handed him his change. "And why in the name of sweet Jesus would you go walking around Murder Row?"

"'Murder Row'," he said. "That's cute." He took his change, pocketed it, and picked up his bag. "You should try Dalt's sometime, Penny."

"Beware Satan, Young MacRae," she said as he backed out the door. "He's real as you or me, and he's shaking us like a dog with a chew toy."

Back in his place at Youngstowne Square, he went straight to the telephone. He dialed the numbers he had for Officer Latt Edwards but couldn't get him on the line. He called the Metro Police dispatcher and left a message for Detective Darrin Hunt.

The light flashed on his answering machine, and he pushed the button, expecting the voice of Mel or that of his mother.

"Hey, Jesus," she said and laughed. "Okay, I'm gonna stop that, I promise. Ezra, this is Sally from the hospital. It's around three-thirty on Sunday. I was thinking maybe we go thrifting for Benny Jack tomorrow—that's Monday. Maybe get him some clothes and shoes? I have all day off, but the thrift stores usually close at six or so. Give me a call this evening or tomorrow morning." She left her number and hung up.

FORTY-FOUR

Hugo drove Perras's IROC-Z, and Perras followed in Lucio's Taurus. They took I-65 North to I-24 and exited at Old Hickory Boulevard. After a couple of turns, Hugo led the way onto a nameless dirt track over which they bumped and ground uphill through woods until it dead-ended after a quarter mile.

"Man, my undercarriage is gonna be all to hell," Perras said when Hugo stood at the driver's window of the Taurus.

"Better the car's than yours," Hugo said. "Cut it off and give me the keys and then stay right there." He pocketed the keys and went to the rear of the Taurus and removed the license plate and tossed it in the back seat of the IROC-Z. He opened the Taurus's trunk and removed the baseball bat Lucio kept there. Then he returned the keys to Perras. "Pull it over to that thicket. Behind it as best you can."

Perras did as he was told, and as soon as he turned off the ignition, Hugo appeared beside the front fender and began slamming the bat into the front windshield.

"Goddammit, Hugo!" Perras shouted as he dove out and scooted away in a wash and rustle of dry leaves.

When the shattered glass fell into the front seats and floorboard, Hugo pulled his pistol from his waistband and fired two close-range shots into the VIN plate. "Won't stop them from identifying it," he said as the gunshots faded through the trees. "But maybe it'll slow them down." He tucked the pistol back into his waistband. "Come on, Murdoch."

"Be better if you burned it." Perras got to his feet and brushed off dead leaves.

217

"Don't want to set the woods on fire." Hugo reached in through the open driver's window and pulled out the keys. "And besides, it's Lucie's," he said and threw the keys down a wooded slope. "Come on."

They returned to Nashville with Hugo still driving Perras's car. But instead of heading for the house on 16th, he drove out West End to the intersection with 31st and turned right up a slight incline. He pulled to the curb and turned off the rumbling engine, leaned forward to look up the side of 110 31st Avenue North and then leaned back.

"Now, tell me again," Hugo said. "What do you know about Ezra MacRae?"

"Huh?"

"MacRae. What do you know about him?"

"Well, I know his name, of course," Perras said.

"Don't be a smartass."

"I told you he lives on Utah Avenue. Youngstowne Square. He's a songwriter, but he cleans pools for a living." He paused and wiped a palm across his lips. "He's from a little town called Reunion—something like that. Up in the North Carolina mountains, I think."

"Probably Runion," Hugo said. "I've been through there."

"Really?"

"There's a fiddle player by the name of Bobby Hicks who lives around there. Played with Bill Monroe and fiddled on a bunch of Ricky Skaggs records." Hugo turned and stared out the driver's window for a moment. "A couple years ago, Nancy and me took a little trip up to Dollywood and then on to Asheville. We headed north from there and tried to find Hicks and ask if he'd play on her first record. But we never found him, and the locals wouldn't direct us." He again leaned forward and looked up the side of the apartment building. "Ate lunch at a good little pizza joint there in Runion."

Perras cleared his throat, opened the car door, and spat. He kept the door slightly open. "That's all I know about MacRae except that he drives a white Ford Tempo that's still got North Carolina tags on it."

"Shut that door." Hugo settled back in his seat again. "Now, remind me where Hunt is in identifying Nancy."

Perras looked ahead for a moment and then closed the car door. "Last I heard, they had nothing but the name Cassie Nance and the assumption that she lived here with Earl Hill."

"What about the car?"

"Nobody's mentioned it."

"You mean to say it's sitting right across the street, and they don't know nothing about it."

"That's what I'm saying, Hugo. If they knew about it, they'd impound it."

"The title's in my name." Hugo looked across the street at his 1986 Buick Grand National, its sleek blackness dusted a greenish yellow with pollen.

"You gonna take it?" Perras asked. "You got the keys?"

"Yeah, I've got both sets. I came by here last Saturday before I surprised her and Earl over on 17th."

"Jesus, Hugo."

"Well, we knew they'd taken Earl's car to meet Burl over at the Stockyard, so once they sat down with their drinks, I left Lucie to keep an eye on them and headed back over here."

Perras stared out the front windshield for a moment. "I'm gonna miss Lucky," he said and turned away to look out the passenger's window. "I wish you hadn't—"

Hugo grabbed the pistol tucked between his thighs and pressed its muzzle just behind Perras's left ear. "Don't you ever mention him again. Not like that."

"All right! All right!" Perras said, his right temple pressed against the window, his hands partway raised. "I won't, Hugo, Jesus."

"I know you won't," Hugo said. "Now, get out."

"What?"

"Get out of the car."

Perras dropped his hands into his lap.

"Now," Hugo said.

Perras opened the door, stood, and stepped up onto the sidewalk. Hugo opened his door and stood, tucked the pistol back in his waistband and pulled at his shirttail to cover it.

"I'm not taking your car," Hugo said across the roof of the IROC-Z. He dropped the keys into the driver's seat and looked left and right and up to the nearest apartment windows above them. "I don't want to see you for a while unless I call or you've got news I need to know." He closed the driver's door. "The first sense I get that they're coming for me, I'll be coming for you. And I'll kill you with my bare hands if it's the last thing I do before they get me." He glared across the roof.

"Well, hey, what if they get on to you because of MacRae being out in the alley? That ain't my fucking fault."

"That's good thinking, Murdoch. Maybe you better make sure that don't happen."

"What's that supposed to mean?" Perras said.

Hugo looked down into the back seat. "Ditch that license plate, will you?"

Perras stared. "Hugo? What'd you mean by that?"

Hugo winked and turned, looked both ways, and crossed to the Buick. He pulled jangling keys from his pocket, unlocked the door, and opened it. He glanced back across 31st at Perras, who still stood staring, and then he sat down behind the wheel and closed the door.

Even though the car had been sitting unoccupied for more than a week—through rain and sunshine, hot temperatures and cold—her scent filled the interior like water. He inserted the key in the ignition and turned it and smiled when the engine immediately came to life. But then he startled when Nancy's voice—Cassie Nance's voice—blasted from the speakers—

She's in love with the boy!

He turned down the volume and listened to the last verse and chorus. Then he ejected the tape, turned the radio off, and read the cassette label. "She might actually have made the bigtime." He glanced down at the gas gauge to see that the Buick had less than an eighth of a tank. "Typical." He shook his head and activated the electronic passenger's window. "Somebody'll make a hit out of that song one of these days." He tossed the cassette to clatter outside on the sidewalk and raised the window, revved the Buick's engine twice and smiled. "Good girl. Let's hit the station on Wedgewood and get you a shower and something to eat."

FORTY-FIVE

Ezra stood over the stovetop, occasionally stirring Kate's pilau and waiting for the pot to return to boiling. He glanced at the clock. 7:36.

He turned toward the window in the kitchen door and saw that the world outside was taking on its eerie after-sunset blend of brightness diffused through the sky and murky shadows below. He lay the wooden spoon beside the pot and looked at the telephone on the wall. He wanted to call Sally, but he knew that wasn't a good idea with Kate in the bathroom.

After calling Latt Edwards and Detective Hunt, he'd sat on the couch waiting for it to be "this evening" when he could call Sally. Then Kate had knocked, shocking him awake, and he'd stumbled up and opened the door to find her standing there with arms full of groceries and her face flushed.

She gave him a peck on the cheek as she pushed past and shoved all the groceries into the fridge.

"I just walked two hours on the Mossy Ridge Loop in Percy Warner." She closed the fridge door. "I'm sweaty, and I'm horny. So, get thee to the boudoir, MacRae." She pushed past him, pulled off her Joan Jett *Up Your Alley* tour shirt and tossed it on the couch. "We're having beef and chicken pilau, but not now."

Thirty minutes later their stomachs growled between the damp sheets, so they tumbled out of bed, took turns peeing and washing their hands, and adjourned to the kitchen, where they sliced beef sausage and chicken, cooked bacon, sautéed onions and celery, browned the meats—he in his Wolfpack wrestling shorts, she in spandex shorts of navy and garnet and a sand-colored, garnet-trimmed sports bra. When the seasoned stock had come to a boil, she'd turned on the oven to preheat and then added rice to the boiling stock.

"Keep that stirred until it comes back to a boil," she said. "Then cover it, put it in the oven, and set the timer for forty-five minutes." She'd pecked him on the cheek again and gone to take a shower.

A knock on the kitchen door startled him back to the moment. His heart thudded when he recognized the shape of a man standing on the dusky patio just the other side of his own reflection in the door's glass panels. He laid the spoon beside the pilau pot, stepped to the door, and flipped the switch for the patio light.

Nothing happened.

He flipped the switch twice more without effect. "Who is it?" He heard Kate's muffled "What?" from the bathroom. "Who's there?" he said.

"Officer Archie Moody, Metro PD," the man outside said. "Latt Edwards asked me to come by and give you a message." The dark figure stepped closer to the kitchen door.

Ezra saw a uniformed torso become clearer in the darkness, the light from the kitchen reflecting from points on a badge, but the face remained shadowed. Wondering *Why the kitchen door?* and whether he'd not heard a knock at the front, he flipped the patio light switch once more, then unlocked and turned the knob.

The uniformed officer charged the door shoulder first and knocked Ezra backward past the range and against the counter beside the fridge. When he tried to bolt into the living room, the intruder tackled him, and both went down in the middle of the floor. The man overwhelmed Ezra and wrapped him up from behind in a combination chokehold and body scissors. He pulled upward on the choke and pushed downward on the scissors, and Ezra felt himself losing consciousness.

And then a naked Kate straddled them, screaming, her wet hair dripping in Ezra's face, her right hand blasting the intruder's eyes and nose and mouth with pepper spray.

Chokehold and body scissors fell away, and Ezra rolled toward the couch, gasping and coughing, nearly taking Kate's left leg from under her.

But Kate stepped over him, refusing to relent with either spraying or screaming.

The shrieks of the attacker-turned-victim sounded as pained as Kate's were outraged. His whole body spasmed. His eyes streamed tears, and he blew globs of mucus down across his mouth and chin and onto the front of his uniform shirt.

"Kate!" Ezra yelled. "Stop!" He stood unsteadily and stepped cautiously around the man's kicking feet, came up behind her, and placed his hands on her biceps. Her screams subsided as the aerosol can began to hiss without spray. They stood together and looked down at the man, amazed at his distress and helplessness.

Loud knocking sounded on the front door. "Open up!" a voice yelled. "Open this goddamned door!"

"Just a second," Ezra answered. He again stepped around the stuttering feet of the incapacitated officer, grabbed Kate's shirt from the couch, and helped her put it on. With another hard cough and his arm around her shoulders, he guided her to the front door and opened it.

Detectives Darrin Hunt and Woody Davidson barged past them into the room and stopped to stare at the downed man in the floor.

"What the hell?" Hunt said. "Perras, what the fuck?"

Detective Davidson dropped to one knee and inspected the incapacitated officer.

Kate turned away from the four men in the living room and went into the kitchen. She set the empty pepper spray can on the counter, covered the boiling pilau, and put on the oven mitts Ezra had ready by the stovetop. She opened the oven door, slid in the covered pot, seemingly unconscious of how her Joan Jett shirt rode up and bared her ass when she bent over, and set the timer for forty-five minutes. Then without a word she walked past the men, went into the bedroom, and closed the door.

Hunt looked at Ezra, who stood with nothing on but the NC State Wolfpack shorts, his skin blotched with red and pink from Perras's attack. "What the hell?" he said again.

Ezra shrugged, and Davidson rose.

The three men stood over the groaning, crying Murdoch Perras, while Ezra described what had just happened. Then Detective Davidson fished keys out of Perras's pocket and soon had him up and out the door for a trip to an emergency room on Harding Pike. Ezra could hear Davidson talking over Perras's groans as they went through the Youngstowne Square complex, telling the neighbors that everything was under control, that they should shut their doors and enjoy the rest of their evening. Detective Hunt told Ezra to check on "the young woman" and then meet him at the kitchen table.

He couldn't tell how Kate was doing. She was dressed in all but her socks and shoes and sitting on the side of the bed.

"How much time is left on the timer?" she asked.

"Don't worry about that," Ezra said. "I'll come get you when it goes off."

"I'm not worried about it."

She didn't say anything more, so he closed the door and sat down at the table with Hunt.

Ezra explained why he'd left his earlier message with the dispatcher—the sighting of the red Taurus parked behind the house at 1619 16ᵗʰ Avenue South.

"The other car was a Chevy IROC-Z?" Hunt asked, his pen hovering over his notepad.

"Yes, black," Ezra said. "It was backed up to the porch, so

I didn't get the tag number." He then told of the prep for the pilau and the knock at the kitchen door soon after Kate went to shower. He described the attack—as much as he could remember—and Kate's rescuing him.

No, he didn't know Murdoch Perras. No, he didn't recall ever meeting him or even seeing him except, now that he thought of it, for a brief moment at the crime scene when Burl Davies was murdered. No, he couldn't imagine any reason for the evening's events. And no, he was pretty sure that Kate didn't know him either. Yes, he would ask her—and yes, "soonest" rather than later.

"Anything else?" Hunt asked.

"Well, there was this one weird thing—last Thursday, I think," Ezra said. He described the wet footprint found on his back step that morning before the funeral of Burl Davies.

"I suppose it could have been Officer Perras checking things out," Hunt said. "Maybe even loosening that patio lightbulb." He made a final note in his notebook and closed it. "Then again, it could have been some neighborhood kid thinking about breaking in or a Peeping Tom." He stood. "I'll ask Perras about it tomorrow."

The timer went off on the oven, and as Detective Hunt stepped into the living room, Ezra turned off both timer and oven and partially opened the oven door.

"You and Ms. Hathaway will need to come to the station tomorrow and make official statements." Hunt stepped out onto the stoop. "I'll have Officer Edwards get in touch." And then he was gone.

Ezra went to the bedroom and found Kate sitting where he'd left her, staring at her toes as she curled them against the carpet.

"Did you know that guy? Murdoch Perras?"

"Fuck no," she said without looking up.

"Supper's ready."

They made an attempt at normalcy, dishing out small bowls

of pilau that they picked at for a few minutes. Eventually they scraped most of their helpings into the trash and went to bed, where they lay side by side and awake until Kate climbed over him, dressed again, and left without a word.

Monday, April 3, 1989

FORTY-SIX

Hugo lay on his back, his head cradled on palms and interlocked fingers. His eyes opened—as if he'd only blinked rather than slept—and took in the play of light on the bedroom's whitewashed ceiling planks, the light not a direct beam through the shower window lined with Lucio's shampoo and bodywash bottles but a diffuse glow. He got out of bed, stepped to the bathroom, and watched the patrol car idling in the alley, its spotlight on the gravel-and-dirt parking area behind his house.

Then the spotlight went dark, and the car rolled slowly forward toward Dorothy Place.

"Damn Murdoch and MacRae," he whispered as he lifted the toilet seat.

When he'd finished and flushed, he returned to the bedroom, and there in the dark, he pulled on clothes he'd laid out to be ready—a pair of black jeans and a plain, long-sleeved black T-shirt, black sneakers, and a camouflage Nashville Sounds baseball cap. An Army-green, top-load duffle bag stood in the corner by the front door, prepacked with a week's worth of clothes, his toiletries, his revolver, and ammo. He slung this on his shoulder and stepped out onto the front porch, where he stood a moment and watched the city-bright night, listened closely to it, and then went down the steps and walked two blocks up 16th to the Buick.

He drove first to Perras's apartment complex, where he took a plastic canister of gasoline from the Buick's trunk, soaked the black IROC-Z, and set it ablaze. Then, after forty-five minutes of aimless driving around to make certain he wasn't being followed, he parked the car in the same spot on 31st where he'd picked it up the previous afternoon. He locked it and again shouldered his duffle, crossed the street, and, using Nancy's keys, let himself into the apartment she'd shared with Earl Hill. He took a beer from their fridge and guzzled it standing in their kitchen. Then he stripped off his clothes, crawled into their bed, and went back to sleep.

They are boys of twelve and eleven, he and Percy Quinn, sleeping out in a tent pitched beneath the magnolia in the Quinns' backyard. He is big for his age and chunky, and "Quinny is skinny," as the taunting chorus goes at school—weekdays and Sundays. Hugo plays seventh-grade football and always wants Quinny to wrestle with him between afterschool practice and supper. Quinny prefers to dance and teaches him to move to the music they hear on WJDX—"Nature Boy," "Feel Like Going Home," "Good Rockin' Tonight." But in the dark tent beneath the magnolia, no music plays, no words sung or said. Instead, rustlings of slight movement and quickened breaths. He takes Quinny in his left hand and settles his head on his friend's narrow chest, matching the pump of his grip to the strong and rapid heartbeat he hears. The thinly skinned ribcage hurts his ear, so he moves his head downward to the softer belly, where the heartbeat recedes to a fainter thumping but does not slow. He feels the aching hollow of his mouth. He feels his lips open and push forward, like a fish's just before it strikes the hooked worm. His tongue emerges and stretches to try and touch, flicking at the musky and humid air of the tent. Quinny settles a hand on top of his head and pushes. He wants to be pushed closer, to be made to close the distance and do he knows not what beyond filling the hollow emptiness of his mouth and releasing the tension of anticipation on the back of his tongue. But he resists, suddenly aware of rumbling tires on Highway 29, suddenly fearful of losing himself so that he misses hearing Mrs. Quinn coming with a treat or a Quinn brother prowling to prank or his own father stumble-stomping toward them across the dark grass. And then Quinny's breath catches, and he throbs four times in Hugo's grip. Both grow still until Quinny's breath steadies and his hand musses Hugo's ginger hair, tugging it affectionately at the crown.

Then Hugo no longer hears a heartbeat. Somehow he knows he is no longer with Quinny in Soso forty-one years before but with his lost Lucie just a moment beyond their last moment.

FORTY-SEVEN

Ezra woke up sore and alone. He looked at his bedside clock and saw that it was 8:17. He rolled to his back and stifled a yawn when he felt the soreness along his jawline and in the muscles of his neck, then lay still a few moments, massaging the places that pained him.

He sat up on the side of the bed, determined to ignore the soreness and solitude, and looked at the window. Although the blinds were closed, he could tell by the light around the edges that the day was cloudy. He reached over and raised the blinds to the top of the window and looked out on the overgrown back corner of Youngstowne Square, where—even under overcast skies—untended grass and shrubs appeared greener every day. Beyond the twenty feet of the complex's landscaping, another one hundred fifty feet of woods extended to a bend in a railway line. He realized that he generally thought of threats as approaching from the front parking area and Utah Avenue, but now he recognized that somebody could approach through the woods from the tracks. He checked to be certain the window was locked and went to his music room to check the lock there as well.

He ran the tips of his fingers across the strings of the Guild in its stand, and as the sound faded, he heard the train coming. He returned to his bedroom and stood watching the flickering in the trees that was all he could see of the train's passing. But hearing the rumble was enough to take him home to Runion, where every place he loved—Mel's house and barn and fields, his parents' house and church, downtown and Stackhouse Park—was within earshot, if not within sight, of a train.

There's a song in that, he thought and picked up his notebook from the nightstand and wrote down two phrases, ALWAYS A TRAIN and TRAINS BECKON ME HOME.

He hadn't called Mel or his parents the previous afternoon as he'd intended. A shivering—akin to the train's flickering in the trees—seemed constant deep inside him, and he knew he needed some "Mel time," as his mother called it. The trauma of the past eight days had been real but disembodied—the horrifying shootings witnessed as if watching them unfold in a movie, the dreams that followed, a voice over the telephone line, threats, sorrows. But during Murdoch Perras's attack, the trauma became carnal, a physical power that had wrestled him to the ground with, he believed, full intention of killing him. The fear made flesh in that moment couldn't be comforted by Mel's disembodied voice on the telephone. Ezra needed to go home, he knew, until this was over.

The train passed, and he turned away from the window just as the telephone began ringing.

"Man, what the hell happened last night?" Latt Edwards asked when Ezra answered. "This place is buzzing."

"Well, I'm supposed to give you a statement, right?"

"That's the word."

"Can we save it 'til then? I gotta get busy putting the day together." Ezra looked down and saw Sally Evans's number written on the pad by the telephone.

"Sure thing," Latt said.

"I'll meet you at the station," Ezra said. "What time's good for you?"

Latt paused, and Ezra guessed he was looking at a schedule or a to-do list.

"How about two o'clock?" Latt said.

"All right, I'll be there with my story straight."

"Wait," Latt said. "You got a daytime number for Kate Hathaway?"

Ezra gave him the number for Billy Keith's office on 18th and for Kate's apartment, said he would see him at two, and disconnected the call.

The shivering inside him took on a slightly different feel as he dialed the number for Sally Evans.

"Hello?" she said.

"Sally?"

"Yes, who's this?"

"It's Ezra. Benny Jack's friend?"

"Oh, Jesus, really?" she said with a laugh in her voice. "Okay, I promise that's it for that joke." She paused. "Unless Benny Jack needs it to go on."

"I'm with you on that," Ezra said. "You still up for hitting some thrift stores?"

"Well, I've already got plans for this morning and the early afternoon," Sally said. "Maybe around three?"

"Afternoon works best for me anyway. How about three-thirty?"

"Perfect."

"And supper after the thrift stores close?"

"Perfect again."

"Great. We can decide where to eat later."

"I need to run now." She gave him an address on Wyoming Avenue. Before he could say that was probably close to him, she said, "Okay, see you then," and was gone.

His weekly pool-cleaning rotation included seven regular stops on Mondays. If everything went well, then he could probably finish all seven before he met Latt at the station to make his statement about the previous evening's attack. He could take pilau and ice water so that he wouldn't have to stop for lunch. As he began packing a lunchbox and thermos featuring images of Yoda, Luke Skywalker, and R2D2 in a scene from *The Empire Strikes Back*, he checked the clock on the range.

8:48.

"Time enough," he said aloud. He brushed his teeth and dressed in jeans, black high-top Chuck Taylors, and a dark blue long-sleeved Music City Pool Management T-shirt for an overcast morning's work.

FORTY-EIGHT

At eleven o'clock, Detectives Hunt and Davidson sat at a window table in the Pancake Pantry and waited for their orders. They'd been discussing the previous evening's adventure in Ezra MacRae's apartment and the troubling surprise of charging one of their own with breaking and entering and assault.

"And that's maybe just for starters," Davidson said before sipping from his coffee cup. "When are you interviewing him?"

"I'll talk to him at two o'clock, after I get yesterday morning's autopsy results from Dr. Harlan." Hunt sipped his ice water. "Was everything all right at the hospital?"

"Yeah, we were there for about an hour and a half altogether. He was mostly fine when I took him downtown."

"She gave him a hell of a spraying."

"That she did," Davidson said. "But here's something for you to check out when you talk to him." He rubbed the bridge of his nose. "When the hospital got him cleaned up, he was still red in and around the eyes, but it was also clear that somebody'd beat the hell out of him since we saw him yesterday morning at that body dump."

"Somebody?"

"He wouldn't say who, but maybe you can find out."

Both leaned back in their chairs as food arrived. The waitress placed rye toast, sliced tomatoes, and three sausage links in front of Hunt and an order of fifteen silver-dollar pancakes with a side of bacon in front of Davidson.

Hunt stared for a moment with a slight smile and a slightly raised eyebrow.

"What?" Davidson tucked a napkin into his collar. "I'm not you."

"I didn't say anything." Hunt began to butter his toast and salt his tomatoes. "Enjoy."

"I had a long night and a busy day already," Davidson said. "Who knows when I'll get a chance to eat again?" He began buttering and syruping the arrangement of small pancakes on his plate. "I got some good stuff this morning, so this is a reward."

"No need to justify it, Woody." Hunt scooted his plate a few inches to the left and put his open notebook on the table beside it. "So, finish your breakfast and then tell me about your morning." He sliced his tomatoes and sausages into the same number of sections each, then forked pieces together and chased them with a bite of buttered toast and alternating sips of coffee and ice water.

In a few minutes, Davidson leaned back again as the waitress took his empty plates away. When she was gone, he leaned forward with elbows and forearms on the table, his own notebook open in front of him. "First stop was the Register of Deeds to look into the house on 16th. Owner is a man named Hugo Rodgers. He's had the place since June of 1977." Davidson took a sip of coffee and watched Hunt scribble in his notebook. "Sorry, that's Rodgers with a *d*. No other real estate in that name in the metro area."

"What do we know about Mr. Rodgers?" Hunt said with a slight twitch of the lips behind his mustache.

"Not much in the way of personality details yet." Davidson drained his coffee cup. "That's my afternoon." He waved off the waitress who suddenly appeared with her refill pot. "No thanks." He watched her walk away and then turned back to Hunt. "I picked up more at the county clerk's office."

In January 1978, Davidson summarized, Rodgers applied

for and received a business license for Rodgers Promotions. The mailing address was a box in the post office nearby on Acklen, but the physical address was Rodgers's property on 16th. Business activity at the physical location was described on the license application as record promotion.

"That's interesting," Hunt said.

"I thought so, too," Davidson said, a slight smile thinning his lips.

"You have a bombshell you're saving, Woody. I know the look you get."

Davidson's smile widened, and his eyebrows danced. "You got me, amigo." He picked up his notebook and began summarizing the rest of what he'd written at the county clerk's office. "A few years after securing the business license—we're in August of '86 now—Hugo Rodgers and a Nancy Castellano applied for a marriage license and then got hitched at the courthouse."

"Nancy Castellano?" Hunt said.

Davidson nodded, his eyebrows dancing again.

"Cassie Nance?" Hunt said.

"That's what I'm thinking." Davidson closed his notebook and took a swig of his ice water. "Hugo Rodgers and Nancy Castellano filed for divorce just after their second anniversary last year."

"Fault grounds?"

The waitress swooped by and laid their ticket on the table.

Davidson watched her walk away again. "Adultery," he said, turning back to Hunt. "They filed a joint petition, and both cited adultery."

"Well, well." Hunt knuckled both sides of his mustache. "If Nancy Castellano became Cassie Nance, then we can safely guess she'd committed adultery with Earl Hill." He sipped the last of his water. "And Rodgers becomes our prime suspect for shooting the two of them."

"That'd make sense."

"I wonder who Rodgers committed his adultery with." Hunt scooted his chair back and stood up. "Maybe Perras can answer that."

"But what does he have to do with this mess?" Davidson asked as he stood up from the table as well.

"I don't know, but last night MacRae said he'd seen a black IROC-Z parked at Rodgers's house yesterday afternoon."

"Perras's?"

"That's what I'm guessing." Hunt pulled his wallet from a back pocket. "And you might not have heard while you were digging through deeds and licenses—"

"What?"

"Patrol let me know that the car was burned to a crisp in the early hours this morning."

"Anybody hurt?"

"No, we had Perras downtown, of course. Slight damage to a couple of nearby vehicles. But Perras apparently always took up a minimum of three spaces for the Chevy and his patrol car, so not much collateral damage."

"Sounds like that ass," Davidson said. "Too bad he's in lockup. I'd like to rassle him a bit." He lifted his water glass. "You think Rodgers torched it?"

"Probably." Hunt tossed a twenty-dollar bill on the table. "Nice work, Woody. Breakfast is on me."

"Good man," Davidson said, crunching ice between his molars. "I'll get you next time."

They exited the Pancake Pantry and walked left on Belcourt Avenue.

"So," Davidson said. "If we're thinking that Hughes's murder a month ago was connected to song charts, the fact that Rodgers is in the record promotion business might tie him in."

"As long as the development of the Hughes case is headed in the right direction, this is definitely interesting news about Rodgers."

"That feels good to me, too," Davidson said. "And you're

thinking that Perras was at Rodgers's house yesterday? That it wasn't just somebody else's Chevy?"

"Between its presence at the address, last night's attack on MacRae, and the car fire, I am."

They crossed the street and walked alongside 20th Avenue South.

"Oh, speaking of cars." Davidson stopped. "Almost forgot. While I was at the county clerk's office, I looked up Rodgers in vehicle registrations." He pulled out his notebook and flipped through it to find the last page he'd written on. "If that red Taurus with the Jersey plates is involved somehow, it's not his."

"No?"

"But he does have a vehicle registration for an '86 Buick Grand National."

"Not seen at the house."

"Maybe his ex got it in the divorce?"

"Maybe," Hunt said. "If that's the case, then we need to take another look around Cassie Nance's address. It might have been parked somewhere around there this whole time."

They crossed the street to a lot on the corner of 20th and Acklen.

"So," Hunt said across the roof of his '85 Fiat 132. "When I get back to the station, I'm going to get somebody to work on two things—the Taurus tag number MacRae gave me last night and a warrant for a forensic search of Rodgers's house."

"If you get the warrant done for later this afternoon, let me know, and I'll meet you there." Davidson unlocked the door of his '87 Ford Ranger. "Meantime, I'm gonna barge in on some of my Music Row contacts to see what I can find out about Rodgers and his wife. Surely to God somebody knows if Nancy Castellano Rodgers and Cassie Nance are the same person."

"Good luck with that. When I get the warrant, I'll leave a message with dispatch." Hunt unlocked the Fiat. "Now I'm gonna go squeeze Perras until he leaks from all orifices."

FORTY-NINE

Ezra MacRae and Sally Evans slid into a booth at Dalt's, ordered supper, and when their Corona Extras arrived, looked at each other across the tabletop and clinked their bottle necks together.

"That was some awesome thrifting," Sally said.

"Benny Jack will be the best dressed man on the streets of Nashville," Ezra said.

They each took a swig of beer and then set down the bottles to await their food.

"What's your prognosis for Mr. Boudreau, Nurse Evans? If I may ask."

"Well, barring divine intervention, he'll be released to rehab either tomorrow or Wednesday. Tomorrow's more likely, given his situation."

"What does that mean?"

"Homeless. Uninsured. You know."

"Where's that gonna leave him?"

"Probably Edgefield Rehab over in east Nashville. That's where most of our cases like Benny Jack go post-op."

They fell into small talk, occasionally taking sips from their beers or ice waters as they chatted and laughed.

"A Nashville native?" Ezra said when she told him she was born and raised there. "I haven't met many of those."

"We're a rare breed."

"You are, for sure." Ezra immediately felt a warmth in his cheeks.

Her smile seemed suddenly shy, and her blue eyes looked askance at him as the waitress arrived with a plate in each hand.

"Cobb Salad with blue cheese and honey mustard on the side?"

"That's me," Sally said.

"And the usual Dalt's Club for you," the waitress said.

Ezra looked at her face but couldn't remember her waiting on him before. "Thanks."

"'The usual'?" Sally said when the waitress turned away.

"I guess I eat here too much and always get the same thing."

They ate without speaking for a couple of minutes.

Ezra washed down a mouthful of sandwich and chips with a swig of Corona Extra. "So, did you train as a nurse here?"

She held up a finger and finished chewing a bite, likewise washing hers down with beer. "No, I did leave Nashville for that. Vandy and MTSU have great nursing programs, but I went to MUSC in Charleston, South Carolina, just for a change of scenery." When Ezra lifted his chin and pursed his lips, staring over her head for a moment, she said, "Medical University of South Carolina."

"Ah, got it," he said. "My parents love Charleston."

"So do I," she said. "I miss it."

When they finished eating, the waitress took their plates, then picked up their empty beer bottles, and refilled their water glasses.

"Maybe you could show me around it one of these days," Ezra said. "Charleston, I mean."

"Maybe." She tucked a wayward, wavy lock of blonde hair behind her ear. "I need to go to the restroom." She slid out of the booth.

Dumbass MacRae, he thought, watching her walk away. *Dumbass, dumbass, dumbass.* He felt a kiss on the top of his head—a kiss exaggerated with a loud "Mwah!"—and then, sensing diners around him turn his way, watched a big man slide into Sally's seat.

"Hey, good looking," the man said.

Ezra recognized the voice coming from the face he didn't know.

"Yeah, it's me," the man almost sang. "Hugo Rodgers."

Ezra stared first into the gleaming blue eyes and then at the hand extended over the table.

"Don't leave me hanging, MacRae," Rodgers said. "Let's press flesh and be friendly."

Ezra glanced around and saw that others had turned back to their own business, then shook the hand, feeling as if he'd been transported into some kind of dream.

"And yeah, that's my real name," Rodgers said. "Your friends in the PD are figuring me out as we speak, so I don't got too much reason to hide it now."

Ezra finally found his voice. "What are you doing—"

"Having dinner, much like yourself and Nurse Sally Evans," Rodgers said.

"What—"

"We need to speed this up a bit, MacRae, so Sally can have her seat back." Rodgers looked toward the restrooms and then back at Ezra. "So, what do I want, you might ask? Besides a roll in the hay with a big strapping boy like you?" He pressed a crumb of something on the table with the pad of a finger, lifted it to his nose, and sniffed it. "Well, besides that, I don't want much anymore." He licked the crumb into his mouth. "But I'll tell you what I don't want," he said. "I don't want to go down in front of Nashville folks. People I've worked with. Carted through the streets like some monster." He jabbed the tip of a straightened index finger against the tabletop. "I don't want to die and be forgot in two shakes." He picked up Sally's water, sniffed the rim of the glass, and took a sip. "Most've already forgotten that poor boy Dixon had shot last month. And they're forgetting Burl as we speak." He took another sip of Sally's water and set down the glass. "I don't want that."

"I thought you killed that guy from *Cash Box*."

"Your brain grabs at the strangest things, MacRae. Must be the songwriter in you." Rodgers turned again in the direction of the restrooms. "If I'm gonna go out in a blaze of glory, I wanna do it somewhere it'll leave an impression." He began to slide out of the booth. "Somewhere they'll tell a good story about it. For years. Maybe make it into a new murder ballad. You ever write one of those?" He dipped his index finger in Sally's glass and then took the fingertip between his lips and sucked off the water. "And in answer to at least one question running around in that handsome noggin of yours, I followed you here from Utah by way of your stop over on Wyoming."

Ezra hung fire.

"Just wanted to give you a kiss, introduce myself, and say I'd be seeing you." Rodgers slid off the edge of the booth bench and stood. He licked two fingers and dipped them into the pocket of his Hawaiian shirt, pulled out two twenty-dollar bills, and dropped them on the table. "Dinner for you and Sally is on old Hugo."

With a glance over his shoulder, Rodgers turned and strode to the exit, disappearing into the evening just as Sally slid into her seat.

"Strangely warmed," she said with a smile.

"What?" Ezra said, blinking himself back to the moment.

"My seat," she said. "It's warmer than I left it, which is weird." She half turned and looked toward Dalt's front door and turned back again. "I saw a man standing here. Did he sit down with you?" She leaned slightly forward over the table and peered into his face. "Are you okay, Ezra?"

"I'm gonna be sick." He scooted out of the booth. He stood unsteadily and then stopped with his hand on the back of his seat. "Don't drink your water."

FIFTY

Hugo stopped outside the Dalt's entrance and turned to see Sally Evans slide into the booth across from Ezra MacRae, who, after only a moment, stood and said something to her and then hustled toward the restroom. He smiled to himself and walked to his car and then headed back toward downtown, taking Harding Pike, which soon became West End. He drove through the 31st Avenue intersection and, a block or so before he reached Centennial Park, turned left into the lot of Cat's Records. After a few steps toward the store's entrance, he stopped and turned and crossed contiguous parking lots back in the direction of 31st and Nancy's apartment. Standing on the corner below the building as if waiting for the light to change for crossing, he looked right toward where his Buick had been parked only a few hours earlier.

A Metro PD patrol car sat darkly on each side of the street.

Hugo stood a moment and then returned to the Buick.

He continued along West End until it became Broadway, crossed over the interstate loop, and entered downtown. Driving slowly as if trying to take in everything around him one last time, he continued until he could see down the incline toward Lower Broadway and the Cumberland River beyond, then turned right onto 8th Avenue South, which he took to Wedgewood, where he again made a right. As he approached 16th Avenue, he slowed and then took the right, and within a few feet, his house came into view, emerging from behind a large Southern magnolia that stood on the edge of his front yard.

The place glowed inside. Two figures stood on the front

porch, silhouetted against the living room's picture window—one round like a sumo wrestler, one thin like a scarecrow.

Hugo drove past and turned left on Edgehill, crossed to 21st, and within ten minutes he was seated in a booth in Brown's Diner.

"Hugo Rodgers," the waitress said as she approached. "I haven't seen you in a while."

"Laurel Dauphin, I haven't been here in a while."

"Where's our Lucky boy?" She handed him a menu.

Hugo held the menu at arm's length. "I think he's beyond cheeseburgers and chicken fingers."

"I had a feeling that might be coming. All that pumping iron and such." She took an order pad from the pocket of her apron. "Made him a great little body, though, you know?" She pulled a pen from her cleavage. "You eating?"

He handed the menu back to her. "I've already eaten onion rings over at Dalt's," he said. "But I can't be in here without having a cheeseburger and a Budweiser."

"Fries?"

"Why not," Hugo said. "Never know when—"

"I'll get your beer." She turned away and spoke to the table beside his. "Y'all still doing okay?" When the couple said they were fine, she veered toward the kitchen window. "Junior! Cheeseburger and fries for Hugo!"

Junior's face appeared in the window. "To go?"

"Not 'to go,' Junior! For Hugo! You need new batteries for your hearing aids?"

"I don't wear hearing aids."

"Well, there it is." She turned toward the patrons as they laughed.

The cheeseburger arrived with pickles speared onto the top bun with a toothpick, grilled onions atop melted Velveeta, mustard squeezing from under the patty, and lettuce hanging out over the bottom bun.

"Looks good," Hugo said to Laurel when she set down one plate with the burger and another with the fries.

"Enjoy," she said and hurried away.

He sat and ate, staring at the empty seat across the booth. When he washed down the last bite of the burger, he seemed not to notice he'd finished and looked down at his plate for more. He kept his fingers curled on his beer glass and looked up as Laurel arrived again.

"You want another?" she said.

"Beer?"

"Beer or burger or anything else," she said.

He downed the last swallow of Budweiser. "Better not," he said. "Just the check, I reckon."

When he paid and stood to leave, Laurel appeared beside him once more, this time with a warm hand on his upper arm and her face looking up into his. "Hugo, you and Lucky be careful, okay? Music Row's turned into a dangerous place lately."

He covered her hand with his. "Thanks, Laurel," he said. "We'll be all right." He turned to leave but stopped and turned back to her. "Hey, y'all got a phone book I can look at?"

He drove past his house once more and found it still brightly lit, but the figures no longer stood on the front porch. Downtown on Broadway again, he continued to 2nd Avenue South and turned left up the hill. He crossed the Cumberland River on the Woodland Street Bridge, passed under the interstates, and turned right on South 5th Street. After two blocks, he turned left on Fatherland and pulled to the curb beside the "City of Edgefield" historical marker. He cracked each window a couple of inches, turned off his headlights and engine, and reclined the seat. After a moment, he sat up again, took his revolver from the glovebox, and checked the cylinder to see it was fully loaded. He put the gun in the floorboard between his legs and just under the edge of the seat and lay back once more and closed his eyes.

FIFTY-ONE

All the lights in 1619 were still on, even though the forensics team had been gone for half an hour. Detectives Hunt and Davidson sat across from each other at the kitchen table with coffees a uniform had brought. Their notebooks lay open beside their cups as they compared and exchanged notes on the afternoon.

"Apparently Hugo Rodgers was a fairly big deal once upon a time," Davidson said. "Pretty successful in the promotion game through most of the seventies and into the eighties, but the good times tapered off over the past seven or eight years."

"Why is that?" Hunt asked.

"I got at least three possible explanations for you." Davidson looked at his notes, then flipped a page. "Probably the simplest is that the Nashville music industry changed a good bit after that cowboy movie came out."

"What cowboy movie?"

"What was it, *Urban Cowboy*?" He looked again at his notes. "The soundtrack went pretty big, and a lot of country records were crossing over to the pop market. Or trying to." He sipped his coffee and then made some small correction to what he'd written earlier in the day. "Of course, that required record promoters like Rodgers to deal with pop stations as well as the country ones they already had in their pockets. Word is from folks who've been around a while that Rodgers didn't like the new sound he was hired to promote or the new people, the pop people, he had to deal with." He pressed his hands flat to the table on either side of his notebook and yawned. "So, the less interested, the less successful."

Hunt jotted down a couple of notes. "All right." He flipped to a fresh page. "Next?"

"Okay, rather than double down on his record promotion business, Rodgers is said to have taken some of his resources for that and put them into trying to make himself a music mogul. Started a production company for recording and a publishing company, neither of which he filed any paperwork for."

"Doesn't seem to be the direction you want to go when you're struggling—taking on more."

"Right. And according to Charlie Lamb, who's done publicity work up and down Music Row for decades now, even though Rodgers had been a pretty good record promoter, he wasn't particularly good at knowing what makes a hit song or how to make a hit record." Davidson took another sip of his coffee and made a face. "So, no, not a good strategy to take some relatively thin talent and spread it even thinner." While Hunt scribbled, Davidson stood up and removed the plastic lid from his coffee cup, found a mug in a cabinet, and poured in the remaining coffee. "Want me to do yours?" he said over the whir of the microwave.

"I'm fine," Hunt said. "Third explanation?"

"A woman." Davidson took his mug from the microwave. "Always a woman, you know, but in this case maybe a man, too." He sat down at the table again. "Long story short, a fellow named Billy Keith—who, by all accounts, operates right on the outside edge of law and ethics—hooked up with this band down from New Jersey, promising to make something out of them. But pretty soon, he dropped them for no reason anybody understands. All of the band but two hoofed it home to Jersey. Those two"—he looked at his notes—"our Nancy Castellano and a guy named Lucio Centopani, fell in with Rodgers. And as we know, Rodgers married Castellano and made some recordings of her. Shopped her around Music Row for a year or two with no success." He sipped his coffee. "Looks like when he failed to make her a star, she split and took up with Hill."

"I have news on Centopani," Hunt said. "But I want to know what you learned."

"Not much," Davidson said. "Just that Rodgers apparently turned his imagined star-making talents on this kid and promoted him under the stage name Lucky Baker. But again, no cigar." He drained the last of his borrowed mug and stood up from the table. "Everybody I talked to who knew anything about this particular situation said Rodgers seemed to get more and more out there as time went on. Some even said he got scary—attitude, behavior, things he'd say." He turned to the sink and turned on the hot water.

"That last bit ties in with what I got from Perras this afternoon," Hunt said.

"Which last bit?"

"The bit about Rodgers being a scary individual."

Davidson put a finger under the tap and squirted dishwashing liquid into the mug. "This case just gets curiouser and curiouser." He yanked a paper towel from the roll hanging under a cabinet and washed the inside of the cup with it.

"It's about to get even more so," Hunt said. "The disfigured body we found yesterday morning is Centopani's."

The mug slipped from Davidson's hand and clattered into the sink without breaking.

"My reaction exactly," Hunt said. "Except I didn't have a mug in my hands." He waited for Davidson to rinse the cup, dry it, set it back in the cupboard, and then sit down again. "Now that the breakables are put away, you might also be interested in Perras's claim that Rodgers and Centopani were lovers, a claim that autopsy findings seem to confirm."

Davidson stared open-mouthed across the table. "These guys never heard of AIDS?" he said at last. He hunched over his notebook and jotted down a few words and tagged them with exclamation points, then looked up at Hunt.

"I don't know," Hunt said. "But I think we have to be careful here. If we begin working from the premise that these fellows' homosexual relationship is a crime, on any level, we're going to prejudice our investigation."

Davidson looked at his notebook again, rolling his pen in his fingers. "Understood." He touched the tip of his pen to the paper but lifted it without writing anything, stood up quickly, and then leaned back against the counter. "Wait a minute. How does Perras know this stuff?"

Hunt drained the last of his coffee. "Perras was friends with these guys, and I'm convinced he's played the mole for Rodgers, whether he knew it or not. What he claims is that Rodgers has some kind of weird power over people." Hunt closed his notebook. "In fact, according to Perras, Rodgers practically ordered last night's attack on MacRae."

"Wow," Davidson said and then looked closely at Hunt. "So, was it Rodgers that beat the shit out of Perras before he got pepper sprayed?"

Hunt stood up and scooted his chair to the table. "I have my suspicions, but he wouldn't say." He stopped and met Davidson's blank stare.

Detective Davidson slowly returned to the moment. "Well, was Perras, like, involved in some sort of threesome with these guys?"

"He also had no comment on that," Hunt said. "The fact that he threw up at the crime scene yesterday morning says something, I think. But again, Woody, we can't operate on that assumption." He turned away toward the living room. "Hit the light when you come out, will you?"

FIFTY-TWO

Ezra sat talking with Sally in the Tempo, parked in front of her house on Wyoming Avenue. When he'd returned to the booth in Dalt's, he told her the whole story—from the murders of Burl Davies and the other two, including the shooting of Benny Jack, to what Hugo Rodgers had said while she was in the restroom.

"He knows where I live?"

"He followed me. Which I guess means that he was watching my apartment."

The drive back to her house had been quiet. Ezra wondered where Rodgers went when he left Dalt's and what he intended to do next, wondered if maybe the man was following them again. He also wondered what Sally was thinking, surprised that she seemed neither angry with him for putting her in this position nor afraid of Rodgers and the threat he posed. He'd wondered as he pulled to the curb outside her house if Mel would like her and if this could be considered a first date and if he should try to kiss her.

"I could come in and sleep on the couch," he said. "Or the floor."

She laughed. "There's no need. My dad has way more guns that he ought to have."

"You live with your parents?"

"They're just here for a couple of weeks. They come every Easter and stay." She picked her purse up from the floorboard and held it in her lap. "They live in Florida now or in their camper on the road." She looked toward the one light shining

251

on the porch and the lamp burning in the window. "I grew up in this house." She turned to him and smiled. "And who could've guessed what trouble Jesus, of all people, would bring to my doorstep."

He leaned his forehead into a palm.

She laughed and leaned over and kissed him on the cheek. "Now that's absolutely the last time." She got out of the car.

He got out too, and met her at the passenger's side back door. He handed her a couple of bags from their thrifting and carried a couple more himself as he walked her to the porch, where they stood underneath a light fixture made mostly of amber glass.

"I had a great time," she said. "Thanks."

"Same here."

"I think Benny Jack will be thrilled with his new threads."

"Me, too."

She made as if to kiss his cheek again, but he turned his head and touched his lips to hers.

"Naughty, naughty." She waggled an index finger in the air between them.

"Naughty Naughty"—John Parr, songwriter.

She turned the handle on the storm door and then stopped and looked back at him. "Of course, if you're afraid to go back to your apartment by yourself, you're welcome to stay here and sleep on the couch." She smiled again. "Or the floor."

When he returned to his place at Youngstowne Square, he doubled his usual checks to be sure nobody was in the apartment with him. Then he dished out and microwaved a small bowl of pilau, grabbed a beer from the fridge, and carried bowl and bottle to the couch, where he pressed the playback button on his answering machine.

The first message was from Stone R. "Got your guitar ready. Good as new. Bring the cash balance and pick it up any day and any time after ten in the morning."

The second message was from Greg Black at Music City Pool Management. "Hey, Ezra, it's Greg at a little after five o'clock. Listen, I know the Pigott pool down on Glen Leven is on your schedule for tomorrow. Just got a call from Mrs. Pigott asking if you can come early rather than late. By noon, if possible. Hope you can swing that."

The image of Cora's curves and cascade of blonde hair shot through him like a lightning strike. But when his mind's eye began to recover from the flash, the image that emerged, steadied, and stayed was of Sally Evans at her front door—a smile on her face, her hand on the storm door's handle.

He rinsed his bowl and fork and beer bottle, left the bowl and fork in the sink, and put the bottle in the trash. Then he stripped off his clothes, brushed his teeth, and crawled into bed, where he lay in limbo a long time between relaxing toward sleep and jolting awake—Sally smiles across the table; Hugo Rodgers kisses the top of his head and disappears into the night; naked Kate curls against him in bed; a policeman chokes him in the living room floor while pilau boils on the stovetop; Mel yawns and lifts him against his belly in front of Ramsey's Funeral Home, his friendly bear hug strong and comforting; Cora touches him by her pool, kimono open to reveal the plunging neckline of her swimsuit; naked Kate blasts her pepper spray; gunfire echoes, blood mists the night air, and bodies fall; Sally stands at the front door, her eyes sparkling beneath the porchlight.

Tuesday, April 4, 1989

FIFTY-THREE

Ezra breathes underwater, somehow, but still feels in a looping state of panic and anxiety. The water of the pool is clear around him, but the floor of the pool is littered with leaves and twigs, scraps of paper, a pistol, guitar picks, a live mouse, toy cars, and a body lying on its right side with its back to Ezra. The man—it is a man's body— wears a red-and-white shirt wreathed with a design of black flowers and blue guitars. The body begins to roll so that its face comes into view. It is Hugo Rodgers, and he is dead. As the face rolls upward from the pool floor, the eyes stare—unmoving and unseeing. The mouth hangs open in a grimace—a death mask.

And then it is not a death mask. The eyes snap to focus on Ezra, and the mouth smiles hungrily.

The shock blinds him for a moment, and when his eyes focus again, Benny Jack floats where Rodgers had been. In an outfit Sally picked for him, he is clean and handsome. His eyes are squeezed shut, and he prays. Bubbles rise from his mouth, and as they rise and pass Ezra, he sees a single word trapped in each—Want. I. To. Home. Go. Home. To. Want. Go. I.

Benny Jack's eyelids snap open, and blood and dirt flow out of the eye sockets.

Ezra raises his face to follow the words of Benny Jack's prayer, hears his own voice praying the same for himself. He sees Cora Pigott and Sally Evans on the surface of the water in swimsuits—Cora's a wash of rainbow colors, Sally's the pale blue of her scrubs. They move on the surface as on a floor—as if they played some game, as if engaged in some struggle.

He tries to clear his eyes of water, focus, and notices that some-
body stands above them on the edge of the pool. He recognizes the
shirt of red and white and black and blue—Hugo Rodgers, risen
from the bottom. Panicked, he tries to scream a warning to Sally
and Cora, but chlorine water catches in his throat, choking him
and threatening to rush into his lungs.

Rodgers extends an arm.

Ezra ducks his head. Looking down again, he notices two things
missing from the bottom of the pool—Benny Jack and the pistol.

He looks up to see Cora and Sally still oblivious to the man who
stands over them and to the muzzle flash.

He begins to drown and screams, "Mel!"

Ezra sat up gasping for air, and when his lungs easily filled, he covered his face with his hands and exhaled between his wrists. He inhaled deeply again and this time tried to blow out the dream's horrible residue. When his heart and lungs steadied themselves, he swung his feet to the floor and sat up on the edge of the bed and looked at the clock.

7:05.

He began to busy his mind with the day as the nightmare's images faded. He could go easy getting ready, check his cleaning supplies and stop by MCPM if necessary, pick up Benny Jack's guitar, and show up at Cora's around 10:30. He'd already given Stone R. both dime bags bought from River Ben. When he checked his wallet for the twenty he would still owe the guitar tech, he had a thought and stood for a moment. Then he went into his bathroom, dug to the back of a drawer, and soon came up with a condom, which he tucked away in the wallet.

By 11:05, he was putting the finishing touches on Cora's pool.

He'd barely gotten started when she'd come out. She was barefoot. Her bouncy blonde waves and flips caught the sunlight. She wore a one-piece swimsuit, black with a band of rainbow colors that fell from her right shoulder strap, crossed her right breast, swirled down across her belly, and rounded her left hip. She seemed to attach that hip to his, staying with him as he cleaned—flirting and touching, making it difficult for him to think. He wanted to tell her that, since their last time at poolside together, he'd met somebody that he really liked. And he'd been to church twice. And he'd become a dangerous man to be close to. But he couldn't hold on to any of these thoughts. She touched him in this or that way and in this or that place, and then she filled his mind, pushing out everything and everybody else. She didn't seem to care if any of the neighbors saw. When he'd put away his gear, she led him through the sliding glass doors and into the cool fragrance of her home.

"We've been needing to do this for a long time, pool boy." She laughed. "We've got a couple hours."

In her bedroom, Ezra lost all his nerve and gave in to the moment. He watched her slide the straps off her shoulders, toss her hair, push the swimsuit down over her hips, and let it fall to the floor.

She stepped out of the pool of black and rainbow fabric. "Your turn," she said.

He pulled out his wallet, placed it on the top of a TV at the foot of the bed, and stripped off his clothes. Then he took up the wallet and fished out the condom.

"We don't need that," she said. "Save it for your new girlfriend."

"What new girlfriend?" he said, suddenly conscious of his nakedness and Cora's.

"The one I hear in your voice and see in your eyes but"— she looked down at his erection—"hasn't quite taken you over all the way."

He felt as if his entire body blushed. "It's not really a thing like that yet," he said.

"Then let's make this one time count, before it becomes a thing like that."

He put a hand on each of her lightly sunburned shoulders and held her at arm's length. "A question?"

"Ask."

"You've definitely got a thing like that—you're married," he said. "So, how is this happening?"

"It's happening because we want it to happen. And because he and I go our own ways when we really, really want to." She raised her arms and brushed his hands from her shoulders. "And right now, I really, really want to."

He picked her up in a bear hug, and when she scissored her legs around his waist, he winced at the little bit of soreness remaining from Sunday night's attack. "I guess I'll have to take your word for it," he said, any pain quickly forgotten.

Unlike Kate's lovemaking, which was intense and under her control, Cora's was a free-for-all of both expected and unexpected sensations and sounds. They laughed and moaned as they wrestled from one corner of her king-sized bed to another.

When the bedside telephone rang a few minutes into the match, they froze and gave each other fake surprised looks and then let it ring. When it stopped, they started again, but after only a few seconds the ringing resumed.

"I should answer," she said with a sigh. She picked up the receiver and put it to her ear as she lay beneath him, her green eyes looking up into his brown. "Hello?"

Ezra was surprised that she didn't sound in the least distracted or out of breath.

"Yes," she said. "I believe he's still here." Then she winked at him. "I think he's just about to finish up." She put her finger to his lips when he almost laughed. "Should I ask him to call you back when he finishes?" She listened, and her face turned serious. "Oh, okay," she said. "Hold on while I go get him." She lay the receiver on the nightstand, and, with a finger to her own lips now, they waited a few seconds. Then she picked up the receiver again and handed it to him.

"Hello, this is Ezra MacRae."

"Ezra, it's Greg. Listen, something serious has happened, and you need to call Sally Evans as soon as you can."

"What is it?"

"I don't know, but she said the police were there."

"Police were where?"

"I don't know that either. Just call her."

"Did she leave a number?"

Greg gave him the number, and Ezra repeated it aloud so that Cora could help him remember. Then he disconnected the call and began dialing Sally, saying each number aloud again as Cora nodded confirmation and smiled beneath him.

"Edgefield Nursing and Rehab," a woman's voice said.

"Hi, is Sally Evans there?"

"Hold on," the woman said. "Here she is."

"Hello? Ezra?" Sally's panicked voice said.

"What's wrong?" he said. "Are you okay?"

"Yes, yes," she said. "I'm okay."

The strangeness of the situation struck him, as Sally filled his ear and Cora filled his eyes. He raised up, straddling her, his knees and calves pressed tightly against her hips and thighs.

Sally said something he either didn't catch or couldn't comprehend.

"Will you say that again?"

"That man has taken Benny Jack," she said. "That man from Dalt's last night. He must've been waiting here at Edgefield. When nobody was looking, he just walked off with him still in the wheelchair."

"Where did he take him?" Ezra said. "I mean, does anybody know?" He looked down at Cora, who offered an exaggerated frown with her bottom lip stuck out and then mouthed the word *Go*.

She steadied him with a hand as he climbed off and let her fingers trail down his thigh as he stood up from the bed.

He forced his attention back to Sally on the line. "And how did you find out?"

"I came with the transport to help Benny Jack feel safe, and I took my eyes off of him too."

"Hey, it's not your fault," he said, standing naked in Cora's bedroom. "It'll be all right."

Sally's voice began to shake. "Can you come get me? Where are you?"

He looked at Cora, who had rolled to her side and lay looking back at him. "Sure, I'll come get you," he said. "I'm at a client's pool down below Berry Hill. Where's Edgefield?"

She gave him the address on South 5th Street in East Nashville. "Please hurry," she said. "Can you take me to your place? Maybe he'll call you like he's done before."

"Sure, I'll be there as soon as I can."

Cora sat up on the side of the disheveled bed. When he handed her the receiver, she laid it in the cradle.

"I won't ask you to explain," she said. "But I'm sorry we couldn't—" She stopped and stood and stretched her arms toward the ceiling, lacing her fingers above her head, arching her back, and flexing the muscles in her legs. "Now we have unfinished business."

"I'd stay if I could," he said, pulling on his underwear.

"Damn right you would." She began picking out clothes and putting on one piece at a time. "So, since we didn't finish, we can't technically call for a rematch, can we?"

"I'll have to look into those rules," he said with a nervous chuckle and buttoned his pants. "I'm sorry in more ways than one, but I've got to find out what's going on." He pulled his long-sleeved MCPM T-shirt over his head and then sat down on the bed to put on his shoes.

"I understand," Cora said. When he stood up from the

bed fully clothed, she embraced him—quick and tight—and released him.

As soon as he was out of her presence and hurrying to get to Sally at Edgefield Nursing and Rehab, he felt guilty about his time with Cora Pigott, guilty and weak. And he was afraid, not about what awaited him at Edgefield and not about what Hugo Rodgers might do to Benny Jack. He was afraid that Sally would know what he'd been doing—that she would look at him and know, that she would smell him and know. He pinched portions of the body and sleeves of his shirt and lifted them to his nose, but he couldn't detect anything other than the odor of chlorine.

When he pulled to the curb in front of the Edgefield facility, Sally hurried across the lawn and got in. She twisted in her seat and hugged his neck, breathing deeply.

This'll be it, he thought.

But she let him go after a moment and settled in her seat. "I think we ought to go to your place," she said. "Did I say that already?"

On the drive to Youngstowne Square, she told the story of what had happened up until the point Hugo Rodgers took Benny Jack. At the hospital, she'd helped him dress in his new clothes, which she said he loved and was immediately proud of. Then she rode in the back of the transport van to help him get settled at the facility. Edgefield's manager and a CNA leader took Sally upstairs to check out a couple of beds they were considering for Benny Jack. While they were gone, the transport driver had to use the restroom and, even though he asked a male CNA he met as he entered the building to look after Benny Jack for a couple of minutes, the young man didn't come outside immediately. Apparently, Rodgers had simply emerged from nowhere and walked away, pushing Benny Jack in front of him.

"How do you know it was him?"

"A patient and another CNA were smoking at an open

window on the second floor and saw it happen. They thought it was just a family member taking a new patient on a stroll until all the commotion. The man had on the same clothes I glimpsed him wearing at Dalt's last night." She quieted when they entered the Sylvan Park area.

After a short drive, he put on his turn signal and entered the Youngstowne Square complex.

"We live close to each other," she said.

"Do you know Penny down at The Store?"

"I love Penny," she said.

"She calls me Young MacRae."

"I'm Sally Goodin'."

"That's an old Woody Guthrie ballad."

"I know."

Inside the apartment, they sat on the couch and waited.

"Did you have lunch?" he asked after a few minutes.

"I didn't," she said. "I couldn't have eaten a little while ago, but I think I could now."

"Well, I have this really good rice dish that a friend and I made a couple nights ago. It's a Lowcountry thing called pilau." He thought for another moment. "And I've got a Chef Boyardee pizza kit—pepperoni, I think."

"Let's do the pizza," she said. "That'll occupy us for a while."

"I like the way you think, Sally," he said.

"Well, I got sick on pilau once in nursing school."

They went into the kitchen and began working through the simple processes. And as they worked, she asked about the pilau and about the friend he'd made it with. He told her about Kate, how their relationship both pleasured and frustrated him, how it had been her obstinate absence that had put him in front of Ave Canora at the moment when Hugo Rodgers had opened fire on Burl Davies, his acquaintances, and Benny Jack.

He slid the pizza into the oven and closed the door and set the timer.

"And you have no idea what you did to upset her so much on Saint Patrick's?"

"No idea," he said. "I guess I get blackout drunk sometimes, so I must've done something in that condition."

"That's not healthy, you know," she said. "Not healthy in so many ways."

"I'm working on it," he said. He almost segued into telling her about Cora Pigott but stopped himself. "Your turn."

She'd had a boyfriend in high school, but that ended when she left for college. She'd had another boyfriend through most of her time in Charleston, but that ended when she finished her degree and returned to Nashville. Since then, she'd dated only a handful of times, and nothing had developed beyond a movie and a meal or two. "Kind of a nurse's curse," she said. "At least it is for me."

When the pizza was ready, they cut it and sat at the table and ate it with glasses of Diet Mountain Dew.

The telephone rang, and they startled and looked at each other. Ezra stood up and went to the living room with Sally following.

"Hello?"

"Hello there, Ezra MacRae, this is your ol' buddy Hugo Rodgers calling from Knoxville."

"What are you doing in Knoxville? Where's Benny Jack?"

"Now don't get your panties in a wad, MacRae. Benny Jack's just fine. He's sitting in the car eating a Happy Meal." He paused for a vehicle to go by. "And we're not doing anything in Knoxville besides stopping at McDonald's and calling you." He paused again for what sounded this time like a motorcycle. "Just passing through. I told Benny Jack I was taking him home to Appalachia, Virginia, but we might make a stop in your Runion."

"What?"

Rodgers chuckled. "Maybe we'll see you there."

The call disconnected.

He stood for a moment, unable to put down the receiver and trying to think what he should do next. He looked at Sally. "He's going to Runion," he said as she took the receiver from him and laid it in the cradle. "I've got to go home."

Sally guided him to the couch and sat beside him. "Take a deep breath and let it out slowly," she said. "Do it with me." She breathed in deeply through her nose, held her breath for a moment, and then blew it out slowly through her mouth. "Come on, do it with me."

Ezra breathed with her three times.

"Okay," she said. "What do we need to do? First things first."

"Okay," he echoed. "I need to get in touch with Detective Hunt and let him know about that call. Maybe call Latt Edwards. I need to call Mel and warn him so that he can get my parents safe." He thought a moment. "I need to call the sheriff's office at home." He paused again. "I need to call the pool company."

Sally stood up and held out her hand. Ezra reached to take it, but she didn't pull him up.

"No, give me the keys to your car."

"What?"

"I'm going to go home and get some clothes."

"What?"

"Ezra, you're going to Runion, and I'm going with you. Benny Jack is likely to need me." She pushed her open hand at him again. "I'll be back by the time you've made your calls and packed."

FIFTY-FOUR

As soon as he'd concluded his Monday afternoon interview of Murdoch Perras, Detective Hunt had obtained a warrant to arrest Hugo Rodgers for murder, with potential other charges pending. Then, as soon as he'd learned late morning Tuesday that Rodgers had taken Benny Jack Boudreau from the rehab facility, Hunt added a count of kidnapping and made certain the warrant information was disseminated to Tennessee fusion centers for further dissemination statewide and to other states as well. Some three hours later, he was waiting for Davidson to return from the restroom and getting coffee, when the telephone on his desk rang.

"Go for Hunt," he said when he picked up the receiver.

"Detective Hunt," the dispatcher said, "I have an Ezra MacRae on the line."

"Thank you," Hunt said. "Put him through." He waited for the change in the sound when the connection switched. "Mr. MacRae, this is Detective Hunt. How—" He flipped open his notebook and picked up his pen.

Davidson returned with two cups of coffee and set one near Hunt's notepad.

Hunt lay down his pen and covered the receiver mic with his palm and whispered, "I hope you washed your hands."

"Hmm?" Davidson grunted but then apparently realized what Hunt said. "Oh, sure."

"You there?" Ezra said in Hunt's ear.

"I'm here." Hunt picked up his pen again. "And you feel

265

confident that Rodgers was telling the truth about being in Knoxville?"

"I guess," Ezra said. "I travel that way a lot. Timeframe seems right—between when he was at Edgefield and when he called."

"Hold on." Hunt finished writing his note. "Anything else?"

Ezra described his encounter with Rodgers at Dalt's the night before and then asked, "How did he know where I live?"

"How do you know he wasn't just at the restaurant by coincidence?"

"He told me."

"Mr. MacRae, you should be aware that we've discovered a leak in our ranks, and we're dealing with it. We believe Rodgers got your information from that source."

"Oh," Ezra said. "It's not Latt, is it? Latt Edwards?"

"No," Hunt said. "It wasn't Officer Edwards. He's a good man."

"I'm glad to hear that," Ezra said.

"All right, Mr. MacRae, if there's nothing else—"

"He said he might go to Runion," Ezra said. "That's where I'm from."

"Yes, we're aware of that—"

"Do I need to call Deputy Boyce?"

"Who?"

"Deputy Davis Boyce. He's with either the Runion Police Department or the Madison County Sheriff's Office. I never know which. Or if there's even a difference."

"No, we'll call him and our colleagues in"—he scanned his notebook—"Appalachia, Virginia, and give them what we have." Hunt wrote *Dep Davis Boyce* in his notebook. "Anything else?"

Ezra hung fire a moment. Then, "Why me? I mean, I can't help wondering why he seems so focused on me."

Hunt looked at the ceiling and then at Davidson. "We're not certain, but we have an idea." He put down his pen and propped his elbows on the desk. "The world that Rodgers has lived in has been coming apart recently. Our thinking is that Burl Davies wasn't the target of the attack you witnessed. The woman that night was Rodgers's ex-wife, and the other man was, well, the other man." He squeezed his eyes shut and pinched the bridge of his nose. "We think that his ex-wife was the real target and that the murder was some sort of intimate moment for him. But maybe it started a downward spiral as well." He took a quick sip of his coffee. "You with me?"

"I think so," Ezra said.

"He's also murdered another man who we think was part of the event that night. He was Rodgers's roommate and maybe even his lover, so that leaves only you and Benny Jack and Hugo, himself, as the last survivors of—"

"What about Curly Crocker?" Ezra asked. "He was in the paper, right?"

"We spoke with Mr. Crocker at the end of last week, and according to what he told us, Rodgers has not approached him." Hunt looked up at Davidson and again covered the mic with a palm. "If Edwards is on duty, ask him to check on Crocker." He pulled his palm from the receiver and then replaced it. "Make sure he checks both Crocker's publisher and his home."

Davidson nodded but didn't leave the side of the desk.

"Mr. MacRae?" Hunt said.

"I'm here."

"We'll get him. You just sit tight." When he heard no response, he drew a deep breath and took another sip of coffee. "All right, I'm going to let you go and then call the Runion and Appalachia jurisdictions and let them know what might be heading their way." He disconnected the call and looked up. "Woody, stop hovering."

"Thanks for including me in that impressive little story you just told MacRae," Davidson said. "You believe that? I mean, it makes sense to me."

267

"Well, if I'm wrong, you'll be included in that as well," Hunt said.

"Then again, Rodgers might just have the hots for MacRae." Davidson sipped his coffee. "You should've told him that."

Hunt angled his notepad so that Davidson could more easily see what he'd written during his talk with Ezra MacRae. "Get this down in yours, contact Edwards about Crocker, and then get dispatch to connect you with those jurisdictions in Virginia and North Carolina." He knuckled his mustache. "Your accent will probably be friendlier to Deputy Boyce and whoever is in Appalachia, so you talk to them."

"Sure thing, boss," Davidson said, twanging his voice like a banjo.

FIFTY-FIVE

Ezra dialed Mel.

"Hello?"

"Hey, Chief, it's me."

"Ez, I was hoping I'd hear from you soon," Mel said with a smile in his voice. "How are things in Witness Protection?"

"Well, they've gotten pretty damned serious, but details will have to wait a few hours. I'm fixing to head home, and I've got a huge favor to ask."

"Ask away."

Ezra briefly described the situation—how the identity of the killer of Burl Davies had been discovered, how it seemed this Hugo Rodgers had taken Benny Jack Boudreau and might be on his way to Runion.

"On his way here?" Mel said.

"Looks like it," Ezra said. "He called me from Knoxville earlier—like thirty minutes ago, I guess—and said he might see me in Runion." Ezra began to pace. "There's no way to know for sure, but if he's less than two hours from getting there—" His voice caught in his throat. "I'm worried about Mama and Papa. And about you."

"He doesn't even know about me, Ez."

"That's probably right, but it won't take more than a couple questions for him to find out about my folks." Ezra stopped pacing. "And about you and me." He sat down on the couch. "Having Benny Jack with him might slow him down some."

269

"It's tough to get ahead of crazy," Mel said. "But we'll do our best. Tell me what you're thinking."

"Can you help my folks figure out what to do? I just spoke to the lead detective on the case here, and he said he'd call the Runion law. I'm guessing they'll think to get Mama and Papa some protection, but I don't know that for sure or how quick they might get to it. What I know is that they'll hear it better from you than from either Deputy Boyce or me."

"I can do that as soon as we're off the line," Mel said. "And I can bring them here to the farm if Davis thinks that's a good idea."

"That works."

"When you get to town, come here first," Mel said.

A knock sounded at Ezra's door.

"Hang on a second. Somebody's here."

"Be careful, Ez," Mel said.

Ezra laid down the receiver and went to the door. He suddenly stepped to the side and put his back against the wall. "Who is it?"

"It's me," Sally said. "I'm ready to go."

He opened the door to find Sally on the stoop with a small suitcase in hand. "All right," he said. "This should be interesting." He turned away and picked up the receiver. "Hey, you there?"

"I'm here, pal. What's all the commotion?"

"Looks like there'll be two of us coming in on you in about four hours. Is that okay?"

"We can make it work. If your folks come, too, that'll make six of us."

"Six?" Ezra asked. "Is Curtis in town?"

"No, he's still up in New York," Mel said. "Caroline's here." He whispered something away from the receiver's microphone. Then, "Stop and snack if you have to, but we'll have something on the table." He paused. "If we're not in the middle of a shootout."

"Lord, let's hope not," Ezra said. "We're leaving here in ten."
His throat tightened again. "Thanks, Chief."
"Y'all drive safe," Mel said. "Love you, Ez."
"Love you too," Ezra said and hung up.

hello river
hello mountain
my its been a while yall
how you been
how you doin
still runnin long and standin tall
i been away
did you notice
that i aint been goin wild
through your shallows
down your steep trails
im feeling like your long lost child
i want sunshine
i want cool breeze
i want fishin line
i want shade trees
i been under the gun
i been prone to roam
tell mama boudreau son
benny jacks comin home
comin home to dirt roads
old heehaw episodes
biscuits and gravy
old hills gone hazy
comin home to feather beds
fryin meats and bakin breads
comin home to the bloodline
happy days and moonshine

i want sunshine
i want cool breeze
i want fishin line
i want shade trees
i been under the gun
i been prone to roam
tell mama boudreau son
benny jacks comin home

FIFTY-SIX

Runion's Deputy Davis Boyce hung up the receiver after his conversation with Nashville's Detective Davidson and wiped his palm across his mouth. He looked up at the ceiling and then at Deputy Maurice Norton. "Well dagnabbit, Maurice, looks like we might have a spot of big city trouble coming our way."

Deputy Norton, a round but tall and powerfully built young man with a light brown complexion and raven hair, set aside the paperback he'd been reading since the morning. "I was wondering, just hearing your side of the conversation."

Boyce briefly described the situation as Davidson had relayed it to him.

"You mean like a serial killer?" Norton said.

"Something like that, I reckon," Boyce said. "Let me think a minute." He looked up at the ceiling again and again wiped his palm across his mouth. "All right, get on the horn to Dan and tell him to take up a position out at the driveway to MacOde Farm. He don't need to be right at the driveway but in sight of it and keep a lookout, especially for a black '86 Buick Grand National. And tell him not to leave there without it being a real emergency."

"Yessir," Norton said. "What about me?"

"I need you to stay here and pay attention to the call-ins, particularly anything that raises your hackles. Keep your ears open." He stood up from his desk. "We should be receiving something over the wire pretty quick now, maybe even pictures of who we're looking out for. So, look up from your book now and then and keep an eye on the street. The Buick's got a Tennessee plate"—he looked down at his desk blotter—"two dash alpha two tango eight one. And we're searching for a big man, mid-fifties to mid-sixties, and a younger fellow, small, maybe in his late thirties."

Deputy Norton looked up from the notes he was taking. "Got it," he said. "What're you gonna do?"

"I'm gonna pay a visit to Reverend and Mrs. MacRae over on Glory Ridge and get them in a protected situation." He took his gun and shoulder holster from the desk drawer and strapped it on, took his jacket from the back of his chair and worked his way into it. He jingled the keys in his pocket. "I'll radio the Sheriff on my way." He turned and started down the hallway toward the rear of the building.

"Be safe, Davis," Norton said. "Got your bullet?"

"I do," Boyce said without turning and stepped out the rear door of Town Hall and into the parking lot on Back Street.

FIFTY-SEVEN

After they exited I-40 at Newport, Ezra drove them into the mountains, following US 25-70 and crossing the French Broad River twice. They descended from a ridge via deep curves into Hot Springs, drove through the small downtown area, and crossed the French Broad a third time. At the end of the bridge, they turned right on Highway 251 and headed toward Runion along the river's edge.

"No straight ways to get here?" Sally Evans asked.

"Afraid not," Ezra said. "You gonna be sick?"

"Not yet."

"If you start feeling like you're gonna be, let me know." He reached over and patted her knee and then let his hand rest there. When Sally put her hand on his and left it, he felt a breathless thrill in his chest. "We're almost home."

They passed Chunn's Tavern and crossed the bridge over the Laurel River's confluence with the French Broad. They rose up through a deep switchback to the right and a sharp curve to the left, and then they were on the north end of Main Street, where Ezra slowed and pulled to the curb and stopped in front of the *Runion Recorder* office and Arrowood Pharmacy, allowing Sally—and himself—a view of the small downtown.

Even though it was only 8:15, Runion's single traffic light was already blinking for the night. The only two places still showing signs of life were on their left—Runion Pizzeria and Town Hall with its jail and legal offices.

"I should go check in with Deputy Boyce if he's around."

Ezra unlatched his seatbelt and opened his door. "Feel free to take the self-guided tour if you want."

As he started across the street, he heard the Tempo's passenger door open and close.

"I'll meet you back here," Sally said from behind him. "Looks like it'll take about five minutes if I do the full tour."

Ezra chuckled to himself and went inside the jail.

A uniformed young man looked up from a book. "Can I help you?"

"Hey, I'm Ezra MacRae. Is Deputy Boyce around?"

"Not right now. He's actually with your parents, getting them hid away with a member of your dad's congregation." The young man stood up and extended a large, beefy hand. "I'm Deputy Maurice Norton."

"Some people call me Maurice"—"The Joker." Ahmet Ertegun, *Eddie Curtis, and Steve Miller, songwriters.*

Ezra shook the deputy's hand. "Do you know which member of the congregation?"

"He didn't say. Probably figures the fewer that knows the better, but I'm sure he'll tell you soon as he can."

"I'm heading over to Mel MacOde's, so he can reach me there," Ezra said. Then, "Are you Sherry Norton's little brother?"

"I'm her youngest brother, yeah, but I don't know about little anymore."

"You look a lot like her," Ezra said. "And I mean that in a good way." He stood for a moment and looked around. "Tell her hello for me, okay?"

Outside, Sally waited by the Tempo, and Ezra crossed to her.

"Mr. MacRae?" Deputy Norton called from the doorway. "Do you know Dan Payne?"

"I think I know who he is," Ezra said. "His little brother Dean was in my class."

"Yeah, well, Deputy Payne is keeping an eye on MacOde

Farm. I'll radio him that y'all are coming, but he might still stop you." He paused. "That's a Ford, right?"

"Tempo," Ezra said. "Deputy Norton, this is my friend, Sally Evans, a nurse from Nashville."

"Welcome to Runion," Deputy Norton said. "Wish it was under less nervous circumstances."

When they were passing the last buildings on the south end of Main Street, Sally said, "Damn, y'all grow them big up here in the mountains."

Highway 251 dropped back down to the riverside, and almost immediately Ezra turned right onto the bridge to Piney Ridge. In the middle, he slowed and pointed up to their left. "That mountain is called Five Finger, and Mel's farm is just in the foothills to the left of it."

"Where do you suppose Rodgers and Benny Jack are?" Sally asked as Ezra eased the Tempo through the switchbacks that lifted them up to Piney Ridge.

"I don't know, but if he didn't go on up into Virginia, he's gotta be around here somewhere."

The road leveled out atop Piney Ridge, and Ezra turned left toward the farm. "He must know that locals like big Deputy Norton will be on the lookout for him. My guess is he'll find some place to hole up for the night and start figuring stuff out in the morning, when he won't be so conspicuous."

"Makes sense to me," Sally said.

He turned right on MacOde Farm Road. "If he knows the general area much, he might have stopped in Newport and gotten a room." He hit his bright lights. "If he slept in his car last night, he probably doesn't want to do that again, especially with Benny Jack in tow."

"I hope he's okay," Sally said. "His bandages are already past due for changing."

The Tempo's headlights reflected off Deputy Dan Payne's patrol car parked a hundred yards or so beyond the entrance to the farm. Ezra turned his lights off and then on again and gave a quick toot of his horn, and Payne's blues flashed half a second in response.

When Ezra parked just to the right of the farmhouse porch and cut the engine, Mel and Caroline stepped out the front door. Mel wasn't in his usual up-on-the-farm attire of black T-shirt and jeans. Instead, he wore a blue denim shirt and khakis. Ezra thought a kind of glow had returned to Mel's countenance that—he realized with a bit of a shock—had been missing for so long that it seemed new rather than recovered. And at this he felt a brief burn of an old jealousy. Beside Mel, Caroline seemed much as Ezra remembered from those days when she and Mel were finishing their schooling and planning a wedding for after graduation—all before the sudden and scandalous breakup. He'd always felt she was jealous of him and was puzzled—even disturbed at times—by the deep friendship Mel and he shared. He believed she would have eventually wedged herself between them and pried them apart if she hadn't first brought on the catastrophe that nearly destroyed Mel.

As they came down the steps, Ezra stood up from the car, unsure how to greet them. But according to the Big Macs' ritual when meeting, Mel immediately lifted him in a bear hug. When he set Ezra down, they cupped the back of each other's neck with their left hands and touched foreheads together. As soon as they let go, Caroline took him in her arms and held him as tightly as Mel had, then kissed him on the cheek, and said in his ear, "Ezra, I'm so happy to see you. I'm so happy—" Her voice caught with emotion. She released him, stepped back, and put her arm around Mel's waist.

These greetings concluded, Ezra introduced Sally, and Mel welcomed the two of them into the house, then closed and locked the door.

"Are you hungry?" Mel asked.

"I hope you like chicken and dumplings." Caroline led the

way to the dining room table. "Oh, Sally, the bathroom is down the hall if you want to wash up. The little back porch is that way, too, if you smoke." She looked at Ezra with a half-smile and a raised eyebrow. "And you're welcome to wash up in the kitchen sink, if you want."

"If you go out the back or the front for any reason," Mel added, "be sure to lock up when you come back in. Them's the house rules until our current situation resolves itself."

When all were washed and refreshed, they sat down to a table laden with the promised chicken and dumplings, a heaping bowl of mashed potatoes, green beans, creamed corn, a tossed salad, and biscuits.

"Not very healthy," Caroline said as they all began to serve themselves and pass bowls around. "But the circumstances, as I understand them, call for comfort."

"Agreed," Sally said.

Against the darkness all understood—to one degree or another—to be lurking outside, they raised their voices in conversation and story and laughter, raised glasses of red wine in celebration and solidarity. They toasted and blessed each other and, in the process, nearly emptied all the bowls and the basket of biscuits.

When headlights swept across the ceiling, they grew quiet, and Ezra and Mel put their napkins in their plates and stood up.

Mel went to the door and turned on the porch light. "Looks like Deputy Boyce," he said. "Caroline, he's always hungry, so you should probably grab another plate and put the leftovers on it."

During their meandering conversation over supper, Mel had said the Sheriff was useless as both lawman and politician. But despite having no experience in law enforcement, the man had been elected based on his dubious claims to business acumen—"I'll clean up the waste in the Sheriff's chair," Mel mocked—and on the questionable entertainment value of his schtick as an angry village idiot. Deputy Boyce, Mel said, essentially led the force of five deputies, three of whom actually seemed to possess some skill and character while the other two were little more than the elected Sheriff's sycophants.

"No women, apparently," Caroline had interjected.

When Mel let Deputy Boyce in and locked the door again, he made introductions. "You know Ezra, of course," he said.

"Of course," Boyce said. "Mr. MacRae and I have history."

"And this is Nurse Sally Evans, Ezra's friend from Nashville, and Caroline Bennett, a friend of mine from back in my NC State days."

Caroline set the plate of leftovers in front of the deputy and asked him what he would like to drink.

"I could use a beer," Boyce said. "But beer and whiskey with home cooking feels a little sacrilegious to me, so I'll just have sweet tea if you don't care."

While Deputy Boyce ate and Sally and Caroline watched him and talked some between themselves, Mel stood on the porch and kept watch as Ezra carried in luggage and Benny Jack's restored guitar. When Ezra and Mel returned to their seats at the table, Caroline and Sally went into the kitchen and returned with pecan pie, French vanilla ice cream, and coffee, dessert plates and mugs.

"Lord, Miss Caroline," Deputy Boyce said as he wiped up the last bit of gravy from the chicken and dumplings and the last of the mashed potatoes with the last of the biscuits.

"Are my folks all right?" Ezra asked as the servings of pie à la mode and coffee began to make their rounds.

"They're good." Deputy Boyce forked a bite of pie into his mouth. "They're worried about you, of course." He sipped his coffee. "I tucked them away way over in the Petersburg area with one of your papa's elders, Otis Fowler and his wife Nina. They're safe."

"Can I call them?"

"I don't see why not. We don't figure this Rodgers fellow to be able to tap a phone, do we?"

"I think you should, Ezra," Sally said.

He carried his dessert plate and coffee upstairs to use the phone in the bedroom he claimed as his own.

The group remaining around the table grew quiet apart from the clink of forks on chinaware and occasional slurps at the rims of coffee cups.

Boyce downed the last swig of coffee and dropped his napkin in his plate and pushed back his chair. "Mars Hill said they'd keep an eye of the Fowler place," he said when Ezra returned to the table. "I've got Dan Payne watching your front here until seven in the morning, and I've got Brent Mack at the office, keeping an eye on things overnight. I sent Maurice Norton home to get some sleep so he can take over for Dan bright and early." He stood up from the table. "Between the four of y'all and the four of us, surely we can handle one loose cannon." He wiped his palm across his mouth and then rested both palms on his hips for a moment. "I surely hope so anyway."

When he'd gone and last pours of wine had been drained, yawns made their way around the table.

"Okay." Mel turned to Sally. "We've got two bedrooms available upstairs. One's my brother Curtis's, who's living up in New York right now, and the other's Ezra's whenever he's here. Caroline and I have our room up there as well. The couch down here folds out into a bed, but I think it's more comfortable not folded out."

"Sally can have my room," Ezra said. "I want to keep close to these doors, front and back, so I'll bed down on the couch."

Sally, Mel, and Caroline disappeared up the stairs. Then Mel reappeared with Ezra's bedding.

"You sure you don't want Curtis's room, Ez."

"I'll be all right, Chief." He leaned and looked past Mel toward the top of the stairs and nodded in that direction. "Things seem to be running smooth with Caroline," he said.

Mel looked over his shoulder toward the stairs as well. "It's weird," he said. "I'm getting used to it already." He set the stack of bedding on one end of the couch. "Maybe too quick. We're doing better, I think, talking it out face to face than we were on the phone."

"I'm happy for you," Ezra said. "Maybe a little jealous."

"Jealous of the relationship or jealous of Caroline?"

"A little of both."

"Don't be," Mel said. "You can have me anytime, Ez."

"You Can Have Me Anytime"—David Foster and Boz Skaggs, songwriters.

Mel winked and pulled Ezra into a bear hug.

"Chief, I can't tell you what it means to have you with me through this." Ezra kissed Mel's cheek as they released the hug.

"We're the Big Macs, Ez. We stick together."

After Mel disappeared up the stairs, followed by the sound of a closing door, a movement on the top step caught Ezra's eye.

Sally then came down three steps, bent below the ceiling line with a smile, and motioned for him to follow. Ezra left the bedding stacked on the couch, double checked both the front and back doors, turned off the downstairs lights, and tiptoed up to her room—his room. They didn't speak but climbed into bed and lay on their backs, side by side in the dark, hands held in the narrow space between them, her right leg laid across his left just above the knee.

Wednesday, April 5, 1989

FIFTY-EIGHT

In the house on MacOde Farm, sleep was a shy and flighty creature. It hid in the shadows beneath and behind furniture, the shadows behind doors, slowly emerging from these and approaching the beds only to duck back into darkness at the least creak or cough in the old house, the least troubled thought.

Sleep crawled through the open windows of Deputy Dan Payne's patrol car and curled up like a cat atop his thinning brown hair, making his head heavy. Throughout the long night, more of its kind rose from the back seat like stowaway assassins and clawed gently at his eyelids.

In the cabin halfway up Lonesome Mountain, sleep lived in only one place and came by only one means—in Deputy Davis Boyce's recliner by means of the tumblers of whiskey that rose and fell, filled and refilled, until he was overtaken where he sat.

To the occupants of the black Buick parked in darkness behind Runion's old mill sleep gave a wide berth.

Most of the sleep in Runion seemed gathered like sheep and corralled for the night in Deputy Maurice Norton's husky frame. He slept soundly and snored loudly, his wife beside him lulled to her own deep sleep by the steady ebb and flow of his ursine roar.

FIFTY-NINE

Mrs. Hazel Ramsey stood behind the combination reference and checkout desk in Runion's Main Street branch of the Madison County Public Library. She'd just finished the Wednesday Children's Storytime and seen the little ones out the door with their mothers and stepmothers and grandmothers and foster mothers when two men came in and approached the desk.

"Good morning, ma'am," the older and larger man said.

"Good morning, gentlemen," Mrs. Ramsey said. "How can I help you?"

"My name's Hugo Rodgers, and I'm wondering if you have any aerial photographs of the area, particularly those parts across the river."

"Piney Ridge?"

"Well, I don't know exactly. We're just passing through, but we like the look of the place. I'm nearing retirement, you see, and looking for a nice community where I can settle myself and my young charge here." He leaned a bit over the desktop and spoke more softly. "He's my retarded cousin, and I have the care of him."

"I see," Mrs. Ramsey said. "Well, I think we do have some photographs. They're not labeled with names of roads and such, but I've lived around here my whole life and can identify most anything you want to know about." She pointed out a table where the men could sit and then went to the map drawers where the photographs were kept. "You just want Piney Ridge?"

"Yes, ma'am," Rodgers said. "For starters."

She brought three enlarged photographs shot from an

airplane and spread them out on the table, adjusting them so that they connected to be as much like a map as possible. "As you can see, here's the bridge that goes over." She looped her index finger across two of the photographs. "And this is Highway 209A that runs from Runion over into Spring Creek."

"Thank you, ma'am." Rodgers seemed to study the photographs for a moment and then looked up. "We actually know somebody from the area. Do you know Ezra MacRae?"

She smiled. "I certainly do. Are y'all from Nashville?"

"Yes, we are. But we want to get out before it turns into another Atlanta, if you know what I mean."

"Or Charlotte," she said. "Yes, I know what you mean. One of our sons lives in Charlotte, and it's a frightening mess to get around in."

"Ezra always talks so fondly about places around here, but I don't know the names of them. When he's here, do you know where he likes to be?"

"Well, his parents—his daddy's a Presbyterian minister, you know—they live up on Glory Ridge, but that's closer to Jewel Hill, where his church is, and not in these pictures." She cocked her head and studied the photos. "His best friend, Melvin MacOde, runs a little family farm over on Piney Ridge. Ezra probably spends more time there than he does with his folks." She smiled. "Those boys are so close."

"Is that farm on here?"

"Let's see." She studied one photograph for a moment and then moved to another. "Of course," she said, again touching the print with a finger. "This here is MacOde Farm Road, and, yes, right here's the farmhouse."

"MacOde Farm." Rodgers turned to Benny Jack. "BJ, did we see a little sign that said there was local honey for sale at a MacOde Farm?"

Benny Jack shrugged and looked away toward the area decorated for the Wednesday Children's Storytime.

"You probably did," Mrs. Ramsey said. "Melvin has to do all manner of things to keep a farm afloat these days. And he does it all by himself."

Rodgers studied the photograph including MacOde Farm for a moment and turned to the adjacent print. "What's this funny looking property here, ma'am?" He pointed to a structure pictured beside 209A.

"Hmm. Yes, that's the Piney Ridge Holiness Tabernacle. The property looks odd in the picture because of the graveyard, which is this area behind the church."

Rodgers studied the two photographs one more moment and then stood up so suddenly that Mrs. Ramsey's breath caught and she took a step back.

"Thank you, ma'am," he said. "You've been oh so helpful." He grabbed Benny Jack by the back of his shirt collar and pulled him up. "Come on, BJ, time to go."

"Have a nice day," Mrs. Ramsey called after them and then began gathering the photographs together for returning to their drawer.

Less than ten minutes later, Deputy Davis Boyce pushed through the library doors. "Morning, Hazel," he said. He'd received faxed images during the night, but they were blurry and less helpful than he'd hoped. He showed them to the librarian. "Let me know if—" He stopped when he saw it in her face.

"They were just—" She put her hand over her mouth.

SIXTY

Ezra enjoyed the easy day, despite the anxiety that seemed to surround them. Every moment, he expected to encounter Hugo Rodgers at the turn of a corner in the house or the barn. He felt he could get too close to the edge of yard or field and be snatched into the shadows lurking just inside the tree line. But these fears couldn't get a firm grip on him. Being home with Mel grounded him in the familiarity of place and sensation, and beneath his anxiety and fear, he felt the love of this landscape and the security in this friendship.

Sally and he had lain mostly awake together through the night, but both seemed to have fallen asleep for an hour or more as the sky grew light and the sun rose. They hadn't made love during the night or in the morning light, even though their bodies remained in constant contact beneath the covers. The day found them laughing and playful as they walked the property or sat on the porch.

Just before noon, Caroline and Sally prepared and packed a lunch for Deputy Maurice Norton. Ezra and Mel walked with them to deliver their goodies.

Norton rose from his patrol car at their approach, thanked them profusely, spread the food on the car's roof, and ate.

When he finished, he tucked everything back into the picnic basket, then reached into the rear floorboard and pulled out a small cooler. "Here," he said. "Why don't y'all take this lunch Alita made for me. It's four Indian tacos, so there's one for each of you." When they tried to refuse, saying that he might want

288

them for an afternoon snack, he told them she'd packed another cooler for that. "These are really just regular tacos except the beef's done a little different and they're wrapped in frybread instead of tortillas or taco shells."

"Any word from downtown?" Ezra asked.

Norton wiped his mouth with a bandana pulled from his back pocket. "Deputy Boyce radioed a little while ago," he told them. "Said he tried to call y'all at the house, but nobody answered. Might've been as y'all were starting on your way down here." He reached through the back window of the patrol car and pulled out a quart jar of iced water. "Said he talked to Hazel Ramsey at the library about ten minutes after she'd had a run-in with the bad guys. They claimed to know you, Mr. MacRae, and were curious about MacOde Farm and the Piney Ridge Holiness Tabernacle property. Deputy Boyce suspicions they intend to come at the farmhouse from the back sometime after dark. Maybe after they think everybody's asleep." He stopped and took three hard pulls straight from the jar, and then replaced the lid. "Said he'd check out the Tabernacle quick as he gets a chance. I think he's betting on finding that Buick parked there by graveyard."

"What should we do?" Caroline said.

"Well, I'd check the house real good when you get back up there."

"I've had a lot of practice at that lately," Ezra said.

"When you've cleared all the rooms, just make sure everything's good and locked up and then stay close this afternoon. If you're outside, then stay on the porch or in the front yard where I can see you." Deputy Norton shifted his weight twice, and his leather belt creaked. "I need to step over here in the woods a minute, but I'll be here until seven or eight this evening. Deputy Boyce'll probably stop by before it gets too late in the day. If I hear anything on the radio, I'll come up to the house and let you know." Again, he shifted his weight and stood a moment with crossed ankles. "Or if you need me or Dan when he takes over, just turn the porchlight on and off a time or two."

"Thanks," Mel said.

"And thanks for the tacos," Sally said. "I'm sure we'll enjoy them."

"I like them best with a Coke." Norton hurried around the rear of the patrol car and lumbered like a bear toward the tree line.

SIXTY-ONE

Hugo eased the Buick under trees adjacent to the graveyard behind Piney Ridge Holiness Tabernacle. He engaged the footbrake and turned off the engine and looked at Benny Jack, who sat half-turned in his seat and gawking with googly eye and open mouth out the back windshield.

"Let's go for a hike," Hugo said.

Benny Jack turned to him with the same expression. "In the graveyard?"

"No, not in the graveyard, you idiot." Hugo opened the car door. "We're going on a hike through these woods here in front of us." He stood up out of the car and then leaned down and looked at Benny Jack. "Now, come on."

They followed what Hugo guessed to be the remnants of an old trail, maybe made by somebody who once lived on or near MacOde Farm and walked to church on Sundays and Wednesdays.

"I'm hungry," Benny Jack said. "And I'm thirsty."

"We don't have anything for you to drink," Hugo said without stopping. "But we're bound to cross a stream somewhere in these woods." He continued walking a few more steps and then stopped. "Did you eat all them crackers I bought you yesterday?"

"Yeah," Benny Jack said. "I ate the last pack for breakfast."

"Well, you should've said something before we got out in the middle of nowhere."

"I wasn't hungry 'til now."

Hugo picked up his pace again. "Well, that's just too bad,"

he said over his shoulder. "Now, come on, fucking douchebag." Hugo felt a sudden pang as that phrase dropped from his lips, accented in the way Lucie had said it to him not even a week before. His throat tightened, and by the light of small flashes like lightning in his brain, he tried to trace the twisted trail from his and Lucie's first drunken steps together between kitchen and bedroom to this walk in the woods with a googly-eyed little man he'd already attempted to kill once and would certainly kill when his current plan came together. *What I wouldn't give*, he thought and wished he were strolling through these dead leaves with Lucie on their way to a secluded cabin where they might relax and be completely themselves.

"I am not," Benny Jack said behind him.

"Not what?"

"I'm not what you called me," Benny Jack said. "I'm a lot of things, but I ain't whatever you said."

"Okay, fine. Come on."

Seven minutes later, Hugo stopped and put his hand out to stop Benny Jack too. "Listen," he said. "I hear a little creek. Come on."

Soon they arrived at the edge of a small stream, and Benny Jack squatted down beside it and cupped water in his hands and drank over and over.

"That's enough, now, you'll make yourself sick," Hugo stepped on a stone in the middle and then stepped to the other side. "Come on."

Benny Jack attempted the same move but slipped and sat down in the middle of the stream. He looked up at Hugo, googly-eyed and grinning. "Ah, that feels good," he said. "Come on in, sir, the water's fine."

"Fucking—" Hugo stopped himself and turned away. "Come on, Boudreau."

Within another hundred yards, Benny Jack was bent over and puking water and bile.

"I told you not to drink too much," Hugo said. "Probably something dead upstream."

Benny Jack retched his hardest at that, but nothing came up. Then he just stayed bent over with his hands braced on his knees. Slowly he recovered his breath and straightened up.

Two plopping sounds and a huff came from behind them, and they turned.

"Is that a goddamn bear?" Benny Jack asked, wide-eyed and open-mouthed again.

Hugo chuckled. "I believe it is."

The bear stood in the middle of the broken path they'd been following around the side of a hill and stared at them as they stared back.

"Is it gonna eat us?" Benny Jack whispered.

Hugo didn't respond.

"Reckon we can pet it?" Benny Jack whispered.

"Better not," Hugo said. "It ain't that big, but it could mess you up." He started to turn away. "Just come around slowly and walk on."

"I can't," Benny Jack said, still staring at the black bear. "I can't move."

Hugo turned and grabbed Benny Jack by a shoulder and yanked him around. "Come on," he said. "We ain't got time for this." He spat in the bear's direction and shouted, "Get from here!"

As they watched, the bear lumbered away toward the stream, stopping every few steps to look back at them.

"I hope you get sicker than hell," Hugo shouted. Then he turned to Benny Jack. "Now, come on. I think we're almost there."

They soon found the small utility barn Hugo had seen on the aerial photograph of MacOde Farm. It was unlocked and mostly empty. Against one wall stood a stack of six small bales of hay.

"Think you can carry one of those?" Hugo asked.

"I can try." Benny Jack tried and couldn't.

Hugo blew a big breath out his nose. "All right then, come

on." He took up a bale in each hand. He stepped outside the barn and then around back, the direction from which they'd come. He looked toward their trail, then up the hill, then down. He scanned along the lower edge of the pasture in which the barn stood. "Down there," he said. "But this way." He led them back the way they'd come until they were inside the tree line. Then he swung right and angled down the hill, taking a flanking position on the barn. He found a mostly level spot where he could stand and see the structure and its surroundings through the branches and new leaves but couldn't see them when he ducked down. "This'll do." He pulled the strings from the bales and spread the hay on top of the leafy ground. "Now, you lay down and get some sleep. I'll be back in a minute."

Hugo returned to the barn by the way they'd come. Back inside, he looked for signs that he and Benny Jack had been there. These he erased as best he could and then returned slowly to the tree line behind the barn, continuing to obscure any other indications of their passage or presence. He made his way back to Benny Jack and found him asleep, so he left the little man at peace and made his way along the tree line in the direction of the MacOde place, remembering that the librarian's photograph had shown this stretch of woods running past the farmhouse and all the way to the road. He wanted to get as close to the house as he could to try and plan for the finale he had in mind.

He smiled to himself at the thought of tables turned, thinking he was the mirror image of Ezra MacRae when Sunday—*just three days ago*—he'd spied on Hugo's house from the alley. He moved forward again, angling a little deeper into the woods to get a look at the front. He crept from tree to tree and then stopped behind one of the larger trunks and peered around to see the four people on the front porch. He was surprised and then not surprised to see Nurse Sally Evans sitting in one of four rocking chairs. In two of the other chairs sat a man and a woman he judged to be about the same age as MacRae. The man he knew would be Melvin MacOde, owner and proprietor of MacOde Farm, the woman likely his wife or girlfriend.

MacRae sat on the edge of the porch at the top of the front steps, leaning back against a timber post and facing the woods and Hugo. He had his right foot planted on the second step down and his left leg stretched out along the lip of the porch. He held a guitar in his lap and occasionally strummed a chord as the four of them talked and laughed.

Hugo watched MacRae for a long time. *A lot of love up there*, he thought. *Lots to love.* He wondered how they could smile and laugh, knowing he was somewhere close by but not knowing just how close. Still, he believed that as night fell all around the house, they would grow quiet as fear rose into their throats. *Been like that since Eden*, he thought. *Since the dark of caves and woods.*

He finally turned back the way he'd come. When he was where he couldn't see the people on the porch, he stopped and listened for their laughter and for any approaching vehicles. Then he crouched as low as he could and ran out of the trees and up to the back door. He stood for a moment pressed against the wall and listened, then peeped through the door's window. He could see through to the front porch and saw enough to know that all four remained in their places. Just inside the front windows was a large living room, where he saw part of a recliner and most of a couch with bedding stacked on one end of it. Other than that, he could see only the short hallway that ran from the living room to this back door, just inside of which, to the right, was a bathroom. He tried the knob but found it locked. Then he turned, crouched low again, and angled away to the tree line.

Benny Jack hadn't stirred.

Hugo stripped off his shirt and lay down beside the little man and tried to nap, but he couldn't get comfortable. After a few minutes of twitching and rolling his shoulders, raising his head at every noise, he began to suspect the problem. He rose and gathered his arms full of leaf-cluttered hay, stepped over Benny Jack, and respread his bedding there. Then he lay down again and slept for over two hours.

He'd dreamed he and Lucie walked in woods together, keeping watch on a bear that circled them while they searched the leafy ground for the keys to the Taurus. The dusky air beneath the trees chilled his naked skin and awakened him. He turned his head to the right and felt his throat tighten to find somebody else—*not Lucie*—beside him. He lay listening, trying to call Lucie back from the fast-fading dream. Then he sat up and roughly shook Benny Jack. "Wake up, boy," he growled. "Got a plan I need to hammer into that pea brain of yours."

SIXTY-TWO

Sunset passed and twilight progressed through its slow fade to dark while the five of them sat around the table—Mel and Caroline, Ezra and Sally, and Deputy Davis Boyce. They talked and laughed over pizza Caroline and Mel had made, and Ezra told stories about the exploits of "the Big Macs," some of which included comical and not-so-comical run-ins with Deputy Boyce.

The lawman had arrived about an hour before sunset, just as the pizzas were going in the oven. He'd easily acquiesced to Caroline's insistence that he stay for supper, but he said that while the pizzas baked, he would take a walk in the direction of the woods between farm and church.

"I've got a utility barn back there," Mel said. "Not much in it these days, but I use it from time to time."

Deputy Boyce wiped his palm across his mouth. "If that barn was on one of them pictures Hazel showed 'em, then I'll wager that's where they're headed if they're not there already."

"It's been there for years, so it's probably in the photos," Mel said. "But what'll you do if they're there?"

"Well, if I can't avoid a confrontation, it'll probably sound like *Gunfight at the O.K. Corral*," Boyce said. "But I'd rather just slip back here without Rodgers seeing me and get hold of Maurice and Dan."

"What if they're not in the barn?" Mel asked.

"You ask a lot of damn questions, Melvin," Boyce said. "If they ain't there, then I ain't gonna traipse around in the dark looking for 'em. We'll just have to let 'em come to us if they're coming."

Boyce had returned from what he called his "little reconnoiterin' stroll" to report that he'd found nothing conclusive. The barn seemed undisturbed. He could see where things had recently passed this way and that through the long pasture grass, but he couldn't find any tracks or footprints. One suspicious trail ran in a straight line between the barn and the woods, but the local potheads, he thought, might have stumbled on the place and partied there from time to time, although he'd seen no specific signs of that.

As the pizzas had come out of the oven, Deputy Boyce popped his slight paunch with the flat of both hands. "My belly's getting the best of my brain," he said. "I need to eat before I can think again."

By the time they finished supper, the windows had lost any sense of outside detail and reflected only the warm light of the interior and the people around the table.

Mel poured more wine for all except Deputy Boyce.

"I'm not much for wine," Boyce had said. He pushed his chair back from the table. "I'm going out to the squad car to radio Deputy Payne. I want him to check on the Buick over at the church—make sure it's still there—before he comes to relieve Norton." He turned the porchlight on and opened the front door. "Not yet as dark as it looks from in here." He turned the porchlight off again.

As the two couples sat around the quiet table, Ezra felt again the strange mixture of safety and anxiety. He picked up a piece of pizza crust Sally had laid aside on her plate, bit it in half, and chased it with the fresh wine Mel had poured.

Then Deputy Boyce was back. "All right, everything seems quiet, but Payne's running a bit late. Once he goes by the Tabernacle—"

"What was that?" Caroline said.

"What was what?" Boyce said.

"Listen," Ezra said. "There it is again." He stood a moment. "Oh, my God, here we go."

"What is it?" Mel said and stood up from the table.

The voice called again, coming closer and growing clearer. "Jesus?"

"It's Benny Jack," Sally said.

Deputy Boyce released the strap on his holster.

"Jesus!" Benny Jack wailed.

Ezra stepped to the door, opened it, turned on the porchlight, and stepped outside.

Benny Jack stood in the yard at the foot of the steps.

"MacRae, you're a sitting duck in the door like that," Deputy Boyce said. "Turn out that light."

Ezra took a step back into the house and turned off the porchlight. "Where's Hugo Rodgers, Benny Jack?"

"Is my Sally in there, Jesus?"

Deputy Boyce nodded at Sally Evans.

"I'm here, Benny Jack," she said. "You need to come in so I can check on your bandages."

"I'm hungry," Benny Jack said as he started up the steps. "And I'm thirsty."

Ezra kept an eye on the googly-eyed little man's progress up the steps and kept glancing out into the darkness to see if he could catch a glimpse of the evil that lurked out there. "Where's Rodgers?" he said again.

Benny Jack reached the porch and stopped. "He told me I could get out if I wanted to. Told me my Sally was here."

"I'm here, Benny Jack," she said again and came forward. "Come in and have something to eat. Then we'll see about your bandages." She put a hand on his elbow and an arm around his shoulder. "Come to the table."

"I'm thirsty, too," Benny Jack said.

Deputy Boyce nodded at Ezra and then at the little man.

"Do you know where Rodgers is?" Ezra asked.

"You mean Satan?" Benny Jack said. "'Cause that's who he is." His eyes widened when Caroline set a plate in front of him with two slices of pizza and followed this with a glass of water.

"Y'all ain't got any Miller?"

Tight smiles appeared among the group around the table.

Mel made a guitar-playing motion at Ezra, who left their circle and tiptoed upstairs. Mel then turned back to Benny Jack. "If you've been traipsing around in the woods, then you need some water before you have beer."

"Whatever." The little man took a big bite of pizza and washed it down with a gulp of water. Then he looked at Mel. "Is this your place? Woods and all?"

"Practically the whole mountain," Mel said.

"We seen a bear, me and Satan." Benny Jack took another bite and another gulp.

"You saw old Black Jack?"

"Who's that?"

"That's my bear."

"It's your bear?"

"He lives on my mountain," Mel said. "He's my bear, I reckon."

"Well, he didn't look that old," Benny Jack said. "Looked like my teddy bear growed up."

"Hey, Benny Jack," Ezra said from the foot of the stairs. "Look here."

The googly-eyed little man turned and stared. "It's my Lonely," he said. "It's beautiful." He left the second piece of pizza and the water and took his guitar from Ezra. He strummed a G. "Yep, it's my Lonely all right. Always in tune."

"And Sally saved this for you." Ezra held out the Coricidin bottle.

"Thank you." Benny Jack took the bottle and slid it on his finger. He turned to Sally. "Thank you, Miss Sally."

"You're welcome," she said.

Ezra felt like he was talking to himself, but still, as Benny Jack moved the slide up and down the strings, he explained how Stone R. had found the guitar's internal structure weakened by the gunshot. He'd stabilized its constitution with new bracings so that the guitar was stronger and sounded better than ever. "I've got a new case for your Lonely, too," he said. "It's upstairs."

"Thank you, Jesus," Benny Jack said. "Thank you for your kindness to a sinner who runs with Satan himself." He wiped tears from his eyes. "I'm late. I'm sorry." He turned to Mel. "Mr. Mel, can I please use your bathroom?"

"Sure," Mel said. He pointed toward the hallway. "It's down that hall, last door on your left. If you get to the back door, you've gone too far."

"Thank you." Benny Jack laid his guitar on its back in the floor. "I'm sorry." He stood and disappeared down the hallway.

"That's a good thing you did, Ezra MacRae." Sally kissed him on the cheek.

"Aw, shucks, Miss Sally," Ezra twanged. "Let's get this out of harm's way." He stooped and picked up the guitar from the floor and looked around the room, then secured it in the seat of the hall tree chair that stood by the dark passageway into which Benny Jack had disappeared.

As he turned back to Sally, he sensed movement behind him but caught it too late to apprehend the threat. Sally's eyes flared and her mouth opened, and then everything froze when the strong left arm of Hugo Rodgers snaked around his throat and tightened into a chokehold. Rodgers jerked Ezra back against his chest and belly. He anchored the hold with his left hand on his right bicep and extended his right arm over Ezra's shoulder and pointed his revolver at the group.

"Thank you, MacRae, you good-looking thing, you," he said and flicked his long tongue around the rim of Ezra's right ear. "Now I got you where I been wanting you." He swung the

301

revolver back and forth. "Only we don't need all these people around." He grunted and cinched the chokehold tighter.

"Let him go!" Sally said.

"Let him go," Rodgers mocked. "Shut the hell up, girl-friend." He swept the gun left to right to cover them all.

Ezra's eyes followed the pointing of the barrel from Sally to Mel to Boyce to Caroline, but when the barrel returned to rest on the deputy, his gaze continued to Mel and then to Sally. They seemed to blur and fade, and he wondered how they were doing that.

"Man, you better ease up," Mel said. "You're gonna be wrestling over two hundred pounds of dead weight in about ten seconds."

"Man, you better shut the hell up too, Far-mer-Mac-Ode-had-a-farm." Rodgers swung the gun again in quick movements like it was a conductor's baton. "Doo-dah, baby, doo-dah," he sang. Then he steadied the gun and swung it back to Deputy Boyce. "I ought to shoot you first, since you've got your own piece." He cocked the hammer on his revolver. "Put your gun down on the floor and kick it over to me."

Boyce paused.

"Do it now, Deputy Dawg."

Ezra felt Rodgers slightly ease up on the chokehold, and the dark edges that had begun to frame his vision retreated. It struck him that the fear he saw in the eyes of Sally and Mel must reflect the fear in his own. The pity he saw mixed with their fear shamed him. He knew from a youth spent wrestling with Mel and Curtis that he ought to know an escape from this hold. He rallied and pushed up on his tiptoes and tried to pry the man's bicep and forearm down from the sides of his throat, but Rodgers only cinched the choke tighter.

"Boy, I'll snap your fucking neck if you don't be still." He tongued the inside of Ezra's right ear and whispered, "Don't make me."

Darkness once more bled into the edges of Ezra's vision.

Rodgers focused again on Davis Boyce, but the pressure Ezra felt on his throat remained.

"I've got six bullets for the six of y'all," Rodgers said. "There ain't gonna be no warning shots."

Boyce did as he was told.

As Rodgers stepped on the gun with his right foot and dragged it behind him, Ezra felt him ease off on the chokehold, and his vision cleared again.

Rodgers thrust Boyce's gun into the shadows beneath the hall tree chair and then kissed Ezra's ear. "You back with me now, darling?" For the first time, he pressed the muzzle of the gun to Ezra's right temple. "I said, are you back with me now, darling?"

"Yes," Ezra said through a constricted throat and gritted teeth.

"Yes, what, darling?"

"Yes, asshole."

Rodgers crowed. "Classic!" He again waved the gun back and forth. "This ain't really going nowhere, y'all," he said. "I mean, it's not even a Mexican standoff. That'd be y'all pointing guns at me while I point mine at Ezra MacRae here. But y'all got nothing to point but your fingers. So, we're just standing."

While Hugo babbled, Ezra's gaze ranged quickly from Caroline around toward Sally but stalled on his own reflection in a mirror just over Mel's right shoulder. His distressed red face shocked him, and he understood the looks on the faces of his friends and the deputy. Shamed again by the sight of his helplessness, he let his gaze wander away from his suffering and stupidly imagined that the front windows, between which Mel had mounted the mirror, framed a scene bright with fields and mountainsides instead of dark with night and the dim reflection of their current situation.

One jolting flex of the chokehold brought Ezra's eyes back to the mirror where they met Hugo's icy blue stare, and he felt a different kind of shock at the man's hungry expression. Rodgers winked and slowly tightened and then slowly eased the choke as he grinned and nuzzled his face closer, scraping his prickly beard across Ezra's ear.

"Look at us," Rodgers whispered. "Oh boy, this turns me on." He winked again and then focused his attention once more on the four arrayed in front of him. "Or how about this?" he said. "Maybe we're waiting for the brains among you"—he swung the gun and licked his lips—"waiting, I say, for the brains among you to explain why I've done what I've done. Like in the detective shows." He pointed the gun at Caroline and said, "Are you the brains, Farmer's Lady?" Then he pointed at Mel but called back over his shoulder, "It sure as hell ain't you, Benny Jack Boudreau." He laughed. "Here's the thing, y'all. This ain't no *Heat of the Night* episode, and I can't tell you why about much of none of it."

"*I Can't Tell You Why*"—*Don Henley, Glenn Frey, and Timothy B. Schmidt, songwriters*. This appeared without effort in Ezra's mind, and he grabbed hold of the clarity, willing himself to keep his brain working.

"I couldn't get Nancy a record deal, and that hurt my pride," Rodgers said. "And then she left me, divorced me. So, double failure—no record deal, no wife."

Ezra felt and heard Hugo's breath catch as if stifling another laugh or a sob.

Rodgers licked his lips again. "And then she showed back up unannounced and found me in bed with Lucie. And for them that don't know, that's Lucio Centopani, aka Lucky Baker." Rodgers stopped again and swallowed hard. "Now, I didn't know why that happened. But it happened over and over again until I loved him." He paused once more and cocked his head to one side, away from Ezra's. "And he loved me for some reason." His mind seemed to go elsewhere for a moment. "Oh, but he was so sick." Then, as if some sudden sound or movement startled him, he snapped back to attention. "So sick. He was gonna get me caught, and then he was gonna die."

The cocked gun continued to drift back and forth along the row of faces facing him.

"Now he's dead, and here I am caught anyway."

Nobody moved.

Rodgers eased his hold so that Ezra seemed simply held rather than choked, and while the gun in his hand oscillated back and forth across the faces of those in front of him, Rodgers locked his eyes on Ezra's in the mirror. "If I could be a million miles away and clear of all this," he said, his voice suddenly a raspy whisper. "And have you there with me."

Ezra sensed a different tightening in his throat, knowing that Hugo's "you" was not some callout to the ghost of his murdered lover.

Rodgers's eyes glistened in the lamplight of the living room. Then they appeared to freeze and harden. "I figured I could take out Nancy and Earl and Burl, but mainly Nancy, and they'd connect it to the hit on that kid from *Cash Box*. Worked for a little while, but then I went and popped that other boy." He stopped and swung the gun around to point at Sally. "Hey, girlfriend, did he die?"

In the mirror, Ezra saw a glow fill the hallway behind Rodgers and then disappear. He glanced at Rodgers's eyes and saw them riveted on Sally, whose voice failed when she tried to speak.

"What?" Rodgers taunted, shaking the gun at her. "Speak up, girlfriend."

Still transfixed by the tableau of Rodgers and himself framed in the mirror, Ezra saw Benny Jack's Lonely rise, not with its flat top or back aimed at Rodgers's head but one of its hips, recently reenforced with new wood. He squeezed his eyes shut.

The crack of wood meeting skin and skull—and the muted hum of strings—filled the room, and the hold on Ezra's throat disappeared.

Just as Mel and Sally lunged forward together to catch Ezra as he slumped down, the first shot cut the air and the mirror between the windows exploded. Like some lightning-quick reversal in a wrestling match, Mel had Ezra's back held tight against his chest and belly as he scrabbled backward, pulling a coughing Ezra away from Rodgers, who staggered and swung the gun and his dazed blue eyes in the direction of Deputy Boyce and Caroline.

A second blow slammed into his head, and the gun fired again.

The bullet hit Boyce in the left shoulder, spinning him halfway around and collapsing him to the floor, where he lay on his back blinking at the ceiling.

"Goddamn devil!" Benny Jack shrieked. "Goddamn Satan!"

With the third blow, the Lonely's neck separated from its body, and Rodgers fell forward onto all fours, almost face to face with Boyce. But he still held the gun in his hand as he shifted his weight to rise.

Benny Jack stood frozen, the Lonely's neck in his hand and its body dangling from the six strings like a dead puppet.

"Why you little cockeyed son of a bitch," Rodgers growled. He struggled to his feet and, still partially crouched, turned— his gun coming around half a beat behind—as a large figure loomed out of the darkness of the hallway and shoved the little man aside.

In that confused moment, when Rodgers must have expected to find the googly-eyed little man cowering in front of him but instead found Deputy Maurice Norton towering over him, he hesitated. And in that split second of hesitation, Norton slapped the gun from his hand and followed with a smack to an unshaven jowl that spun Rodgers around. Caught up in the deputy's massive arms, the killer's entire face reddened and his head seemed to balloon away from the body flailing beneath the same chokehold Rodgers had so effectively applied to Lucio and Ezra.

Hugo's body quickly stilled, and his watery blue gaze fell to Ezra on the floor where Mel held him and Sally shielded him. As they stared at each other, Ezra tried to read the expression in the startled and startling eyes he'd first seen when they turned to him as a masked Rodgers stood above a kneeling Burl Davies in the middle of Music Square West. He tried to imagine what thoughts or feelings—if any—moved behind the killer's icy eyes that now began to fade with his consciousness. Neither broke the stare until Rodgers's gaze slid slowly off Ezra's face and seemed to slump to the floor.

When the big man he held went limp, Deputy Norton released the hold and spread his arms and backed away like a fighter being waved off a knocked out opponent.

Hugo Rodgers collapsed in a heap and lay twisted and unconscious, his mouth agape but sucking air.

Somehow through the ringing in his ears, Ezra heard Benny Jack whispering into the sudden stunned quiet, to nobody in particular, "I'm sorry. I'm sorry. I'm sorry."

Saturday, April 8, 1989

SIXTY-THREE

The morning broke beautifully clear but cold.

Still feeling the house too close, the memories of the violent presence of Hugo Rodgers and of his final brokenness too much with them, Ezra and the rest dressed in sweaters pulled from closet shelves and sweatshirts dug out of drawers and took their coffee in the sunlight on the front porch. They'd made it a temporary act of worship—pagan as it seemed—to reach or jump up and touch the overhead porchlight sconce every time any of them walked in or out the front door. The light's periodic goings on and off Wednesday evening had caught Deputy Norton's attention enough to cause him to walk up the hill after his relief arrived—"just for a looksee," he said. He'd crept far enough up the front steps to see the situation playing out in the living room and, reasoning that Rodgers had come in from the back, had gone around the house in hopes that the door there was still unlocked. He'd been just easing it open—hoping that it wouldn't squeak or screech—when Benny Jack dealt the first blow with his Lonely and the first shot rang out.

Not long after the chaos of that moment, the local rescue squad left for the hospital in Asheville with a stabilized and ornery Deputy Boyce in the back, followed out of the MacOde Farm driveway by Deputies Norton and Payne with a handcuffed and still groggy Hugo Rodgers in the backseat. Another car waited in the road for these two vehicles to depart and then rolled slowly up the driveway and parked beside Deputy Boyce's patrol car. Detective Woody Davidson and Officer Latt

Edwards emerged from the dark sedan and stretched, their hands straining for the stars and their bestial grunts drumming like Ruffed Grouse in the mountain night. After hearing the telling and retelling of the evening's events, Davidson had returned to a rented upstairs room at Chunn's Tavern in Runion and Edwards had eventually settled down on Mel MacOde's living room couch.

Despite Benny Jack's seemingly hundreds of apologies for unlocking the back door when he'd pretended to need the bathroom, they'd celebrated him as a hero, right alongside Deputy Norton. But even as he sat in the Saturday morning sun—swallowed up in one of Mel's N.C. State sweatshirts and wrapped in a quilt Mel's mother had made, drinking hot chocolate, his broken Lonely in the case at his feet—he continued to apologize every few minutes.

"Mr. Mel, I'm so sorry for letting goddamn Satan in your pretty house."

"That's all right, Benny Jack," Mel said almost every time. "You sure dealt with that devil when it counted, didn't you?"

"Reckon I did," Benny Jack responded. "I reckon I did."

Although the apologies to Mel continued, Benny Jack had been convinced, for the most part, to stop calling Ezra *Jesus*. But for some reason he couldn't be persuaded to call him *Ezra* and generally just called him *sir*. Nobody could understand why, and Benny Jack seemed unable or unwilling to explain it.

"Benny Jack?" Ezra said.

"Yessir?"

"That devil told me he was taking you home to Appalachia, Virginia."

"Yessir."

"Did you want to go home?"

"I reckon I did."

They all sat quietly for a while, except for Caroline, who brought refills of coffee and hot chocolate.

Ezra stood and stretched. "Chief, I'm gonna make some long-distance calls and run up your phone bill, okay?"

"I appreciate you telling me this time," Mel said and winked at Sally.

"Come on, Sally," Ezra said. "You can make some, too. It'll be fun."

He led her upstairs and sat down on the side of the bed. She closed the door behind them, lingered there a moment, and then surprised him by sitting in his lap and kicking off her shoes. He looked up at her with a raised eyebrow. "Nurse Evans, I admire your bedside manner."

"Who are we calling?" she said with a smile.

"First off, information for Appalachia, Virginia, to see if we can get hold of anybody named Boudreau."

One call to information led to three more calls to Boudreau households, the third of which provided the number for Benny Jack's paternal grandmother, Alison Boudreau, who spoke with an odd but distinctly English accent. When Ezra identified himself and said he was a couple hours south of her in North Carolina and had her grandson with him, she interrupted. "Can I send someone to get him?"

"Well." Ezra paused, locking eyes with the blonde and blue-eyed woman sitting on his lap. "His friend Sally and I were thinking about driving him up there." He raised both eyebrows, and she nodded. "But can we agree that if he chooses not to stay then he can come back with us?"

Alison Boudreau said she would try to be agreeable to that.

"One other thing," Ezra said. "Do you have a guitar thereabouts that he can play while I get his repaired again?" He winked at Sally. "He broke it over Satan's head a couple nights ago."

Mrs. Boudreau seemed not even to notice what he said. "He can play mine whenever I'm not playing it. His cousin Elderberry makes guitars, so you won't need to worry about getting it fixed. I'm sure Elderberry can see to it."

After Ezra wrote down Mrs. Boudreau's directions, he ended the call and turned to Sally. "You up for a road trip? We can get back here this evening, or we can take our stuff and head home to Nashville from there."

"Let's come back here." She slid off his lap, then immediately pushed him down on the bed and straddled him—her knees against his lower ribs, her calves along his sides, her sock-feet toes burrowing in under his buttocks. Then she pulled the red sweater off over her head. "Is this okay?"

"More than," he said. "*More Than This,*" Bryan Ferry, *songwriter.* "Should we lock the door?"

"I did when we came in," she said.

You know there's nothing more than this. He smiled up at her. "You mean, this was premeditated?"

"I've been meditating on it since you first showed up at the hospital," she said and rolled off and bridged on shoulders and heels to unbutton and push down her jeans.

"So have I," Ezra said and sat up and began tugging at his own warm clothes.

They sat around a large table in the middle of the Runion Pizzeria—Ezra, Sally, Benny Jack, Latt, Davidson, Caroline, and Mel. Scraps of the three large pizzas they'd ordered—the Appalachian Mountain Special, the Cow Tipper, and the Ghosts of Avalon—littered silver pans surrounded by a clutter of drink glasses and coffee cups.

Davidson wiped his mouth and cleared his throat. "MacRae." He scooted his chair back a few inches from the table. "I didn't want to tell you this before you ate, but you ought to know that Edwards found Curly Crocker dead at his home the afternoon you left to come here." He paused and stared across the table at Ezra. "He'd been dead a little while, maybe since last weekend."

Ezra sat and stared back at Davidson a moment. "Rodgers?"

"Seems likely," Davidson said. "Autopsy's pending, but Crocker was strangled somehow."

Ezra shifted his gaze to Latt and then to Mel.

"Somebody you knew?" Mel asked.

"No," Ezra said. "I mean, only by reputation. He's a bigtime Music Row songwriter for Jamboree Music." He glanced toward the jukebox. "He was the only other witness—besides me and Benny Jack—to those Easter morning shootings." He put a hand on Sally's thigh, raised his glass, and slurped the last of his drink through the straw. "I guess I was next," he said.

"That's not necessarily the case," Latt said. "It could've been—"

"I don't think he wants you dead," Davidson said. "He has a hard-on for you, MacRae, no doubt about it." He glanced at Sally and Caroline. "Pardon the expression, ladies."

"Nurses don't embarrass that easily," Sally said.

"Nor do farm women," Caroline said.

"I think that was obvious the other night," Mel said. "What the detective just suggested, I mean."

Ezra glanced at Mel to find him looking back with a slightly raised eyebrow.

The table fell quiet.

Ezra held his friend's gaze and tried to follow the sense of the words running through his mind. *Remember, Ez, nobody loves you better than me. Not your mama, not your papa, not your three-eyed cousin Whoppa. . . . I'll remember you, my handsome young man. . . . So, what do I want, you might ask? Besides a roll in the hay with big strapping boy like you? . . . You can have me anytime, Ez. . . . I've been meditating on it since you first showed up at the hospital. . . . Oh boy, this turns me on. . . . If I could be a million miles away and clear of all this. And have you there with me. . . . Love you, Ez—*

Caroline cleared her throat. "Should we look for a Curly Crocker song on the jukebox?"

"Officer Edwards and me don't have time." Davidson scooted his chair further from the table. "What's our waitress's name?"

"Hannah," Mel said.

"Hannah?" Ezra called to her before the detective could. "I think we'd better be hitting the road."

"Hitting the road," Hannah Henderson said as she approached, flipping through the tickets on her order pad. "Better be hitting the road."

Davidson and Edwards returned to Town Hall to meet the Sheriff for a second round of questioning Hugo Rodgers. They planned to complete the paperwork for extradition to Tennessee and take him home with them the next day. Mel and Caroline promised to have supper ready for everybody that evening, saying they would probably eat around seven o'clock. The two of them then returned to MacOde Farm for an afternoon on horseback.

Ezra, Sally, and Benny Jack walked down Main Street to Aslan's Wardrobe for more thrifting. They found a couple of Runion State T-shirts and a rare find in local-hero merchandise—a T-shirt picturing Gabriel Tanner & Lonesome Star. While Sally helped Benny Jack look for jeans, another shirt or two, maybe a sport coat, and possibly another pair of shoes, Ezra walked down to Cowart's Department Store, where he borrowed a bag from Julia Cowart and filled it with socks, a couple packs each of white T-shirts, and flannel boxers. Back at the front, he dumped the bag on the checkout counter.

Julia began tallying up his purchases. "Apart from the socks," she said, "you know everything here is too small for you, right?"

"Yeah, yeah, they're for somebody else."

"Heard about what happened over at Mel's the other night," she said as she took his money. "Everybody all right?"

"Everybody's fine, Julia, thanks. It was crazy."

"I'll bet," she said. "Even by Bloody Madison County standards."

"Hey, have you heard anything about how Deputy Boyce is doing?"

"Oh, Davis'll be fine," Julia said. "You know he's immortal, right?"

Sally and Benny Jack stepped out of the thrift store just as Ezra returned along the sidewalk.

"We ready to hit the road?" Ezra said.

"I think so," Sally said.

Benny Jack remained quiet.

"Well, let's get on."

In the public parking lot adjacent to the pizzeria, they put their bags of clothes in the trunk of the Tempo. Then Ezra unlocked and opened the passenger door, reached in and unlocked the back door on that side, which he then opened for Benny Jack, who fell into the seat and yanked the door out of Ezra's hand to slam it shut. Ezra and Sally looked at each other. He held the door open until she was inside and closed it behind her.

As he stepped around the rear of the car, he stopped and looked up. In one of the barred windows on an upper floor of the jail, a window surrounded by the loopy letters of the mural's "Greetings," he thought he could see the silhouette of a head and shoulders. He wondered if that silhouette might be Hugo, and a chill ran down his spine. He gave a little wave and then continued around the car and got in.

"All set?" He turned the key in the ignition and glanced in the rearview at Benny Jack, who sat with his eyes closed and his head laid back. He turned to Sally, who gave him a smile and a wink. He backed out of the space, navigated behind the Post Office and the WHMM radio studio, and then turned left on Lonesome Mountain Road.

SIXTY-FOUR

Hugo pressed the left side of his face against the plexiglass and watched Ezra MacRae's car until he couldn't see it anymore. They'd had another of those moments, he thought, like when MacRae had been in the alley behind his house and like when he'd been in the woods next to the MacOde place and watched MacRae on the porch. But this time—unlike those others—their eyes had met. He wondered why it should be that, just when he'd discovered himself and tasted the possibilities of life, he must lose it all. And all was lost, he knew. *Oh*, he might meet Ezra MacRae face-to-face one last time, truly locking eyes with him from witness box to defendant table. But, then again, he might not.

He heard voices and the shuffling of feet approaching.

"Stand right there, Rodgers," one of the voices said. "And put your hands behind your back, please."

When Hugo did so, two deputies whose names he didn't remember unlocked the cell door and entered. He knew that he could easily take out both of them, and if they'd had guns on them, he might have done so. But the big detective from Nashville was downstairs, as was that big deputy who'd choked him out at the farmhouse, so he just stood and let them put the handcuffs on him.

316

SIXTY-FIVE

As they made their way north and west along Madison County mountain roads, Ezra pointed out to Sally the various landmarks of local history and of his growing up in this place. He kept Benny Jack in the rearview, but the little man still sat with closed eyes and seemed focused on trying to look like he was asleep.

At the end of Belva Bridge, Ezra turned left and took the meandering Asheville Highway into Tennessee. They entered Greeneville and then left it via Baileyton Road, a two-lane that continued through the countryside to I-81. As soon as they cleared the entrance ramp and hurried north with the interstate traffic, Benny Jack stirred and spoke. "You know why I stopped calling you Jesus?"

Sally turned in her seat, and Ezra faced Benny Jack in the rearview. "Wasn't it that we convinced you my name's Ezra?"

"No." He looked at Sally and then met Ezra's gaze in the rearview. "It's because you lied to me in the hospital."

Ezra and Sally looked at each other, and then she turned back to Benny Jack. "I don't remember hearing any lies," she said.

"You weren't there. It was just me and him." He turned back to meet Ezra's eyes. "Jesus wouldn't lie. Ain't that right?"

"Sounds right to me," Ezra said.

The little man laid his head back again, turned, and looked out the window as they passed a tractor trailer.

Ezra saw Benny Jack's Adam's apple rise and fall as he swallowed.

"You said you wasn't gonna take my Sally away from me," he said. "And now, sir, you've gone and done it."

Ezra glanced at Sally, who looked back at him with raised eyebrows. "Well, now," Ezra said at last. "I don't remember saying that exactly." He turned on his signal to take the Kingsport exit. "We talked about how she only had eyes for you in that hospital room, and then you sang for us." He glanced at Sally. "Remember?"

"I do remember," she said. "It was a beautiful little concert."

After easing into the flow of traffic toward Kingsport, Ezra glanced again at the rearview. "Wasn't that it?" he said.

Benny Jack stared out the window and said nothing.

> i remember the night
> i got paid fifty dollars
> to split between lonely and me
> i was gonna use my half
> on my pretty girl sally
> but im in the grave cold as can be

They'd all been mostly quiet through the hour since Benny Jack shut down the last time. But as they entered Appalachia, Virginia, movement in the rearview caught Ezra's attention, and he glanced to see the little man sitting up and watching wide-eyed as they rolled along West Main Street.

Ezra caught Sally's attention and cut his eyes toward the backseat.

She turned around. "Is this looking familiar to you?" she said.

"It sure is, Miss Sally."

"How long since you've been here?" Ezra asked.

"Jesus, I don't know," Benny Jack said. "That's the real Jesus, not you."

"Understood." Ezra pulled Alison Boudreau's directions out of his shirt pocket and glanced at them, but Sally laid her hand on his. He looked at her.

Wait, she mouthed.

"We're on West Main Street," Benny Jack said, seemingly trying to see everything at once. "Now, just up here in the middle of this big curve we'll be on East Main Street." He scooted to the middle of the back seat and leaned up between Sally and Ezra. "Get ready to turn that way." A hand shot out in front of Ezra's face with a finger pointing to the left.

"All right," Ezra said.

"Turn, turn," Benny Jack said. "Jesus, turn right here. I mean, turn left right here."

"Okay," Ezra said as Sally laughed.

"Okay, now pretty quick down here, you're gonna wanna take a right on Boggs Avenue." Benny Jack rested his left hand on Ezra's right shoulder for a moment and then began a rapid patting. "Okay, now turn right right here."

"Yessir," Ezra said and made the maneuver.

"And that's it," Benny Jack said. "Stay on Boggs Avenue, and I'll tell you when we're coming up on Mama Boudreau's place."

They continued between a handful of houses that stood on either side of Boggs, and then they were quickly out into the countryside again, driving through a valley between forested hills.

Benny Jack was soon patting Ezra's shoulder again. "Get ready, get ready! It's just up here at that next mailbox."

Alison Boudreau came out the front door and onto the porch as soon as they pulled in the driveway. With a wave of her hand, she motioned them forward into the yard and then came down the porch steps.

Ezra stopped and turned off the car, and Sally and he opened their doors and got out.

In the back seat, Benny Jack seemed frozen in place, his face turned to his grandmother as she hurried across the yard.

Mama Boudreau had voluminous white-blonde hair that erupted from her head and poured down over her shoulders. Her thin face was lit by blue eyes and a wide, large-toothed smile outlined with red lipstick. She wore a yellow sweatshirt emblazoned with the words *Hindman Settlement School* in white lettering, slim black slacks, and red pumps with French heels.

Sally opened Benny Jack's door and helped him out as his grandmother rounded the rear of the car, her arms already opening wide. Benny Jack collapsed against her, his body shaking with sobs.

"My lovely boy, we have missed you so much," Mama Boudreau said, pressing his head to her breast. "Welcome home." She kept her arms wrapped tightly around him and kissed the top of his head as he cried. "It's all right. You're home now. You're safe." When he stilled, she turned him toward the house and, with an arm around his shoulders, walked him in that direction. They started up the steps, and she raised her voice and spoke without turning. "You darlings come in when you're ready."

Ezra and Sally met at the rear of the car, where he opened the lid of the trunk to retrieve the bags of clothes and the broken Lonely in its case.

She kissed him on the cheek. "This is another good thing you did, Ezra MacRae," she said. "Better be careful or you're going to infatuate me."

"How many good things does that take?"

She laughed and closed the trunk lid. "Can't tell you, pal," she said, and they walked across the yard together.

Inside Mama Boudreau's house, the air was rich with aromas wafting from the kitchen and rising from a dining room table filled with steaming bowls of mashed potatoes and green beans and creamed corn, plates of fried chicken and trout and ham, hot biscuits and cool Cornish pasties. The top of the sideboard buffet was covered with cans of soda, pitchers of tea—sweet and unsweet—and water, a pot of coffee, and desserts—a chocolate cake, a coconut cake, a chocolate pie, a chess pie, and a platter of no-bake chocolate cookies.

A woman introduced as Benny Jack's Auntie Ophelia had the management of table and buffet. "What can I offer you to drink?" she asked.

Ezra carefully accepted the cup of coffee she brought him. "Y'all did all this in two hours?"

"Lord, no," Ophelia said. "Mama gets these notions. We've been cooking nonstop since Wednesday evening."

Over the next while, the front yard filled with hobbling cars and pickups, and the house filled with cousins and other relations, many of whom arrived with instrument cases hanging from their hands or tucked under their arms. Most seemed versions of Benny Jack and Mama Boudreau—small frames, knotty joints, handsome faces with sharp features. All warmly welcomed the return of Benny Jack, and several took Ezra or Sally aside to thank them for bringing him home.

"How long has he been gone?" Sally asked a large man introduced as "Cousin Clatie's Bill."

"Well, let's see." Bill scratched in the beard under his jaw. "Me and Benny Jack finished school together in sixty-eight. Then his daddy died in the Farmington mine that November." He lifted his cap and rubbed a hand across his bald pate and settled the cap again. "He must've left out of here not long after that. Maybe about this time in sixty-nine?"

"Twenty years," Sally said.

"Pretty much right on the nose, I reckon."

Ezra arrived from the direction of the table. "Twenty years is what he told me the first time I met him," Ezra said. "So he's, what, forty years old?"

"About that," Bill said.

Ezra cupped his left hand under his chin as he bit into a Cornish pasty. "Not your regular mountain fare," he said. "Delicious."

"We love those," Bill said. "That's one of the things that sets this family apart around here."

"I'm guessing that music's another family specialty."

"Yep."

The gathering moved outside, where one end of the porch became a stage while the other end and the near edge of the yard below became dance floors. Three guitars, a banjo, a mandolin, and two fiddles were joined by two tin whistles and a riddle drum. Dancing feet added rhythm to instrumentals that alternately rollicked or lilted or cried. Everybody sang when a song called for singing.

Benny Jack sat next to Mama Boudreau and held her guitar in his lap and slid his Coricidin bottle up and down its neck. His broken Lonely lay in its open case at his feet, and his cousin Elderberry squatted there looking it over.

"Wish we had a camera," Sally said as they danced in the yard to a slow song.

"So do I," Ezra said, pulling his gaze away from Benny Jack and looking into Sally's blue eyes.

"You should borrow a guitar and play one of your songs for us."

"Well, thank you for thinking of that, my dear," Ezra said as he spun Sally and gazed again at the collection of instruments and players. "But I'd rather just absorb and enjoy."

At the end of their second hour on the Boudreau homestead, Ezra and Sally spread their goodbyes and thanks all around and then walked with Benny Jack to the Tempo.

Alison Boudreau watched them from the top of the porch steps, her penciled eyebrows knit together and her lips pursed.

"Mama Boudreau said you could come back to Nashville with us, if you wanted to," Ezra said. "But I'm sure she'd love to have you stay with her."

Benny Jack didn't answer for a moment but instead opened his arms to hug Sally and then Ezra and then Sally again. "Jesus."

He blinked a tear down his cheek. "Don't you reckon I ought to stay here and take care of her? She's getting on." He paused. "I mean you this time, sir."

Ezra felt warm tears brimming in his own eyes. "I reckon that would be good, my friend," he said.

Benny Jack nodded once, hugged Sally again, and shook Ezra's hand. Then he turned back to the house, matching his grandmother's sudden smile tooth for tooth.

Ezra backed the Tempo around and pulled to the edge of Boggs Avenue. Then he leaned up and took his notebook from his back pocket and handed it to Sally. "Will you find a blank page and write down the number on that mailbox, please?"

"Got a pen?"

He fished one out of the door pocket and handed it to her. "And before you go looking for lyrics about you, there aren't any." He turned left onto Boggs without looking at her. "Not yet." He drove them toward Appalachia, he with a hand on her knee and she with a hand on top of his. He'd rolled down his window, and through it he listened to the music from the Boudreau porch long after the sound of it sank beneath the hum of his wheels on the blacktop and the rush of the wind in his ears.

Epilogue

That Sunday morning, the day after they'd carried Benny Jack Boudreau into the bosom of his family in Appalachia, Virginia, Ezra and Sally joined Mel and Caroline in a pew near the front of the Jewel Hill Presbyterian Church. Ezra's Papa, the Reverend Ephraim MacRae, preached on Psalm 30 and how God can get a person—"a songwriter like King David, perhaps," he'd said—out of a mess and deliver him from enemies that would celebrate his destruction, deliver him "from mourning to dancing and from drowning in lamentations to bursting with song."

After the final hymn was sung and the closing prayer was prayed, after the congregation members shook hands with their minister and left the parking lot, the remaining six gathered at the open doors.

Ezra raised a hand and squeezed his father's shoulder. "Hell of a sermon, Papa," he said.

"Thank you, son." Ephraim looked at Sally and shook his head.

"Come on, you two," Sarah MacRae said. "Ride with me to lunch."

"Mama, I'm not sure Sally is ready for your driving. We can come on with Mel and Caroline."

"They're doing something else for a few minutes, I think."

Ezra turned to look at Mel.

"We'll be along soon," Mel said.

"As will I," Ephraim MacRae said.

"Well, Mrs. MacRae—"

"Sarah, dear."

"Sarah," Sally said. "Your son hasn't ridden with me yet, so he doesn't know what I'm ready for."

Sarah MacRae laughed and pulled the keys from her purse and handed them to Sally. "Then why don't you drive us?"

"No way this can be good." Ezra followed them toward his mother's Volkswagen Cabriolet as his father took Mel and Caroline back inside the church.

They stayed one more night at MacOde Farm and returned to Nashville on Monday.

For a time after Hugo Rodgers's "not guilty" plea at his arraignment the following Thursday, they found themselves often talking—at Dalt's, at his place or hers, walking the streets of Sylvan Park together—about what it would be like to answer questions from the prosecution or the defense as Rodgers sat and stared at them. The dread of testifying at trial competed with the fear that Rodgers might escape custody and come after them.

But then it was over.

One evening before a late double date, at a kitchen table cluttered with Whataburger trash and beer bottles, Ezra learned that no trial would take place. At the preliminary hearing, Latt said, Rodgers changed his plea to guilty on four counts of first-degree murder and two counts of attempted murder, along with several lesser crimes—desecration of a body, kidnapping, assault, arson, and breaking and entering. Initial charges for sodomy were dropped. A sentencing hearing was scheduled for late June, and Latt said he expected that by then a plea deal would take the death penalty off the table but remand Rodgers to the Riverbend Maximum Security Institution for the rest of his natural life.

Daisy Davies moved into her late husband's Ave Canora office and became energetically involved in the day-to-day operations of her publishing company. She and Mark Williamson became a formidable team of songpluggers up and down Music Row. By the time Ezra and Sally traveled to Runion for Mel and Caroline's wedding at MacOde Farm on the first Saturday in September, Daisy and Mark had received solid responses to several of Ezra's songs. Four had been put on hold for final recording consideration—"The Sweetest Rose" for Vince Gill, "As Long as I Can Dream" for T. Graham Brown, "No Other Love" for Clint Black, and "Night of the Stranger" for

Heart. Others were scheduled for recording in late October or early November—"Rita's Cantina" by Doug Stone, "Dealing with Destiny" by Exile, and "One Chance" by The Spyders. Newcomers Chauncey Tripper and Rhianna Oaks had already recorded "Big Rain's Coming" in June. The single was scheduled for release to radio in late September, and the song would appear on each singer's MCA Records debut, both scheduled for release in November. The single hit number one on *Billboard* and *Cash Box* country charts and climbed into the top ten on the adult contemporary charts of both trade magazines. At the same time, the video ran in heavy rotation on both CMT and VH1.

One Friday, more than halfway through the following year —1990—and a week before Mel and Caroline MacOde were scheduled to visit Nashville to celebrate their first wedding anniversary, Ezra received mail from ASCAP. As soon as he removed it from the mailbox and recognized what it was, he stood in the gravel of the Youngstowne Square parking lot and carefully tore open the end of the envelope. Inside he found a check for $23,669.52 in performance royalties, most of it for "Big Rain's Coming." He stuffed it quickly back inside the envelope and looked around. Then he pulled it out again and stared at it. He pushed the check back inside the envelope once more, folded it, and stuffed it in the front pocket of his jeans. He headed for his apartment, eyes warily watching around corners and scanning the woods in back. Once inside, he did something that he hadn't since those days when Hugo Rodgers was on the loose—he searched the apartment thoroughly, checking out all the places where somebody might hide. Those old searches were for murderers. This one was for thieves. When he was certain he was alone, he got his Guild six-string from the music room. He pulled the folded envelope from his pocket and removed the check again and flattened it out on the kitchen table. Then he sat down.

"Look what we did," he said at last to the guitar in his lap. He raised his face toward the ceiling and closed his eyes as if to pray. "Have you checked your mail, Benny Jack?" He imagined the family gathered on Mama Boudreau's front porch, just as Sally and he had left them almost a year and a half before, gathered with their guitars and fiddles and other instruments as they played "Jole Blon," Benny Jack sliding through the interludes with his rebuilt Lonely and his Coricidin bottle, the unopened envelope from ASCAP lying on the porch floor beside a foot tapping out of time.

Some seven months later, on another Easter Sunday morning, a haggard man in filthy jeans and blue work shirt, stepped up onto the apartment stoop and knocked on the front door. When a young blonde woman with a baby on her hip stood in the open doorway and looked at him, his blue eyes widened for a moment and then narrowed in a smile.

"Good morning, young lady," he said. "I'm so sorry to bother you, but I'm wondering if Ezra is around."

She glanced back over her shoulder toward an open bathroom door and then turned back. "I don't know who that is," she said.

"Beg your pardon, ma'am, I thought he lived here."

"My husband Jeffrey's in the shower."

"You don't know Ezra MacRae?"

"No, I don't," she said. "We're getting ready for church."

The man studied her up and down and looked over her shoulder toward the sound of a shower. "I'm so sorry," he said again. "Do you mind if I ask how long y'all've lived here?"

"We've been here since the first of the year." She shifted the baby and said again, "We're getting ready for church."

With the squeaky croak of a valve, the shower stopped.

"Well, I hope y'all have a blessed Easter service." The man began backing down the steps. "I'm sorry to have bothered you."

She closed the door without responding and locked it, then

carried the baby into her bedroom. A movement at the window caught her eye, and she looked to see the stranger entering the woods at the back of the Youngstowne Square property.

Then Jeffrey stood naked in the doorway, toweling his thick black hair. "Your turn, honey," he said.

She looked out the window for another moment before she turned and handed him the baby and started for the door.

"What were you looking at?" Jeffrey stepped to the window.

"There was a man come to the front door asking for somebody I never heard of." She returned to stand beside him at the window. "When I came in here to lay out the baby's clothes, I saw him heading into the woods."

They stood together and watched the man reach the train tracks and turn east.

"Those look like prison blues he's wearing," Jeffery said.

"And just how would you know that?" She smacked him playfully on the butt and lightly pinched the baby's cheek. "Y'all better be dressed by the time I get out of the shower."

"Who did you say he was asking about?" Jeffrey asked.

She turned away from the window and pulled her T-shirt off over her head as she headed for the door. "I don't even remember," she said. "Nobody I ever heard of."

THREE OF FOUR ESCAPEES RETURNED TO NASHVILLE PRISON

SHEILA WISSNER and CINDY ROWLAND

Staff Writers

NASHVILLE - Three of four inmates who escaped from Nashville's Riverbend Maximum Security Prison on March 30 have been captured.

Two of the four escapees, 33-year-old Milton Ramos and 32-year-old Benjamin "River Ben" Bennett had been released from their cells in order to serve meals to Muslim prisoners observing Ramadan. The situation unfolded when the two overpowered unarmed guards, according to Pam Hobbins, corrections spokesperson.

"Ramos was armed with a crude knife, and he and Bennett forced the unarmed guards into the laundry room, took their radios and jackets, and secured them with handcuffs and leg irons to the permanent tables where the clean clothes are folded," Hobbins said.

The two proceeded to overpower a third unarmed guard in the control room, then opened the cell doors of two other prisoners, 29-year-old Kevin Steele and 55-year-old Hugo Rodgers, along with another door to the outside, according to officials.

Prison officials further stated that the escapees used two mattresses taken from the cells and a ladder from maintenance to scale the 12-foot fence and cross the razor wire at the top.

No guards were seriously injured during the escape. Officials were alerted to the situation when the guards failed to report in according to schedule.

"The Easter weekend did not affect staffing," Hobbins said.

Ramos and Bennett were taken without incident behind a pawn shop on Charlotte Pike early Easter Sunday morning.

Ramos was serving seven years for burglary. Bennett was serving life with the possibility of parole for habitual criminality.

Steele was captured just before press time. He was serving a 48-year sentence for second-degree murder and robbery.

A reward of $5,000 had been immediately offered for Steele's capture and the friends to whom Steele fled after his escape "snitched him out for the money," according to Capt. Michael Tyler of the TN Department of Corrections.

Steele was knocked out of a West Park tree he had climbed in an attempt to avoid capture. He fell into Richland Creek and was immediately apprehended.

Rodgers was still at large at press time. He is considered extremely dangerous. If seen, do not attempt to apprehend or communicate with him and instead call 911.

Acknowledgments

Thanks to Madville Publishing for making *Streets of Nashville* possible. This book is better after its encounter with fiction acquisitions reviewer Mike Hilbig, line editor and proofreader Liz Evans, and, most of all, editor Kim Davis. Thanks also to fellow Madvillians (not mad villains) Linda Parsons and Susan O'Dell Underwood for continual support.

Thanks to Wildacres Retreat in Little Switzerland, NC, specifically to Resident Manager Wendy Burns and staff, for the wonderful writing residency during which the first draft of Streets was completed. Thanks also to fellow writing resident Dr. Han VanderHart for great conversations at residency mealtimes and to the black bear I met on the Wildacres Loop Trail, a beast that made it into these pages as soon as I made it safely back to Laurel Cabin.

Much appreciation goes to members of the 2021 novel session at Hindman Appalachian Writers' Workshop—Annette Saunooke Clapsaddle (leader), Judith Hoover, George Hovis, Patricia Hudson, Maria Klouda, Linda McAuliffe, Lisa McCormack, Cathy Rigg Monetti, Tonja Reynolds, Teresa Rimer, Shea Sims, Zoe Strecker, Jayne Moore Waldrop, and Anna Walker. #savebennyjack

I'm grateful to readers who offered early enthusiastic and encouraging responses to the work in progress—Joe Plemmons, the first to read it; workshop colleagues Tamara Baxter and Tess Lloyd, who lived with *Streets* drafts every month for a couple of years; Michael Briggs, whose reading and critique were particularly helpful in the development of character Hugo Rodgers. Chris McGinley and Tonja Reynolds offered invaluable guidance in the construction of my query letter as I set out looking for Madville. C.W. Blackwell and Alex Kenna were the first pros to read it and offer kind words.

Thanks to Maurice Manning and his Bucolics for providing the epigraph and inspiring the form for Benny Jack's lyrics.

Special thanks go to Sgt. Robert Nielson of Metro Nashville PD for generous guidance through procedural issues. Mistakes in this area are mine.

I continue to appreciate the support I receive from my colleagues in the Department of Literature and Language at East Tennessee State University and the many amazing creatives in the ETSU-adjacent community.

Last but not least, thanks, as always, to Leesa for her enduring love and commitment, for her patience and encouragement when the muse is upon me and the blue screen is in front of me—she knows what that last bit means.

About the Author

Michael Amos Cody was born in the South Carolina Lowcountry and raised in the North Carolina highlands. He spent his twenties writing songs in Nashville and his thirties in school. He's the author of the novel *Gabriel's Songbook* (Pisgah Press 2017) and short fiction that has appeared in *Yemassee*, *Tampa Review*, *Still: The Journal*, and elsewhere. His short story collection, *A Twilight Reel* (Pisgah Press 2021) won the Short Story / Anthology category of the Feathered Quill Book Awards 2022. Cody lives with his wife Leesa in Jonesborough, Tennessee, and teaches in the Department of Literature and Language at East Tennessee State University.